PRAISE FOR ADRIAN VAN YOUNG

"*Shadows in Summerland* is an extraordinary novel certain to enchant readers of Sarah Waters as well as those looking for a thrilling and transporting gothic tale rich in atmosphere and unforgettable characters, dead and alive. Like the novel's illusive photographs, author Adrian Van Young captures the limitless wonder and dark mysticism of the 19th century with incredibly authentic detail. *Shadows in Summerland* is sure to keep readers awake until the witching hour, in the company of an unforgettable cast of characters—spiritualists, photographers and their vapours, a couple on trial for their lives, a girl who sees ghosts, and the enchanting ghosts themselves."

—Julia Fierro, author of *Cutting Teeth*

"Fans of Adrian Van Young's Gothic short stories will find a lot to admire in his debut novel, a horror-filled historical riff on 19th-century séances, spirit photography, and mediumism. William Mumler emerges here as a memorably monstrous entrepreneur, exploiting the living and the dead alike, and moving with equal ease among drawing rooms, darkrooms, and freshly dug graves. In charting his social striving in a milieu of Bostonian clairvoyants and con artists, Van Young has produced a witty and disturbing horror novel: it's as if Henry James had written an issue of *Tales From the Crypt*."

—Bennett Sims, author of *A Questionable Shape*

"*Shadows in Summerland* is a rich, strange, elegant novel of the supernatural, firmly rooted in the best of classic gothic fiction. Adrian Van Young is a peerless storyteller with a magician-like ability to shift the borders of the reader's consciousness with his prose, effortlessly evoking not only the bare-knuckled rawness of 19th-century New England, but the candlelit borders between the world of the living and the world of the dead. A superb achievement of weird fiction by a burgeoning master."

—Michael Rowe, Shirley Jackson Award-nominated author of *Wild Fell* and *Enter, Night*

FIRST EDITION

Shadows in Summerland © 2016 by Adrian Van Young
Cover artwork © 2016 by Erik Mohr
Cover and interior design © 2016 by Samantha Beiko

Distributed in Canada by
Publishers Group Canada
76 Stafford Street, Unit 300
Toronto, Ontario, M6J 2S1
Toll Free: 800-747-8147
e-mail: info@pgcbooks.ca

Distributed in the U.S. by
Consortium Book Sales & Distribution
34 Thirteenth Avenue, NE, Suite 101
Minneapolis, MN 55413
Phone: (612) 746-2600
e-mail: sales.orders@cbsd.com

Library and Archives Canada Cataloguing in Publication

Van Young, Adrian, author

Shadows in Summerland / Adrian Van Young.

Issued in print and electronic formats.

ISBN 978-1-77148-383-4 (paperback).--ISBN 978-1-77148-384-1 (pdf)

I. Title.

PS3622.A45S53 2016   813'.6   C2016-900934-3

C2016-900935-1

CHIZINE PUBLICATIONS
Toronto, Canada
www.chizinepub.com
info@chizinepub.com

Edited by Sandra Kasturi
Proofread by Tove Nielsen

Canada Council   Conseil des arts
for the Arts   du Canada

We acknowledge the support of the Canada Council for the Arts which last year invested $20.1 million in writing and publishing throughout Canada.

ONTARIO ARTS COUNCIL
CONSEIL DES ARTS DE L'ONTARIO

an Ontario government agency
un organisme du gouvernement de l'Ontario

Published with the generous assistance of the Ontario Arts Council.

Printed in Canada

SHADOWS IN SUMMERLAND

ChiZine Publications

SHADOWS IN SUMMERLAND

A NOVEL

ADRIAN VAN YOUNG

for my parents and Darcy, as ever

The more intently the ghosts gazed, the less
Could they distinguish whose features were;
The Devil himself seem'd puzzled even to guess;
They varied like a dream—now here, now there;
And several people swore from out the press,
They knew him perfectly; and one could swear
He was his father; upon which another
Was sure he was his mother's cousin's brother:

Another, that he was a duke, or knight,
An orator, a lawyer, or a priest,
A nabob, a man-midwife; but the wight
Mysterious changed his countenance at least
As oft as they their minds; though in full sight
He stood, the puzzle was only increased;
The man was a phantasmagoria in
Himself—he was so volatile and thin.

—Lord Byron, *The Phantasmagoria*

Mumler's face is one of the few from which one fails to gather any trace of character. It is calm and fathomless, and although it would be harsh to say that it is unprepossessing, it is yet a face which one would scarcely be able to believe in at first sight.

—*The New York Daily Tribune*, 1869

MUMLER IN THE DOCK
October 1861

I sit here before you unjustly accused. I sit here at your mercy, reader.

We three sit before you, a congress of rogues, and all our fates are intertwined.

There is I, William Mumler, the spirit photographer. There is Hannah, my wife, who can reckon the dead. There is William Guay, our Poughkeepsian friend, who has up to this juncture protected our interests. And these are just the tattered souls who sit here left and right of me in the Year of Our Spirit 1861, bearing credible witness, in Suffolk Court's dock.

Publically we are accused of fraud and larceny most foul.

Privately we are accused of a murder that cannot be publically proven on account of the fact that the man it concerns cannot be verified as dead.

Put forward uniquely, such charges might crush us. Taken together, they cancel each other.

For now we sit here in our cells—mute, incoordinate, fearing the worst. The jail is a piece of well-meant legislation, the new human way to prohibit and punish—four long wings of Quincy granite branching from an octagon with enormous arched windows admitting Charles Street where people, in their freedom, go. Not so William Mumler, confined behind bars, impotent and indisposed, his head inclined into a storm of rapists, pickpockets, cardsharps and abusers in a ten by four space where the sunlight itself, shining raggedly into the arms of the cross, has not the slightest character, the slightest touch of heaven in it. While forever the knocking of implements, scratching, the grunting of a hundred apes, those sad and headstrong bouts of sound that men fallen into the sere will enact.

And though I am not one of them, I am neither, however, completely *not* guilty.

But I didn't bamboozle American mourners, and I didn't murder the man that they say.

It is these crimes and these alone for which I am brought here to answer today.

THE BOOK OF
THE SPIRITS

MESSAGE DEPARTMENT

What moves our tongues to speak your names, you mortals who tend on the ways of the spirits? Why do we shiver if not to feel cold and why lament if not bereaved? Why do we wander if not to discover and why watch over if not to guard? And would you believe us, you passers among us who cannot hear our ceaseless pleas, that we shiver and sadden and wander and watch because we cannot help but do? And would it pain you in your beds, in which you sleep to wake again, that all of these and more but stir the same collective nerve of us, a network of spirits, each bound to the next—each spirit a story, each story an absence, each absence a loss in the world, a bleak room, a beggar's shack we pace amidst? So what do we say to you? What do we say, you mortals, you breathers, you feelers, you babes? What do we say to all of you to whom at last the answer matters?

HANNAH AT CLAYHEAD

August 1845

Born half-dead, so I've been told. Not a single tearless cry. Pulled me out backwards, strangling on my mother. Then lifted me into the light for a breath.

Took one in. So here I am.

Ghastly and purple: some flower in ruin. Or a big withered beet. Or a corpse flower: yes. Passed down to my mother who held me aloft to the various shades in the room.

Little girls forget, see nothing. This was not the case with me. For here is my mother, a young woman then. Middle of her dress undone. One of her breasts spilling out of the gap to let down milk between my lips. Resting over her sternum, a cameo portrait that held a face not unlike hers. In careful inks. With charcoal depth. The Maier flute below the nose. The hard flattened cheekbones. The widely spaced eyes.

And here is my father in pouting grey clothes. Muttering a benediction. Petting me along my sides. Always reeking of fish, not enough, far too many. The inherited curse of grey fish, caught in nets, resting pickled and smoked on others' tables.

There was tribulation living in his lungs, even then. Starting, already, to tatter him.

Nights the ocean smote our island. Hurtling against the rocks. Our house stood at Clayhead, a perilous clime. Where before your every step, above the mottle of the rock-beds, you could fairly hear the snapping of your bones as you fell. The year after I came, a lighthouse went up. So many salmoners lost to the waves. Unluckier families than me and my own accepting cold bratwurst and strudel.

Saw others, too. Not the salmoners. Others. Earlier, even, than anyone guessed.

They made a very queer parade through those first couple of years of my life in the vale.

Stupid and stubborn. Confused in their movement. Lummox shadows trundling by. Asked me of things about which I knew nothing. Never seemed to look at me for long, or directly. Stood in dark rooms, turned into the corner. Distractedly perched on the edge of the bed. Walked up to doors where they paused for a moment, unsure of the thing that they sought. Turned around.

But I was not the only one. Mother saw them, too.

Claudette.

Gaunt as a birch. Undappled grey eyes. Tight about the thin, chapped mouth. High-collared dresses all the colours of a rainstorm. Hair long and dark as a river at night. Corded wood the same as father. Levered our trap from the deep April ruts. Hoisted great cauldrons of stew from the fire without a bit of broth the lesser. They said when Claudette pushed me out, she lowered her legs, very still, from the stirrups and rested her feet on the floor. When she sat on a chair in her kitchen dominion and carved her figures out of soap, I felt that nothing could displace the bucket wedged between her knees. These figures she kept in a drawer in her bedroom. Latch was always snug in place. Yet still I sensed the dolls sometimes. Seeing my way through her room with their eye-nubs.

Nights my mother sang to me. A song without rhythm. Yet music it was. Said that it came from the Bible, my mother. Her Bible and hers alone.

"Your hair is like a flock of goats, moving down the slopes of Gilead. Your teeth are like a flock of ewes and every one bears each its twin."

Tapping with her fingers on the surface of my teeth, she would kiss my forehead and would let her lips linger. Would kiss me and brush back the goats in my hair. Spilling them, scrabbling, down onto my shoulders. While just outside the ocean waves dashed and murmured on the rocks. Light from the lighthouse, magnesium, molten, cutting back and forth above us. Flickering into the room's darkest corners. Darting again out to sea.

Who came first.

The governess. Out wandering among the dunes.

Me there with my mother, the two of us watching, as the girl in the Grecian-bend bustle came on. My mother stood facing away from the sea. A tepid winter sun behind her. Yet the light was enough to determine her shadow, which stretched, twice her height, inland from the cliff. The figure approached us not head-on, but rather instead from an easterly tack. Coming up over the waist-high dunes between Clayhead and the ocean. Hair half piled upon her head, half straggling about her shoulders. Nostrils raw. Skin pale to translucence. Bright, blue veins reaching under her scalp. But as she approached, drawing closer and closer, I found I could only see her less. Perspective of her shifting clockwise unless I stood completely still.

Mother was without this problem. She followed the girl steadily with her eyes. And pivoted where she stood, my mother, to match the figure's every motion. Matched them, and ticked like a sundial behind them, as though to keep the figure within range.

"Where are my children? Lavinia? Miss Pearl?" said the girl into her cold, cupped hands.

"And where is my stick for biting on?

"Where is the Doctor and where are his salts?

"Why am I dizzy so close to the sea when *precisely* sea-air was prescribed me?"

And my mother replied, "Go home to God. You are long overdue at His side, darling girl."

"Is that where they have gone—to God?"

"So will we all one day," said mother.

A pause from the her. A thoughtful pause. A human pause, it seemed, at first, and I remember thinking: *I can really* know *them, can't I? Know them like my flesh and blood.*

"Did falling sickness land me here?"

"Like as not, it was," said mother.

"Then where's my stick for biting, miss? Don't you know I'll be needing it soon?" said the girl.

Standing there pinching the tulle of her dress. Waiting for the fit to come. And then when it didn't she muttered away. And that was the last time I saw her.

Mother knelt down, drew a sharp arm around me. "You're looking at them wrong," said she.

I was then four. Said I, "How's that?"

"You're trying to trick yourself into seeing them."

"They squirm a lot."

"It's *these* that squirm." Mother pointed at her eyes. "Let them do the work they'll do. Learn to trust in what you've got."

"What's that?" said I.

"The ken."

"The ken?"

"The ken," said my mother, but said nothing more.

MUMLER ON DRESS

To the true gentleman, it should go without saying that his physical appearance is an index of his character. His mode of dress concurrent with the rigour of his hygiene and the neatness of his grooming are pre-eminently vital. The American gentleman is no different, and so is honour-bound to be that which his country boasts of him. Sober, strong, self-governing, with nary a hint of anything that beggars immodest regard from his fellows: the foppish or brigandly wearing of jewellery, the compassing of one's top-hat with bands of sealskin, silk or satin, the adoption of a formal coat that finds the wearer out-of-season, and so the wrongs accumulate until the scoundrel is consumed. But in the American gentleman, lo, such conflagration need not rage. This prodigy of taste and tact should refrain from not only arraying his wealth if he is blessed enough to have it but moreover still from discussing its prospects or making it known in any way. In mind as in make as in manner, this man, and never the tierce, in him, shall cleave. He should be neat in the extreme—his moustache trimmed, his frock-coat smart— inviting no further impression whatever than that, precisely, which he is: a gentleman about his business, a gentleman to be admired.

MUMLER ON THE UP AND UP

July 1859

In the summer of 1859 with all of life's prospects assembled before me, I was sent to deliver a cameo necklace to the Sunderlands of Exeter Street in Back Bay.

The necklace was silver and dripping with cameos after the Egyptian fashion, with forget-me-nots cut into the mounting and four amethysts ranged around.

In the jewellery shop where I worked with my father off Newspaper Row in the heart of downtown, I had a name for all of them who came peacocking through the door. I would whisper it, seethingly, under my breath no sooner had the door swung closed—a door that bore upon its glass the words Mumler & Sons, my unthinkable future—coming and going, and going and coming, I would utter my withering secret aloud: "Lahngworthies, Lahngworthies, every last one." I would murder the A as they did on Cape Cod, these Spiritists and womanists and anti-Sabba-whatsit-nists, Boston Brahmins each and all, these people who bought jewellery to gussy up their worthless lives. They wrought nothing, did nothing, squandered the triumph of having more than most—than me. They were contemptible in that.

And yet I kept an open mind.

I, William Jr., was the shop's chief engraver, not because of my father but rather my hands, quick and exacting for all they were stubby, sweeter than a barren maid to the baubles and chains that came under their care. When I came down the stairs from the modest apartment that my father allowed me above the workshop, the other craftsmen on the floor would turn their eyes in shame from me.

Such was my estate on that red-letter day in June of 1859 as I walked down the Green in between the house-fronts past the old and tyrannical names of the street-signs.

Moving west there was Berkeley, Clarendon, Dartmouth, until Exeter came like the edge of a cliff; I stood, nervous despite myself, in front of a puddingstone sliver of house that matched the address on the ticket.

I checked on the state of the cargo I carried and went up to knock on the door.

A servant girl answered, took my name and led me to sit in the carpeted foyer on a couch with a hideous pattern of tulips directly across from a grandfather clock. Though I was early at the house by no more than a couple of minutes, still I must wait for those scrupulous hands to light on the hour I was set to arrive. Beyond a sort of canted screen between the parlour and the foyer I saw a figure in rotation, Mrs. Lucretia or her lady, preparing the room for my coming.

I got my calling cards in order.

Mrs. Sunderland seemed to emerge from the screen like some sort of fairy the way I perceived it, though really she slipped through the sliver of space between the screen's edge and the parlour's doorway, tailored to her size exactly. She took my card, glanced at it, scanned me lengthwise and to my surprise took my hand in her own. My hand had been swollen with heat from my pocket, yet there in the cave of her palms it contracted.

She was little and lithe in the way she was made, her hair curly as barrel liquorice. She had a pretty, cramped face just showing its lines.

She glided off beyond the screen and once I had followed her, wrenching the thing to fit my magnanimous bulk past its edge, she motioned I sit on a second low couch within her lace-curtained and cool inner sanctum. My hostess sat across from me in a brocaded wingback that bore her aloft a couple of feet above the floor. I found I was squinting because of the sun which her lady had let through the drapes as I waited, slanting over the top of her mistress's chair and shining down into my eyes.

Set between our sets of legs was a table with coffee and small pastries on it.

"Let's have it then, Mr. Mumler," she said.

I took out the necklace and showed it to her in a fan on the flats of my hands.

"Would you?" she said as she rose and then I. She inclined her head foreword. "Obligingly, sir."

Careful to maintain a suitable distance, I fastened the chain below her hair. She shook back her hair and began to process before a gleaming Cheval mirror.

"I take it you are pleased?"

"Oh, quite. And tonight I shall give it a coming-out party."

"Special occasion?"

"A speaker," she said. "Miss Fanny A. Conant. She's on at the Banner of Light. Do you know her?"

"A Spiritist," I said.

"A Spirit-*ual*-ist," my host corrected. "She is to speak and hold a sitting." Finished inspecting herself at the mirror, she sat once again in her chair. "Are you familiar with our movement?"

"As much as I've read in the papers," I said.

Sitting again, I crossed my legs and tented my fingers upon my left knee. My hostess's eyes flickered over me briefly.

"Oh we are frightfully disorganized," the lady said quickly. "We are buffeted by skeptics almost constantly, you know. And yet we are always accepting of strays."

"I am not wed to any faith. You see, I cannot be a stray."

"We Spiritualists," she said, "are more. Though I grant you that faith might have something to do with it. Are you learned, for example, on the question of woman?"

"I am learned on the answer of woman," I said.

"Really, Mr. Mumler. What a wicked thing to say. You're in the habit of saying such things, I imagine? And yet anyway," she gave pause, "you're not boring. Maybe a little passé, but not that."

"I've liked our talk myself," I said. "So much, in fact, I would like to discount you. Half-price let us say for the necklace, Lucretia?"

Her nostrils flared a little then. She did not answer for a moment.

"Oh you may call me that," she said. "You may call me Missus L. But the size of your offer, you see—it's indecent."

"You are busy enough as it is," I pressed on, "what with all your women and their questions, Mrs. Sunderland. I won't be the cause of your falling behind all on account of some ornament."

"We've been privileged enough to afford it," she said with a curious ruffle of her dress.

This fanning of her feathers done, she smiled and moved onto the edge of her chair. And I detected in that movement an apologetic tremor or anyway one of explanation—*I could not help myself, you see*—as though she were now more embarrassed for me than she'd been for herself just a moment ago when I had implied that she'd needed my help.

But why, you will ask, did I wish to discount her when I was not my father and my father was not me—when I gave not a fig for La*h*ngworthies like Lucretia, with their frivolous neckwear and parlour revivals?

Here is the reason: I wished to deceive her.

I wished to infiltrate her graces under the pretence that I stood in worship of her. I wanted to smirk at the plush of her world, to see its frailty from inside. And I wanted, I think, to avail myself of her, to channel her relations and resources and connections towards higher, purer aims than hers.

Decisively, I raised my hand and I blocked out the sun slanting into my eyes. I said to her: "Madam, I see."

Leaning closer toward me still, she spoke in that same vital fog of apology: "But surely there's—oh, let me see . . ." She counted on her well-kept fingers. "Yes, surely an eleventh place can be made in our circle for one such as you. Unless you are elsewise committed?" she said.

"When you call it a sitting," I said, leaning forward, "is it not a *séance* you mean, Mrs. Sunderland? Complete with planchette, levitating violins, chilly hands upon one's shoulder?"

"The way you say it, Mr. Mumler, I should think you had decided we were charlatans already. There must exist in all of us a modicum of childlike wonder."

"I would very much like to feel *that*. I will come."

I lightly, gamely, slapped my thigh. Then appeared to go gloomy; I did a faint laugh.

"Mr. Mumler, what is it?"

I held out a moment, looking away from her briefly, then back. "Seeing I will be your guest, the price does not agree with me. Nor would it agree with my father," I said. "Bless him that he made me, Ma'am, but my father has never been partial to bargains."

"I can see that you will not relent," said my hostess. "And a most welcome tyranny, dear Mr. Mumler. Half of half, all right?" She smiled. "I would gladly meet you at a quarter."

"Do you stand firm in that?" I said.

Mrs. Sunderland frowned. "Why as firm as you stand. As you've stood, Mr. Mumler, against every reversal."

Which is why later on, in the hours before supper, under the guise of receiving a shipment of various gemstones arriving at Lowell, I dropped in at Fisk's at the top of Copp's Hill, thinking it would relax me some.

Fisk's was—no polite way to say it—a brothel.

Last house on the right on Snowhill Street and just round the way from Copp's Hill Cemetery, Fisk's had been my hideaway from the day-in-day-out-ness of Mumler & Sons. There was brandy and laudanum and beer and sweet wine. Cigar smoke and opium smoke muddled oddly. There were soft, low-backed couches on which to extend while Women of Erin and Women of Ham and Celestial Women made love in your ear. I loved the ease of it. I loved its transaction.

I came there often twice a week.

Sometimes I would even pass up on the girls—Madam Fisk didn't mind if you kept buying brandies—and sit in the shadows alone, watching others, a light tipple in me, at ease in my skin.

I would sample diversely when I had the urge (yellow Fang and black Bertha and olive Aida) though I mostly returned to the red-curtained room of a fair, Irish girl named Brianna O'Brennan.

Her name in Gaelic meant "Sad Hills." She had told me this one night in what was verily an outpouring.

I would think of her hunched at the foot of the bed, her hair too short to hide her nipples, opening and closing her legs on her soreness, as if to hide the thing we'd done.

But she was not the only one who felt the darkened edge of something—just the faintest pollutant of sadness or shame in the wake of our nighttime and noontime encounters.

Let us call it, then, The Sadness, sharp in me from time to time.

I felt it then, and feel it now, and shall feel it, I am wholly sure, till *I* die. In the bedrooms of Fisk's it would moulder in me as soon as I had spent myself, giving rise to gloomy thoughts that begged the point of all this searching. Not for something high-minded but pleasure itself, which seemed to me flagrant, deceitful, outrageous.

But then I would remind myself that Brianna O'Brennan was only a whore.

Which brings us back to Madam Fisk's on the day I delivered Lucretia her necklace, aware that in only a couple of hours I would find myself deep in the enemy's camp. I needed Brianna. I needed release. I needed somebody to pour me a drink. And with this in mind I arrived at the brothel, unfrequented in these working hours and never on afternoons past by me, so that the house Negro, a man named Bill Christian, launched from the wall he'd been leaning on smoking, thinking perhaps that I might be The Law.

"Mist' Mumler," he said. "Come by early today."

"Pressing business, Bill," I said.

"Brianna just now waking up."

"A loyal gent at arms, is Bill."

Bill assessed me carefully, looking to see was I drunk or unhinged. He was charged to size up every one of Fisk's clients, whether or not they were his friends and I knew that he wasn't above the heave-ho, if situations came to that.

Once in a gin-fog I'd seen him do violence to the face of man who'd refused to pay Madam. Bill had been smashing his face on the brick. First his nose, cocked to the side. Then his lips, rent down the middle. Then his nose stove in entire, a syphilitic pit of blood.

He was also a gorgeous male specimen, Bill—the handsomest Negro in all of the Hub. The bones and sinews of his face were overlaid with darkest satin and his plum-coloured lips were in perfect proportion. He smiled at the women and smiled at the men and he smiled at nobody at all on the street. It was Bill Christian's armour—a pre-emptive smile, not just for white people but everyone breathing. Reaching me his flask of gin, he showed it to me now.

I drank.

"Here's to life with both eyes open."

"One closed and one open," I said as I swallowed, "to throw the bastards off their guard."

Bill opened the door and revealed me the staircase that led to the parlour crisscrossed with low couches. Standing there against the light, Bill looked like the sculpture by Charles Cordier of the Moor in the turban and Renaissance beads, and for a brief moment I felt overjoyed to be welcomed by him in this halcyon place—some sultan's dominion, all columns and incense, giggling ladies of the veil, the prince who took a little gin and called me warmly by my name.

Off of the receiving parlour, Fisk's became a long red hall. The place had used to have a wall that split up the floor into separate apartments but the wall had been felled and replaced with a hall that ran between the eight-some rooms. When you walked down the hallway, as I now was walking, passing by the curtained rooms, there was a sort of temple hush, a feeling of going past saints in their niches.

When I came to Brianna's room, I saw that she was not alone. A man with skin as white as hers was mounted stride her, bombarding her groin. He had a wide constellation of moles on his back and his head was as dark as a Kilkenny mare's. They were having their way in pantomime—plunging limbs and soundless cries. Behind her lover's lunging shoulder Brianna's pale face would rise up now and then, the lips retracted slightly on the dark filmy teeth and the sharp chin appearing to quiver with pleasure. Yet I detected something different in the splay of her legs, in the way that her face, every time it emerged, was fixed on a point resolutely before it, which I took to be her lover's eyes. And oh it was a stolen sight, such that I couldn't look away.

I fumbled myself and I clung to the curtain.

We all of us happily shuddered together, becurtained Willy Mumler and the beast with two backs.

HANNAH FULL
OF GRACE
January 1859

And then one day it happened: Grace.

Her parents kept the Shoreham Inn.

But the first house we shared was the Kingdomtide Church. Perched by North Light, at the edge of the sea.

All nave, it was, the Kingdomtide. And seemed, like its faithful, to sit there on faith. Not least for the buck and the scourge of the wind, butting at the walls year round. Nor the waves of the ocean that footed the cliffs, so high in a storm that they dashed the pine roof.

Glad to remind us, Reverend Hascall. Raised up from a boy on these raked-over shores. Salt-blooded, it was said of him, with long veins of seaweed investing his flesh. Really a reedy and stoop-shouldered man with a pale freckled face and a muzzle of whiskers.

Abner Hascall, his father, my mother's good shepherd.

His father, *her* mother's, progressing through time.

Earlier that October, the North Lighthouse had been ripped from its moorings by terrible winds. A couple of salmon dinghies had been lost along with it. Each of them packed with island men. Could not place out in the storm what part was rock and what part harbour. What remained of the boats and the men and the lighthouse were still being dredged from the base of the cliff. Already to show we were not beat, a new lighthouse was underway.

The Sunday after construction began, the Reverend Hascall assembled the flock. Those sober and not made their way to the church, where last week's storm had made the path leading up to the building a treacherous porridge. Wallows in the places where the lighthouse cornice-stones had hammered upon the rain-slick earth.

German and English, mostly, we. Methodists, nearly to the last. The women in bonnets and dark trimless dresses. Mirthless to the very bone their charging, pale and thin-lipped faces. Sitting father to children, clan by clan.

So were they arranged today and likewise did we go among them.

Maiers walking. Maier women. My mother and I with our far swampy stares.

The first thing that our eyes perceived down the dark avenue of parishioners sitting: the Christ in perfect agony, suspended in back of the pulpit.

All this I saw, and then a stall. Families milling, children laughing. A man in the back just beside where I stood—not in the back row, but against the back wall—raised and lowered his arm in a curious gesture. Seemed to be a man alone. No family about or even near him. No reason for him to be there as he was, sinister and sad.

Brown, striped trousers. Wide-brimmed hat. A hat, at that, inside God's house. Also, a darkness to his figure. Not a swarthiness, exactly, but a boldness or solidity. And I saw that his clothes were soaking wet, the sort of wet that never dries, the water running down his chest to pool about his untied brogues. Coming away in sticky braids every time he raised his hand, bulbs and fronds of brownish kelp. I even thought I smelled the brine.

"Ignore him, child. Go take your seat."

But the drowned man continued to stand there, not speaking. Trickling like a statue in a garden.

"He is gone. He is no one," said my mother. "Open up your hymnal, girl."

"Said the two sisters of Bethany to Jesus, Oh, Lord. Lazarus our brother lies ill," said the Reverend. "He whom you *love* lies ill, they said, and wiped off his feet with their hair. Answered Jesus to Mary, Martha, calmly. Slowly, so they heard his words. Said He to the sisters, Take ye heart. Lazarus's illness leads not to death. *Lazarus's illness* leads instead to God's glory. That the true Son of God, who I am, may restore him. That I may raise—yes, raise!—him up. That he might awaken, said God, for I wish it. Sure as I stand before you now . . ."

Turned in my pew when the hymn started up and saw in a flash that the drowned man was gone. And yet I glimpsed, three rows behind, arrayed between her handsome parents, a girl my age unknown to me with a curious look on her face.

It was mirth.

Mother as stiff as a dressmaker's doll. Listening to Revered Hascall. Or appearing to listen to him, anyway. The muscles of her face lightly tensed, then relaxed.

Tremendous coil of auburn hair. That was the first thing I noticed of Grace.

That and a small bony, rarified face. The cold of the church showing pink on her cheeks.

Her mother was all but the promise of her. With a bloom of dark hair and long, slender neck. The man beside her very still. Fingers meshed across his ribs. But with something of wryness in his eyes. Not smugness, exactly, but something amused, as Reverend Hascall raised his own.

"Hannah, don't stare," mother managed to say.

Already we had this in common: aloneness. Letting the curse fall where it may.

"Hannah, go see to your mother," said father as we filed down the aisle once the service had ended.

Mother's brow gone reflective with sweat. Her lips dry.

Grace's first words: "Is your mother all right?"

My eyes went darting, panicky. As though the voice were in my head. Then I saw that the girl had detached from her parents, was suddenly standing in my path.

"Just a little faint," said I.

"Some calomel, then," said Grace. "For the purges. A fair warning, though: it will dry out the eyes."

Mother leaned against a pew-back, half aware of where she was. Father ahead, looking back in vexation, eager to smoke in the cold with his friends.

"We shall help her together, all right?" said Grace. "Here, Ma'am." Alongside her. "Now cling to my arm."

Said mother: "You're kind." And accepted the arm. Accepted with a rigid smile.

"I'm Grace," said Grace. "Now tell me yours."

Said I: "I am Hannah Maier."

"You have immensely kind eyes, Hannah Maier. Are you kind?"

"I would like to think so, miss."

"Don't call me miss. Say Grace," said she. "Say Grace"—the girl laughed—"as you do at your table."

"Grace then," said I, leading mother along. Continued out into the muck of the churchyard.

Father in a pack of men. Rocking on his cork-soled shoes. Lot of them smoking wordlessly with the grotty intentness of gamblers.

"You think that the Reverend is silly?" said I.

"Was I that bad at covering up?"

"*I* think that the Reverend is silly," said I.

"The Reverend!" said she. "Why the Reverend's delightful. Verily, a human torch! You will have to come down to the inn," said the girl. "My parents have taken it over, you've heard?"

"I hadn't," said I.

Which of course was a lie. Everyone in town had heard. The pretty girl from Providence whose father wore a silver fob.

"In two days' time, I shall gladly receive you."

Nodded and opened my mouth, but no words.

"Good!" said Grace. "We will talk and be splendid. I will take you on a tour of every mouse-hole in the house. Are you all right to walk, Miss Maier?

"Go on," said mother. "Go. You're kind."

I was, for the first time, embarrassed of her while Grace wheeled around in her peach-coloured dress. A few pretty strands coming loose from her coil and riding the sea air, electric with cold.

"So nice to have met you," she cried, walking backwards, holding her skirts above the mud.

The last time that I saw her she was standing with her parents in the nearly empty lintel of the church-house.

Mother sat beside me on the carriage-ride home. Bonnet cast over her face for the light. A series of ruts and the trap started up. Tipping me suddenly into her ribs.

"All mother needs is a nice darkened room. Ain't that the truth of it, mother?" said father. "A nice darkened room with a nice warmed-up cloth to chase off them mean winter headaches."

Gin-fug heavy, on the wind. Father's arm crooked as he reached in his coat. Sunday the Lord's day but also a day when father went to sleep at five.

Up ahead another trap. Crossing the road that bisected the mountain.

"Ho, Pieter," said father. "Get on with them nags."

The man driving smiled and the trap cut across.

"Fleeter of foot than yours," called Pieter.

Brood of three boys with a woman in back. A frieze of longsuffering faces theirs from all this riding in the open. And Pieter himself, who was somehow familiar. Who had, at some point, taken soup in our kitchen. Or stood with father in the hall for as long as it took them to take down a cup. But when I saw his face emerge from underneath his wide-brimmed hat, I knew him for the drowned man with the kelp in his hair that I'd seen earlier at the back of the church. Sure as Lazarus walked, here was Pieter, the drowned man, steering his carriage off into the trees.

MUMLER ON THE NIGHT-SIDE
July 1859

By the time I arrived at the Sunderlands' house at the chosen time of six o'clock, I have to admit I was decently tight from all I'd drunk at Fisk's with Bill.

The day had that devil-may-careness, you see.

All of the street-facing windows were bright with lamps and guttered flames alike, the curtain faintly parted on the parlour of the house where schools of well-dressed bodies moved. It wasn't my hostess who answered the door, but a man whom I took for her husband LaRoy—unaffiliated mesmerist, reform innovator and owner of the Banner's sister-paper in Athens, "The Spiritual Philosopher." Tall and stooped was this LaRoy, his golden beard made weak by white, a funnel for hearing held up at one ear.

"Why, you must be the champion of Lucretia's afternoon," said the man upon taking my name, over-loudly. "You needn't have favoured her so in your pricing. But come, take a sherry. We are just circulating. Mrs. Conant's address will commence in a tice."

"Thank you for including me," I told the old goat.

"Nonesuch, nonesuch," Mr. Sunderland said. "We have daughters, you know! Well come in, sir! Come in!"

He dithered close by me while two comely maids turned me out of my coat and then into the parlour.

I grant it was strange that LaRoy Sunderland and not one of these maids met with me at the door, and yet I adduced it as part of their plan to position themselves as the salt of the earth—not moneyed Back Bay carpetbaggers but Boston progressives in every respect.

So why not start with me, I thought. *Willy Mumler, who's waited so long in the wings.*

LaRoy Sunderland was a rigorous host, however hugely hard of hearing. He did his best to introduce me to the fourteen-odd assembled with the repeated combination of a facilitated handshake and ten words or less on their chief-most achievements: phrenology, literature, banking, priest-craft. The parlour was broad with strong light in its sconces, which made the sherry glasses blinding. The sherry helped to give me balance; another glass more balance still. Bespectacled faces, and faces with beards, and faces with beautiful lips, and with wrinkles, looming, retreating, extending their hands, nodding to LaRoy, their host.

Aside from LaRoy and Lucretia there were: the Sunderland daughters, Cordelia and Sarah; a man in a cello-shaped waistcoat with tails who wore dollops of rouge upon his cheeks whom I had heard from somewhere near was the modern heir apparent to the stage, Josiah Jefferson; Unitarian Reverend John M. Spear, tieless in a smoking vest and at his side a Negro boy made strange by spectacles and tweeds; a blind and reanimate mummy, F. Bly, whose specialized field was the head and its contours; a dark and dourly handsome woman with her hair gathered up in a sort of sleek harp.

LaRoy told me this woman here was the trance-speaking medium Fanny A. Conant.

Mrs. Sunderland volubly recognized me from across the packed room and came fluttering over. Along her way, she flapped her hands, as though she were chiding the air in between us.

"I see you've met William—our craftsman," she said. "Isn't he perfectly novel? Say, Reverend."

"The very spice of life," said Spear.

"And just the dose we need," she said. "Did you know, Mr. Mumler, that Reverend Spear's faith is so much confined to the loftier classes, it has a branch for normal folk that is totally identical in polity and practice?"

"Universalists," I said.

Lucretia and Spear nodded at me, impressed.

"My point exactly," said Lucretia. "Mr. Mumler proves my point. I wonder, John, would you have him or are his hands too rough for prayer?"

"We'd be lucky to have such a man in our ranks."

"You sound like you're insisting, Reverend."

"She believes in The Spirit alone," he addressed me. "Anything other is cause for amusement. But shouldn't we let Mr. Mumler decide if he needs metaphysical comforts, Lucretia?"

"I am in need of a sherry," I said.

Which elicited a garnish of sparse, polite laughter.

"I myself enjoy the privilege of parishioner, sirs," said the young professorial Negro beside him. "And I came up from Beacon Hill."

"Came *down* from Beacon Hill, dear Phineas." Spear gave a titled, uncomfortable smile. "Came up by way of down, of course, is what the young man means to say. Yet here the fellow stands!" he said and clapped his hand upon his shoulder. "Whichever direction, we're happy you've made it."

In the barely congenial silence that followed, I made good on my proposal of another glass of sherry and, under the guise of returning said glass to a sideboard stacked with others like it, I wandered afield of John Spear and his minion to make a closer study of the Sunderlands' house.

Here was the hall with its framed eminences, which led to yet another and another after that. A couple of liveried servants went by, bearing two towers of folded-up napkins. Removing myself from the wings of the house, I traced my way back to the parlour and past it; I passed a dressing room and washroom, and a nursery and bedroom, and from there an obliqueness of further rooms still, each one darker than the last.

I was happily and irretrievably lost.

At the end of some hall angled off of some other, I passed a larger, lighted room that seemed to be a library. The library was very calm, a self-contained and womblike place, and voices from the cocktail party floated from the hall. Inside I was faced with the back of a man who was moving around against the window. He was busy with something, some sort of appliance, conducting it now here, now there. The appliance itself was five feet high, its bottom a juncture of three spindly legs. At the top of the legs was a sort of dark box, a shaded cyclopean eye at its centre. To the right of the man was a cloth-covered table that held an upright wooden drawer over which the man started to brood and concoct to what purpose I could not say.

I shifted in the doorway then; the busy stranger turned around.

"I do say, sir," the stranger said, his hands held up at his lapels. "You've given a fellow a scare just now. I expected Miss Conant but you—have we met?"

"I expect that we haven't. William Mumler."

He lowered his hands and stepped back toward the window. "Taking a tour of the house, are you, sir?"

"Yes, I thought I would take one before the address but it seems that I've gotten myself badly lost. I'm a reader, you see." And I swept the high shelves. "Such rooms are a sort of safe harbour for me."

The man appeared to soften some; he gainsaid the step he had taken away.

"Algernon Child," the man said. "Pleasure's mine. Algernon Child of the PSAI."

He was minutely fashioned but willowy too—no trace of stoutness in his genes—and wore above his bloodless mouth a thin and sharply trimmed moustache. And when I accepted his hand which he thrust to compensate how he was made, I found the hand met to be shockingly rough, the hand of a man who has laboured his worth since a very young age at the pick or the stylus.

"The PSAI," I said. "A Spiritist association?"

The short man gave a little scoff. "Whatever your views on that," he said. "No, sir, I am in photographs. Pristine, living records. The Photographic Section of the American Institute, you may have heard our name said round."

"It's a camera then."

"Of the wet plate variety. You've yet to be immortalized?"

"Now there is a pleasure I'd like to have greatly. Though I have seen the end result." He watched as I circled the camera up close. "You're not a believer, why palaver here?"

"I meant no insult, Mr. Mumler."

"You have given none, sir. My inquiry is rational."

"An initiate, then! Oh they've tried, sir, they've tried. But I am not one to yield so gamely. And as for your question, a man's got to eat, to pay his landlady, to frolic, you know. I am privately indentured."

"You're moonlighting, then?"

"I am here to take a portrait of the speaker, Fanny Conant."

"And this?" I asked him of the table, upon which sat the upright drawer.

"A bath of silver nitrate and potassium," he said. "To fix the negative, you see. Which reminds me—ah curses—it must be done soaking." He rushed the table, seized the drawer. "Mr. Mumler, might I borrow your shade for a moment? Forgive me for saying, you make ample shade. Over here. Now stand just so. And shadow my path, if you will, to the slide."

We humped our way across the room to where the prized appliance stood. Mr. Child rose on his toes to insert the glass plate in the back of the camera.

"Now the widow's weeds," he said, retrieving a large cloth of felt from the couch and placing it over the box with the plate. "There she stands, Mr. Mumler. The veil hanging o'er. Ready to enact her magic. I do say, sir, I've taken shots but for whatever reason she always beguiles me."

"Darkness and light," said a voice from behind us. "That, and the dependable reaction of the chemicals. Mr. Child, Mr. Mumler," said Fanny A. Conant, appearing to glide through the library door. "I'm not very long now from being expected. Wouldn't you rather hold off, Mr. Child?"

"Better not, Ma'am. I'll be quick, don't you worry."

"Prefer that I should sit or stand?"

"Sit, Ma'am," he said.

"Won't the window shed light?"

"Yes, Ma'am—well, no. There's a backdrop for that. You're keen to every detail, Ma'am."

"How is it that you know my name?" I asked her as she went to sit.

She fixed me with her pale blue eyes; they were housed in a long handsome face, strongly white, with a cluster of little dark moles at her hairline.

"It was because I didn't know I asked Lucretia who you were. You'll agree one should know every face in one's audience."

"And who *is* Mr. Mumler?" Child said, on a grin. "He's rather a mystery to me, who just met him."

"He's a jeweller on Washington Street," said Miss Conant. "Our hostess is decked in the spoils of his talent. But let us turn no soul away. So welcome, Mr. Mumler, to the new dispensation."

Algernon exposed the plate. We were left to wait out three long minutes of stillness. This he'd explained as the optimal time for the image to make itself known on the glass.

In the portrait she is looking at the camera directly, her arms hanging shapeless and free in her lap.

Fanny Conant's address saw the clock once around, though I have little recollection of her actual words. What I do recall, at the half-hour mark, was a break in those words to admit Mr. Child, who arrived in the parlour in unnatural fluster. Moving regrettably in my direction, he attempted and failed to not crush people's toes.

Meanwhile Fanny down in front, at a raised music stand that stood in for a podium, was somewhere in the neighbourhood of "spiritual affinities," which she had named a precondition for the marriage of souls. The spiritual affinities, she claimed, *must* be realized; the spiritual affinities, she harmonized, were all. The marriage contract, else-wise, guarded legal prostitution, conceived by the husband, fulfilled by the wife.

She let her notes fall from the stand to the floor as she rapidly covered her points.

"An ultraist with uteromania," said Algernon Child, who had fetched up beside me.

"An ultraist with what?" I said.

"An ultraist—a radical," said Algernon, sweating. "And yet you'll observe that she speaks out of trance. Have you seen Cora Hatch? She's a savoury one, Cora. But *never* speaks outside the trance. Damp as she gets when the spirit's upon her—"

"—do hush," said the head-doctor, Bly, in the back.

I could see he was blind by the way that he gazed just right of the place we were actually sitting.

"Sorry, uncle, sorry," said Algernon Child. "Keen as a bat in Brazilia he is."

"Uteromania?" I said.

Frowning, he answered me: "Womb disease, sir. For the womb has gone *tilted*, you see, in the victim, leaving her defenceless to the creep of strong opinions. A most common disease among Spiritists, sir. These Coras and Kates selling ghosts by the dollar."

"And Fannys," I said.

"Yes, Fannys," he said, observing Fanny Conant speechifying for a moment. "They say a third sex will be born," he continued, "with all of this thumping of manicured hands. But looking at her—yes, looking at her."

"I find her to be very sleek."

"No one's denying *that*," said Child. "But Mr. Mumler, really, I saw the way you looked at her."

"Looked at her when?"

"The library," he whispered. "You wanted to throttle her blind when she spoke."

"I wanted nothing of the sort. And I cannot pretend that I do not resent it."

"Forgive me, Mr. Mumler. I've offended you twice."

"Lucky for you, I am not a hard man or I should have to throttle *you*." I elbowed him gently in the ribs, at which he gave a little start. "Your profession," I said, "is remarkable, sir. If you're staying for dinner, I'd like to discuss it."

"Oh look, she is finished," said Child, striking out. "Let's make a prospect of the dining room, sir. I could never on earth forgive myself if I ended up trapped beside F. Bly."

The "sitting" was set to take place in the parlour and, after our supper was cleared, we repaired there. I'd fallen in with Mr. Child, and we walked arm to arm, trading looks, in the herd. Others shuffled on in front, Fanny and Lucretia leading. LaRoy Sunderland went in back with his horn like some mild and oblivious prophet.

The lighting in that place had changed. I saw red shades on all the lamps. Clearly, the servants had been busy, constructing that room's ambience. The table where we went to sit was half of the size of the one where we'd eaten, a perfect little cherry round. Upon it was a black lace cloth.

I sat flanked by Reverend Spear and of course Mr. Child the Perpetual Friend, whose palms were slick when we joined hands. We were seated intermittently women and men, with several more men in attendance. This arrangement was according to the charge of each guest, negatives and positives, women to men, so that the "telegraph of souls" could optimally transmit itself.

The rows of shaded lamps went softer. Hands were clasped the circle round. The medium Fanny began to intone toward a dim and indefinite point past her nose. A series of sharp, hollow sounds—gaunt sounds—came from somewhere underneath us. Many of the eyes were closed, but several, including my own, remained open.

Miss Conant spoke up, "We are testing the batteries."

The gaunt sounds continued, more rapidly now. But after a while they petered out.

Then Fanny Conant began to look different. What can only be described as a physical awkwardness came over her person. Her arms grew slack, she tipped gradually forward and the hands that she held seemed to tether her there. She hung for a moment, then slowly came up. She appeared to grow out of the dark like a rose.

"Has Vashti come into the form?" she said. "Vashti of the massacre of Yellow Stone River? Oh come to us, Vashti, in paint and rawhide. Come with all your bright, black hair. Bring us tidings from your shores. Come and unveil to us beautiful truths."

"Vashti is receptive," she continued with a groan.

"And is Vashti alone?" said Mrs. Lucretia.

"Vashti is never alone," answered Fanny. "Vashti has come here arm in arm with a spirit of exceeding purity."

"Is it male or female?" said LaRoy over-loudly, tilting his funnel toward Miss Conant.

"One rap for no. Three raps for yes. And two if the spirit cannot answer. I ask on behalf of LaRoy Sunderland, is the attendant spirit male?"

One rap was heard.

"Is it female?" said Fanny.

Three this time.

"Female, then," she said serenely. "Of what relation is the spirit under inquiry," she said, "to persons sitting round this table? A mother?" (One rap) "A sister?" (One rap) "A daughter?" (One rap) "A friend?"

Here three.

These raps I discerned every second more keenly were coming from *under* the small parlour table, though by what trick or agency I couldn't then hazard a guess, I must say. I scanned the darkness at my feet, saw only my thighs, Mr. Child's and the Reverend's. Our chairs had been set very close at the table and no one had thought to move his back.

"And what did Madam do in life?" said LaRoy Sunderland with still more animation.

"One of us wants to know," said Fanny, "what was your station in life, oh spirit? Were you a mother?" (One rap) "A seamstress?" (One rap) "A reformer?" said Fanny. (One rap again)

"A poet?" said LaRoy. (Three raps) "Hark she is a poet, friends!"

The actor, Mr. Jefferson, shifted in his chair, his dusky eyelids firmly closed.

"Kindly ask *Vooshti*," he said to the medium, "if her poetry translates one sphere to the next? Will she privilege us with a couplet or two?"

"*Vashti* has come and gone," said Fanny. "A summer's breeze laden with pollen, is Vashti. It is just your familiar that speaks. Ask of her."

"Oh eloquent spirit," the actor pronounced. "Oh Poetess Most Byronesque! Might I have the morbid privilege of hearing how it was you died?"

Fanny betrayed the slightest frown. "An *actor* begs your leave, oh spirit, to hear in what manner you quit this existence? Did you die by so-called natural causes or did you die by violent ones?"

"Why must the spirit take care I'm an actor? What has that to do with the way that it died?"

"Perhaps," said Lucretia, eyes still closed, a smile melting across her face, "the spirit wishes to keep track of when you are speaking your lines, and when earnest."

There came in the wake of her words three raps and the actor stood up from his chair in surprise; he sat just as quickly, as though he'd been stretching.

"Natural causes, then," said Fanny. "If ever they can be to those they afflict. Tell us oh righteous, benevolent spirit, not only your manner of death but its name."

A whooshing sound was heard off-stage; it was like someone breathing in a sickly, laboured way. Its origin was somewhere behind Fanny Conant's shoulders. This I could tell on account of her hair, which was very gently blowing in the airstream.

"I died with ground glass in my lungs, says the spirit. I died of a chill that spread all through me. But it is beautiful to pass from this earth, says the spirit. Beautiful to be here among you, she says. And yet all the same I don't wish to come back unless it were to die again. LaRoy, I am here, says the spirit. Am happy. And please—oh, please—wish Moses well."

Joining the whooshing there came, all around us, the ringing of one and then two bells and yet a third and fourth in concert, until all four both high and low were ringing in the darkness with a staggered regularity, changing their distance and height ring to ring. For a couple of us, this proved too much. Neighbours' hands at once were dropped, eyes pried open, heads thrown back and laughing delight projected up to hear those tinny imps of sound.

Lucretia emitted a long, sultry giggle, and touched the flesh below her throat.

Mr. Sunderland was sitting with his elbows on the table, weeping and smiling at once, like a madman.

"Her name," he announced, "is Mabel Warren. The heart of Mr. Moses Dow, she worked for a time at his Waverley Magazine. Died of lung fever. A ghastly affair. Moses almost gone to ruin. Oh welcome, thrice welcome, most pined-for of spirits! Welcome, Mabel Warren, to the dayside," he cried.

And LaRoy Sunderland threw up his hands. And Brockton and Spear laughed deep in their throats. And Bly looked up with feeble awe, rotating his head after objects unseen. Lucretia pretended to swoon in her seat and J. Jefferson made to hold her.

Fanny never broke composure. And never broke the chain of hands. She nodded serenely round the group as if we had all of us risen and thanked her.

She was, so far as I could tell, an expert, unabashed hoax.

"Done," said Miss Conant. "Our Vashti takes flight, the cherished Mabel Warren with her. Resurrect me not, she says, unless it were to die again. Resurrect only this night's revelation. Embosom it deep within your soul."

Since neither Child nor I had funds to hire a cab to take downtown, we decided to split the annoyance by walking, Algernon to Blackstone Square and I to the workshop on Newspaper Row.

At Algernon's door we went up for a brandy.

I noticed at once that his rooms were more modest—partly based in where he lived but also the surfeit of books and wall-hangings that made his walls seem close upon.

The hangings were all of them camera portraits; original negatives most likely.

An arrangement of triplets, all grown men, the selfsame widow's peak and necktie.

An earthbound trapezist who looked to be wearing a spotted pair of lady's bloomers.

A beautiful woman with long dark hair, parting and brushing it a la Madonna.

A trim pair of dandies with mutton-chop whiskers lighting each the other's pipe.

A duck-hunting party.

An actor in blackface.

A man giving a temperance pledge.

An angelic maiden no older than ten lying in state on a bed pocked with roses, the roses themselves—which were coloured somehow—making out the edges of a latticed, gilt frame.

And especially pretty, dear reader, this last. It bore a resemblance to Cora Christine, though nowhere even half as lovely—erotic locus of my days, as cousins are, when boys are small.

Had I told you of Cora? Well, maybe I didn't.

Cora Christine was my cousin, you see. She drowned when she was ten years old. Unluckily, I had been there. My father had been drunk of course, as he so often was on the weekends those days, my mother sodden with her syrup. My Uncle Asa, too, was there but he'd been dozing at the time and I was the only one out on the water to see the spot where she went down. There'd been no body, only fragments: the bright purple bow that she'd worn in her hair; her Godey Lady's book, still tented. More terrible even than her being dead was the fact that my cousin had ceased to exist, for I had seen her heaving head blinking out of existence beneath the dark waves. A short and unfussy *tchau* had been hers in the Lutheran church where she'd gone as a girl, while out in the churchyard our family had watched as Cora's stainless, unplaned box had gone in its sling of guy-ropes to the bottom and how Cora, not in it, had seemed so exposed, so naked to all those watching eyes that I had been the first one there to rain a handful on her coffin. While this print of the girl more or less Cora's age in her tiny white coffin surrounded by flowers had revealed to me, whether I knew it or not, a sight that I had longed to see: a flesh and blood person respectfully dead and laid to rest in sainted ground.

Though the roses, too bloody, seemed gaudy to me. And the funeral dress was much too busy. And the angle at which the portrait had been taken would probably have been much better had the portraitist arranged himself to give the box a bird's eyes view.

This would have achieved the intended effect of her soul taking leave of her body.

It's said that artists know their art—can remember, precisely, the moment it touched them—when it approached and took their hands with promise shining in its eyes.

I cannot boast of such romance. And yet, in certain ways, I can.

That picture of the sweet dead girl—the picture promised more, you see.

It was my favourite of the bunch and turning away from the wall I confessed it.

"Thank you, Willy, yes," he said, approaching my chair with two glasses of brandy. "This was a girl who had died in her sleep. Not sixteen and simply died—what you might call a tragic mystery. Her parents commissioned a number of copies to hand out to guests at the lip of her grave."

"How much did you charge?"

"For the *cartes de visite*?"

"If that is the word for reproductions."

"Six dollars, usually, face to face. Price breaks for the larger orders."

"You could charge more," I said and rose and toured the pictures, sipping brandy.

"Thank you?" Child shrugged. "I aspire to, of course."

"You are quite welcome, sir. But you could. And you must."

"I'll charge as much when I have earned it."

"And your pictures will sell themselves short, I should say."

"How much do *you* charge? For a necklace," he said.

"As much or as little as seems advantageous."

"And yet you are one to tell me," said Child, "to overcharge someone right there, eye to eye."

"You may *under*charge him, too," I said. "You may feasibly charge any sum that you wish. It is the smallest asking price that yields, in time, the greatest gain."

I drained my glass and looked at him with calculated vagueness.

"Will you tutor me in this?" I said. "What with your talent and my acumen, we'd reinvent the game completely."

"No, not I," he said. "*I* can't. I was never so much as taught myself."

"Self-taught, then?" I said. "Impressive."

Algernon declined to speak.

"Then how, man?" I said. "You sound like me. Enough damned evading. Come out with it then."

"I came up under Abraham Bogardus of New York. He is president now of the PSAI. Here was a man who taught me much by assisting me, you might say, in comparatively little. And in that, sir, I must abide. If you wish to go it, you'll go it alone."

"That is what he'd want, would he, this Abraham Bogardus of the PSAI?"

"I am altogether certain of that." Child nodded. "*Mr.* Bogardus," he said, "was a prodigy. He had what is called the lambent eye."

"A smirking tyrant was your master. And yet you are the better man."

"Be careful what you say," said Child. "You pay me a backhanded compliment, sir."

"I pay you only what is due. Pity it should be backhanded."

"You and your quipping again," said Child. "I do say, sir, it tires one out."

"Yes," I allowed. "I can see how it might. Clearly, you mean me to forfeit this round."

When I spoke I was facing the wall of framed portraits and Algernon couldn't see my face—or could he, perhaps, in the glare of the panes, see the curl of my lip and the flare of my nostrils, which were not so much signs of defeat, I should say, as the throes of a need to regroup and revalue.

"Forfeit and yet . . ." I turned around. "I would very much like to still be friends."

"It goes without saying, I hope," he smiled, "that I should want the very same."

"Then all I will ask you is this," I said. "What is the best kind of glass for the plates?"

After some hesitation, he said, "Patent British. Now let us talk of other things."

And talk we did, for several hours, into the watches of the night: of the slavery question, of the rumblings of war, of P.T. Barnum's Feejee Mermaid, of aperitifs and cordials, of garters and bustles, of Hawthorne and Melville and E.A. Poe, of the slow decline of Child's South End and the precipitate rise of the Back Bay. When finally I stood to leave Child shadowed me, on a swerve, to the door. I was drunk too, and exceedingly tired, the sort that claims you all at once, and my coat was leaden on my shoulders on my way down the stairs and out into the street.

Child stood in the doorway, smiling weakly, one arm hid behind his back. The pavement of Athens was starting to grey in the first of the mid-summer morning.

"Willy, I want you to have this," he said.

He handed me a pamphlet-book, with the following thinly printed title: *A Practical Guide to the Collodion Process: Describing the Method of Obtaining Collodion Negatives and of Printing Them* by George Washington Wilson.

"Willy, I want you to keep it," he said, pronouncing "keep" like "sheep," poor man, and thrusting the book between my hands as if I might elsewise refuse it. "I am glad, sir, most glad, to have met you tonight."

And giving my shoulder a squeeze, shut the door.

I wandered Boston in a haze. Early-shifters everywhere. A woman with a basket struggling through her front door. At the end of their rounds, a few plainclothes policemen. Labourers whistling in the mist. A couple of shabby young Micks in their cups. I felt the ragged pull of drink and lung-smoke caking up in me, but this time the emptied-out feeling was different, for there was something in beside it: the skinny book beneath my coat—the images that I had seen.

MISS CONANT IN CAPTIVITY

March 1850

At night they would empty the schoolhouse of children and have me up upon the stage. The stage, in this case, was a dining room table pushed against the schoolhouse wall.

They brought in coal-lanterns and lined the walls with them so nothing would escape their eyes.

The chair that I sat in on top of the table was hard and high-backed to encourage my posture. Below the chair's seat there were two pillows, on which they said to rest my feet.

The gentlemen lurked below the stage, some of them sitting and some of them standing. Certain of the standers had their hips tilted forward, their arms folded over their chests, their lips pursed.

"Permission to work the rap is granted," said a man toward the front named Shadrach Barnes.

He was shaggy-haired and blond and big—a healthy urgent country dog.

He was also a Professor at the College of Troy. He had come all the way to Roundot just to meet me.

"Permission to work the rap," he said, "has been granted the lady, assuming she's able."

He started to walk toward the head of the table, his stethoscope swinging on his chest. I let him get a foot away before I gave a single rap. He froze for a moment, assessing the sound, then began to come toward me again with new purpose. 1, 2, 3, 4, 5, 6, 7, I rapped in succession to make him walk faster, though I'd rested the muscles in my feet before his hands could get at me.

"Do it one more time," he said.

I shook my head that I would not.

"Surely, Miss Conant can give us reason explaining *why* she cannot rap."

"The spirits won't speak on command," I explained. "The spirits resent such ultimatums."

"The test conditions are not right?"

"The test conditions are too much."

"The spirits are prone to stage-fright, then? The spirits are seized by performance anxiety? Why the spirits are not unlike an actress, struggling to recite her lines."

"The spirits will not humour you if you persist in making fun."

"The spirits will not or *you* will not?"

"The spirits respond *through* the medium, sir."

"Not of, but through. Not will not, but cannot. Such muddy distinctions want candor, Miss Conant."

At a loss, I shook my head.

"Confess then," said Barnes, stepping back from the table, gesturing with the hand he'd withdrawn from my foot.

The sessions went on for a week in that schoolroom. They happened long after the classes let out, somewhat past the supper hour. Shadrach Barnes was always there with the likes of the Minister Willets and others: a county judge, some aldermen, a man who'd gotten rich in coal.

Roundot was black with coal dust to the elbows. The mountains and gorges were crisscrossed with chutes. The lives of the miners, our fathers, were hard. Everyone had to do her part. I had heard of the raps from a friend of a friend, and that latter friend from the friend of another, the travelling word come down from Hydesville, courtesy of the sisters Fox.

The following sessions went much like the first. I sat there on the table on the chair beneath the pillow. People came to hear the rap, leaning in close at the top of the table. They leaned in and listened intently and long, like men listening for the sea in a shell. Some of them would smell the air, the space around my feet and legs, breathing in as much of me as decency permitted.

The men called themselves an "impartial committee"—convened in faith to break my will. Other girls who worked the rap had drawn other committees that went on for weeks but I was the first one in all of Roundot who had summoned a college professor from Troy.

Before the fourth session they took me to the basement of the school. A pack of women waited there. These were the wives of the well-to-do men heading up the inquiry. They guided me into a small anteroom that was furnished to look like a janitor's bedroom and had me lie down on a small iron bed where they started to paw beneath my clothes. They were weak pecking hens and they found nothing on me. Two of them drifted away to report. When these two returned, they conferred with the rest, too far away for me to hear.

They said to wait there on the bed. The six or so women went upstairs.

Shadrach Barnes came through the door. He was in his shirtsleeves with the stethoscope hanging. He stood in the door peering at me intently before turning around to shoot the chain. At last he sat down at the end of the bed. All of me tensed at him being so near. The bed was child-sized, almost too short to hold me, even shorter with a body perched there at the end. He readied up his stethoscope. And then, gently, he found my heart. He listened a minute, moved down to my lungs.

He drove his hand between my legs.

I gasped at the pressure and tried to fold inward, my instinct to pull, to shrink away, but the strong hand continued to grope at my lap. I made a sort of whining sound I didn't recognize as me, and again and again tried to jackknife my body against Barnes' hands, which were holding me down. I slowly retreated from what was occurring, so queer and unreal it was happening to me. I tired of kicking out my legs and lowered them onto the mattress again. And I felt a sort of warming or a summons settle in beneath the terror and the shame. The mortification of this man, touching me where no one touched, where I had scarcely touched myself, not for never wanting to but rather because I had never known how. I hated the feeling and willed it away but it was like a far off bell—at once too faint to scrutinize and too persistent dismiss.

Shadrach did not make a sound. He seemed intent that I should feel him. He worked as if it pained him to—to cause me this, to cause on me.

Sharply, he removed his hand and folded it beneath his thigh.

"I allow that you're clever," he told me abruptly. "Cleverer than most, perhaps. But sure as I sit before you now, I am every bit your match."

"You will find me out?" I said.

Shadrach Barnes did not respond.

"You will find me out," I gasped. "Yes, you, *good sir*, will find me out. I suppose in the meantime that I'm not to speak of what you did to me tonight?"

I waited a moment for him to respond. Instead, he stowed his instruments and rose and drew his coat about him.

"Do you like it?" he said.

"I despise it," I answered.

"Not me," he said and spread his arms to take in the bedframe, the walls. "Your new room."

HANNAH IN HER PERFECT INNOCENCE
February 1859

Twenty-two rooms in the New Shoreham Inn. Thresholds to lintels, mine and Grace's. Though the Fanshawes were hopeful their logbook would fill when news of the inn's better qualities carried. To Providence, Boston, wherever it was that people left to end up here.

A typical room in the inn was as follows. A carved oaken door with a knob of tooled brass. Pushed open, a dusk of untenanted air. Half the time smelling of wax or glass polish, at which Grace and I pinched our noses and clucked.

Continuing, we closed our eyes, not wanting to exhaust the room. And just through the door would encounter the coat-hook. Dipping, then rising again from the wall. So different, I thought, from the one in my house where father hung his fishing tackle. Our hook for hanging, the Shoreham's for show—an elegant, curtailing spiral.

The best coat-hooks, we both agreed, were in rooms 3, 14 and 20.

Now on to the couch. Of the fainting variety. Brocaded pillows ranged across. The cushions themselves not much for sitting: a kind of flimsy tautness, not soft and not hard. Hands clamped on the arms, we pressed our bottoms, twisted and ground them down onto the satin. And when we rose would count away how long it took the mark to fade.

The best fainting couches for making designs were in rooms 8 and 11.

The vanity with the clearest mirror an unbreakable tie between rooms 6 and 12.

From morning to evening, empty rooms. Each emptier than the next one, it seemed. Their air vibratory with people that could, if only they chose to, be in them.

Once, from New Hampshire, a land-speculator, hoping to build some kind of mill.

Once, heading home to its native Nantucket, a whaler with salt-stains from faraway seas.

And once, above the vanity amidst the chill of room 16, a skinny, old woman in only a nightdress, writing her nephew a letter.

The woman's hair like shreds of cloud. Pitted, yellow scalp beneath. Wrote with her nose nearly touching the page. The interstices of her spine. The top of one onion-skinned, lace-slippered foot was juddering upon the boards.

"Oh come, Hannah, come!" shouted Grace behind me.

She ran toward the woman. Breath caught in my throat.

Grace flounced, laughing, on the bed: "A wooden bed! It barely creaks!"

The woman's shoulders seizing, dropping. Her metal point pen falling onto the desk. It rolled with a dark, hollow sound off the edge.

"To the best of your knowledge," began the old woman, "what time can a lady expect the Express?"

"The Express?" said I.

"The mail carrier, dear? We are distant out here but the Orient, hardly."

"I couldn't say the time for sure."

"Then know you," said she, "Mr. Stuart of Quincy? Or know you my sister, Amelia Stuart?"

"No ma'am, I am sorry," I said to the woman.

"Mr. Stuart, you might be aware, is my nephew? Amelia Stuart's only boy? And mightn't you guess we are scheduled to meet upon the wharf at six o'clock? Oh what will he think when he comes there, sweet boy, and his old Auntie Reeves isn't waiting to meet him?"

"Who are you talking to, Hannah?" said Grace.

Didn't answer her at first but drifted closer to the woman. My shadow, taller, moved ahead. It seemed to be attracted to the woman in the nightdress. And her face, which had been slurred at first and altogether indistinct, grew sharper the closer my shadow advanced until, all at once, it was painfully so.

Some fever gripped her. Soaked and trembling. A U-shape of sweat on the front of her gown. Behold her red and haggard eyes. And a knob of a chin—a malicious chin, even—drawing the composite of those features like a funnel.

An ache began to heighten in the lining of my lungs.

"Which is why, don't you see, I must catch the Express? To notify my nephew David? Does that not . . . *resonate* with you, child?" said the woman. "Do I still seem to you such a dotty old fool?"

"There is a woman," said I. "Over there, at the mirror."

"A woman?" said Grace. Getting up from the bed. Hanging on the nearest post.

"An older sort," said I. "She is writing her nephew a letter."

"Is she terribly, terribly old?" said Grace. "Say, is she a hag or a sort of grand dame?"

"Her face is . . . distinguished. A very fine face."

"What's our grand dame's name?" said Grace.

The old woman seemed to hear Grace but her eyes stayed on me.

"Lutheria E. K. Reeves?" said she. "Have you not heard my name said round? How my husband Mr. Chesterton Reeves owns the dandiest tailor's in all of the Hub? You *are* familiar with him then? I trust *your fathers* wear his hats?"

"Lutheria . . . E.K. . . . Reeves," said I.

The ache boiling up from my lungs to my chest and from there to my throat and up into my nose. Amassing itself, like the eye of a storm, around a fixed point in my forehead.

"Hannah, are you all right?" asked Grace.

"I think I might sit down."

"Would you like to sit here?" said Lutheria Reeves. Getting up from her seat with a curious spryness.

And yet I found I could not budge.

"Is my chair so distasteful to you?" said the woman. "Faint, then, wherever you wish, foolish girl!"

How long I slept I could not say. Though it must have been two or more minutes at least. Grace had that look to her, you see: panic shading over into quiet dejection. Thirty seconds was one thing, but two minutes, three. Who could be said to return from three minutes.

What I saw first: two large, damp eyes, surmounted by a coil of hair.

"Hannah—oh Hannah, you're back," shouted Grace. "Where in the world did you go, you queer thing?"

The pain I felt had lessened some. An unspecific aching at the margins of my head.

"You feared I were dead," I said to Grace. "You feared I were dead and it made you so *sad*."

"Why of course I was, Hannah. Irreparably sad! What would you have me be, you goose?"

And then I looked down at my dress. Web of snot was on the front. Or what I figured must be snot. But this was white and thicker stuff, like you might use to bake a cake. It was hanging in ropes from my bust to my bodice, trembling beneath my breath.

"Grace. Oh Grace. I am disgusting."

"*You*," she said, "are Grace's goose."

Did I manage to smile. Then I said, "So I am."

"And a goose must think well of itself," said my friend, "if it wants to be more than a bird, after all. A goose, Hannah Maier, must look in the mirror and ruffle its feathers, grey and white."

Thomas Unger, stable-boy. Trampled to death by a spooked draft horse. A garland of hoof-shaped dents and bruises. Gleaming spots among the gore.

Mr. Isaac Hardy, prospector in fishes. Stung by an eel as he strolled on our reefs. The bottoms of his trousers cut away to vent the swelling. Mumbling, shivering. Red-nosed with ague.

Abby Blackwell, walking circles. Clutching at her broken neck. Not completely askew but not quite hinging right. As though she were looking, forever, askance. In half-mourning now for her husband and son, died March of 1823, yet still the wound of all she'd lost could in no way have stung her the fresher.

Relations always sordid ones. Grace and I discussed them often.

Would describe them to Grace who would file them away to be given a part in the drama.

Mr. Isaac Hardy and the widow Abby Blackwell were childhood lovers prized adrift. But she was a widow on false information. Mr. Hardy was alive! Yet Abby's mother, Mrs. Reeves, she disapproved of Hardy's people and thus concealed the knowledge of his being alive in hopes that she would marry in a lateral direction. Thomas Unger, of course, with his Teuton last name, was Blackwell and Hardy's unmentionable child. And unbeknownst to *all* the players was Mrs. Reeves' massive fortune, promised to her daughter when she passed from the vale but in reality *kept* from Mr. Hardy, which Mrs. Reeves effected through a clause in her will that gave her daughter sole inheritance.

The best rooms for bearing witness to a thrilling confrontation were 7, 13 and 21, in that order.

Every day that the roadways were clear that December I travelled downhill to the New Shoreham Inn. Wrapped to the eyes in my double-thick woolens and over that an old serge cape. Too stiff with accumulate damp to ripple, it acted as a kind of sail, and frequently I found myself among the frozen rutted marshes at the edge of the road. Blowing in from the east, whole climates of sea-spray that slowly soaked my clothes and hair. Out west of the cliffs, Providence and places like it. Like leviathans scared to show their humps. Birds taking wing from their homes in the cliff-face and fanning out over the water due east.

Towelled off my hair and my face with my scarf. Explaining to Grace when she asked, and she did, that the cart that I had ridden in to get there was uncovered.

"Then you must arrange for a covered one, Hannah. Come thaw out your bones by our fire."

The Fanshawe's was a peerless fire. Burning for hours in its hearth of cut stone. Carpet and curtains and dresser wallpaper. Tables here and there throughout, each of them topped with a white latticed cloth. On one of them, to make an ashtray, the varnished and hollowed-out hoof of a deer. Paintings of people so out of the common, so different from me and my life up at Clayhead, they might've been characters in a book whose ending I would never read.

Grace's father there sometimes, drinking brandy or tea by the fire in his housecoat. Cordial enough, though not warm in the slightest. The only thing warm in that room was the fire.

"Grace," he said. "Hannah." His eyes dark and heavy. A Meerschaum smoking on his knee.

Mrs. Fanshawe in and out, possessed by a sort of directionless energy. Their charwoman Willa was thorough enough that Grace's mother never cleaned, but Mrs. Fanshawe *seemed* to clean, mainly rearranging things, until she retired to read one of her novels in a chair catty-corner to her husband's by the fire. She'd acknowledged me once, on the first day she met me. Had yet to repeat the gesture since. But then she barely spoke to Grace, except to command her around the apartment:

"Your overshoes, Grace, are in the hall. Wouldn't you love to remove them for mother?

"The crystal decanter. Pour mother a drink? And don't come down the stairs so fast?"

The few times I saw her familiar with Grace she acted at pains or by some imposition. Calling Grace over, embracing her fiercely. Then letting her free with a quick dry kiss.

After a while, they stopped showing in church. Though Grace would come herself sometimes. The place where they'd sat in the pews was saved for them until it began to grow narrow. Then closed.

MISS CONANT UNDER FIRE

March 1850

"What is it that bolsters this Spiritualism?" Shadrach Barnes asked the committee of men. "It comes from out of the mouths of babes and those same babes contend it true."

He swept his arm past where I sat. I felt raw and alone so high up on my chair though I mightn't have been there at all, in a way, for I sensed the proceedings might carry themselves from beginning to end far removed from my presence.

"I am told that the wage of a Roundot mineworker is five dollars a day," Barnes said. "Five dollars a day, less the cost of his tools, to brave the darkness and the depths."

Amos Edwards, front and centre, who co-owned the mine with his brother Elijah, shifted a little in his seat and slowly crossed his legs.

"Fanny, behind me, garners double. Double and then some," said Barnes. "Six sittings a day, one hour for a sitting, two dollars an hour—that's a twelve-dollar take. Fanny, a girl of seventeen, making two times as much as the grown men of Roundot, and then in the comfort of her parlour, where the air is as crisp and as clear as a bell. As crisp and as clear as a bell," he repeated, "unless you count the Spirits in it."

Laughter took the small committee, none so loud as Amos Edwards. Shadrach Barnes paced back and forth, careful not to turn around.

"Roundot might've called many men to its aid. I, of course, am only one. And being that man which Roundot chose, to wit, a disciple of science and reason, I have studied long and hard for three days past inside this room to determine for all, to the best of my knowing, whether Fanny Conant can communicate with spirits. My inquiries have focused on the rap, by and large, the so-called grammar of the spirits. The inhuman sound that they use to express the sort of words I'm saying now. Yet far *too* human, I should say. As I have tried, gamely, to prove. And yet which due to some vile cunning, some legerdemain unknown to me, Fanny Conant has concealed and still conceals how it is made. But what can we really expect from a girl who claims to commune with the dead?" said Barnes. "It is a question I ask, gentlemen, not of you, but rather instead of Fanny Conant, who has only to look inside herself to see the evil of her ways."

"Here, here," said Amos Edwards, rising slightly from his chair. "Tell us what evils afflict her, Professor."

"I myself have developed a number of theories on how Miss Conant works the trick. Medically speaking," Barnes said and gave pause to finger the mandible prongs of his scope, "the rappings themselves may be ascribed to one of several dislocations. The ankles, the toes, the hips, the fingers, and most favourable to this end, sirs, *the knees*. Why the knees? Since wide, the knees. The knees are the broadest and thus the most pliable, specifically the tibia and femur," he said. "The former grates upon the latter when the muscles either side of the former are exerted, producing a percussive sound, and ample force to jar a table. Fanny Conant effects—or *affects*, I should say—a quite ingenious jamboree. Fanny is for the bandstand, sirs, to herald with flautists the coming of spring!"

The laughter came bolder this time, more relaxed. The gentlemen were settling in. I felt my eyes begin to dart, searching out the room's egresses.

Where were my parents? They had profited from me. And then they too had been too scared. Their daughter, held below the town and brought every night to the church of the elders. Or maybe they waited, distraught but resigned, in front of the great double doors in the dark. If I were to stand on the tips of my toes to see through the window surmounting the lintel, might I have seen them on *their* toes attempting as hard as they could to be near me?

Shadrach Barnes was down below. He was binding my feet with a sort of thick bandage. He did not speak as he did this, and I could see only the crown of his head. He wrapped and clipped and tied the bandage without ever once looking up at my face.

"Of course, when they do it in China," he said, "the women inflict it on themselves. The effect of the binding is purely cosmetic. They like to go on slender feet."

"Be sure she's not *too* nimble, sir," said the Minister Willets, his eyes resting on me. "She isn't far from getting up and bolting through that door."

"She is just about right, I think," said Barnes, and tightened the knot that he'd made in the bandage.

There was a fiddling at the door, and then it burst open, admitting the nighttime.

Someone laughed invisibly.

An object trailing smoke rolled in.

And as it rolled, the door slammed shut, and the room was suspended a moment in silence. One of the aldermen gathered himself and he walked down the aisle to survey what it was. His footsteps sounded very loud. The object was still trailing smoke when he reached it and then it exploded in his face. It was fondly what the boys would call a sparkling torpedo.

The alderman yelled and shot upright. He clutched his eyes and limped away. A couple of local Roundot boys separated from the darkness beyond the open door.

They carried torpedoes of all shapes and sizes, ones to lob and ones to hold, and they lit them at once, as in some ceremony, and came on holding flames like monks.

The women, who'd been standing in the back of the room, who I'd hardly been aware were there, cried and came forward, a tide of them, running, to tamp the things before they went. The mine-owner, Edwards, looked shrewdly content. He leaned and whispered something in the county judge's ear.

Shadrach Barnes stood patiently, his hand upon his chin.

The pack of torpedoes went up, a sortie. The women, too late, fled clutching their bonnets. The room was filled with brilliant shapes and oppressively violent cracks and bangs. I stared for a moment, unable to move. And then I remembered my feet, lashed together.

Sweat was spreading through my clothes and trickling down my bandaged legs.

Shadrach Barnes was still, like me. He was standing at the head of the long line of tables and watching the proceedings down the middle of the aisle. He stood with his arms crossed, his necktie bunched up, strange, wild lights playing over his face.

"Now wasn't that a proper shock?" said one of the wives, who had mounted the table and was holding protectively onto my arm. "I trust you're holding up all right through all of these hooligan antics, Miss Conant."

Please don't make me go downstairs, I tried to convey with my eyes, without speaking, but the woman would not look at me, as if she'd been instructed.

I tried to pull my right arm free, but the woman who held it was uniquely strong so I hauled myself off of my chair into space, not caring what happened, just wanting my freedom, and I went swinging out in a sort of drunk circle anchored by the strong one's arm. A second woman joined the first upon the stage and wrenched me back, assisted by a stouter third. I kicked with my legs but they targeted no one, just lifted me slightly off the ground.

"This isn't right," I think I yelled. My voice was unthinkably loud in the silence. "This isn't right. This isn't right."

"Do not be alarmed," said Shadrach Barnes. "Miss Conant is afflicted with the bilious derangement. It is yet another symptom of the mediomania that compels her to sit there and lie to our faces. Spiritualism, womanism, bloomerism, abolition—all variants of the selfsame affliction. And now, gentlemen, they have driven her mad."

Everyone nodded thoughtfully as I was dragged across the room.

"Go easy now, miss," said one of the women. "You'll only make it harder on yourself if you fight."

"Motion to reconvene," said Barnes, "when I have dredged this mystery further. Thanks to you boys for the most rousing show. And to the rest of you, goodnight."

MUMLER AT HOME
August 1859

In the nineteen years that I'd lived there and even now I do no longer, I am incapable of entering the Charles River house where my parents have lived for three decades without holding my breath for as long as I can, my knuckles jammed into my nostrils.

It is not any smell in particular, reader, that drives me to blunt my olfactory organ, as you will doubtless be expecting based on other tales you've read—tales of little innocents imprisoned in some manor where they are subject to the tortures of a cruel, demented aunt and who only need smell the linseed oil that auntie used to dry her letters to send them headlong into fugues of remembrance from which they can never completely return.

No—since you ask, I am not one of those.

It is nothing so disturbing or evocative as that which makes me plug my nostrils up. Though I have often wished it were given the doldrums of my boyhood where a breath of the gruesome or macabre would have been better than nothing at all.

Which is what my parents' house smelled like, not to say it had no smell; it was rather a medley, all woven together, so no smell rose above the rest.

First would come that of my father's meerschaum, a resinous and bitter reek that was strongest in the parlour and the bedroom where he slept. Next came my mother, a sour-sweet putrescence like some garden fruit in suspended decay, a polite simile for the gin and then laudanum which she had been using to temper her pain since the "pond incident," several years ago now. And weaving in among these notes, if the rare parlour casement was open that day, was the smell of the river gone brackish in summer or faintly metallic in the cold, along with the wind-carried smell of the hospital: orchids, ammonia, alcohol, death. And then the dust, dust everywhere, little bits of us Mumler's flaking off day by day, collecting on the ceilings and the stones in the walls like an extension of our claim on that place, of our unhappiness.

I would venture to say, if it isn't forgone, that this is the place where The Sadness was born.

On the day that I speak of, these smells became one, in the same hanging cloud, when I entered the house. My father wouldn't be at home, I knew from his twelve-hour days at the shop, which would give me some much-needed time with my mother whom I hadn't called on in a number of weeks. Her murky bedroom was upstairs, separated from my father's by a span of dark hallway. Thusly had they *always* slept. Or ever since the fateful night that they battered their bodies together, made me. And it seemed darker now midday than Boston proper was at night, the churchlike panes above the stairs veiled with blood-red floor-length curtains, giving the hallway a battlefield haze—an artificial, gory twilight.

My mother's door was locked of course, so like a good boy Willy knocked.

She opened the door in her *robe de chambre*, a yellow affair in dire need of a wash, and the woman inside it hollow-eyed, with a malarial air of intensity.

"Oh, Willy. *Entre, entre*," she said, running a corpse-maiden's hand through my hair. "I was just—reading, thinking, breathing. How many breaths, dear, we must take in a day."

"Are you feeling all right today, mother? Not worse?"

"Not worse and not better. Not *well*, anyway. My arm, you see. It comes and goes."

"Of course," I said. "It must be awful."

In the winter of 1855, my mother slipped and broke her arm on an icy embankment beside Walden Pond. I was eighteen years old and I saw the whole thing. It shook me a little, I'm happy to say. A host of bystanders, including myself, were gathered around her when daddy returned with three cones of chestnuts side-stacked in his arms. (Mother's chestnuts went to me, which made the evening seem worthwhile.) I knelt beside her in the snow and clung to her hand through the height of her pain. She lay abed the next few weeks in a fog of good-natured self-pity, slept mostly.

"I've been to the chemist's," I said.

"Have you really?"

"You knew I'd have been to the chemist's." I smiled.

"I rather thought you had," she said, backing away to sit down on the bed. "But then again, Willy, it could be you hadn't. It could be you hadn't and nothing in hand and I'd have been forced to abide in your company."

"Well today I can offer you both," I said, beginning to reach inside my pocket but mother got up jerkily and stumbled across the carpet toward me.

"Have you slimmed a bit, Willy, since last time I saw you?"

She pressed my arm back to my side, where it hung.

"A mother knows, Willy. A mother takes note. Your clothes seem to hang on your frame, well, more smartly."

I drew the vial out of my coat and approached her, the cork-end extended.

"Perhaps I've not been sleeping much. I'm on a new hobby of late," I informed her. "Now can't you kindly take this please—"

But mother proceeded to race to the curtain where she stood with her hand trembling on the chord.

"Here's the problem, dear. You drift. Your mind is defective somehow, I suppose. So many talents, so little commitment. What would your father have to say?"

"What wouldn't he say?" I answered dully.

"He'd say, wake up!" she shrieked at me, drew the bedroom curtain wide and cackled as light deluged the room. "He'd say, wake up, and look around. Your life's estate lies here—before you."

She seemed barely able to withstand the sun, so fiercely did it flood at first and stood in a sort of perpetual wince, half wilting away from and half leaning into the smoulder of hot July light from the street.

I tossed the vial up, let it turn in the air and land with the lightest of smacks in my palm. But before I could do this again she ran toward me and sheltered the vial in the cave of her hand.

"I accept!" said my mother. "I will keep it safe, Willy. On reserve for the really bad days, don't you know."

"But not before you've tallied up."

"No, never before that," she said. "Though I seem to need all in my arsenal lately to make good work of just one column. But enough about me and my weaknesses, Willy. Methinks that you pity your mummy too much! Where are the ladies—the *beautiful* ladies—who are destined to steal your regard clean away?"

"They are here and there," I said. "But you, mother, are everywhere."

"Oh Willy. Don't sport. I am just in one spot. I have been in one spot—right here—for some months."

And then suddenly she grew silent, my mother, as though she had remembered something and her boudoir glaze of resignation seemed to leave her all at once. It was replaced by something strange and yet something I felt I knew, a sort of half-remembered fear whose ghost flitted across her eyes like a swimmer in moonlight traversing a pond but not without ripples disturbing the dark, fanning to the farther shores.

"Poor courageous, kindly thing." I took up her arm and made with her to bed. "Let us get you snug and sound and if the pain is in you dosed. And then—"

"—hands off. Hands off, I said!" She wrenched from my grasp with fear plain in her eyes. "I can put myself to bed! Well can I withstand such pains! If I need you to help me with either," she cried, "by God I will tell you myself, horrid boy."

Then she went limp. Mother swooned and I caught her. I caught her and brought her, a-mumble, to bed. En route, I felt her untrimmed nails scratching along the inside of my forearm. I drew back the covers, and tucked her beneath them, and levered her head to support it with pillows. And when her eyes began to flutter, I poured from her pitcher of cloudy night-water and sweetened the murk with four droplets of laudanum.

This cupful I poured in the purse of her lip then titled her head back until it went down.

With mother asleep or nearly so, I tried to tidy up the room. First I pulled the curtains closed to spare her eyes that wicked light. Next I collected the old drinking glasses, took them downstairs to the kitchen and slopped them. Last I amassed all the blood-besmirched tissues and gave them to the wastebasket then returned to the bed, where I re-ensconced mother, smoothing down the counterpane and brushing back her sticky hair.

And yet it was strange I felt nothing at all apart from the urge to keep on, to keep moving. I'd attended, delivered, assured and made good. I must get on to other things.

And that is what sets me apart, I suppose, makes me the kind of man I am.

HANNAH NOT A MOMENT AGO
February 1859

Grace and I along the cliffs while mother watched us from the porch.

Usual talk along usual lines: the bachelor. The widow. The orphan. The will. The evil hag athwart them all.

But none of them were in that place. The freezing, arid land unrolled.

Yet I pretended they were there to fill my ears with Grace's laughter.

"She comes for you tonight," cried Grace. "With her imbecile's sleeves and a face like Ophelia."

"Fibber, she does not," cried I.

She was running ahead of me, calling behind her. "Seek out Mr. Hardy then!"

"Seek *who*?"

"Seek Mr. Hardy. So he may protect you."

I caught up to Grace and ran in very near. So near, in fact, our elbows touched. Peeling away while she laughed and cried out: "Beware the black spinster, Lutheria Reeves."

Later, ran to rags, we stood. The both of us screening our eyes, looking inland.

"Do you think she can see us?"

"Yes," I said.

"She seems to see more than most people, your mother."

Knowing this true, I resolved to say nothing.

"How lovely that must be," said Grace.

"That my mother is able to see us?"

"No," answered Grace. "To be seen. To be noticed. I sometimes fear *my* mother can't."

"And yet they love you, Grace," said I. "Even I can see that much."

"*Your* parents?" said Grace, breaking into a smile.

"It was your parents I meant," I said.

"We don't choose them, you know. Our parents. And yet they appear, for all that, to choose us."

"I have chosen you," said I. And when Grace didn't answer: "Just as you've chosen me."

A queer sort of smile on her face when I said that. A mirthless exposure of teeth.

"Then I shall take you at your word. Take you and not let you go. Not ever."

And she ran toward the ocean, displaying her arms, whirling around at the edge, circling back.

From the edge of our porch here were Grace and my father. Cresting the rise that wound down into town. Hunkered figures stamped in tandem. Father sawed the reins and cursed. What, I imagined, would they say to each other, hollering over the wind off the mountain.

Walking backward through the door, the threshold creaked beneath my foot.

"Hannah, come in here a moment," said mother.

I paused at the edge of the room, looking down.

On a bench turned away from the table she sat. The bucket wedged between her calves. Flurries of soap from the figure she carved unwinding slowly down the air.

"You sapped yourself but good today."

"And Grace?" said I.

"A peach," said she. "But Hannah, I wonder." Blew soap from her hands. "Do you think she can see them the same as you do?"

"She sees." Arms crossed. "Grace *sees*."

"Grace *sees* because Grace is your friend," said my mother.

"But it's only a game. A stupid story. I'll tell it to you, if you like."

"It is no game. So hold your tongue. Come sit over here as I asked you to, child."

I did as she said. On a chair next to her. She continued to shape out the figure unyielding. "Now what is it, Hannah, that you and Grace see?"

"Wonderful people," said I.

"What kind?"

"Sad people, mostly. And some mad. Others of them do not speak."

"I trust you remember the girl," said my mother. "The one that we saw long ago, you and I."

"Out there?" said I. Motioning to the window, beyond which stretched the ocean dunes.

"That poor child had lost her way."

"She died," said I.

"She had," said mother. "Died—and yet you *saw* her, child."

"Why is it only us that see?"

"If I knew that." Stopped carving. Hard and pale and very still. "It's the ken that decides, I expect," she continued. "Picks us each and every one. Touches us, child. Right here. On the eyes. And ever after that, we *see*."

"And the others," said I, "who do not speak. The ones who watch, are they dead too?"

"Mostly dead," said she. "God keep them."

"Like Lazarus, then?"

"Like that."

"*Mostly* dead?"

She paused. "Yes, child."

"So, part alive?"

Knife angled down. Hands in her lap as she thought what to tell me. "When Lazarus was taken ill and all were sure that he would die. Not dead, mind you, but very ill. With Martha and Mary watching over. Jesus"—she dusted off her work—"bearing down hard on the city of Bethany. Tell me, child: what was he then?"

"Before Jesus touched him?"

She nodded.

"I can't . . ."

"You *can*. Think, child."

"Alive and dead?"

"He was neither." She smiled. "He was nothing at all. And yet he looked like me or you. *This* is one of those," said she.

Brushing the last of the soap-dust away. Revealing a man in a hat and galoshes. A man whom I instantly knew.

It was Pieter.

"You saw him, child. The same as I. And yet we know: he walks and breathes. Pieter," said she, "will be your first. Pieter is for you to keep."

She handed me Pieter, still grainy with shavings. And this a highly detailed likeness. Right down to the kelp woven into his hair, the vertical jag of his nose and his lips scrolling from beneath his hat. The crown of that hat a bit rumpled in dampness. The face itself puzzled, a little bit sad.

"Is Pieter sick?" I asked. "Like Lazarus?"

Turning the figure about in my hands.

"He *may* be sick. Or injured."

"Or very, very old," said I.

"Yes, that too," said she. Down-looking. Shaking the soap from out her skirts. "Or Pieter may be well. Quite healthy. Until one day not too far off . . ."

"Pieter will be dead," said I. "Dead but alive, like poor, poor Thomas."

"Perhaps *undead* describes it better. That is what Pieter is now. Undead."

"But what if I keep him safe and dry?"

"It won't do him a bit of good. This doll which is yours, which you hold in your hands, is only for you to remember him by."

"Then you carve them," said I, "so you will not forget them?"

"I carve them because they are real. Real to me. And I would be foolish indeed to dismiss it." She looked at me a moment, searching. "I spared you as long as I possibly could."

Father went out on the water that March and came home every night for supper. In need of a drink or sometimes four after hours upon hours on the newly warm ocean. Casting the fishnets and hand-over-handing and bailing them landward and casting again. And then they would rest at the end of the day while spilling the guts of those fish on the rocks. Father's hook so slathered up that even wiped clean, left to dry overnight, it stunk the whole front of the house to high heaven.

Nights I heard my parents seething. Louder sometimes than the wind. Until, in the small hours of the night, their anger turned into exhaustion and sadness.

"Promise you won't go," said mother. "Promise you won't get on that boat."

"Know how daft that sounds, Claudette? Sometimes—I swear—I might be living with a madwoman."

Left my bed and crossed the house. Came to stand before their door. Something, however, had warned me off knocking. Knocking or turning the knob. I could not.

"Your hair is like a flock goats, moving down the slopes of Gilead. Your teeth are like a flock of ewes and every one bears each its twin. Your lips are like a crimson thread. Your lips are lovely," said my father. "Your cheeks are like the halves of a pomegranate, darling, behind the fresh drew of your veil. "

Strangers on the road to Shoreham. Lurking in its muddy streets. Furtive, silent, grizzled men half-shrouded in dirty mist. Watched the road like highwaymen who lacked the impetus to rob. Wandering between the buildings. Standing at the mouths of alleys. Perched on a hitch-post in front of the bait house. Wet hair obscuring embarrassed, pale faces. The same four or five, I became fairly certain. It was something I read in their posture, their height.

Inklings of the shadow-Pieter—the one who didn't fish with father.

The curve of his hat-brim, the jag of his face, the seaweed twining in his hair.

They were not like the spinster Lutheria Reeves, and they were not like Mr. Hardy.

They were not like the widow Blackwell, untying her noose from the beams.

Holding her high-collared dress at the neck in nesting rings of pearl and jet, two locks of hair— one blonde and one brown—crossed under glass like a family crest.

Grace right beside me. Her eyes wide as mine.

"Is she positively radiant this morning?" said she. "She must be now she's heard the news."

"The news?"

"That Mr. Hardy lives!"

"Radiant," said I. "But sad."

"Probably, she can't believe it."

"She's waited so long for this moment," I said.

"She *daren't* believe it, of course," Grace added.

The widow stood and looped the noose. "Tell me, girl: will it be quick? How long till I am with my boys?"

Farther I went into room 22. Up ahead, like ink, my shadow. Approaching the chair that the widow stood on, which shook a bit beneath her weight.

"Is Mr. Hardly there as well?"

"Presently he comes," said I.

"Who comes?" said our lady of silk and grey rope, the course of the noose through her hands never ceasing. "Bowen? John? Is that who comes? But oh why *now*, my cherished boys? Why now, as I stand on this chair unafraid, prepared at last to come to you?"

Remembering my mother's words: *Hannah, I carve them because they are real. And I would be foolish indeed to dismiss it.* And angry at her suddenly for presuming to tell me what was real. For keeping it from me, this blessing or curse, until she could no longer.

I would know the widow Blackwell for myself, then.

I would touch her.

I would touch, let's say, her brooch.

Began to move toward where she stood.

"When they meet at the heart of the room, they shall kiss. Kiss—and with such passion, Hannah!" This as Grace turned from the widow to face me. Catching my shoulders, her face very close.

And before I was conscious of having desired it, so pure and so simple a thing, we were kissing. No more than a second. The briefest of pressures. Grace's lips and mine, conjoined. A humid smell like baking bread or wine or brandied raisins.

Bliss.

And a closeness I sought to increase, bit by bit. Until her body gave a hitch.

Grace pulled away from my lips and stepped back with something dangling from her chin.

And here came the itch, rising up from my lungs. The tide of pain not far behind. And looking up I realized that I had been foolish to gainsay my mother for three feet away, standing full in my shadow, was the widow Abby Blackwell looking me in the face. Her head bent at angles it mightn't have bent at. The bruise on her neck a deep purple up close. Tiny globes of nervous sweat were standing out across her brow.

I veered toward the window away from my friend. Who was wiping her chin. Looking at me in horror. The stuff I'd sneezed or spit on her in a sort of sticky web between her fingers.

Here was the cold dingy street of New Shoreham. But in that room the sun was bright. So bright it meant to break my eyes. So bright that Abby Blackwell, now reflected in the casement, was blurred about her darkened edges. And Grace behind her, coming toward me, somehow not squinting at all in the glare.

MUMLER AND CHILD
August 1859

Child and I met on a blustery night in the Atwood and Bacon Oyster House.

I sat at the bar with a brandy and water—it was my second of the hour—and was blessed with a view of Child struggling inside in his soaking greatcoat with his hair in his face, one hand wrenching at his collar, the other one absently holding the door so wind and rain came swirling in and a pinched deputation of waiters rushed up to make the bumbler more at home. He noticed me, sat on the neighbouring stool. Lightning raked across the sky and imprinted on the surface of the sidewalk-facing windows. In the stutter that came before the thunder, through curtains on curtains of slant-falling rain, a couple strolling arm in arm disentangled themselves to dash for cover. Child, who was sponging his face with a napkin, followed my gaze to the couple and smiled.

"Enjoying the scenery, are we, Willy—safe and tight and dry?" he said.

"But wouldn't it make a splendid picture. Lovers flee the angry gods."

Child scoffed at this. "Man and woman in a storm. What have the gods and their anger to do with it?"

"Why that was poetry," I said. "And poetry must mark its passage. The artist—the true one—must never depict except for what he feels or sees."

Child said, "Baudelaire, if I'm not mistaken. Let nature speak for itself—there's another."

"Who said that?"

"I did," said Child. "And every picture-maker from Bogardus to Daguerre."

"Bogardus—your teacher?"

"The same," answered Child. He flagged down the barkeep: "What he's drinking, please."

"Let nature speak for itself," I continued. "Doesn't that strike you a tad over-literal?"

"Certainly," said Child. "Why not?" He cut a playful eye at me. "I should say you've used that book, so eager to out with opinions and theories."

"Here and there. *About*," I said.

"About, mostly, I'd say," said Child.

"All of that aside," I said, "why shouldn't the artist *inflect* on his art? Infuse it with his unique essence? Why shouldn't he devote himself to *being* an artist above everything? To making a living, yes, there's that, but also enriching that living with *something*—some part of himself that he cannot divorce or distance from the thing he sees."

"A story for you about tetchy old Abe."

"The darksome man revealed," I said.

"Hardly a warlock, if that's what you mean. And hardly cloaks himself in shadow. In fact he is the opposite: a straightforward man of essentials. Of facts. When Abe began to tutor me, initially, at least—"

"Tutor you in what?" I said. "I'd thought he insisted you go it alone."

"That was photography, strictly," said Child. "Before that he served as my life-drawing teacher at the College of Art right here in Boston. The camera was for him back then a sort of photogenic pencil. He practised in secret, a dubious hobby. I don't think anybody knew. So it *was* necromancy of a sort, I suppose. Though it was hyper-scientific, hyper-real, hyper-rare."

"And when did he usher you into the circle—reveal to you his eldritch dabblings?"

"He didn't reveal them at first," said Child. "Bogardus had us sketching snowflakes."

"From life?" I said.

"See, that was it. It wasn't really life at all. We were meant to imagine—approximate—snowflakes according to what he called our fancy. And the outcome was always imperfect, all wrong. Like pie-shaped parlour lace, our flakes."

"And yours?"

"Mine were best in the class," Child said. "And yet still lacking by his standards. But then one night in late December he pulled me aside after class had let out and he led me out into a terrible storm. Flakes were falling all around. Real and symmetrical ones—perfect flakes. Perfect and yet we had sketched them all wrong. Have you ever seen snowfall up close?"

"On my nose."

"I mean, beneath a microscope."

I think I almost laughed at him, but then I saw he spoke in earnest.

"It looks like something wrought in iron. Or else the finest fine-spun glass. Indestructible-seeming and yet so frail . . ." He returned to himself with a sip of his brandy. "At any rate he had me sit. On a commonplace bench on The Common itself. It was one of those evenings—hellaciously cold. We were the only souls abroad. Abe held out one black-gloved hand, contrived to settle there: one flake. And he told me to draw. And he sounded, well—angry. And so I drew, slowly at first, until that lovely flake was gone. It had melted on the leather, you see—disappeared. So Abe caught another and told me: *Draw faster*. And I tried—oh, I tried!— but I couldn't, you see, for this new flake had melted too. I'd no more been able to capture its essence than Abe had the poor thing itself, in his palm. It was," his voice hoarsened, "a glorious mystery."

"But photography solved all that?"

He nodded. "To his and my thinking it changed more than art—more than made *science* of art or vice-versa. It had changed the very terms of existence, we were certain. Changed even—dare we think it—death. *Lovers flee the angry gods.* . . ." He said it with a hint of mocking.

I felt my mouth projecting down. "Yes," I said. "What of them, sir?"

"The poetry, Willy, is in the process. The process is inside the camera. The camera is the best rebuke to all our man-dreamt foolishness. It captures the mystery without all the meddling!—our human need for explanation. For that is what poetry is, in effect: a futile explanation of what cannot be explained."

This time I caught the barkeep's eye.

Our oysters had arrived or were arriving at the table in a foul and sloshing sea of brine and as Child fished for one, then another, to drink them, I quietly ordered not two but three brandies, planning to fob off the extra on Child when the order was brought and could not be recalled.

"Photography doesn't need poets," said Child. "All that it properly needs are photographers."

Poor Willy Mumler, a man of few friends. I'm guessing why may be divined.

I have long been a lone timber wolf, you might say, howling my contentment at the moon's yellow vagueness. Scrappier, scurvier wolves come abreast, sniffing my backside, the pads of my claws and I have a mind to draw blood and regroup unless the courtship can be made on my terms.

But I didn't strike out against Algernon Child. I sat and listened to his nonsense. I sat and listened to this man rail against the elations that I had conceived.

If only I'd heeded the lupine in me then all that came after might have been avoided.

MISS CONANT CAST IN LEAD

March 1850

My first couple of hours in the basement that night I lay on my back with my eyes on the ceiling. The room was intensely dark and airless. I could not see my lifted hand.

I woke, suddenly, to a key in a lock. Someone came on in the light of the hall. He cut a bedraggled shadow in the door, like a man weighted down by the heft of his life. His hair and the long pointy beard that he wore rendered blonde in the light and the room went to blackness.

Then I heard him in the darkness, edging his way toward the bed.

I tried to back up but he came on too fast. And yet he didn't use his hands. He used just himself, his own bulk, to tip toward me, and he buried his head in my breast like a cat.

I accepted the weight and we lay, like stacked wood. He curled a leg up and then over my hip, his face still nuzzling in my breast. He didn't kiss or bite, just pressed and possibly smelled me, his nose in the fabric.

I saw him through feeling his warmth and his weight.

I saw him though he was not there.

I felt the rise and fall of him, the vast proportions of his chest. I wanted to stop him, to thrust him away and tried to for a time, I think, my arms reaching out for some fixed point of purchase.

"You lovely child," he said to me. "You lovely, lovely child."

He moaned.

"Tell me I am small," he whispered. "Tell me I am barely there."

I cradled his face and I peered at it closely.

His eyes were shut tight, like a child in night terror. I ran my fingers over them: the eyeballs lightly spasming, the lashes heavy on the cheek. I touched his nose, his mouth, his beard and all the while he lay so still. His eyes began to open slowly. He seemed to want to see me there.

But then, before his iris showed, I had lowered his head to my breast.

The inquiry continued for another two weeks. This was what they told me after. But a week, I found out, is no longer a week when the days no longer feed each other.

That was all it was: existence.

I heard the feet of youngsters, skidding, the marching of the teachers as they gathered them to hand. Sometimes a squeal or a bark of commandment sifted through the boards like dust. Some of the boys, I could only assume, were the very same ones who had lobbed the torpedoes.

One of the teachers from the school would bring me what remained of suppers. She was a fat and buxom woman who put me in mind of a South Indies icon, gliding along despite her girth, then crossing her arms to watch me eat.

When the sounds of the schoolhouse went silent above me, the wives of the men of the spirit committee would come to clean my face and hair.

"My dear," said Shadrach Barnes one night. "Today you must give up the trick."

But he spoke without heat. And his words, they lacked purpose. He only seemed to say them as a matter of course. So Amos Edwards stepped in then to take up Shadrach Barnes' slackness. He walked along the table with a queer erratic violence as if his movements were not his.

"To me," he said, "the greatest mystery is what Fanny Conant is trying to prove. The girl speaks in sophistries, riddles, evasions. Sometimes she declines to speak! Yet what she wants is clear enough. There is precious little mystery in Miss Conant's motivations." And the coal-baron turned to address me directly, facing away from the men of the crowd. "Frederick Conant works my mine. Frederick Conant is your father. And Frederick has come into more than a penny since when you first beheld these spirits."

Roughly his fingers encircled my ankle and dragged it, wriggling, from the stage. I nearly lost my balance then, tottering upon the chair.

Barnes came on a couple of steps.

Edwards presented my foot to the crowd, jerking me down bit by bit from the stage.

"This cheap, vile enchantress," he said. "This soubrette—"

"—I say, sir," said Shadrach Barnes.

"You say what?" said Edwards, spinning. All of the archness was gone from his face. "You say a great deal, *Doctor* Barnes, but what of it. What has any of it come to while we sit here like fools!"

"You are tired," said Barnes. "I understand. We are all of us equally tired, Mr. Edwards. And yet we are all of us men, after all. Gentlemen, once upon a time."

Amos Edwards cleared his throat. "Of course," he said and stepped away.

Shadrach took me down that night but did not stay to lie beside me. He seemed at once protective of me and terribly worried what others might think.

And then I awoke to a scratch at the lock. Soon he'd be crossing the room to sit down. And yet he seemed timid or possibly drunk—his key, I mean, the way it scratched. They had gotten him drunk. They had put notions in him. *Find where she sleeps and defile her*, they had told him.

The person who entered was not him.

This person was thinner, and shorter, and balder. He moved jerkily, as if he were nervous, as if he were conscious of me through the dark.

"Say your name," I told the shape.

I heard it catch a breath, then nothing.

It turned sideways and closed the door. There was something familiar in its profile. I braced myself against the bed, curling my hands into claws.

That was when Amos Edwards' face loomed like an unhealthy moon from the dark. His hair stood in wings along his head. His teeth were yellow, strong and clenched. He was breathing roughly from his nose, with pauses in between the breaths. Before he even reached the bed I smelled the liquor in his pores.

"Let us see, girl. Let us see," this man was saying, bearing down.

I clawed at his face, but he remained. And then he was wrenching at my clothes.

"Let us see. Let us see. Let us see. Let us see."

He whispered it fiercely, fumbling with his belt.

With one of his hands he had me pinned. The other one fished inside his pants.

He did not seem to really want me. There was no heat beneath his skin. He was doing this not out of wanting to do it but rather because I had wanted it less.

Then there was a blinding light. Edwards stopped fumbling, his trousers half down. He turned around to see the source and as he rotated away, it grew brighter.

Shadrach Barnes stood in the door.

"Mr. Edwards, a moment?" he said from the hallway.

"Hem," said the other. "If you might—with the door . . ."

"I shall not budge until you do."

Shakily, slowly, Edwards rose, refastened his belt and walked toward Barnes.

I was sitting there stiff with my hair in a tangle, my dress still up around my thighs.

Then the room was dark again and I could hear the two of them conversing in the corridor. I heard one of them and, much later, the other making up the basement stairs.

I lay there benumbed and yet calm in the dark. I could still smell the scent of the coal-baron's liquor. And I would lie there, gaining strength, rebuilding from the inside out so that when someone came for me it wouldn't be me that they found lying there but an artefact, an icon, a figure of lead whose aspect they would flee before.

So let them come and come again. Let them fall on me in legions. Let them think they'd used me up when it was I who would sap them.

"It's time for you to go, Miss Conant."

Shadrach Barnes stood in the hall. A cadre of shadow-shapes shifted behind him.

"Go," I think I said. "Go where?"

"It is no longer safe for you here," said Barnes.

"Was it ever?" I said. I was laughing at Barnes. "Or only now that *he* has come?"

"It has never been safe," said Shadrach Barnes with something naked in his voice. "It has never, for a moment, been safe for you here."

"And what if I'm content to stay? What if I am not afraid?"

"I don't doubt that you aren't," he said. "But you are not in your right mind."

"My mind," I said and tasted scorn, "feels as right to me as ever."

"The girl is in shock," he said, not to me. "Prepare yourselves. She'll not go easy."

"You're right, but still you're wrong," I said. "Not all of you together would be able to lift me!"

"We will do our best," he said, distracted by something occurring behind him.

I struggled upright at his words, eager for what, I could not say. The figures behind him clustered forward, shifting in the light.

"Try to make me go. Just try. I have lead all through my bones!"

"Mrs. Edwards, Mrs. Willets, Mrs. Jaffrey," said Barnes, stepping away from the door. "On my mark."

The women filed in then broke apart. I sensed them pushing past me in the dark air of the room. I extended my arms as a sleepwalker might, waiting for them to brush my fingers, and when one did I pushed her back.

"Keep away," I yelled at her.

"Please don't do that, Fanny dear."

"Kindly calm yourself, Miss Conant. We are here are *your* behalf."

Edwards' wife came in from the left. Her neck was an urn; she was big-boned and strong. She seized both my arms at the wrists, pinching hard, and pinioned them behind my back.

"Do you know what he did? Your husband?"

"Miss Conant, for goodness' sake," said Barnes.

Jaffrey's and Willets' wives were upon me, dragging me off of the bed toward the door.

"Any minute," I said, "your arms will tire! And then you'll have to set me down!"

HANNAH IN FLIGHT
March 1859

Father went fishing that Friday like normal. But Saturday morning had still not returned. Mother sat at the table, surveying the bluffs, when slightly after dawn I woke.

Haggard this morning, her hard, changeless face. As if she'd been there through the night. As if she had had company that only let her rest come dawn.

While out across the blue-locked land a pale blue light, by shades, amassed.

"Maybe," said I, "he came and went when both of us were still asleep. Or maybe he slept in town. At Heinrich's house or at the Inn."

Mother had nothing to say in response. As soon as I sat down, she gathered me to her. She'd let her hair down from its usual bun. Which, rather than soften her face, made it strange.

"Forgive me, child," said she. So softly. "I have done a foolish thing."

"Mother?"

"Forgive me first. We'll need each other soon," said she.

"We need each other now," I said.

And then she smiled, not sad but sweet. "It was so with *my* mother and me. Have I told you? I haven't, I think. And why would I, before. Well once upon a time . . ." She paused and seemed to wince past something sharp. "She needed me more than a mother *should* need. She needed me more than I was, at the time. She needed me—like faith—like God. She needed me terribly," said my mother. "And that is how they broke her, Hannah. In her terrible moment of needing me most."

"Broke her?" said I.

"Without falter," said she.

"Broke her because she saw?"

"Because *they* could not see. Could not see or saw too clearly. But not out of envy. No, Hannah, not that. It was effortless, really. They were simply afraid."

The sun crested a shelf of cloud. Migrating, aimlessly, over the dunes.

"Was she as old as you are now?"

Silent a moment. Considering closely. "She was nearly as old as that widow," said she, "that you and Grace have often seen."

I thought of Abby Blackwell's face. The date of the death of her two darling boys. Yet even so I realized I did not know my mother's age. Nor either the age of the woman just like her, trapped behind the locket's glass.

"You've never seen her since?" said I.

My mother shook her head. "Not once. When they broke her, they broke her in secret, you see. Broke her on a bed of fire. And I have seen a thousand women—sisters, daughters, mothers, all. A thousand strangers, dear to others, every time that I saw her. A prank, I've often wondered since. The strangest cruelest kind."

While past the window, through the mist, upright shapes of men were moving. Fanned abreast and creeping toward as though we were a flock of quail. Slowed their footsteps to a shuffle. Coyly they approached our gate. Their hands folded across their thighs or held from view behind their backs. In the centre one's hand, a familiar object. And only when we came outside to meet the men upon our porch I recognized my father's hook, streaked brown and green from a night in the ocean.

Heinrich's the only corpse they found. This in the wake of a whole day of searching.

Little taller than a dwarf and pulped by the currents beyond recognition, a wonder they found him at all, I was told, by the men who brought my father's hook. As to whether or not their dinghy sunk or broke apart upon the cliffs or flipped in the path of the charging nor'easter, none of them had lived to tell.

No sign of Hermann. Otto. Pieter. All of them were simply gone.

The Clayhead darkness long and deep out of which, slow to sleep, I could conjure my father. Floating upright out to sea. Man in the shape of a cross from above. Ready to sell his very soul for just a nip of something strong. *A thimbleful*, he begged the sun. Taking its leave of the world. Of my father. *Just a blessed taste*, said he, *so I can rest my eyes and sleep.*

Time or tide would tell, I thought, when I woke up on Sunday with father still gone.

And this I had hoped to see made covenant in every face at Sunday service.

But what I saw was wholly different. What I saw made me afraid. When the long avenue of familiar faces down which we walked to take our pew was titled, just slightly, toward me and my mother. As if we had some pull on them. As if our blood called out to theirs and told them where to turn their heads.

Mother pale and clearly anxious. *I have done a foolish thing.*

All throughout the hymns we sat, trying not to rub our necks.

The Revered Hascall in ascension. Light through the windows igniting his hair. The pointy shoulders of his coat were flexing like a pair of wings.

"Woe betide our little town in what is yet its grimmest season. Five more men, this Friday past, swallowed by the vasty deeps. Five more widows. Five more orphans. Sitting here among us now." The Reverend Hascall raised his finger. "Woe betide, yet woe be damned."

A gasp went up among the pews.

"Yes, my children, woe be damned. Believe your ears. They hear me right. So let us turn now to the story of Samuel, when Saul of Israel was king. On the evening of the battle with the godless Philistines, Saul and his three bravest generals waited. And Saul the King said: *I must conference with Samuel and conference with that man tonight for he and only he, said Saul, can say why God has turned away.* But Samuel the King was dead. And Saul did not deny this fact. Nor either deny to his men, as he spoke, that he *was* wise though dead he be.

"There is a medium at Endor, said one. So they went.

"To a creature of night Saul came by night. For she *was* a creature, this woman of Endor! She thrived, like nightshade, in a cave! She feasted on rats and sometimes dogs! She conjured Samuel out of the ground! And Saul, he opened up his eyes, beheld the newly risen man. Beheld him in *his* robes of woe, with the stink of the witch's curse upon him.

"And Samuel asked him: *King Saul of the Israelites, why have you disturbed my sleep?*"

Here the Reverend Hascall paused. In his rumpled black suit, fingering for the passage.

"*Suffer not a witch to live*, commanded God down unto Moses. Suffer not a witch to live and yet King Saul had done far worse. Can you say, any one of you here in this church, the words of Samuel to Saul?"

Said the Reverend: "Can *you*?"

Eyes on me and mother.

"But Reverend," said she, rising out of her pew.

Another voice amid the crowd: "The Medium at Endor lives! She lives to curse us all our lives, having brought this doom upon us!"

"Speaks lies," said another. "Her tongue is forked."

"She came to my house," said another. "She *knew*. She warned me my husband would drown in the storm!"

"And mine," said Pieter's wife, atremble. Standing in her wrinkled dress. "She told me to keep him at home. My Pieter. She begged me to keep him at home. She knew."

"I wanted to help you," said mother. "I tried . . ."

Shielding me behind her hands.

"Wanted to *help* us." Hascall laughed. "Sprinkle not our wounds with salt. Speak one of you, if she will not, the words of Samuel to Saul?"

Silence now inside the church where all had retaken their seats save for mother. The Reverend Hascall raised his arms and trembled that the words should come.

"Samuel told him: *You. Shall. Fail. For God has turned His face away. Your armies in their thousands will be routed and enslaved. And those who live—who should resist—God will smite their ruin all.*"

Mother standing. Now she knelt. And held me tight amid her arms.

"Mercy upon us," she told them. "Please, mercy. My child, my one, not fifteen years."

Drawing me in toward the neck of her dress until that dress became my world. The bombazine a cataract. As dark as Abby Blackwell's veil.

While through the shadow of the cloth the Reverend sweated far above. His hair plastered across his brow. His suit as rumpled as a flag. The sound of his breath in between his chapped lips the loudest one in hearing in the high room of the church.

But then the dress was wrenched from me and we were moving down the aisle. The bodies near too dense to pass. Her back to mine, my back to hers, we circled each other like soldiers in strife.

Christ the Son, His lesson learned, was watching us go from Him wanly, forlornly.

When I saw, at the opposite end of the church, reflected there as in a mirror, another kind of unwell man who did not hang like Christ but stood. And not in the centre like Christ, but due right. Where before, I recalled, he had stood to the left. Just as now he spoke to me where once he'd kept completely mute. The kelp still flowing from his hair in that same moist and ragged wig. And the saltwater, too, in a steady cascade from out the bottoms of his trousers.

"Girls?" he whispered. "Girls? Seen Nils? The harbourmaster, Nils Von Schafer? Can everyone not see for miles that we are in for wicked weather?

"Oh why am I so *wet*," said he, "when I have been trying all day to get dry? And why does Inga look so sad when I am not ten feet away? So put your wrist into it, girls and tap her so she turns her head?"

It wasn't fair, not one bit fair, and I couldn't help it, I called out: "He's here! Your husband Pieter's here—" said I before my mother's hand came shushing.

And that is when the widow sobbed. Or something like a sob, I thought.

I felt my mother's bones contract. She raked what I now saw was spit through the full flowing ends of her hair and then from it.

"Get out of this place," I heard now from the pulpit. "Like your mother before you, get out and be gone!"

The aisle of the righteous contracted before us. Narrower and more and more. The faces tightened. Angry, fixed. While the thrusting front-parts of the people blockaded.

"All of you, get back!" said mother. Brandishing her hands as claws. And clearing a circle she lifted me up and thrust me from her, toward the door. Only to have the defile close upon her, her hand coming unclasped from mine.

And the people appeared to be eating my mother. Collapsing, viciously, *on* her. Both sides of the aisle like two halves of a jaw that appeared to be chewing my mother right up. When in among them, slow at first, a rout began to manifest. Bubbling and spilling, then flowing more freely. A hand and then a torso bucked. Murmurs, some vexed, some amazed, at her strength.

Mother burst from all their arms.

The Reverend screaming: "Hold her, there! Christians! Countrymen! Hold fast!"

She heaved them off. Like corded wood. And spread herself before me, panting. Her bombazine dress torn away at the collar. Her hair a nest of Clayhead shrubs. And a long slanted gash down the side of her face from fishing hook or fingernail in which at last, done gathering at last, the bright red blood began to seep.

"You're ugly!" said mother. "You're all of you ugly!"

It made the people shrink from her. Not least of all Inga, the spitter of curses. Screened behind her three stout boys.

The dead man still standing against the south wall. Entreating his widow. His head in his hands: "Oh why are you crying—my Inga, my life?"

The last of the townspeople parting before us. Gratefully, almost, revealing the door.

Mother drove the trap uphill.

"But what about our things?" said I.

"What things we can manage," said mother, "we'll bring."

"And what about *people*?" said I.

"What about them."

"What about my friend?"

My mother said something too soft to be heard. And then her face slackened. She said something louder. Not repeating her first words, I saw by her lips, but endeavouring new ones more kind than before.

"Remember her address," said mother.

And drove.

And drove and drove, on through the fog. The grade becoming ever steeper. West of the cliffs lay the broad looming backs of places I might soon be in. Until up ahead in the road stood a dead man. Not labouring upward but standing to face us. Wearing only his shirt and suspenders and pants. About to flag us down, it seemed. But mother neither stopped nor slowed. And just before we came abreast freed one of her hands up to cover my eyes. But not soon enough to protect me from father. Alone of his kind in the dark icy road.

Standing in his supper-clothes. Calling out something that we never heard.

Staring after the trap, when I turned back, with wonder profound and benumbed in his eyes.

The mist closing in as we crested the summit. Obscuring the trees and the town far below.

MISS CONANT ON FAITH
March 1850

We marched arm in arm through the dark to the station. Shadrach Barnes went on ahead, once in a while turning back to survey us.

I smelled spruces and pines. I smelled cold mountain dirt. And I felt the cool breath of the dark on my face.

"You shouldn't have struggled," said Edwards' wife.

"You poor, bedeviled thing," said Willets.

The Devil take you to his bed, I did not say to either of them.

I had left Roundot only once. It had been with my parents to visit my cousins who lived up north in Buffalo. That place had been a clanging mess: so much commotion to so little purpose. The train, I remembered, had snaked through the mountains from a point of departure not far off. Pebbles and larger, jagged stones had tumbled away from the tracks into blackness.

The train depot platform at first appeared empty. At the opposite end of it, starkly described beneath the platform's single lamp, a bell-shaped figure stood and waited. It shifted around to present us its front. Its lace-trimmed black-and-scarlet dress performed an arc about its ankles. Shadrach Barnes was first to greet it. They addressed one another— Professor meet Shape—inaudibly and, I perceived, with solemnity.

Though I wasn't aware that we had stopped, Barnes signalled for us to make our way forward. I struggled against the hardy matrons, doing my little kick and lift. It was a woman, this was clear, and her dress was plum-coloured, with lacy, black trim.

One of the matrons was bearing a lantern. Every time it rose and dipped it blotted the woman, revealed her again.

"You're all but a slip of girl, aren't you, dearie? You never said she'd be so little."

The way she spoke was mealy-mouthed. I'd never heard her kind of voice—not in Roundot or Buffalo. Even in dreams.

"You're taking her to sit in parlours, not to serve out years hard labour. I should think that her size wouldn't matter," said Barnes.

"I am merely commenting," she said and knelt down.

The matrons had let go my arms. Up close the woman's face was broad; her jaw was as hard as a man's, her teeth square. She wouldn't have looked that out of place among the other Roundot women. And yet there was a calmness or patience about her. Her eyes were clear yet almost sleepy.

"She will more than do, I think. Mr. Barnes," she said, "you have my thanks."

The coal baron's wife and the minister's left me, shuffling away from their posts at my sides.

I stood between the woman and the terrors I had come from. Where were my parents? I wanted to run. There was something occurring here and now that could not be reversed or undone, I was certain.

And so, as I felt I must do, I cried out. I cried out pure and loud and long. And cried for so long that Professor Barnes grimaced. His top lip drew up from his teeth.

But she smiled.

"You're not shy, are you?" she said, warming my cheeks with her palm.

MUMLER IN THE DARKROOM
September 1859

Around the time that I met Child and photography first took my hand approached the anniversary of when I'd started stealing from the Mumler family business.

My adventures and successes in embezzlement started with a gold-plated timepiece I'd glimpsed on Commercial and that I obtained through titrations of credit over the course of the fortnight that followed. I say and have said and still say the word "credit" for this was all it was at first—or at least as pertains to my parents, the victims, who saw no deficit in gains. This was how I managed it: I'd simply overcharge the client. I'd conceived of a series of installments that would, all told, afford the fob and for every knickknack that I sold in those weeks I would overcharge the client in accordance with my object.

A little fogged with laudanum, my mother's bookkeeping squared up.

So it was that a number of other accents would join the golden fob that year: silk neckties from Provencal, a stunning pair of ruby cufflinks, a velvet smoking jacket, a deadly pair of Oxford spats that provoked, I was sure as I walked about town, the light murmuring and applause of awed strangers.

Which isn't to say I cared for *things*, the vacant glory that they promised, but rather that, much like the money I made for doing what I loved to do, I saw my outfitting in fey *accoutre* as another advantage to hang round my neck in the headlong and gauntleted dash toward my calling. Patrons are keener to offer a boost if they can be met at halfway on the ladder.

My pockets, they whistled; my fancy, it roared. And oh the threadbare days of youth!

So disparage me, reader, a profligate crook, as well to do for being young.

My father did. My father frowned. My father bent his eye on me. And I fed him with fibs about where the bulk came from, that I had won it playing Monte with the Irish, and so on.

But then came Brianna and with her new pastures—pastures of drinking and smoking and swerving through Boston streets made raw by dawn that cost me several dollars more than the ones I'd been confined to in the bleak house of my boyhood and that needed a fresh change of clothes now and then, preferably French and ingeniously slimming.

New appetites brought new deceits—or new expedience, let's say. Like a criminal dentist I started to scavenge the more bejewelled of my commissions. Garnet, I soon found, could be passed off as ruby; amethyst, sapphire; moissanite, diamond; shaved and burnished rounds of glass for Poseidon's own pearls from the nacre-rich deep.

These so-called gems I sold to pawnshops, to fingersmiths and confidence men in back alleys.

Boston's Lahngworthies were never the wiser—they pouted, and cooed, and rejoiced in their treasures. They gladly paid their doctored quotes, often with a little bonus and left overcharged, overdressed, overjoyed.

The only legitimate commerce I did in in summer or fall of 1859 was the modest under-charging of Lucretia for her necklace.

The reason was this: photography was expensive.

My deliverance, my calling, an absolute racket! For once you had purchased the camera itself there were numberless tools of the trade still to gather, none of them common and none of them cheap. You first needed lenses of varying thickness—a single for landscapes, a double for portraits—and these must be ordered from Ross's of London whose manufacture process, it was said, reigned supreme. Though if not bought from Mr. Ross—as I couldn't do barring certain bankruptcy—then you had to seek out Lerebours or Secretan, with the former preferential in the matter of focus. Oh! and you needed paper, Canson Frere's or Turner's brand, and a porcelain bath to hold the sheet, and a glass bath for holding the nitrate of silver as it washed the sheet to etch the light, and press frames for printing, glass funnels for straining, and a piece of wash leather to clean off the plates, and then the plates of glass themselves to fit inside the camera slide, and a graduated measure and small scales and weights. That was just the hardware, dry.

The chemicals cost me even more!

Chloride of gold, spirits of wine, Iodide of Potassium, alcohol, Aether, Pyrogallic and Glacial Acetic, both acids. Not to mention the Collodion and Nitrate of Silver. If either weren't completely pure, as the blood of a virgin or infant must be before it trickles down the altar, the process might as well be doomed.

The camera must be level, the plates well-positioned. The exposure must not be too long but neither must it be too short. And the plates—oh, the plates!—they must always be clean and only handled at the edges lest the photograph's subject be joined, in the print, by a foggy and underdressed thumbprint.

I liked to call him Mr. Thumb.

He was a sort of foggy dumpling hovering beside my head when I was my subject, as I often was. You see, I would expose the plate but then I would grow anxious at the seconds ticking by and so I would dash through the frame prematurely on my way to secure the reactioning slide.

In these early attempts at depicting myself, Mr. Thumb is more nearly the sitter than I.

There is scarcely the round edge of one of my heels, in most of these prints, caught fleeing the scene.

Yet I still needed sitters; I needed a muse.

So one night at the edge of fall in the wake of a couple of frustrating endeavours I visited Fisk's at the top of Copp's Hill where Bill Christian, as always, waited.

Bill was the son of a Fort Hill mortician, a fact he'd only told me lately. He'd always asked after my mother and father, whomever else I might hold dear, and I would tell him all were fine, and he would say the same of his.

"Still making them dead folk look decent," he'd said a couple of weeks before that night. "And wants to make me next in line. But I'll be damned if trussing death stacks up to any kind of life. To us, who have gone our own way," he had toasted. "Me with watch-dogging and you with the girls."

Tonight however he demurred, not much disposed toward conversation, barely letting me sip from his trusty gin flask before bringing the door wide and showing me down.

Downstairs, I poured myself a drink and settled on my favourite couch, which permitted a view of the room's panorama.

My plan had been, initially, to chase that drink with several more and with some liquor in my guts to see about a decent whore—Brianna O' Brennan, if she was in house—then crawl back to the jewellery shop to get some rest before my shift. But life, as such, was not to be.

A clamour went up in the parlour's far corner.

A skinny man with crow-black hair rose up from the couch he'd been sprawling upon and started berating a feminine form positioned with her back to me. The sweep of purple crinolines and the fever-dream height of Pagoda-style sleeves told me this was Madam Fisk. He yelled with some manner of foreign pronouncement, English-speaking, perhaps but not born of these shores.

"Pay, must I? Cough up? Pipe down? When she is mine and I am hers? If you will make me pay," he said, "then I will yell till I am hoarse."

That was when I recognized him.

Never before had I seen him head-on but only that once, hard at work from behind, his Irish paleness pummeling between Brianna's freckled thighs.

Madam was trying to talk the man down, pushing her palm at him slowly while whispering. But the Irishman grew every second more angry.

"Make me pay to see my girl, you dunderheaded cunt?" he cried. "When me and she have all but died to be together on these shores?"

I swallowed my brandy, rose up from my chair and tapped Madam Fisk on the shoulder. She turned.

"If I might, Madam Fisk, have a word with this man?"

"Don't trouble yourself, Mr. Mumler," she said.

"Aye, what's that, you tub of guts?" said the Irish while straining past Madam to see me. "Wants to have a word with me, I'll give him words enough to eat."

"At least, then, allow me to try," I told Madam. "What may come of it, Madam, I take on myself."

"You're a tolerant man, Mr. Mumler," she said and groggily wandered away from the scene.

Brianna's drunken paramour tripped over the edge of the couch coming toward me, performing a skidding and one-legged hop as brandy sloshed out of his glass on the carpet. Out of the corner of my eye, I saw Madam Fisk pour a gin at the bar.

"So speak, you Christmas hog," he said.

I put my arm around his shoulder.

"You're angry now and rightly so. Maybe even a little embarrassed," I said. He tried to shrug me off of him but I gritted myself and bore down. "Have a name?"

"To some," he said.

"Care to share it?"

"Fuck off."

"Care to share your name with *him*?" I said and nodded at the stairs.

"Not much in the habit of talking to niggers."

"In the habit of fighting them fist over fist?"

"Eamon," he said. "My name is Eamon."

"Eamon, let me ask you this. When she comes through that door, your girl, in a terrible flush of just having been fucked—and she comes in that parlour, her Johnny behind her and catches you here fathoms deep in your cups, who among the three of you do you reckon that pitiful scene will hurt most? Not Brianna, on the clock. Not the Johnny, freshly fucked. Neither one of them," I said, "is going to bat an eye at you."

"You know her name," he said, "my Bri."

I did not contradict his words. "I know it from experience for I have had your Bri myself."

He flinched at that, I do admit and I fully expected him, reader, to strike me. Beatific and patient, I'd lowered my eyes and made my peace with earthly pain. But the jar from the Irishman's fist never came.

I opened my eyes.

He was just staring at me.

And then a gloomy lassitude consumed his person on the spot: his shoulders slumped, his eyes turned down, why even his clothes seem to hang on him sadly. He might've let go what was left of his drink had I not gotten under him, bearing him up, and with one arm around his neck, the other one entwined with his as he struggled to walk while still drinking his brandy, we crossed the room of staring men and the whores who would have them and disappeared streetward.

On our way up the stairs onto Snowhill Street proper, a storm of applause filtered up from the parlour. The Irishman's face underwent a contortion, and when the applause died away there was laughter. And then the door was opening, Bill Christian behind it, spotlit by the lantern.

My, the Negro was a sight, in his spats and suspenders and black stovepipe hat, the light angling off of his plunging cheekbones in such a way they looked stone-carved. Eamon seemed strangely to no longer need me and rushed at Bill Christian headlong up the stairs, waving the drained brandy snifter absurdly as though he meant to have at Bill, but Bill sidled by him, as lithe as a dancer and let him go tumbling into the street, the glass flying from him and shattering brightly upon the cobblestones beyond.

Eamon righted, whirled around.

Bill said: "Come on, you Irish sprat."

But the Irishman stood in the shadows and heaved. Bill Christian made a cigarette.

"This devil of Africa guarding the gates, what else might I expect?" said Eamon. He straightened his coat and wiped spit from his lips. "We really do reside in hell."

When Eamon had shambled away through the night, I crossed the street and kicked the glass. Bill had lit his cigarette and was puffing away at it, propped on the wall.

"His liver exceeded his will, I should guess."

"He was only a gentleman gone out of hand."

"A gentleman, you call that, Bill?"

"Customer of Madam Fisk's."

"You commanded yourself with both honour and grace."

"The customer always come first," said Bill Christian.

"Face first sometimes, Bill?" I said.

He flashed the armour-plated smile before his expression went gloomy and distant, and I saw that he wasn't unflappable, Bill. He was, of everything, ashamed.

"I saw you there that night," he said. "I delivered that gentleman just what he asked for."

"Can I ask you a question, Bill?" He nodded, ground his cigarette. "When people talk to you like that, how does it make you feel?" I said.

Bill considered the question I'd asked him a moment, smoke still trailing from his nose.

"It's like I'm breathing?" said Bill Christian. "It's like I'm standing there, alive? Like my eyes look at things and my ears they hear things and my hair keeps on growing as every man's does but I'm absent, I reckon. I'm not really there. Like if they had a mind to they'd brush me aside."

"That's a shame," I said to Bill. "Photogenic man like you."

It would be more than several hours before Bill showed up at my rooms and, indeed, when I first had invited him there on the offer of taking his picture pro bono, it was anyone's guess if he'd actually come.

But lo, before the dawn, Bill came.

He stood tired and abashed out on Washington Street, his shift having ended a mere hour before and he scraped off his shoes (though he wore spatterdashes) before gaining the hallway and climbing the stairs. He'd also waxed and combed his hair into a clerk-ish sideways part and, in spite of the darkness surrounding his eyes, had cinched his cravat all the way to the collar.

I too had outfitted myself for the moment, abstaining from brandy in favour of coffee, laving water on my face, erecting the tripod, preparing the slides and arranging the screen at an angle to sunlight, which was just then beginning to pour through the blinds, even going so far as to pour out the fluids that I would need later to finish the prints.

The place, for all that it was not, looked not unlike a studio.

"Power of whatsits you got up in here. Photography," said Bill. "Some racket."

"Care to discover the function of each?"

Bill made a pass around the room, stopping near objects to peer at them closer.

"Let's start with my picture," Bill rubbed at his eyes, "and then Mist' Mumler can give me the tour."

So I ushered Bill over to sit on the stool. I asked that he remove his coat and then to put it on again; had him cradle his hat chimney-up in his lap and then to reverse it to hang toward the floor; had him loosen, a little, his scarlet cravat and told him to smile if it put him at ease.

"Another question, Bill," I said, "if I may be so bold to ask."

I was standing, at this point, behind the tripod with Bill dead-to-rights in the eye of the box. I'd never seen him look so awkward, exhausted and stripped of his back-alley wiles. It was all I could do not to fill up his ears with the vulnerable, beautiful poetry of him.

I would make sure to title the portrait, of course, before I next saw Algernon: Black Apollo on his Throne; The Whorehouse Negro, End of Shift.

But I begged off a moment, arranging the plate. "How much do you see in an evening at Fisk's?"

"Different night to night," said Bill. "Two greenbacks an hour as a base, normally little extra on the side."

"I should think that your talents are wasted," I said, "for such a mediocre fee."

"*Talents*," uttered Bill. "That's rich. Teaching drunks and whoremongers to work on their manners."

"A talent by another name."

"You want to call it that," said Bill, "I am too damn exhausted to argue with you."

And that was when I thought it best to capture Bill's image, exposing the plate.

"Congratulations, Bill," I said. "You're the finest and first in a long line of icons."

Bill said: "You just took my picture!" The smile was bashful, broad and strong.

"You don't sound glad to hear it, Bill."

"I weren't expecting—*that*," he said and ran a hand across his hair. "Now all you got to do is soak it?"

I briefly demurred: *all* that I had to do. My irritation must've shown.

But Bill was intent on the now-exposed slide, which I drew from the back of the box and submerged. His soft dark eyes worked tirelessly, tracking the plate as it moved through the air.

"A good long soak is all," I said. "And Bill will emerge, if the mixture is proper."

"How much do you charge for them cards de visit?"

"So Bill is keener than he seems."

"I live in the city of Boston, don't I?"

"It's *cartes de visite*," I inflected with relish. "And I have not devised a sum. How much would you charge," I asked Bill, "were you me?"

He considered the prospect. "Fifteen for a dozen."

"A little steep for novice work."

"Speak for yourself, Mist' Mumler," said Bill. "I may be a Negro, but novice I ain't."

We had carried out maybe a dozen exposures before the sun hovered in force over Athens. Between us the process felt glad and ecstatic, like brothers at play in a father's wardrobe, inciting each other: just one more silk necktie, just one more wool greatcoat before he comes in.

After the final exposure we sat in the midst of my new photographic equipment and shared what was left of a bottle of bourbon I kept on reserve for occasions like these. We sat for what seemed like a very long time, drinking eighty-five-proof with the sun on our cheeks, not really even getting drunk so much as just feeling the bite of the liquor, our shirtsleeves bundled up, eyes raw.

As though taking its cue from the shift in the light, The Sadness expanded, enormous in me.

"Have you ever lost someone you loved?" I asked Bill.

"Name for me a man who hasn't."

"But I am asking *you*," I said, with a bit of a barb to my voice. "You, Bill. My cousin Cora died. Quite young. And I could've saved her but then, well, I didn't and I suppose I sometimes feel . . ."

"As if you had done it yourself," said Bill Christian.

"Indeed." I glanced at him. "Sometimes."

"How was it she died, Mist' Mumler?" he said.

"She drowned, Bill," I told him. "In that very ocean." I nodded at the east window. "I was twelve and she was ten. Holiday in Nantasket. Our parents were drunk. We were swimming, my cousin and I and—she vanished. We never even found her bones."

Bill had been watching the light cultivate, moving quietly, mutably over the boards and he looked at me now from the sides of his eyes.

"My mama," he said. "Coming here, from down South."

"You lost her at what age?"

"Can't say."

"Can't say how old—"

"No, sir," said Bill. "I'm twenty-eight or nine, I reckon. But then I can't say that she's dead, well, at all." And here he appeared to grow wordlessly angry; he dazzled the world with his smile, sipped his bourbon. "You asked me had I lost someone and I just told you that," he said.

"Care to tell me how?" I said.

"We were near to Ohio, it come down upon us. The men we had with us was certified scoundrels. White men, river men. Ferrymen, they were called. But mostly just jackals, dyed white in their fur. Like as not they'd sell us back the very place we'd run off from or cut down the lot of us, triple their shares. Toss our bodies in Old Muddy. And camping out there on some sandbar some night between Kentucky and Ohio, mama set her mind on something. But when she waked up, shaking daddy and me, holding the key to our chains in her hand . . . And it was like she *knew*," said Bill. "But wouldn't—*dursn't*—pass the cup." Bill Christian winced and licked his lips. "We were already fighting upriver without her."

So Bill and I were not so different—fugitives of former lives. The sun drew focus on the pane and the dew burned away, irretrievably lost.

The best picture I took that day has Bill with his hat pointed up in his lap, his torso tending slightly left, the smile he has brandished to fend off the world just beginning to show at the sides of his mouth; an unassuming, lovely smile. The other ten pictures were botches, I fear—or anyway not up to snuff. I disposed of them quickly, with flinching remonstrance, in the dimly lit alley that bordered the shop.

Mr. Thumb is on the scene in most of these aborted prints, seeming to glare at Bill out of the shadows.

In one, he hovers at Bill's shoulder. While in yet another he lurks at Bill's feet. While another one still has him waiting off-stage for rehearsal to end and the show to begin, furtive in his shroud of night-fog, studying my every move.

MESSAGE DEPARTMENT

What of these companions she keeps, our familiar, amid the dim of wintry rooms? We speak of the widow and so of her sons, the lighthouse keeper in his cap, the eel-stung surveyor marooned under bedclothes, the lady at her long dispatch, and so we ask these broken ones how they can suffer to be seen when they especially and alone can never know the mortal cost? And ask again, we shambling dead, we pious and we unconsoled, if Hannah of unending eyes can see the precipice she toes? Or Fanny Conant in her cell prevailed upon by men to speak, can you bleak mortals comprehend the heresy of Fanny's creed that fond and long departed love might raise its bones and thenceforth be? While in among the darksome dens that heal the wanting souls of men, what strange affection all the same this Mumler courts in wanton girls who have no name or provenance beyond their office of an hour? In hunger sharp and fancy dull where goes he, now, upon his way? Up the hill and down again, past plots where paupers fall to dust, what sweet removal from this world does Mumler in motion, in furious motion, in ruthless and furious motion pursue?

HANNAH AT THE WHARF-SIDE
September 1859

Boston from the start was this: a fleetness of shades without object or aim. So many I could scarcely count. For every being made of flesh, a double of shadow beside or behind him.

We had been there, my mother and I, for five months.

We lived on the wharf among fish and more fish. How the first place we saw on the boat coming in was also where we made our home. We had set up a stall, which was profitless, really.

It sold not fish by statuettes.

Drifts of soap behind our stall. Making squeaky our floors. In our shoes and our hair. Trails of it sliding from our skirts and leading the way to our door, in the evening.

Shaped like children, family pets. Like heads of state. Like former lovers.

Also, that first month ashore, a fine remembrance of my father. Standing spraddle-legged in boots. Fishhook hanging from his hand. By a narrowing thread from the top of his shoulder, the net of spring salmon that he'd never caught. His salt-stung eyes. His puckered face, a barge for albatross and gulls. Father shrinking in the rain, where mother had placed him, his visage. To melt.

Suds of him bubbling into the gutter.

With the weather still warm we extended the tenting. Slept on palettes in the back.

But poverty is seldom slow. It tends to happen just like that. Such was the case with my mother and I. With winter coming on, we starved.

Old potatoes. Blackened bread. Rusty well water perfumed with an onion.

Mother hardly seemed to mind. It was more than just pride. In my mother, a relish. A life of privation a life to be lived.

Could barely get out of my nightgown those days for fear of looking at my ribs.

Mother's cameo necklace occurred to me often. Sole precious thing not of soap that we owned. Its mould of jet. Its silver backing. Its long romantic, linking chain.

Mother only took it off for fear of tarnish when she bathed. Her single monthly luxury, in a tub loaned to her by the fruit-seller's son. The water she'd heat with the driftwood she found along the harbour's filthy beach, some of it so sodden through she must burn other wood to dry wood to be burned. And then she would sit in her loan of a washtub, washcloth draped upon her eyes.

The necklace was the only thing.

I could filch it. Or filch it and hide it for later. Could claim it was stolen. Could tell her: a shame. Exchange it for money and money for food. Not sustenance but human food.

For we were humans after all. Not Maiers. Not bitches of Satan. But women.

At the end of the month, as she soaked in her bath, I stalked the necklace like a cat. It hung on a nail just in back of the tub.

With her long ropy arms hanging over the lip, my mother shifted, sighed, subsided.

Last time I had disobeyed her, Grace had flinched from my embrace. Grace had flinched, and I had swooned, the Widow Blackwell in my face, and everything from that point on was a long falling out of the life I once knew, and I would be foolish, colossally foolish, to slip that necklace off its nail.

Had never once strayed from the wharf-side, our home. Had heard tell of Boston, but never once seen it. But now I was in it, I could not ignore it. Rousting me from every side.

Yes, had heard tell of Boston when we lived at Clayhead. Mostly from menfolk, who'd gone there with fish. How two men in Boston had twelve years been neighbours—waked and slept and ate twelve years—

while only in the thirteenth year had come to discover, in fact, they were brothers. Beaten by the city into numbness of each other.

Now I saw how this could be.

Granite, puddingstone, and brick. Awnings striped and checked and solid. Ragged, evil-looking churches. Hotels as high as the heavens were low. Mansard friezes so lifelike they squirmed with change as you approached. And vendors, vendors everywhere. Of leather, tobacco, candy, nuts, men's top hats and women's scarves. Rows and bins of children's toys, as finely wrought in wood and paint as the figures that we carved in soap.

The cameo necklace surprisingly heavy, tolling down between my breasts.

Bostonian at twelve o'clock. Boy a couple years my junior. Trousers and shirtsleeves, a charcoal grey vest. Face gaunted and red with cold.

Foot traffic broke and flowed around us.

"Has missus got the time?" said he.

"I haven't got a watch," said I.

"I beg your pardon." Second stranger. Halting then veering around me, lips clenched.

"How can you tell by the moon, then?" said he. "Isn't there some way to tell by the moon?"

"I'm sorry, but I must keep walking," I said and whirled around to take my leave, and heard back behind me the questioning voice: "What's the deviled problem, then? Aren't I fit to know the time?"

Turned to watch the dead boy fade behind a veil of jostling bodies.

I stopped at the corner of Washington Street. Admiring the cuts, very clean, of the buildings. How bright and regular the lamps. When suddenly something, a clanging chimera with coal-smoke boiling from its base came tolling its onslaught in high, hollow rings, bristling with people that clung to its flanks or dangled from its rearward parts. Could not move from off the curb. People queuing up behind me. One block up the creature stopped, rejected about a dozen captives and when they had safely alighted moved on.

The ring of the thing in diminishing pitch.

A foreign pressure on my elbow. "Miss," said a man's voice, "I say, are you well?"

Harvest blond and fair-complexioned. Hatted, coated, gloved and caned. Handsome, I guess you would call him—yes, that. Near all of his person inclining toward mine.

"Are you ill?" the man said. "May I help you along?"

"Be at peace," I told the man. Like my mother might say. "You are missed at God's side."

"I say, are you looking for something? Some business?"

"I'm sorry," said I. "But I . . ."

"Thought what?"

A beat in which we watched each other.

"I'm looking for," I searched, "a jeweller's."

"Washington Street is the ticket," said he. He took my arm and started walking. "Not too far and not too close. Though I should say, your arm in mine and on such a fine night, in its infancy yet . . ."

"We must hurry," said I.

"To the jeweller's?" said he. "They're open late all down this street."

"But I must get back to my mother," said I. "She's very old and very weak."

"An angel of mercy, are you, then? And what must be your sainted name? Which leads me to ask, now I think of it, miss—"

"—but really, sir, we must push on—"

"—Saint Cordelia, perhaps? Or Constance, yes? You strike me, somehow, as some manner of C. Up ahead is a place that I know," said the man. "Many say they do good work. Grant me your hand for a kiss if you're going."

"I couldn't," said I.

And broke into a run. The young man grabbed my elbow hard.

He whispered at me: "Slattern bitch." And then with a last violent squeeze let me go.

Running along the storefronts. Tripping. My chin scraping against the road. Rising again with a faint beard of blood. Faceplate of the locket cracked. A trickle of blood from the scrape on my chin getting smeared by the chain there, a greasy red fan.

I broke my eyes against the gloom. Squinting while running to make out the storefronts.

Mumler and Sons, I read, in script. Wasn't that a German name. The printed pane began to shake as someone descended the stairs to receive me.

Did not bear much speculation, the big bearded man who came down to the door. Remains of something formal on: rolled shirtsleeves, a loose cravat, a vest of dusty, greenish-black. Wiping his hands with a towel in the foyer. Thick, dark eyebrows slightly arched.

"You're open," said I.

"No, miss. We are closed."

"I was told you were open."

"You were misinformed, sadly."

"Still you answered. There you are."

I was shocked at the sound of my own indignation.

"Which surprises you, does it?" said he, on a smirk. "As if I could ignore such ringing. The devil's own summons you gave me, I'm sure, and yet there is some *doubt* I'd come?"

Why would this shrewd fat man not help me. How could he be so cold, so cruel. The night's events, like staggered waves suspended at their crests from breaking. Fright after fright after fright. And I wept. So rarely if ever. Surprising myself. Tears streaming cold off the end of my chin.

MUMLER AND HANNAH
September 1859

The girl was weeping, frightened, bleeding.

It was rather an overreaction, I thought, to hearing that the shop was closed. And yet you never knew how close some ladies wore their jewellery—most of the time for the sake of a flirt, while for others it was their ward and ensign. Yet she wasn't unlovely, I'll give her that much, and I was not a man of stone.

I beckoned her up and then over the threshold.

Not a little irritated was I still in any case, having closed the shop early to tinker at pictures and was midway through soaking, at that precise moment, the fourth in a series of six of Bill Christian. I had her sit upon the couch where mournfully she scrubbed her hands.

"Custom or repair?" I said.

"Neither, sir," the girl said. "I have come with a sale. A cameo necklace of silver and jet. It's faceplate is broken, but that's only glass. I am sure you can fix it," she said, "and resell?"

"If it's an assessment you're asking," I said, "I might prevail to grant you that. But a resale, I'm sorry, is out of the question. We're strictly custom and repair."

"Won't you kindly look?" she said. "If you won't look, you'll never know."

She fumbled the necklace, her eyes still on mine. She was capable of anything, it seemed, in that moment. I should probably get her a cloth for her chin; her décolletage sported a bright swatch of blood. When she'd taken the necklace from off of her neck she waited a moment then held it up, swaying.

Its faceplate was shattered indeed, rim to rim, and the glass cleared away save a rind at the edges. The portrait, set in jet, was sound, as well the portrait's silver backing.

"You'd do better to have it repaired then resold. Here, I'll say twenty-and-five at the margin. Yes, twenty-and-five would do it nicely."

"And not repaired," the pale girl said. "What would it fetch me not repaired?"

"Exceedingly lucky you'd be to see ten. Bit of fingersmith's chattel. Of course I know of other shops that move such items in and out. In the North End, for instance, or else down the wharves, the northern slopes of Beacon Hill . . ."

"And in order for *you* to accept it?" she said.

"But we are not a pawnshop, Miss."

"Is that your assessment?"

"I've not made it yet."

"And will you make it now?" she said.

With her long fish's mouth and her widely spaced eyes, she wasn't quite pretty—no, not in the least. But fascinating, nonetheless; innocent and alien and terribly desperate.

"I'd require half an hour of your time," I said then.

She coloured deeply, looked away.

"Oh, it's nothing like that, not at all," I assured her. "A touch *outré*, if you must know, seeing it's on business grounds but really very innocent, I think, in the scheme, a personal hobby of mine . . ." I trailed off. "In the night, when it suits me, you see, I take pictures."

"And you're asking to take one of me in exchange?"

"You read me like a hand of Tarot."

"Why, I'm not sure . . ." She touched her hair. A wisp of it loosened and shaded her brow.

"So long as I'm breaking house rules," I announced, "the least you might say is the name I'm to call you?"

And looking up she barked it out, as though she'd been holding it in her whole life.

In the first in the series she sits there alone, looking off to the side, studying her surroundings. Her gaze is not at staring height but dithering along the floor—a gaze that finally finds my shoe, tapping the time that will mark the exposure.

In the next she seems to know her purpose and she stares comfortably at the camera, mouth set. She is either oblivious to the fact that the device on four legs is engraving her image or knows its usage all too well and could not be less curious of it. I'm looking down through the top of the box and seeing her there at the end of it, watching. My foot has stopped tapping. There is only we two. I find that I am hard as ruby.

In exposure the third she is still looking forward yet now to the left and slightly up, which gives her eyes the strange effect of appearing rolled-white like the eyes of a horse. Her shadow on the white backdrop could not be rendered more distinctly. I am standing by the tripod, dutifully changing the slide, looking at her, though if you were to trace her gaze it would fall wide of where I stand. At this point I'd said to her, "Hannah, where are you? Miss Hannah, Miss Hannah. Come back to yourself."

The final picture in this series has me standing over her, holding her up. When the plate was exposed she'd begun to tip forward and I'd quitted my place to be sure that she didn't. The camera, which could not be stopped, had etched this tableau anyway, awkward and tender in all the wrong balance, a botched composition were it not for the girl. The girl who stands there just behind us, quizzical of eye and mouth, her tiny hand held up palm out and roughly at a level with her glossy, dark head; it could be a gesture of greeting or warning. The wrinkles on her palm are pruned. She wears a bathing costume, too, that clings to her as though still damp and her head, which I described as glossy, appears so because of her shining, wet hair. Her face is intensely yet guardedly pale—the shaded pale of human bone or a white wedding dress in the lee of a coffin. Her expression, however, is hard to pin down. She seems confused, to say the least. She seems, like the waif who prefigured her coming, to dwell half here, half somewhere else.

Yet one thing I am sure of, reader. I, who hunch before the lens. I, who curl my bulk round Hannah. I, who appear to be shielding her, reader, from what she sees, from what she shows me.

I, William Mumler, do testify now as certain as I walk and breathe that the figure in the photo is my dead cousin Cora on the day that she drowned, near a decade before.

MISS CONANT IN RESIDENCE
September 1859

"Shall I describe him once again?"

"Oh yes," the woman said. "Describe him."

Her eyes were bright above her scars, one down and one across her cheek. They'd been given to her by her brute of a husband over the course of too many years married. All day I would watch as her kind came and went on the narrow, dark stairway below the street level. Once in a while one of them, such as her, would knock for me and take a sitting.

I closed my eyes and laid my hands palms up, wrists down on the cherry wood table.

"He stands about five-five," I said.

The woman grinned and shut her eyes. "A beanpole of a boy," she said.

"So skinny," I said, "he appears almost taller."

Breathing in, she gave a nod.

"The spirit continues to grow, to develop, when all the flesh has sloughed away."

"Lordy, how I doted on him."

"He died before his time," I said.

"So very long before," she said.

"He died by the hand of his father," I said.

"His father—my husband, whose name was Orestes. What sphere is he in now?" she said.

"He dwells between spheres two and three. He is dressed in pure wisdom, that sphere's final medium." My foot started its rightward creep. "Fertile plateaus. And Elysian gardens. Groves flooded with light

. . ."—still creeping—". . . where every single branch and leaf unfurls its own transcendent song."

My toe found out the weighted chord that worked the window's shade if pulled.

A jerk of my ankle toward me: there. A beam of light cut through the dark.

"Continue to rest your eyes," I said.

"Would it blind me," she asked me, "to look on my Tommy? Oh how I want to be with him!" she said.

"Continue to rest your eyes, please, miss."

Holding the drawing chord in place I produced with my left foot a series of raps.

"The affirmative sequence," I said. And she gasped. "He wishes, I think, to tell you something."

I pitched my head about, eyes closed.

". . . wants nothing so much as to see you," I said. ". . . it is the despair in your voice, Tommy says . . . mother, he says, pretty please, don't be sad . . . I am already two times the man you imagine . . . here in the Summerland . . ."

"Yes?" said the woman.

". . . among its gardens, streams and groves . . ."

"Pretty, pretty please," she said. "Always so polite, my boy."

". . . there is no sadness here," I said. ". . . only the light of the Univercoelum . . . it burns away being . . . knowing, too . . . until all there is . . ."

"*Is*, Tommy?"

". . . is grace."

"Oh, happy, happy day," she said. "Oh Tommy, my love, my darling boy."

Ever so slightly, I opened my eyes and saw that the woman was weeping with violence.

"Are Tommy's wounds healed? All his bruises and cuts? There were so many bruises and cuts when he died. Orestes stepped away . . ." she said. "He was standing over something in the corner and he . . . Oh . . ."

I toed at the chord with my foot till it tautened. The window shade started to scroll down again.

"The doorway is closing," I said. "Tommy fades. Tommy says, Mother, I must hurry home."

"Make it stay open," she said, "yet a while. *You* can keep it open, can't you?"

"Tommy has no proper say in the matter of when he comes and goes. Tommy is a wisp of cloud upon the firmament of—"

"—no please don't," the woman cried. "Please don't let my Tommy go."

"Tommy is no more," I said. "Tommy is gone. There remains only Vashti. And yet Vashti is going too. Going back to her elders as Tommy before her. Denizens of the upper spheres—beings of utter, unbearable purity . . ."

She was whispering, "Damn you. Goddaaaamn you to hell. Goddaaaaaamn you to hell, Orestes Quint."

I dropped my head, opened my eyes. I waited for her to return to herself.

Before the working day was out, hearsay of our meeting would carry downstairs. And the women beneath would come like rats to raven at their futures past.

Through a part in her hair, she looked up at me, squinting.

"I hate for you to see me this way."

"Really," I said, "you must think nothing of it."

Sitting up straighter, she said, "Shouldn't I?"

I was thinking what to say to her. I laid a dry hand upon hers, which was damp. So here were moments, brief and few, where tenderness became a scepter.

That's when Constance gave a knock.

"A Mr. Mumler here to see you."

"I'll be off," said the woman with scars and got up.

The jeweller was here, I now remembered. We'd met at some Sunderland function or other. I arched my neck and smoothed my skirts and bade that Constance let him in.

Walking across the wooden floor, the jeweller seemed to fill the room, not just on account of his size but his presence, which was—how to describe it?

Well.

His tread was light for one so large. He wore his beard full; it looked healthy and growing. A writing-slate-sized dossier flapped and waved against his thigh. He carried his head very high in the air and yet without a hint of malice; it was rather as though he were combing the ceiling for something amusing he never quite found.

Passing the woman with the scars, the jeweller lightly doffed his hat, muttered something gentlemanly and fixed her with one of the most curious smiles that I have seen in quite some time. He smiled at her mildly, politely at first, until he met her in the door and the mildness turned into a boyish disorder that drew his lips clear up the sides of his face.

He irritated me of course, but then he also made me laugh.

He was Henry VIII in the portrait by Holbein, come to visit Anne Boleyn.

"Charmed, Miss Conant. Charmed as ever. Do you recall the night we met? You were an hour or so answering the question of woman and then we all spoke to a dead girl together."

"I seem to have some recollection," I said, "of unbelievers in our midst."

"The sole fact you retained?" he said.

The jeweller sat across from me in a chair that was likely still warm from the woman. He balanced the leather dossier upon his solid hocks of thighs.

"Throughout the history of your movement, how many spirits have been *seen*?"

"I'm not sure what you mean," I said. "*Seen* is a dubious term, after all. People have sensed and felt and heard, which amounts all in all to perceiving, I think—"

"—but seen?"

"Yes seen. What of it, sir? Seen with the eyes? Or the ears, sir, the heart."

"You Spiritists equivocate."

"We *Spiritualists* have liberal leanings."

"And liberal definitions, too."

"I suppose you have come here today with some purpose?"

"Vital one indeed," he said. "Though perhaps you had better just see for yourself."

He rafted the dossier over the table, and watched until I had it open.

There were numerous photographs under the leather. As I looked at the man in the first, which was Mumler, bent over the woman half hidden by hair, I felt I was looking at something uncouth or something pornographic even.

That was when I saw the girl.

She stood, in her bathing costume, in the background. In her bathing costume, mind you, in a jeweller's workroom and holding up beside her face one still and outward facing palm. A trope, I had learned, in the

Eastern religions which told the viewer: *Do not fear.*

The man could not have looked more earnest. He was jiggling his legs with nervousness or with excitement.

"Am I meant to attest to your skill as a humbug?"

"If you wish," said the jeweller. "If a humbug I am."

"If Barnum, sir, may graft a fin to match the rear parts of a chimp then what is to keep you from causing a girl to resemble a manifested spirit?"

"So you grant she resembles a spirit," he said.

"Resembles one but that is all."

"She drowned when she was ten," he said. "That girl that you see in the print, who's my cousin."

"You took it yourself, I'm assuming?" I said.

"Took it," he said. "Exposed and developed."

There was something of doubt in his voice. "And?" I said.

"Took it and yet, I did not *make* it."

"I wasn't aware of a difference," I said.

"The woman I am hunched around. That is the woman who made it," he said.

I watched his finger going down to tap, at two, upon her figure.

"You want me to endorse it then?"

"I want you to more than endorse it," he said. "I want you to print it in your paper. I want you to print it for all of the Hub and I want you to label it first of its kind."

"And what makes you think I would ever do that?"

The jeweller appraised me. "That look on your face."

"The look on my face when I look at the picture?"

"Not that," said the jeweller. "When you look at me."

MESSAGE DEPARTMENT

What future is enshrined in us, you base pretenders to our pain? What makes you mortals put us on that we the worn might live again? You schemers and you squanderers, you walkers in the garb of flesh, how can you love us, we the dead to whom you speak in darkened rooms, when profits warm your outstretched hands the more with every cold untruth, compelling you to whisper now and evermore to those that grieve? You speak by the right hand but act from the left, then cry false feeling down the wind, yet who among you, kin to none, will say in truth the lies of men? So see you, then, the mockery that is this life's immortal truth? You Fanny Conants, William Mumlers, peddlers of the spirit all, who flout the very love you seek, so seek we all in mortal clothes, with leaden shoes and glowing paints and counterpane tableaus of doom and harps and horns and weeping strings and chiffoniers with players stocked and braided hair and shattered glass and phantoms lurking in a box? And yet we spirits ask you now, you innocents of boundless dark, resounding with such grim echoes as only spirits, grimmer, mark, how little matters if at all the good or else the ill of men when all go to their slim reward, their puppetry, their endless ends and none the wiser to regard, across the void, where they began? And so why speak we dead at all? Why squander this, our eloquence? What smoulders in us, we the snuffed, that we should beggar heartlessness when hearts in us by darkness kept as well beat once if ever beat, that slow and falter, gloam and swoon, until they cease and cease and cease?

MISS CONANT IN DEVELOPMENT
May 1856

Rap once for no, three times for yes, and five if you wish the alphabet. If the session is successful, thank the spirits for their kindness; if it is unsuccessful, curse the lot of them for tricksters. Make your feet and knees your friends and be sure they are always warm, for feet and knees too cold and cramped will never work a proper rap. Always maintain perfect posture. Never concede to be shut in a cabinet. Be wary of writers and college professors. Do not speak outside the trance. Wear a dress that shows your neck but wear a skirt that hides your feet. Watch the face but not the eyes. Invest in harps and horns and strings. Do not be afraid to put a little sap in it. Often pray and always sing. Repeat words and phrases. Say: Harmony, Beauty, Comfort for the Ills of Life. Condition your palms not to sweat. Exude grace. Never take more than a glass of red wine.

Miss Cluer and I sat across from each other. E.H.B. sat in the middle, observing. Even at so young an age—both of us were just sixteen—E.H.B. would call us Miss. This was no different for small girls of ten.

"Miss Cluer, you have lost your daughter. Your daughter was five when she died. It was measles. Miss Cluer has sought you out, Miss Conant. She's heard that you can see beyond. Your signal job," said E.H.B., "is making that beyond seem closer. Make it local, in a word. Make beyond a place, Miss Conant, that she can go to in her heart and yet make it one, if you possibly can, that she will require you to show her around. Comfort and confidence first, dear girls, but loyalty second, third and fourth. Loyalty is the sweet, soft milk that draws them here like hungry cats."

E.H.B. held up one hand, the other inching up to join it.

"Comfort and confidence first," we recited. "Loyalty second, third and fourth."

"Such a lovely harmony!" E.H.B. clapped her hands and we smiled at her weakly. "Miss Conant," she said, "engage Miss Cluer. What are you going to ask her first?"

"Who were you hoping to speak to tonight?"

"Who were you hoping to *contact*, Miss Conant. If mediumship is to be a profession we must use professional words, mustn't we?"

"Who were you hoping to contact, Miss Cluer?"

"Splendid, Miss Conant! Miss Cluer, your answer?"

Susie Cluer was a strange one. She was a tall and awkward girl who did not understand her body; her posture in the séance room was, for our teacher, an ongoing nightmare. It was also her habit to mumble her lines which is why, in our sessions, I was often the leader.

"You tell me," said Susie Cluer.

"Please enunciate, Miss Cluer. Who were you hoping to contact tonight?"

"Whoever you think best," said Susie. "I sit here at your expertise."

"Miss Cluer, you've listened! Now you go, Miss Conant."

"I am sensing a presence. It knows you, Miss Cluer."

"Less purposeful, Miss Conant, please. Are you not in the grip of a mesmeric trance?"

"I am . . . sensing . . . a presence. It . . . knows you, Miss Cluer."

Susie peeked out from beneath her lank bangs. "What kind of a presence?" she said, more assured.

"A female presence," I responded, but already our teacher was clucking her tongue.

"Let Miss Cluer guess, Miss Conant. Tell her: a presence longed for and beloved."

"A presence longed for and beloved," I amended.

"Is the spirit male?" said Susie.

I rapped once with my toes, in the negative sequence.

"Is it female, then?" said Susie.

"Quicker, girls!" said E.H.B.

I rapped my toes three times for yes.

"Is the spirit old?"

(One rap.)

"Is the spirit young?"

(Now three.)

E.H.B. held up her palm. "If my memory serves, me Miss Conant," she said, "you're ambidextrous in your talents. In that case don't be shy about it. Your clients shall want variation."

I rolled my eyes about the room, rendered passive by the trance.

"Excellent!" said E.H.B. "Let her heartbeat race a bit. And now begin to feed her, slowly."

I rapped twice with my toes and three times with my knees for a total of five at which E.H.B. beamed. "The alphabet is motioned for. So spell for us your name," I said. "Oh bountiful, womanly rose of the Summerland, gladden our hearts with your name," I cried out.

"Now you are laying it on a bit thick. But markedly improved, Miss Conant. Miss Cluer, what shall be her name?"

"Theodora," said Miss Cluer.

It was a name I recognized as that of the sister who'd brought Susie here. This was after their parents had died in a fire or so the rumour got around, and Susie was remanded to her older sister's keeping. That had been two years ago. The sister had gone to Baltimore to prepare, Susie said, for her railroad arrival, while in the meantime getting by at what her sister had informed her was a sort of acting college. On the day she had been in too much of a hurry to shake the hand of E.H.B., Susie's sister told her this before running to catch her train.

"Let it be Theodora then. Miss Conant, watch Miss Cluer's face."

Her eyes were wide and wet and red.

"Never look into the eyes," said our teacher. "A girl will get lost in the eyes of a mourner. There is such emptiness, you see. And yet such boundless, gorgeous hope."

"You think that she is dead to you. And yet . . ." I gave pause ". . . she is not far away."

E.H.B. considered this. "Forceful, Miss Conant and yet it wants finish. Is not far away and—what?"

"Your daughter's closer than you know. Come with me," I said. "I'll take you."

"I will conduct you, Miss Conant. *Conduct.* That it what you lack sometimes. But all in all a good attempt. Do you feel less alone in the world, Miss Cluer?"

Wednesday was mail-day and saw me abroad, walking the dimly lit halls with a basket. Every able-bodied girl had a job that she was bound to as a tenant of the basement and so it was in place of rent that I went room to room with my parcels of mail. Sometimes the women didn't answer and I would leave the parcel at the base of the door. Other times they answered in the middle of a session or some other task, such as keeping their books, and briskly accepted the bound correspondence while speaking or looking back over their shoulders. And still other times they seemed happy to see me or not surprised at any rate, and came to the door in their *robe de chambre*, smelling like powder and calling me dear.

Many of their names I knew. Rebecca R. Rynders. Lavinia Wilburne. Fredericka Marvin. Lucie May Beebe.

But they were housecats, strung with bells. I was a stray come to stand at the glass. It was my job to bring them the things that they needed, the things that they couldn't acquire for themselves.

One day a man opened one of the doors. He saw me, said nothing, turned back to the room.

"Of course, I understand, Miss Marvin. Not for everyone, you know! But why not keep my card on hand?"

By way of response, Miss Marvin said something I couldn't quite catch where I stood in the hall.

"Auditions, don't you know," he said. "The call of fame is loudest in the daytime, I suppose. Direc-*tors*," he said in a sonorous voice and laid his hand upon his chest.

I peeked through the door and around the man's body. Miss Marvin was powdered and blushed, at the bureau. And almost in spite of herself she smiled at the gentleman posing in her door. It wasn't long before she saw me, beckoned that I leave her mail. The man and I passed one another en route. He watched as I knelt to deposit the parcel.

"*Un facteur la femme,*" he said. "Now that isn't something you see every day."

He leaned on the wall, legs crossed at the ankles. He had an urgent, pointy face and he rifled his pockets, not looking away. He brought out what appeared to be the workings of a cigarette.

"Is she a friend of yours, Miss Marvin?"

"I deliver her mail, if you call that a friend."

"But you must wonder who I am. Josiah Jefferson." He bowed. "An actor of the stage, by trade. I love to have a little hash. And all of you girls are so pretty, you know. Do you talk to spirits, *Madame Le Facteur?*"

In the flare of the match that he put to this cigarette, I saw his well-groomed eyebrows rise. His face was unnaturally gay, too expectant. It looked to be lightly made up at some angles. Brushstrokes of blush, thin layer of powder, black pencil about the eyes.

"I have done my share," I said.

"Ah-ha," said the actor. "A rising apprentice. Yes, I remember mine too well. Richard the Third, Mr. Phineas Pankhurst and him, he had done all the titans, you know. And there I was, a runty turnip, trying to soak up the man's natural light. Do you have clients of your own? Miss Marvin has hers. I am one of them, clearly. What did you say that your name was, my dear?"

"I hadn't," I said.

"Go right ahead."

"You may call me Fanny."

"That's a good girl," he said.

There was a pause in which he watched me.

"Fanny," he said, uncrossing his legs and coming erect with a tight little smile. "How should you like to appear at a party?"

"*Appear* at a party?"

"Attend one," he said.

He stood a moment, smoking stiffly. And then his face birthed a maniacal smile. He pointed at me with the cigarette, waving. "You're keen to every word, aren't you?"

"Actors have parties backstage, Mr. Jefferson. I gather that you mean a séance?"

"Why yes, I'd forgotten. You're terribly earnest. All you Spiritualists, you know. It's a séance of sorts," said the actor. "Tomorrow. Rather last minute, I know, but I thought . . ."

"I had better ask my guardian, hadn't I, Mr. Jefferson?"

"It's a private engagement. Other girls. And yet I feel I could be clearer? No, you are not the flambish sort. You've a head on your shoulders. That's clear as it sounds. But want a little daring, don't you?"

"All I wish to know," I said, "is what you propose I'm to do at this party."

"To sit and be present," he said. "That is all. An opera might explain it best."

"An opera?" I said. "Is there going to be singing?"

"A few notes here and there," he said. "But that's not why I bring up opera. Opera is drama, performance of course and yet it's unique in the way that it's staged. Do you know why that is, my dear?"

"Baritones," I said, "and altos?"

The actor looked taken aback at my words. I watched him attempt to get centred again.

"Extras," he told me. "Whole choruses of them."

Bizarrely, I found I was smiling at him. He'd asked Miss Marvin too, I saw, but she'd elected not to do.

"My dear, you must admit," he said. "Spiritualism *is* high drama. I should think you'd be a natural."

"To sit and be present," I said. "And that's all?"

"Perchance to learn," he said. "To live. To do, for once, the unexpected. Why don't I leave you the address, all right? You can decide at your leisure that way."

He rifled some more in his pockets, down-looking. He didn't seem so threatening then. He wrote in his daybook and tore out the page and unfolded himself from the wall. I leaned forward to take the scrap but he held it just short of my hand, shook it lightly.

"Come any time after midnight," he said. "And you may even bring a friend."

"If I decide to come," I said, "then you will see me there, on time. And if I do not, you'll not see me again. That is because I'll have made my decision."

"Shall I write you the password?"

"You may say it," I said.

"You'll remember it, will you?"

"Yes," I said.

"Samuel. One. Twenty-eight," he pronounced.

I recognized the verse myself. It was Samuel consulting the witch in the cave. It was a passage from the Bible much quoted at the Center sole evidence of our faith in the verses.

The man stood there observing me, as if to make sure I had heard him correctly. When he was satisfied he smiled and donned a black hat with a silken green band. "Well, then," he said. "I shall see you or not see you. Good afternoon to you, Miss Fanny."

All throughout our conversation I'd been pressing myself more and more to the wall. Stepping away, I staggered forward, almost upending my basket of mail.

"Oh, and Miss Fanny." The man turned around. "I'd almost forgotten to mention attire. It needn't be anything fancy," he said, "but don't forget to wear a mask."

Tomorrow was tomorrow. I decided I would go. But I would not go there alone. With me would come Susie Cluer, whom I told of the party in between practice sessions.

"Why must we wear masks?" she said. "Is it a costume party, Fanny?"

"We must look our best," I said. "That is probably all he meant."

"Where are we going to find masks?" said the orphan.

Since Rynders was a frivolous and impolite woman, hers were the sheets that I brought to meet Susie. And not only those but a few of her bedclothes.

Susie launched forward to cover them up. "Fanny," she said and began giggling wildly. "Fanny, you are much too much."

With a scissors I took from Miss Beebe's sewing basket, we started to construct our masks. Feline, I think, was the evening's motif, with the eyes slanting up and the nose a triangle. Over the linen we draped lace and sewed it on loosely to border the face holes. We wore the masks and arched our necks. In the mirror we appeared to glimmer.

After an hour of pretending to sleep, we crept among our sleeping mates. We left through the window, no more than a scraping, toting our lace-covered masks in a sack. The dresses we wore were the dresses we wore. Mine was blue and Susie's brown. We looked like dowdy runaways. We had no coin to ride the trolley.

The house bordered a kind of park. There might've been water farther on. I'd expected the lighting to be more aggressive; the hour was aggressive, the offer itself. But the light in the windows was rich and inviting. Somewhere inside a piano was babbling. The sound of someone, somewhere, laughing was as steady and recurrent as the crickets in the yard.

"Suppose it's time," said Susie Cluer.

I handed her her homemade mask. We donned them while facing away from each other and then turned around to admire and inspect them. Susie resembled a raving madwoman gone out to preach in the streets in a tea-cloth. "*Tray* mysterious," she said.

For all the house seemed flush with guests, the door was considerably long in the answering. A small compartment opened in the top of the door, but a voice didn't speak right away. There was laughing. That, and bits of conversation, floated out into the night.

"Yes, well, you can't blame her, can you? Why I should think she knew full well!" And then: "Recite the charm to enter."

"Samuel. One. Twenty-eight," I pronounced, just as the man had pronounced in the hall.

The compartment swung shut and the door opened in. A woman in an evening dress of dark and sparkling blue stood there. And she must've been wearing nice shoes, with additions, for Susie and I, neither one of us short, stared into her starry bodice. Her face was turned away from us, her voice still engaged with a presence behind her. A contraption of satin and feathers and wire enclosed the borders of her head. Beyond her milled a modest crowd. Every face there was obscured by a mask and every mask was sipping something.

"Get in with you, chickens. Get in," said the woman.

She presented the room with a sweep of her arm.

"I have come as night," she said.

She swirled the cosmos of her skirts.

"We are Sleep," I said.

She gasped. "Of course! Harvest," she said to the woman behind her, "come see darling Sleep. They're twins!"

Harvest, with feathers like high, healthy wheat, looked us up and down and said: "Rather sleep-inducing, I should say, Madam Night."

"Pay this one no mind," said Night. "Harvest answers only to the tyrant of fashion. Harvest scoffs at everything that doesn't grace the pages of her Godey's Lady Book."

Susie, who would be red with shame underneath her tattered linen, shifted her gaze between me and the door. I suddenly felt awful for her. So much of life had been hidden from Susie and yet our ward, our basement mates, trivial girls such as these, even me, we all of us expected her to know exactly how to act. It didn't seem the least bit fair. In point of fact, it made me angry.

I pointed to the feathers at the top of Harvest's mask.

"You're due for a trimming, aren't you?" I said. "Children will get lost in *that*."

"Children of your height," she said.

I studied her a moment for some weak spot, some chink.

"If I am such a child," I said, "then how have I managed to rankle you so? Why, I can see it in your eyes. Right amidst those holes," I said and walked a bit closer, my fingers extended.

My index and my middle twirled as if they meant to prod her blind.

"Come, Madam Harvest. Let's venture elsewhere." The one called Night took Harvest's arm and they wandered away through the crowd.

By the time the shock of that moment wore off, I felt I understood it better. Tonight was not a night for names; nor either was it one for faces. Here was an evening for beauty and boldness; contempt, if it arrived at that. Here was an evening in which everything save the evening itself would be better forgotten.

"She's drunk," I told Susie. "She slurred—did you hear?"

"Do we appear that silly, Fanny?"

"Susie," I said and turned to her. Not caring what it looked like, I grasped her thin shoulders. "Susie," I repeated. "We are guests in this house. We are guests of Mr. Jefferson. Remember?"

She nodded.

"How else could I have known the charm? How else could I have known the address? Tell me, Susie. How?"

I waited.

"No other way, I suppose," Susie said.

"Now." I set her shoulders level. "Let us venture elsewhere, Miss Cluer. *Allons-y.*"

Arm in arm, we circulated. Susie kept her shoulders straight.

The party, or séance—whatever it was—was smaller in number than I'd thought. Apart from us and Night and Harvest, there were five other women, give or take, outweighed by fifteen, twenty men. Drinks were tilting everywhere and not a single slab of beefsteak. One woman and many men were swaying around a small piano, making a mess of Auld Lang Syne. The masks of the men were plain white or plain black, with strange wailing holes at the bottom for mouths. It was almost unexpected when the eyeholes showed eyes. All were moist and red with drink.

Apart from the guests grouped around the piano, the rest of the people stood in pairs. Night stood with a shorter man. The lips of his mask were long and pursed. He turned his head in my direction, nodded a beat and then turned back to Night. On a blue fainting couch in the corner of the room, Harvest had stretched out her legs. A man in a black mask resembling a lion leaned in above her and pounced, left her giggling. Her skirts came up above her knees. He scanned the room and pounced again.

A man approached. His mask was gold, the eyes and mouth outlined in black. It struck me as vaguely Oriental, what a Japanese prince would wear at court. He approached from a sideboard infested with bottles, through a haze of cigar and pipe smoke, with glasses.

"You ladies look lost without something to sip on."

I politely declined. Susie Cluer accepted.

"And now I have done my good deed for the night. Vice," he bellowed, "do your worst!"

He drank off the drink he'd intended for me, holding his head back a moment too long. For a while it appeared he was watching the ceiling, transfixed by the lights through the holes in his mask.

"Sirens and Satyrs, friends and lovers, your attention," said a voice.

It came from a man toward the back of the room. Could this be Mr. Jefferson? He'd seemed to emerge from behind the piano, though I didn't recognize him from the singers around it. This man's mask was small and stubbed, like the face of a dog or a pig without whiskers. The butchering of Auld Lang Syne stopped bleeding and died as the man took the floor.

"What is championed in heaven is strange here on earth. Spirits walk among us, friends. Spirits speak to us, console us. But can a spirit love?" he said.

"I have seen them love!" said someone. "I have seen their limbs entwined."

"Your husband?" said a second voice. "Husbands like a little lark!"

"Where is this gentleman's wife?" said the first voice. "I should like to pity her."

"Now, now," said the man in the animal's mask. "Plenty of time for jousting later. To the neighbouring room," said the man, herding sideways. "To the neighbouring room. And let no one go thirsty!"

And Susie Cluer, sure enough, was making herself a second drink. The man in the mask like a Japanese prince hovered around her, lunging, laughing.

I had never tasted spirits or wine in my life. Tonight, of course, would be no different. But I'd smelled it before on men's breath, in their pores—had seen the change it wrought in them. As well it might've been to drink, but Susie Cluer was not me.

Already she walked with the hitch in her step. Her legs became less and less hers every minute. She chatted with the gold-masked man: coquetry and platitudes. Every so often as she walked, laughing and twirling her arms at her sides, I pictured her face beneath her mask, its gaunt and unassuming features.

The room we arrived in was large, with high ceilings. It was dark save for the mischief of a grand old candelabra. The wallpaper showed a nature scene—thickets of saplings clung with vines. The saplings were yellow or red or bright orange, while the trellis of vines went from light to dark blue the closer you moved toward the seam of the wall. Floor to ceiling sections of the wall were draped in bed sheets, and these all had a squarish look, as if something hard were concealed underneath them. Whatever function it had served, the room was bare of all but couches. Four of them—long, blood red and plush—were arranged in a sort of diamond shape. The candelabra hung above the middle of the diamond. A window was open somewhere in the house and the sheets on the wall rippled some in a breeze.

"Gentleman, ladies, right this way. Positives and negatives, as best you can manage. Though we appear to have a surplus of the former on our hands," said the man in a mask like a dog or a pig, standing at the centre of the diamond, directing. "No matter, no matter. As best you can manage. There's a lady, there's a gent. Two by two—not three!" he said, motioning to Susie, gold-mask, and myself. "Sir—King Midas—Croesus, yes, if you might sit *between* these ladies. These Circes in sackcloth— these bonny beekeepers—these monuments to tattered lace . . ."

He continued to call out the guests one by one and one by one they hastened past, outrunning the spotlight to sit on a couch.

To my right was the man in the black and gold mask and on his right sat Susie Cluer. On my left was the man in the mask of a lion, watching me with bright green eyes.

The man was bigger than I'd thought. And he wasn't well-muscled so much as just generous. His stockiness expressed itself in a slab of firm flesh, segmented by waistcoat.

"I hear that you're called Sleep," he said. "I take it she's your better half?"

I nodded to him that this was so. I heard Susie laugh, pause to sip, laugh again.

"Which makes you what?"

"I beg your pardon."

"If she is *half* of sleep," he said, "then I should wonder, what are you?"

"Wakefulness, perhaps," I said.

His eyes had a warm squintiness through the holes.

"I am called the Lion in the Meadow," he said.

I said, "Your mask is very black. A nighttime meadow, I suppose?"

"Velvet," he said.

"May I touch it?"

"Of course."

The Lion in the Meadow leaned a little closer toward me. I touched my fingers to his snout. He nuzzled his face against my fingers and they slid from the snout to the lips, down the chin. Going over the hole that allowed him to breathe, I felt him panting through the mask.

"Let no man or woman speak false of the spirits," said the man in the mask of a pig or a dog. "Let no man proclaim that they stalk the far shore, parched and lonely strangers to the wonder that is love. Nor let him proclaim to his bosom companion who walks beside him through the vale that the spirits, our guardians, command us these words: Go in want through this brief life. If he cannot speak true of them, then let him speak no more, I say. If he cannot speak true of them, then let him speak the truth of love. Yes, let him speak the truth of love, which does not expire with the husk of the body, no more than it expires or fades under the thralldom of marriage," he said. "Or the scorn of ill health. Or the winter of age. Close your many eyes," he said, "that you might come as one to see."

I myself did not so do. Other people might have though.

This was once a library, I thought to myself as the man stepped aside. And then he extended his arm like a showman.

A series of figures filed into the room.

The lighting, as I said, was dim. So it was difficult initially to tell them for human. They might've been kangaroos or cats. They had that sleek, agile uprightness. They made a circuit of the room, skipping along the walls, hands clasped. Masks rotated after them or else they did not move an inch.

"Continue to close your eyes, my friends. Feel the breeze these spirits make. Feel their ecstasy, their force. Sense them around you with all but your eyes."

The maybe ten figures passed once, then again. "Oh my," said the people on couches and laughed. A garland of girls all wearing dark gauze—in nothing *but* dark gauze, I saw—circled the couches around and around, and started at last to use their fingers. They trailed them along the people's shoulders. They ran them up and down their arms. They touched their ears, where earrings hung. They teased them up their trembling throats. They stood in back of people's chairs, and the gauze that they wore had a luminous look.

"See only the backs of your eyelids, my friends," said the man in a mask of a pig or a dog.

Susie Cluer would be smiling. Susie Cluer would be blushing. Susie Cluer would be trembling, her hand in the hand of the Japanese prince.

One girl brushed a lady's hair, working her fingers through the thickness and as the woman's face tipped back she started to braid it, strand by strand. Now a lady bared her throat. Now a gentleman slumped forward. Now another laughed then groaned as a woman fell over him, kissing his mouth.

The man in the black and gold mask turned to Susie but the mouth of her mask was too small for a kiss. He hiked it up and kissed her cruelly. While Susie kissed, ginger at first, a woman in gauze came around to the man and started to stroke his naked ears. The man in the leonine mask held my hand. And that's when I saw that his body was wrenched toward one of the women in gauze just behind him. Sort of nibbling his jawline, she leaned in between us. The jaw was as brassy and proud as an axe.

The maestro had partnered with one of the girls. They waltzed the diamond point to point. One woman rose from her place on the couch and danced all alone in their wake, her arms swaying. Her fingertips were pale and sharp. They seemed to rend the darkened air.

And then I felt myself get up. The man in the leonine mask and myself were crossing the diamond en route to the door. Before us went Susie and Black and Gold Mask, their arms around each other's shoulders. At first I thought that he was leading, and then I felt I wasn't sure, and finally I had the thought that Susie was supporting him.

An indistinct, persistent bell was singing just outside my ken.

I thought at Susie: *Turn around. Oh turn around, you foolish girl.*

"Miss Sleep," said the man at my side, turning toward me. "I should say I'm new to this. I don't often come to such functions, you see."

We passed through the doorway and into a hall. The way was long, the lighting sparse. Susie and Black and Gold Mask went before us, twenty paces by my guess.

"What I mean," said the Lion in the Meadow, voice muffled, "I am a gentleman, you see." And then the bravado came back to his voice: "As much as Miss Sleep is a lady, I'm sure."

Susie turned around again. Susie, stumbling, called my name. And then her face appeared to plummet. It was as though she'd fallen through a gulf in the floor. She cried in delight. She was on the man's shoulders. And he was running with her full tilt down the hall.

"Farewell, Sister Sleep," she cried.

And that was the last time I saw Susie Cluer.

Later when she made her plans; and later when I saw her on the night that she left; and yet later still when I saw her again, standing on the sidewalk looking up at the building before she picked her way downtown to meet the man that she called Jeffs, the man in the mask of the Japanese prince. Or maybe it was another man.

None of them were her. Not Susie. Susie was that other girl. Susie was that wriggling thing, borne away on shoulders down a dimly lit hall.

And so it was not Susie either, several years after that night, when a woman washed up on the shores of the Charles, tangled in among its trash.

HANNAH SINCERELY

October 1859

A letter I received from Grace in care of Mrs. Eva Heinrich.

Mrs. Prury's School for Girls
Camden, Maine

April 16, 1859

> Dear Hannah,
>
> Here are as many words I know that get at the heart of this place I am held in.
>
> Dejected. Deleterious. Depressing. Despondent. Disagreeable. Dismal. Dratted. Dread.
>
> And those are just a couple of D's, presented in good alphabetical order. Synonyms, I've lately learned from a lesson I left not two hours past. They are far too many classes here. Far _too few_ of girls like you.
>
> I've thought of you often since leaving the Island and wonder where you've got off to. Most important, however, is that you are safe and in a place that suits you better.
>
> Here is something that I wrote that attempts to answer many questions. For one, Mr. Hardy. Is he still in the dark as to the widow's whereabouts? <u>Doesn't</u> he need her after all? Can we really believe that he'd give up so quickly?
>
> That lighthouse keeper, for another. Mightn't he have grown a heart? And decided to buck Mrs. Reeves, his conspirator? For might Mrs. Reeves have exceeded her

bounds and estranged in the process her most faithful friend, allying him with Mr. Hardy? Why, even scheming lighthouse keepers must possess a sort of heart.

I think you will find the below satisfactory to the task of addressing some of these. And if you yourself feel inclined to contribute, I'll insist that you do in the form of Act II.

HANNAH IN CONFIDENCE
October 1859

Breath. Appetite. Hours awake and asleep.

What is a life to the person who lives it.

Any less or more real whether shared or unshared. Released, at last, from lips that speak. Pumped out of the heart like heart's blood or heart's poison.

Else before too long it were.

The way he listened and absorbed. The way he made himself a vessel. Leaning back in his chair with his massive legs crossed, sighting me along his nose. And when I shifted under that. Feeling too much seen by him.

William.

Who said not a word of himself while the pictures were born in the small room adjoining.

William.

Who made sure I stayed in my seat when the dead came to visit me, blowing against me.

William.

To whom I had gladly returned since that first frightened evening, the front of me bloody.

To make more pictures. Be with someone. Feel the feeling of control. We agreed it had something to do with my shadow. Reflecting the light of the dead on the lens.

The cameo necklace now missing for days. William was making it lovely again. Told mother, however, that it had been stolen. A harbour rat had crept around and snatched it from its hanging nail and though I had chased him I hadn't caught up. Going back through the maze of our heated pursuit I had gotten myself, I told mother, quite lost. And that is why I'd come back late. My chin bloody. My hair mussed up.

By the third or fourth time that I left her to see him, I suspected she knew that a man was involved. Though never in the way she thought.

A man who heard me when I spoke. A man who called me by my name.

But never touched me. Not like that. Unless it was to set my shoulders. Brush my hair back. Gird my spine.

Conclusion the first: I could realize the dead. See them and hear them and talk to them, yes, as I had always known I could. But also manifest them with my presence, with my being. Some process in me that agreed with the camera.

Conclusion the second: unlike I'd supposed, the visitations weren't all random

Beloved enough by the dead one in question, it would gambol and romp through your life like a puppy. Reviled enough or else supposed of having done that dead one ill, it was likely to insult you in a key you couldn't hear. Curse your name to total strangers.

That second night. The jeweller's rooms. The box and the screen. The developing drawers. The chemicals, secret and strange, in their phials.

Said the jeweller: "I think we will get her again."

Said the jeweller: "Sweet Hannah. I'm glad that you've come."

First things first: a glass of something. Dark as honey that has dried. Yet not at all sweet to the tongue. Splutter-worthy. Opened up a space in me.

It was the stuff that Mr. Fanshawe had been drinking, I remembered, when me and Grace had caught him dozing, sipped out of his half-filled glass.

William drank a second glassful. Moving with energy over the boards. Sipping his liquor between little tasks such as moving the screen and adjusting the stool and making sure the plates were clean and seeing that the velvet cloth fluttered evenly over the top of the box. His beard would move ahead of him like a shadow-play Satan. The swell of his stomach. What furniture the room had held marshalled off to the edges before I'd arrived. The photographic implements carried into the now empty space to replace them.

"What do you feel in this moment?" said he.

"I feel a fullness—here," said I and touched myself below my ribs.

"And what about now, with the light on your face?"

I told him: "It's moving. It's travelling up."

"Too warm?" said he.

I shook my head.

"The wooden stool agrees with you?"

"It helps me lift my spine," said I.

"What spirit will you manifest?"

"I cannot tell you that," said I. "They come and go just as they please."

"That girl," said he. "The other night. It would very much please me to see her again."

He finished off his drink. Watched me.

"Are you going to begin taking pictures?" said I.

He poured himself another drink. Exposed a series: one, two, three.

The ken was moving in my throat. My mouth. My nose. My eyes. My brain. The room became a trembling place of light impending, breaking through. The skin backlit, the blood beneath. The blood beneath the waiting skin. So it was through the centre, the secret not-region between the membrane and the light, that the dead ones migrated. Distressed and confused. Held there a moment in darkness like amber.

A man with a toothpick and wiry red hair whose stomach had turned on a bad piece of meat.

A woman in a pretty dress who had taken a letter file, sliced up her arms.

A boy of ten-and-seven years who'd been struck on Tremont by a runaway carriage.

But never the girl from our first time together. William insisted that she was his cousin.

Cora, he'd told me that first night, *who drowned*.

Reminded me of someone else. Reminded me of someone loved.

Her ball gown of a bathing dress. Her slightly sad and high-pitched laugh. The hair that kept her slightly damp. As though from a washing. As though from a fever.

But it couldn't be Grace because Grace wasn't dead. Grace had been shipped to a girls' school in Maine. To talk and eat with others girls. To sleep near girls who were not me.

Eventually that second night, thin-witted from too many snifters of brandy, the jeweller announced that he needed to sit. Slept like my father, his head twisted back. His arms extended on the couch.

And sitting there while Willy slept, I thought I heard the scrape of steps. Barefoot wispy quickened steps. Encompassing the little room.

A swatch of something purple, maybe.

It slipped from the darkness and then back again.

The ache—with violence!—in my lungs. Powerfully, I coughed and sneezed.

Stood up from the couch and called out: "Grace!"

In spite of all, I called her name. And I had cried that name so loud that Willy Mumler, sleeping, stirred.

But the girl had stopped circling. The shadows were silent. As suddenly silent as my soul.

Some part of me had known, of course. Grace Fanshawe, my friend, was dead.

Had always known. When we first met. Would die one day before her time. Too lovely at last to remain on this earth. Standing with her parents in the doorway of the church. Whirling away toward the sea, crying out.

Meningitis it might be. Which ate through girls of Grace's age. Which would travel too fast through the ranks of a school. Which clogged the ears and swelled the brain. And in its grip, at last, so died. That explained why, in the picture we'd made, she'd been feverish and soaking. So thin and so pale. Would Grace's bunkmates, unafraid, have knelt with her and held her hands. Or would they have cowered away in the corner, afraid of catching what she had.

MUMLER CONVERTED

I have often heard it said and I will say it now, myself, that Spiritualists are radicals. Spiritualists are vocal sorts. Spiritualists are manly women. Spiritualists are girlish men. Spiritualists are barn-burners of every conceivable checker and stripe. They are socialites and profiteers. Spiritualists are death-indentured, morbid to their turned-out toes. Spiritualists are woodland mystics, rolling bones in cavern floors, and Spiritualists are vaudevillians, Levites of the trap and the travelling show. Spiritualists are dress reformers. Spiritualists are foes of marriage. They are hypocrites but realists, too. Spiritualists are hopers, dreamers, immoderate cosmic philosophers all, and they are supernaturalists, depending on your view of things. Spiritualists are black occultists. Spiritualists are optimists. Spiritualists are soft inventors—they are lily-white shamans and unlettered doctors. Spiritualists are *très* naïve. Spiritualists are young and old. Spiritualists are, wholly, fools.

Spiritualists are many things, but Spiritualists are rarely liars. They have no reason to be such—a fact that I could now speak to.

Spiritualists are merely there. They gaze, and in that act, know all.

MISS CONANT IN A CORRESPONDENCE

Centre for the Diffusion of Spiritual Knowledge
Boston, Massachusetts

November 6th, 1859

Dear Reverend Davis,

I hope this letter finds you blessed with family and vigour, the Great Spirit grant it. You probably do not know me though I know you through works and deeds. You are a credit to our faith, any Spiritualist here to Ohio will tell you. I have read and enjoyed your compendium works—Harmonial Philosophy—in especial your essay, "The Mission of Woman," on which I have spoken a number of times.

I am writing you now in regard to a man who's been making an interesting stir in New England.

William H. Mumler, the man this concerns, is a jeweller on Washington Street in this city. During the day he repairs emerald brooches and then in the evening he dabbles at pictures. These pictures, whose singular, Spiritual nature may well have reached your ears by now, I am scheduled to print in the Banner of Light, a publication you support. These pictures are remarkable; not only technically, however. In them, William Mumler claims to have captured the spirits of people long dead. More often than not they are dear to the sitters—that the sitters, with longing, have conjured them forth.

Whatever good these pictures prove, I am convinced they are a fraud.

But you must judge that for yourself. So I enclose one for you here.

Our movement is tender, so tender, my brother. Going forward we must take great pains to protect it.

Your Sister in Spirit,

Fanny Conant, Trance-Speaker

MISS CONANT IN FELLOWSHIP

November 1859

E.H.B.'s chambers were on the top floor. I'd received word from Constance to go there at once. I brought with me a galley of *The Banner of Light*, published monthly at the Center, in which I'd made good on my reticent promise of featuring the jeweller's picture.

The caption: *Spirit Picture Taken! Endorsed by the Medium Fanny A. Conant!*

I found her engaged in preparing a session—"making up" the séance room.

Rounding the end of a cherry wood table with her polishing cloth barely touching the top, she was humming in tuneless, domestic low tones. Beneath four lamps with crimson shades positioned at its cardinal corners, the séance table streamed with light.

"You wanted to see me, Mrs. Britten."

"This *Mumler*," she said.

"Mrs. Sunderland's friend."

"Oh, curse it all, Fanny, this *is* rather awkward." E.H.B. was English and you could not mistake it whenever a critter came up in her throat. "Help me, Fanny, if you will. My joints don't hinge as once they did."

She knelt again below the wood and scrabbled for something just under the surface. I knelt and I followed her hand underneath, feeling along her until I had found it—a confluence of wire extensions centred in an iron ring, every one of these wires fastened each to a corner where they ran to the bases of four standing lamps. If any of these wires were tugged the ring would function as a pulley, feeding the wires toward the head of the table and bringing the lamps to the ground with a crash.

Kneeling, I ushered the wire to its limit and fitted it over the base of the lamp.

Next I found out the rectangular leaves that boxed in the legs and concealed their oiled castors. The slightest push from E.H.B. would set the table gliding like a stateroom pianola.

"The lengths we're driven to," she said, "to insure that our ravings are heard by the public."

"Is William Mumler such a threat?" I said to E.H.B. abruptly.

Not responding to me straightaway, she said, "*That*." Then she crossed to the wall opposite where she stopped. "I rather thought—we thought, us girls—it seemed premature to go to print at this stage. At least until we have the tale of how he made this spirit picture. What with so many liberties poised in the balance—ours and the Negroes who live south of here . . . Can you hear me, Miss Moss?" she spoke into the wall. "What about when I say: *in peace*? What about when I say: *harmonium*?"

I heard movement behind the wood.

"What about when I say: *washed clean*?"

At that the panel opened out and a girl by the name of Miss Moss ventured forth, lifting her skirts above the cut. She did it with a certain grace—a certain grace, I'll grant her that. Now she stood there businesslike, her finger pressed against her lips. "Your words were muffled, Mrs. Britten. Clearest when you said: *washed clean*."

Miss Moss was one of several girls who were on at the Centre for the Diffusion of Spiritual Knowledge—the CDSK, as we called it for short. Such girls, whom we employed as spies in séance rooms beneath trapdoors, or in the crush of lecture halls would feed or perform us the things that we needed, the trickeries inside our trade. Miss Moss was only one of these. But the one thing that bothered me more than her angling to become a trance-speaker as I had become was the secret that we had entrusted her with and so had we with all the girls: that the spirits were only a means to an end, a way to enshrine the ascendance of woman; how this ascendance had its gambits, no different than anything.

E.H.B. said, "Very well. Washed clean shall be our watchword then. Are you wretchedly cared for back there, I should ask? It must be incredibly dusty and dark."

"I've lain in wait in tighter spots. The chair is a welcome addition, Mrs. Britten."

"You're very welcome, dear," she said. "Now off to clothes and make-up with you."

E.H.B. watched until Miss Moss was gone. "A premier actress of the parlour. Prodigy at touching shoulders."

I felt my mood sour and my mouth project down. E.H.B. must've noticed; she looked at me large-eyed. I think that she meant it to seem like a kindness, but all that I saw was advantage and shrewdness. Miss Moss was a pretty addition, no more, to the ranks of our weary and roundabout circus. She would enter the trance, as we players all did. She would do this and never completely return.

"Tell me what it is I should do and I'll do it."

"You make this far too easy, Fanny."

"I will not print it then," I said.

"You needn't go *that* far," she said. "You must only allow us to meet with him, Fanny. Katherine Fox and yourself, as you're probably aware, are speaking together a week from today. I wonder if they shouldn't come. Do you happen to have it with you, Fanny?"

"The picture?" I said.

"Should you happen to have it."

I folded the galley out before her. She scrutinized then lightly traced the image of the jeweller's cousin.

"She becomes rather faint past the waist, doesn't she? I wonder *is* this Mumler clever. And the woman looks faintly familiar somehow. As if I had known her in some other life."

"I will fetch her along with the jeweller," I said.

"Many thanks for that, my dear. I should like to perceive round the corner, is why. So much unexpected floats into our midst and I would hate, frankly, to add to it much. *Constance?*" E.H.B. called sharply. "Are you hearing what we're saying, dear?"

"As a spring," said a voice hidden somewhere beneath us.

"And how has your research been coming along?"

"Perfectly well, Mrs. Britten," it said, and the room erupted neatly with a feminine form who stepped from a trapdoor concealed in the grain. As predicted, it was Constance. Than subtle Miss Moss she was starker by far—a hawkish, uncomplaining girl. And though she was every last bit as ambitious, at least she wasn't coy about it. She held an extensive notation of papers, foxed at the edges from reading downstairs. She scrolled down the names on the page with her finger.

"Horace Greeley will be there."

She spoke only to E.H.B.

"Horace Greeley . . ."

"He and Mary. Lost their only son to croup."

"Their *only* son?"

"Well, Raphael."

"We had better remember their names, hadn't we?"

"The Spirit protect you this evening," I said.

"Miss Conant," said Constance, and turned to regard me with what I can only describe as intensity. It was loneliness, learned. It was rivalry, given—perverse and burning kin to love. I'd have ventured to say that the girl hated me had I not known her look so well, having worn it myself for three years, in the basement, walking these halls with my basket of mail.

All that I heard as I turned from the room was the shuddering crack of the floor tipping closed.

HANNAH AT MELODEON
December 1859

Mother would not go with me to the Spiritist lecture with William Mumler.

Because I was a woman now. William a man. Mother would not come between us.

Until.

When Willy came to call. Beard combed out from him in waves. Ruby cufflinks at his wrists. Beyond them stretched two white silk gloves. Withdrew from his coat to complete the ensemble, beneath a brief and private smile, mother's cameo necklace. Buffed high and repaired. And then held it open for her to step into.

No explanation, of course, why he had it. Why he and not me had presented it to her.

Watching me as she thanked him. "So lovely," she said. "More lovely even than before."

Now we travelled there together. Willy up front and Bill Christian in back. Rode between Bill and my stern island mother while Willy narrated the passing landscape.

Here the airy reservoir. There the Tremont House Hotel. Armoury-Ticknor on the left from which the Hub dispatched its books.

Melodeon loomed up at us. Clean and carved and bright. Reins ho.

Mumler and Willy fetched up at the train where they lifted a bulky suitcase to the curb.

A man of some proportion met with Willy at the doors. Did not seem to recognize him. Wore a crimson coat with tails. Carnation stabbed in his lapel.

"Help you, sir?" said crimson-coat.

"We're here for Katherine Fox's lecture."

Said crimson-coat: "That's two hours off."

"Miss Conant will forget such things! It was her that instructed me, sir: be here early. And bring your billings with you, please. *Please*"—he touched the bulky case—"is what she would say to you now, were she present."

"I'm afraid that I can't, sir, instructions or no. Not without Miss Conant here."

Willy Mumler smiled. Moved in: "A private word, if you don't mind."

The two of them in low cahoots. His white glove relaxed on the broad crimson back.

Now crimson-coat was laughing strangely. Looking me from toe to crown.

"Spiritualism," said the man. "It is the purveyor of our age."

And then we were in through the carved double doors. Into the hall and the suitcase was open. Open between them, the jeweller and Bill. They rafted it before them like a banner they were hanging. Out from it came little cards that they placed on the first of the seats in each row.

Willy turned back as they went down the aisles.

"You're gifted," said he. "There's no arguing that. In a couple of hours hence you'll be famous, my girl!"

Looking down I saw myself. Tipping out of Willy's grasp. My eyelids fluttering and sick. My island skin—so poor, so pale. While Grace. Just behind me. Just there, by my chair. Her auburn hair gone dark and wet. Extending one pale, wrinkled palm toward the camera. On every seat, this same tableau, stretching onward toward the stage.

These items, I knew, were called *cartes de visite*. Everyone in house would have one.

And then I thought, *Lift up your face.* Marvel of this place that held us. Gold leaf as far as the eye could make out. Chandeliered and tin-stamped ceiling. Sweep of the seat-rows reflected above, wider the higher they climbed toward the rafters.

Turnout enough for the show to begin. Some forward-sitting. Some slumped in their seats. Some of them standing, hands folded before them.

A thin man in coattails who might be an usher standing with his back to me.

But no: unbidden, dead. He turned. The dark and curtained stage receded.

"The Scottish play or Lear they're on? Which do *you* prefer, my dear? Now where was I sitting?" The man scratched his chin. "Where is my wife, Berenice? Have you seen her? Can I be such a muddle-pate that I have banged my face up laughing?"

The curtain parted on the stage.

A pale girl appeared. Wore a bell-shape of hair. Lowering her crinolines. The curve of her bending, re-bending the fabric. The shallow crescent of her back. She was testing for strength or for comfort, it seemed, a polished wingback chair. Stage-centre. And having took my breath from me the curtain closed. The vision gone.

Say your name, I might have said.

The girl was alive, there was no doubt about it.

I had to wrench my gaze away. For here was mother on my right. Presenting me one of the *cartes de visite*. Who'd seen me see the pretty girl. Who'd seen me blush for want of her. Here was my mother who knew everything. About Willy, photography. Taking the locket. Stillness of her. Watching me.

"People are going to know you now. It doesn't flatter you to stare. Stand up straight," said she. "Smile, Hannah. Pay these poor lost souls no mind."

MISS CONANT AT MELODEON

December 1859

The calm of Melodeon's green room was stifling. Like a covey of schoolmarms we sat, trim and trussed: E.H.B., Constance, Miss Moss and myself. Several of us sipped at coffee, except E.H.B., who was partial to tea.

The Englishwoman pecked her cup. "Well," she said. She smoothed her skirts. "Isn't this silence the grandest illusion."

"Who will name the theme?" said Constance.

"I would gladly," said Miss Moss.

"Miss Moss, if you'll recall," said Constance, "often names the evening's theme. If she is permitted to do it too often people will begin to talk."

"Constance's point is a fair one, Mrs. Britten. I need not *always* have the privilege."

"What does Fanny Conant think?" said E.H.B., her eyebrows raised.

I thought I did not like Miss Moss. Her false modesty was a bunion to me. We were false every day about so much besides I did not see the purpose now.

"Why not Constance then," I said. "Our faithful want variety. If Constance is to make her name we must provide her avenues."

"I submit to your judgement," Miss Moss said at large while Constance attempted to not look triumphant.

There came a knock upon the door.

"Samuel. One. Twenty-eight," someone called.

E.H.B. said: "We are ready and waiting!"

An assemblage of people filed inside, chief among them Katherine Fox, the songbird of tonight's event. Trailing behind with his hat in his hands as if he had no business there was the owner of the CDSK, Horace Day, who did not seem to recognize me.

I had met Katherine Fox one time when she was serving on a panel at the Rutland Free Convention. That had been a year ago. The occasion had not accomplished much. The womanists and Spiritualists, neither alike nor different really, had come away opponents of "despotic sensualism," a rather swirling resolution. The Fox girl had sat there, slim-waisted and pale, aloof of the opinions that were dragging her down. Apart from nightly demonstrations in which she'd entreated the spirits for aid, she'd said hardly a word all week.

It hadn't been for arrogance. Rather she'd seemed lost for words. She'd seemed to orbit in and out of the many scouring conversations, as if her attention were constantly drifting and once in a while must be gathered to hand.

She struck me, tonight, as little different. Mrs. Greeley, her handler, announced her. She entered. She dressed a little flambishly, her milky neck and arms exposed. Her waist was as slight as a puddingstone column. Her face was alarmingly round, her mouth small, her large and liquid eyes wide-spaced above a plunging nose. Her skin was pale but thick as cream; I could only assume there were veins underneath it. There was a sort of murkiness or hint of disease that kept her from appearing pretty.

It was hard to imagine I had her to thank for the lifestyle that I now enjoyed.

Greeley was a baroness. She kept close by her ward, arms tensed. Her husband, Horace Greeley, owned the *New York Tribune*. He had yet to write in to the *Banner of Light*. Indeed he was known to support other papers, the *Herald of Progress* primary among them, whose pages had been teeming with the raid on Brown's Ferry while my own, to no end, had promoted this night. I wondered if she knew my name. I wondered if she knew my title.

Constance and Miss Moss were rising, abdicating their seats for Fox and Greeley. Horace A. Day was a gentleman's hat rotating lengthwise between two hands.

E.H.B. had stood to greet them. "How lovely to see you again, Mrs. Greeley. Miss Fox, your ladyship, I'm charmed."

"Mrs. Britten," said Fox and then sat down with a faint taking out of her skirts.

As though she'd barely noticed him, E.H.B. said: "Mr. Day."

The gentlemen nodded. We echoed our mentor:

"Mr. Day."

"Mr. Day."

"Mr. Day."

He was awkward a moment beneath our attentions. He bankrolled the Center—in fact, owned the building—a staunch devotee of "progressive endeavours," though Spiritualism, trance-speaking, all that, appeared to fill him with unease.

Mrs. Greeley sought our hands. Engaged with my own she announced, "Plucky Fanny! A handshake befitting those strong raps she makes. Take note of her, Katherine. Her style is robust."

"I too speak to spirits directly, Mrs. Greeley, if that is what you mean," said Fox.

"To them or through them?" I said.

"To them, Miss." She spoke to me but looked at Greeley. "And then I speak through them to whoever listens."

"You don't rap with your toes?" I said.

"I'm not sure what you mean," said Fox.

"And I don't suppose that you speak out of trance. Horrors, we should come to that. Airing our thoughts and opinions as ours."

Katherine Fox was silent in the process of responding. E.H.B. was smiling stiffly. Mr. Day, uncomfortable, had fled the vicinity, shoes sounding off.

"Katherine's a purist and Fanny's, well, *modern*. Now can't the two exist at once? Which makes me think," said E.H.B., "you might show Katherine round the stage."

"I will fumble around it myself," said Kate Fox.

Mr. Day peered through the chink in the curtain. Reporting back he told us of a man down in the aisles, pamphleting the music hall, row after row.

MUMLER AT MELODEON
December 1859

Oh what a sensation it made down below from where we were sitting, high up in the shadows. Like a single, twitching organism, the La*h*ngworthies looked at them close, hissed about them and dutifully passed them down the rows, thinking, perhaps, it was some sort of ploy until they turned the photographs and saw my stamp upon the back. Below the stamp was printed this: "Endorsed by the Society of Spiritual Development. Fanny A. Conant, Trance-Speaker, March 5th."

Which is why, this time around the clock, I listened intently to Fanny's address, not that it was difficult to grant that lady your attentions. But it seemed vital for me to absorb what she said—to be able to quote her verbatim if called for—if I wished to know her as wholeheartedly as she'd determined to know me. For it was she who'd called me here to be vetted by those at the top of her movement: the homely redcoat whom they called E.H.B. and the financier Mr. Day, among others.

The address began with her standing there still and gently lit upon the stage. The footlamps had dimmed to a dark pumpkin shade.

"Someone name the theme," she said.

A multitude of hands went up.

"What does it mean?" said the girl from the wharves.

"Electing the topic she'll speak on, my dear. Have you one of your own to suggest?" I said.

But my idle flirtation was lost on the girl who pursed her long mouth and turned back to the stage.

Some of the men there began to call out. They were pitching their voices, their hands at their mouths. .

"Harper's Ferry!" cried a voice. "Harper's Ferry! Harper's Ferry! Free John Brown and string up Lee."

But Fanny Conant did not blink. The shouted words seemed foreign to her. And I followed her gaze to a chair just below me, a chair that held a person in it, discernible from where I sat as all but a headful of shining brown hair.

The woman stood. I recognized her. She was one of that cohort who lived at the Center where I had gone to badger Fanny—a Fanny-in-training, or so it appeared. The woman was a single plank in the soaring and fraudulent edifice of them, though religion, I realized, could start with one act; the voice of one person pitched up from a crowd.

"Dress reform," the woman said, as if she had lived and might die by those words.

Fanny hesitated for a moment in responding.

The woman repeated, "Dress reform. What do you say to that, Miss Conant?"

"Take a stand on slavery first!"

Fanny shaded her eyes with her hands, peered before her. The voice had seemed to galvanize her. Blinking her eyes while attempting to see through the haze of cigar smoke that coated the seats, Fanny advanced to the lip of the stage.

"Take a stand on slavery, sir? That will not be hard," she said. "We women are slaves to the dresses we wear. There's your slavery, stamped and paid for! They bind the flesh—they bind the self. They *blind* us, good sir, to the fact we are bound."

And with that she was off on a dashing tirade. She spoke of the criminal imp of high fashion. And she spoke of the bodice tight with lace. And she spoke of the hot and early grave that a widow's mourning costume perpetrated on the body. And she spoke of Florence Fashionhunter. And she spoke of the drama "The Fatal Cosmetic." And she spoke of the prison of powders and pleats that marked the century before.

I realized amusedly she had not for one moment gone into the trance.

Sitting to either side of me, the girl and her mother were listening intently. They looked petrified in their big velvet seats, as if she were forcing them back with her words.

On stage a long and awkward bell was ringing Fanny Conant down and the trance-speaker, meanwhile, was talking so fast that I halfway expected my face to catch fire.

Katherine Fox replaced Miss Conant.

The legend of her went like this:

Katherine Fox of Rochester, Spiritualism's own midwife, who, with her sister Maggie Fox in the small, shingled house where they lived in New York had claimed as girls to hear a sound they ascribed to the soul of an unhappy ghost—a peddler who'd been murdered there in the red basement mud of the Fox sisters' house. The sound had been a rapping one; a forceful drumming on the boards. The men in the family had dug and dug down. The remains of a person—somebody—was found.

When Kate Fox took the stage that night, she channelled the spirit of Zachary Taylor, tactical scourge of Monterey and the twelfth president of the nation. She twitched and rolled her eyes about, like a *somnambule*, underneath their pale lids.

"Old Rough and Ready entreats you," said Fox. "Take all of ye heart in these trying, dark times."

I thought to myself: *What a mortification, this long and untenanted life of the soul.*

The evening having run its course, we waited for the hall to clear: Hannah, her mother, Bill Christian, and I. We waited not quite in the wings—that would prove too fitting, reader!—but rather in back of the orchestra rear, huddled in the shadows there. For we should keep something of mystery about us, not to speak of modesty, if we were going to measure up to what we had proven in prints to be true. And if we should happen to miss crossing paths with the Spiritualists on the way to the doors, then that would be an awful shame, and one I'd explain in a letter to Fanny the first chance I got in the next several days.

But entrances are always simple; exits are the thing to watch.

Our main complication was Algernon Child, who moved from some hidden dimension stage left. He rebounded from me, saying, "Willy!" too gladly.

We shared an overlong handshake, Child's free hand gripping my elbow, while Hannah stood some distance back, confused and dismayed at the little man's ardour.

The last time I'd see him, for oysters and drinks, I'd felt for him only a muted distaste with a thimble of grudging affection mixed in it. But now that I was in the place where I was on the way to the person that I was becoming, the distaste had settled into a repulsion. And attendant upon it, the instinct to flee. But the small man prevented this only too well, kneading my shoulder with vulgar goodwill. I felt, through the arm of my coat and my shirt, the coarseness of his strangler's hands.

"Too, too long, my friend!" he said. "Was Fanny Conant not magnetic?"

"This is Hannah," I said.

And he grappled her hand. "The apple of your camera's eye! As shiny, fresh and sweet as any. Willy is such—well *you* know, Hannah. So many fair birds never flocked round a steeple—"

"—Mr. Child," I cut in, "shall we go for a drink?"

"The five of us then," exclaimed Algernon Child. "I should love to parlay with your cohorts in art."

"Why not just us," I said to Child. "Hannah and her mother are exhausted, I should think. Bill," I shifted my focus to him, "now can't you see them back downtown?"

Bill leaned on the wall with his legs crossed before him, brandishing that flinty smile.

"Yessuh, Massa William," said Bill, smiling broader.

"Now, Bill."

"Bill show dem girls right home."

"We should really be going." I captured Child's arm. "As you can see, the show is done."

Bill's backhanded minstrelsy, that was one thing; Child in the same room with Hannah, another. Suffice to say, it made me nervous, two worlds intersecting beyond my control, not to mention the fact that I felt, well, possessive of Hannah and her special talent.

"Ladies," said Bill, in a sardonic drawl. "Your equipage ready whenever y'all needs it."

"What Bill here means of course," I said, "is do you even need to ask."

A hackney ride later, arrived in Child's room, I noticed three things right away. First was that some of the photographs there hung just askew upon their mounts. Second was that below these few a half-drunk brandy bottle stood. And third was that one of the slant-hanging photos—the one of the men wearing waxy moustaches and lighting each the other's pipes—had been stove at the centre and left to lean there, a labyrinth of spidered glass.

Which meant that Child *was* plenty drunk. Drunk and, what's more, he had meant to conceal it and had done this by way of a Browser breath-mint or a good scouring out of the tonsils.

"Congratulations are in order. Shall I pour us that drink?"

"I should like that. Yes," I said.

"Everyone's abuzz, you know." Decanting the bottle, he slopped out two fingers. "*You* weren't in the crowd when the show had let out so you wouldn't know what a racket you'd made. You'll have a customer or twenty in the morning, I expect."

He reached the brandy glass my way. "You thimble-rigging imp!" he said, pointing a finger at me, laughing. "That waif of a girl. Bit of double exposure. Foggy nether regions for effect. Very clever."

"Well I have you to thank," I said.

"Don't be ridiculous, Willy," he said. "I was only, well, musing ironically, eh?"

"Is everything all right?" I said, trying my best to solicit catharsis.

"All right?" he said and paced. "All right." He walked along the bank of pictures. "Little upset hereabouts." He passed a hand over the wall's disarray. "Had I mentioned I'm a false? Had I mentioned I'm base? Had I mentioned . . ." he half said, half choked, "I'm a liar?"

"A liar," I said. "In what respect?"

He lifted the smashed picture frame from the wall and set it on the sideboard near the bottle of brandy. Sipping his drink, he hunched over the table and started to pick out the loose shards of glass. He held a large, serrated bit between his thumb and index finger, and turned it in the light, inspecting.

"I wouldn't expect you to," he said. "To understand my lie, I mean."

He drained his glass and poured again. He must be at loose ends the way he was drinking. He fitted the picture-frame's shard into place. I was suddenly feeling more generous toward him.

"The truth," he said and turned toward me. "I never was a member of the PSAI."

"Not a member?" I said.

"Though I told you I was. Granted at the time," he said, "my work was up for nomination."

"And now?" I said.

"Declined," he said. "Abraham Bogardus is a principled man. If he granted me entry on grounds of affection, what should people come to think? I don't resent you either, Willy. You *do* know that, don't you?" he said.

"Of course, Algernon. Naturally, as you say."

"Even with Washington Wilson's book I was over a year learning how to take pictures. You took half of one, if that. It's a marvellous portrait. A wet-plate Fuseli. Tad dishonest"—his eyes grew intense—"but still brilliant."

I did not like where he was going. My sympathy turned to a wary embarrassment—more on his behalf than mine.

"When did you hear the news?" I said. "About them declining your pictures, I mean."

He winced at this, as if I'd struck him. And seemed to retreat within himself. Calmly, he lowered his hands to the table and let them rest a while, palms down. And then, just as calmly, he turned up one hand and swept the picture from the top. It hit the floor sideways and skidded across all the way to the wall where it slammed and deflected, sending up a spray of glass that seemed to emit from the wainscoting.

"Tonight," he said. "I heard tonight."

I observed him a moment. He appeared to feel better.

"I am sorry to hear that, Algernon."

And he wordlessly nodded, his face to the side.

When I left his apartment, due north for my own, I'll say I was in better spirits—though you must think me monstrous, reader, for taking such pleasure in Algernon's pain. I was conscious, of course, I should *not* be this way—that my dislike of him should've fallen from me right along with the pride that had drawn my contempt.

But I wasn't that person. I was rather this other. I could not be another way.

So it was when I turned onto Washington Street and saw a man-shape skulking there, I thought it must be Algernon who had outpaced me here to engage me in strife. But as I drew closer, I saw it was not on account of a number of mustering tells: the height was all wrong, it was taller, the figure, and skinner even than Algernon was, and the figure was dressed rather shabbily, too, a brace of banged-up bags about him—a gasping ruin of a hat, like some creature struck dead in the road by a carriage, was being pulled taut at the brim by two hands which I saw in the gaslight were covered with scabs.

"Mister Mumler?" he said in a strange, clotted drawl, as though too many bones were at work in his mouth. "Mister Mumler of Washington Street, the photographer?"

"I am known for my work in the jewel trade," I said, "But yes, since you ask"—and I blushed—"I am he."

He doffed his hat and grinned, the man, and held it by its brim again.

"Are you taking sittings tonight?" said the man.

"It's really rather late for that."

"Tomorrow?" he asked me.

"Who wishes to know?"

"I will come back then," he said.

"How can you be sure *I* will be there?" I said.

"Tomorrow will be very good."

He screwed the hat upon his head and nodded at me sharply once, and arraying his parcels of luggage about him like enormous, dark acorns on some tree of night, he loped in his gentle abjection away. And so he moved out far beyond me, this man, in the very same moment he entered my life.

GUAY IN DEMAND
January 1860

He had set Buffalo on the boil, says His Seership. From Poughkeepsie to Boston I'd gone at his word to see was this Mumler the gospel indeed and I'd taken a journey as long as the soul's across the Seven Spheres toward Light.

To see him I must go at night, I had been told by folks that knew. Not because his arts were dark but just because those were his hours.

I says to him that second time: "My name is William too," says I. "William Guay," says I, "of New York State. And I am come to you tonight by leave of His Seership, the Reverend Davis."

"*Andrew* Jackson Davis, then?" And William Mumler paused, amused. "I presume that you carry the papers to prove it."

I took out the badge of His Seership's estate like a Pinkerton's shield on the flat of my hand and I showed it to Mumler inspecting amused while we stood in the room just beyond the apartment.

"But won't you come inside," says he.

The badge of His Seership's good standing aside he told me to wait where I was in the hall and then the jeweller left the room and I sat hunching there in the ticking of night with my face in the face of the grandfather clock. I cut my eyes—I paced about. My hands became mad frothing things at my sides. And so I rose and followed him to where a sitting was in session.

There was a larger woman posing. She wore the things a widow wears. Mumler cut the box at her. Hannah the shop girl and later his wife stood off a ways behind the shot and her shadow fell over the big woman's toes with the snap and the scrape of the slide being drawn.

"Do not stand on ceremony. Join us, Mister Guay," says he.

The woman posing looked alarmed but Mumler waved she need not be. And then she was upright arranging her crepe as if she had been in the act or been weeping.

I am a hot becalmless soul. I am an unwashed man and hidden. I felt my face take on some blood that Mumler did not make me leave.

"As you are into everything then you may as well come to the closet," says he.

And thereunto he led the way while always smiling back at me to where Hannah the pale girl was hunched in the darkness performing something with the plate. She rose with it cupped in her dress like a chick and handed it to William Mumler who administered a substance called the iron preparation.

He washed it and then held it up to the light.

It was a brawler of a man who now stood there beside the woman. He was large with an aura of riches about him.

William Mumler says to me, "A gruesome sort of man," he says.

"Is he that woman's husband, sir?"

"Your guess is as good as my own," Mumler says. "Why don't we go ask his wife."

So we came out the two of us and I had gone a little slurred for it is not an easy thing to tell a widow: *Here's your husband.*

But "Here's your husband," Mumler says and then the woman clasped her heart.

"My Isaac was hairless before the Lord took him. The tumours, don't you know," says she. "But aside from that rather unpleasant detail, it looks like him in all respects."

At which point she started in crying, the widow, and pressed the plate against her chest.

His Seership had told me to keep up a record, no more than some jottings says he, for our reference and this I did of Mumler's process.

Here are a few of the things that I noticed:

—Hannah goes in the room

—and then Mumler goes in

—when they come out together he holds the plate with him

—the c-something fluid

—then the plate in the bath

—he takes it out again to dry it

—with his right hand he takes it

—fits it into the camera

—he gives it the light then

—1, 2, 3

Why did he send me, you says to yourself. Why did he send William Guay?

Send a William find a William. That is probably why he did.

William, my child, go to Boston, he told me. *Go seek out our favour there. As well it were for you to cross an Ocean of Darkness toward Far Shores of Knowing. And so shall you return as One: Harmonious. Wise. Indivisible.*

MISS CONANT AND MUMLER

February 1860

So I would go to him this time. It was I who requested the meeting.

I went.

The time was mid-evening. The man looked exhausted. I sensed I was first in a long string of clients. Photographers must eat of course. But only when the jewellers earn.

He was sitting there waiting for me at his desk. Rather, more of a workbench repurposed as one. Even in his own rooms and so late in the evening—it was well after eight, when he said he'd be free—his coat was buttoned all the way, his hands encased by white silk gloves.

A moment passed before I saw her, the pale girl standing near the door.

When I'd entered the room she had been there behind me, her hair hanging slightly in front of her face. For all of a moment it made me uneasy, but soon the feeling went from me.

She had this sweetness to her eyes—grey mixed in with bits of green.

"You're here with some concern?" he said. "Your telegram sounded concerned, so I ask."

"And how may writing, lacking speech, impress you as concerned?" I said.

"Its terseness, I reckon," said Mumler and shrugged. *"Should like to have a word with you."*

"To be perfectly honest." I harboured a breath. "I am irritated with you, Mister Mumler."

I saw recognition, then nothingness, vast. He fingered the blotter. He wanted a drink.

"For handing out the pictures in Melodeon," he said. "I'm truly sad about all that."

"I have come here to hear that you're sorry. . . ." I said.

"And now that I have said I am?"

"Have you?" said I. "Have you *said* that?"

The jeweller smiled at me and shrugged.

"Rather than hearing you beg for forgiveness," I said to the jeweller, still standing above him, "I would like to propose an alliance between us."

"What kind?" he said.

"Say, a business alliance."

"Is that not one we have already?"

"Something official," I said. "On the books. Something that, weekly, we both might commit to. A column," I told him, "a blending of talents. I grow tired of speaking through spirits," I said.

"And yet," Mumler countered, "that is your profession."

"I am a womanist," I said. "The spirits, all that, are a means to an end. I have positions that want grounding. Dress reform, marriage, the feting of woman. The freeing of woman," I said, "by my hand."

He considered a moment. He did not deny it—deny that it needed to happen, I mean. He said: "Spirit pictures are only of spirits. They meddle not in woman's plight."

"They are evidential," I said. "And that matters. Images affect, you see. People, for better or worse, Mr. Mumler, aspire to recognize the real."

"And so I print pictures," he said, "of the dead."

"You take the pictures, I print them," I said, "in the Banner of Light, publication of mention. You and *she* take the pictures," I nodded to Hannah," and I pair them with a message to the sitter from beyond. Yet along with the fluff that they normally say—dear one, take heed, etcetera—I outline the aims of progressive religion, which Spiritualism is, at root. I will call it: the Message Department," I said.

"You will outfit the spirits with captions?" he said.

"They will be transcriptions—direct ones—from death on what the living might accomplish."

He appraised me a moment in calculant silence. "Hannah," he said. "What do you make of this?"

I found myself surprised he'd asked her.

"I think that, well, Willy, it's fine. It sounds fine."

"A contract, then. To make it binding," said William Mumler, his gaze fixing me.

I said: "I have made one in printing your pictures." But Henry by Holbein would not be backed down. So I said: "Very well."

"Here's a pen for you. Wield it." He slid one, with paper, toward me. Then sat back. "Transcribe what follows, then," he said.

"I do attest . . ." he started in and I began to write apace, ". . . that the manifestations of William H. Mumler, photographic portraitist of eminence and licence . . ." The bottom of his voice dropped out, obtaining new texture, new depths of announcement: ". . . are as faithful *and* artful—please underline that."

I scribbled headlong in pursuit of his words

". . . are as faithful and artful toward Beauty and Truth as any life-drawing or atlas put forth on behalf . . ."

"You will have to slow down."

And he stopped. I arrived at the end of the phrase and looked up.

". . . put forth on behalf of the earth's living record."

"Signed," he said.

"My name?"

"Indeed. Signed," he said, "In Spirit Bonds . . . Fanny A. Conant . . . Trance-Speaker. The date."

The minute I finished he reached for the paper and mostly ripped it from my hands. He did it with such strength and speed that the pen trailed away from the line I was writing. He took up the paper and shook it to dry it. He observed its completion. He set it before him.

Hannah was looking up, semi-surprised, from the tattered storm-cloud of her hair.

The jeweller rose out of his chair and came around to draw my own. As I stood and the chair scudded back on the boards I felt his eyes below my waist.

I thought, *It is a part of me.*

I turned around, and there he was.

Before the door he took my hands and held them for a moment, waiting. And then when the gesture was going too long, he treasured them up to his lips and he kissed one. I was not at all sure why I let him do this. He held my right and writing hand between his rabbit paws of gloves and he seemed to want to trap it or to understand it fully the way he held it to his lips.

But then the jeweller parted his. My index finger slipped inside. My instinct was to draw it out, but something slowed my doing so and I felt him applying the minutest pressure as my finger emerged from his mouth at the knuckle. Hannah was standing there, watching us gently, as the rows of his teeth grazed the length of my bone.

MUMLER IN HIS CASTLE
May 1860

All through May of 1860, with the heat in a bell-shape enclosing the city, so many people came and went from my Washington studios through the night that I might have been running the most brazen flophouse Athens had to offer up.

After closing was the time, when I'd go upstairs and attend to my pictures. And so my passion had its patrons—scores upon scores of the lately bereaved.

Mr. Jonathan Ewell of the Wells Fargo Bank seeking news of his sister, burned down by consumption. Mr. A. Baker, the suave Saratogan, whose son had been killed by a mishandled gun. Mrs. Isaac Babbit of Babbit's Brand Metals in search of her husband, gone patchy with tumours, never mind that the man who appeared in the picture possessed a virile head of hair.

Some of them bore the grim wages of death—of their drownings and shootings and wastings away—while others still appeared intact with no more than sadness to mark them as other. All of them wrenched from the frame of the shot like vampires before the sun, their hands held up before their faces, clawing against the bright fog of magnesium. They looked embarrassed, pious, awkward—too tired, at last, to not be seen.

Did Ewell see his sister? Mr. Baker, his son? Mrs. Babbitt, Mister? Well.

Absolutely yet not necessarily, reader. They saw the thing they wished to see. For there *were* people in the frame, just not the ones their loved ones said and the mind—oh the mind—will do desperate things to insure that it sees what it wants to, believe me.

Cue the girl who carved soap statues. She would stand at an angle—
the angle, in fact—to the client sitting on his stool so that her shadow in
its falling subtly grazed the path of light. She darkened the path of the
shot; she controlled it. It was her shot, all said and done. And sometimes
before I inserted the plate she would spit on the front of the glass, just
a dribble, and I would pay the spit about until it was absorbed. Always
she did this in dark and in secret, in the closet where I kept the plates,
the bright thin line depending down to pool upon the good French glass.
She did it with her back to me, her shoulders hunched up and her head
slightly down. The spit, she said, was to insure that "the dead ones," as
she called them, showed up in the prints. When I had asked her why
these "dead ones" were never the ones that the sitters desired, she had
seemed at a loss to explain the conundrum.

"The dead ones," she told me—her word for the figures, but never
spirits, never *ghosts*— "the dead ones go where they will go."

Her behaviours in the studio were eerie and intense precisely because
of their lonely covertness and due to this fact, I had come to believe, as
close to authentic as ever existed. When the sitters arrived, she'd grow
furtive and bloodless and then as the visit drew on quite abstracted,
hearkening to sights or sounds that no one there save her perceived.

But maybe I'm getting ahead of myself.

Had I mentioned that she and her mother moved in not less than a
month from the show at Melodeon? Well there you have it.

We were three—Maiers and Mumlers, all under one roof.

A number of causes preceded this change, some of them spoken and
some of them not. First came the demands of our mutual business.
The spirits in no way appeared without Hannah and everywhere that
Hannah went her mother went also.

But the second and unspoken reason was this: Claudette wanted
Hannah, one year short of twenty, to clarify the nature of our murky
attachment and what better way to shed light on the thing than by
trapping us all in the same house together.

Halcyon days, were they not, eager reader? You do not need to answer
that.

But life is not all lust and glory. People will get in the way.

One person I'm sure I have already mentioned—the proselytizer,
William Guay. He came to me pimply, mean-tongued and abashed from
the liminal reaches of New York. He claimed he had come on behalf of
our Pope, Andrew Jackson Davis, the Seer of Poughkeepsie, who'd heard

about my photographs. When I asked how, Guay told me letters—sent to the Reverend by Spiritualist patrons.

Bad enough he shared my name. That was the first of our misfortunes. He stood there gangly in the door, as if I should be glad to see him.

He seemed to have no concept of the thing I was about. Photographs were magic to him. He asked the name of every item, then pursed his lips to record it to memory. His face was long, and very thin, a brittle and immobile disk. His every move about my rooms seemed practiced and a little strange, and I couldn't decide in the end, was he daft, or did he just pretend to be?

He had also just given me five hundred dollars, courtesy of Jackson Davis.

I told him he might shadow me for a week and I booked him a shit rooming house in the town.

HANNAH AND KATE
July 1860

Second time I saw Kate Fox was at a night of entertainments in the Sunderlands' parlour.

"Our hosts are LaRoy and Lucretia," said Willy as we approached the lofty house.

"The woman with the curls?" said I.

"The woman," said he, "who is missing her mother. But yes, the woman with the curls."

"I seem to remember them, Willy," said I.

At the door to the house: "Mrs. Sunderland, Ma'am. You honour us greatly," said I, "as your guests."

"You're welcome, I'm sure," said the girl in the foyer. A private and embarrassed smile.

The jeweller whispered in my ear: "That isn't Mrs. Sunderland."

"I'm ridiculous, Willy," said I. "Will she tell?"

"They don't pay her to gossip, Hannah."

First thing I saw in the Sunderland's parlour: the fresh snowy face and the bell-shape of hair. Grouped about her, people. Milling. Glasses of wine and champagne in their hands. The woman's name was Katherine Fox. I'd seen her stand upon a stage. She'd spoken words, as best I knew. Though I could not recall their theme.

The party guests stared at me. Called me by Mumler.

The room was outfitted for some kind of viewing. A screen or a bed-sheet draped over the window before a couple of rows of chairs. We sat in the left bank of chairs, toward the back.

I watched Kate Fox sit down in front. While Fanny Conant sat behind us.

When I turned to see Fanny arranging herself, she was staring at me in a high trance of ease.

Willy with a glass of sherry. "This will make work of your nerves. Now drink up."

A man whom I had yet to meet yet whom I remembered was some sort of actor. Seated in coattails just right of the stage. Cleared his actor's throat to speak: "Since we've yet to lay hands on Mr. Muybridge's Zoopraxiscope we must make do for now with the old-fashioned kind. Gentlemen, ladies. Most honoured of guests. We project for you now *Le Fantasmagorie*."

"Look right at the wall," said the spirit photographer. "Otherwise, you're bound to miss them."

"Courageous assembled, I give to you now: the Bloody Nun of Saint-Germain."

Something flickered on the wall. A sort of flaming leaf, I thought. Still more of these shapes came to flicker in turn. Until without warning one swerved into focus. The blades of it melted away and it lengthened. Became a head atop two shoulders. Stringy hair about the face. Or was it blood. The Bloody Nun. She groped and yearned for us in terror.

No sooner than she was replaced.

"The Ghost of Banquo and Macbeth."

A man at a table. Got up like a knight. Shielding his face from some spectre above him.

A muffled *ting*. The jeweller's finger. Knocking the rim of my glass that I drink.

We sat through: *The Nightmare. The Death of Lord Lyttleton. Medusa Beheaded. The Rape of Leda by the Swan.*

Willy went to get more wine. And that was when there came a shift. The air around me shifted, say. In Willy's place was Katherine Fox.

The smell of her a piney smell. The smell of Clayhead's pines in May. The folds of our skirts feeding over our thighs where they mingled like skins in the gap there between us.

"Do you find them unsettling—these pictures?" said she.

"Only strange," I said to her, "that people laugh to see them shown."

"*I* find them unsettling. Must they be so bloody? Spiritualism, so it seems, must always have a lot of blood." She paused a beat, then gave a sigh. "Mediumship—what a circus," she said.

Shockingly quickly she drank down her sherry. Her fine white throat, in blue lapels, went swallowing after the last of the liquor.

"You are just starting out. Have you clients?" said she.

"Fairly many clients, Ma'am."

"Clients come and go," said she. "Since the spirits first rapped in my ears as a girl we Fox sisters have been booked solid."

"Rapped," said I. "I've heard it, Ma'am. The rap," said I, "what does it mean?"

"Do they not rap for you?" said Kate.

"They—well . . ." I blushed. "They might rap yet."

"They always like to give a rap. Rapping is their grammar, dear. Go ahead and ask Miss Conant. She is a most dexterous rapper, I'm certain."

"The dead ones, they—I mean, the spirits. Mostly they just come," said I.

"They come to us in different ways. So who's to say what form they take."

The Destruction of Pompeii. Osiris Enthroned. The Witch of Endor in her Cave.

GUAY IN ECSTASY
October 1860

Man is the sum of the natural world. The Six Great Principles show this. They are Wisdom—Utility—Justice—Power—Beauty—Aspiration—Harmony, in that order. Harmony being the last and the highest for it is closest to the wishes of the Positive Mind.

Or Divine Architect. Or Great Spirit. Or God.

For William Mumler was His agent. Listen please while I explain.

Take a camera say and point it. Point it at a tree why not—and tell that tree to keep still please—and make what is called, and what *is*, an exposure. Now do as William Mumler does. Take the plate. Wash it. Pour the so-called preparation. And when you're done: observe.

That tree.

It is all of it there in its fullest expression. No more and no less than the Positive Mind had in mind for that tree when He made it exist is missing from the picture you have taken of the tree.

To see it there exults your heart.

I wrote to His Seership to tell Him as much and His Seership writes back: *Stay as long as you need.*

Packages arrived for me in three days' time at my shabby hotel.

There are two kinds of prophets at large in this world, I thought as I crouched at the base of the stairs and watched the little darkened square that showed the front of Mumler's rooms. The first kind of prophet holds forth in the day and humbles a crowd with the marvels he's seen, yet who can say that this man's words are not the raptures of the crowd. The second kind he has no crowd—he has no mount—and speaks at night—and then speaks only to himself in a room as dark as William Mumler's. No one can say they were prophets, these men, for no one has been there to witness their marvels. Isn't this a tragedy and yet a triumph even so.

Maybe if I stayed right here in my little hideout at the base of the stairs. Maybe if I stayed right here in my base Mental State en route to the next then I could say in years to come that I had been the first to see.

MUMLER IN STRAITS
October 1860

It was late, very late, and I stood in my closet.

An ancient elm that grew out back tattooed its fingers on the roof, while somewhere beyond it a stray dog was barking, bleak and unsure of its meal.

Cora's picture had come out.

Not the one I took with Hannah, where she stands in my rooms in her bathing costume, but rather another, when Cora still lived, a year or so before she didn't. Stuffed into a frilly dress, she is arranged beside her mother, a Christmas scene behind them both. Cora is making her signature gesture: the hand palm out before the face. Although here—as opposed the ghost photograph, where the gesture seems mystical, pushing Beyond—it is Cora upset at the shot being taken, that she has been made to stand still for so long.

Some nights I am given to petting this portrait, allowing its secretive shades to flow through me. And tonight with the dog and the tree on the roof, the Sadness between them, was one of those nights

As though on cue, there came a knock. I stowed away Cora, began for the door.

Pictures of Wilson and Babbit and Baker were in resplendence on my rack and as I left I locked the door and slipped the key inside my coat. I made the creaky trip downstairs and opened the door to the dark vestibule. Algernon was on the steps, hair ruffling in the breezes.

"Willy," he said, leaning into the chill.

He was, I could see, on a powerful tear. His eyes were scorched with sleeplessness and countless days of brandy waste, and his normally neat *accoutre* appeared rumpled.

"You're drunk."

"At ease inside my skin," said Child.

I scanned the darkened autumn street.

"Well aren't you going to ask me in?"

But there was someone else outside, attending Willy Mumler's fortunes.

A shape was all I saw at first, a hatted head, I think it was, that breached in the light of the narrowing door. I stopped the door from coming closed, and I lunged around Child to the edge of the steps, and I asked of the darkness below me: "Who goes?"

The head did not respond at first while the foot-sounds attempted to quiet themselves. Child reemerged, leaning over the railing.

"Deliver thyself from yon darkness," he yelled.

"Beg pardon, sirs, it's only I!" He came out from under the steps. "William Guay!"

"William," I said, "come shake Algernon's hand."

Child offered his hand in a slow, wincing way and William Guay grasped it in his, over-zealous.

"Algernon's a friend," I said. "Mr. Guay," I addressed Algernon, "a consultant."

"Consulting the moon in its phases," said Child.

"I'm sorry I startled you, sirs," said Guay. "And now I'll leave you to your business."

"Don't be absurd, man. Remain, sir, remain." Child shifted his eyes from me to Guay. "I myself have come here on a technical question."

"The ladies are sleeping," I said. "You'll be silent?"

"For those magical ladies," said Child. "As the snow."

And so we ascended with me at the top, Algernon behind me, William Guay at his heels. Though scarcely had Algernon entered my rooms than he barked his shin, hard, on a knobby settee and went stumbling over the carpet, wheeze-howling. This seemed to amuse him to no end. William Guay came to my side and attended to Child while I saw to the door. When I turned from the bolt he was hunched above Child while the drunk man laughed beneath his arm.

"So," I said and crossed my own. "What can I do for you gentlemen, quickly?"

"A drink," said Child, "would be most welcome."

"My instincts say you've had enough."

"Sanctimoniousness *and* covertness," said Child. "Are there no limits to your gifts?"

We shared an awkward pause at that. But the drunker the better, after all, if he was intent upon snooping around, and I walked to the sideboard set next to the couch to pilfer my best brandy stores as insurance.

"Well I can't speak for Mr. Guay." Algernon nodded at Guay, and then paused. "But if I must, why don't I start with a fine little phrase that I've learned. Listen here: Sir David Brewster's Ghost," he said.

"And what, pray tell, is that?" said I.

And here his voice turned deadly sober. "A figure in white is introduced to the frame of the shot and as quickly withdrawn. This creates the *impression* of something phantasmal. The sitter sits still, while the shape is in motion. But I narrate too much, I can see by your face. So let me say it plain," he said.

And here he came in very close and prodded in between my eyes.

"You, sir, are a fraud," he said. "*That's* Sir David Brewster's Ghost. A cheap and fraudulent effect dreamed up by a fraud with a fraud's ingenuity."

"Lower your voice, for God's sake, man."

"I suppose for the ladies," said Child. "*Ladies*, pfah! Do I owe them my silence then? Those ladies, so called, they have been instrumental in making Mr. Mumler's ghost! One stands with her back to the sitter, just so. Her shadow reflects the light indeed! Her shadow conceals a smaller one—the shadow of a young accomplice—yes the shadow of one," he paused a beat to walk his fingers through the air, "who circles the curtain, obscured from the sitter, and then . . ." he paused to sip his drink.

Guay said: "Needn't argue, sirs. You needn't raise your voices so."

"*He* is the one who must answer," said Child, "for this mockery of the progress of man."

"This boy that you speak of who creeps round the curtain. This boy who makes the ghost," I said. "I wonder, Mr. Child, *this child*. Where does he hide when the sitting's in session?"

"Any number of places," said Child, sipping faster, his drink pattering on the carpet like blood. "Behind the curtain, as I said. And if not there then in the bedroom. And if not *there*, why not the closet?"

"The closet," I said, "is not the bedroom. The closet is dark and very small. The closet is filled with breakables. The closet has a creaking door. Why I should expect that the sitter would hear him, this devious, subtle and sure-footed boy."

"Why not show me, then?" he said.

I started to lead Mr. Child toward the closet. The foremost reason being this: I did not have a thing to hide. Guay followed behind and then we were inside, and I motioned for him to attend to the door. He paused a moment, dubious. Then utter darkness took the room.

"What did you . . ." I cleared my throat. "What were you hoping to see?" I asked Child.

"Light a lamp, for God's sake, man."

"Of course," I said, and turned around, fumbling along the sink.

Something slipped off of the counter and crashed. A gas-flame came up toward the front of the room and William Guay rose from a hunkered position. The flame wavered over his pale, hollow cheeks but I could not make out his eyes.

"What was that that broke?" Child said.

"Ought to watch our feet, I reckon."

Guay set the lantern on top of the shelf and retreated back into the shadows again.

Child knelt on the floor and he rooted round. He came up with a shattered plate. It wavered at first in the light of the lamp and then I saw which one it was: a picture of Mr. A. Baker I'd taken in which the man's son stands in back of his father. How I hadn't seen it before was outrageous and yet, in a way, it made ludicrous sense, for if my sitters had been duped into seeing their darlings who weren't in fact there, then why should I have been immune from *not* seeing someone familiar who was? For looking now at Algernon with that shard of the portrait extended before him, I saw that the man in the picture was *him*. He was holding a print of himself in his hand.

And yet it was not *really* him. For the Algernon Child in the picture was dead.

A waifish young man in a worn-looking coat, dark blood running down from the top of his head (recall that Mr. Baker's son had been killed when his pistol misfired at head-height). Oh belabour my stammering heart at such horrors, I saw it could be no one else—right down to the tangle of hair on Child's brow, his thin mustache, his thwarted smile!

Algernon said dreamily: "When have I ever sat for you?"

He turned in the light of the lamp and said, "I—"

But that one word was all he said.

He lurched at me unnaturally as blood ran down into his eyes. He attempted to wipe it away, but fell sideways.

Guay rose from the dark behind Algernon Child. Algernon bucked forward, groping. And then a single, errant beam reflected off the lantern glass and I saw that the thing in Guay's hands was my tripod, streaming with bloodshed, unshod at the joint. Already he was leveraging to get against the closet door , still holding the tripod he'd lodged in Child's head—the back of his head, where his skull met his spine.

Guay wrenched the killing object free. There was a gentle sucking sound. Child dropped to his hands and his knees on the ground.

"Well don't just stand there. Finish it," I think I said to Guay, who startled.

Child's shoulder blades beneath his shirt were flexing like a pair of wings, his forearms shaking with the strain of holding his upper-torso upright. He was muttering also some manner of gibberish—something like: "Mmmrrrepee *peeeze*"—but I was too busy just grasping the basics to figure out what thing he meant. Guay scrambled around on the floor for a moment, got ahold of the rest of the shattered glass plate and embraced Algernon with the serrated edge. But there was no need.

He collapsed to the floor.

Absently I pawed the shelf and came up with a ratty towel that I placed near the body. I think I did it daintily, as if the pool of gore were hot.

"Right," I said. "All right," I said. "First things first, let's get him covered."

And when he didn't seem to hear: "Your coat, Mr. Guay, would be ideal."

There was no time to clean the room. So I swaddled Child's head from the back with Guay's coat—a dowdy rag but dark enough.

And then it came to me "Our shoes."

"Our shoes, Mr. Mumler?"

"They're covered in blood."

So the burden of caution must fall, then, to me. I made an island near the door and here we sat to clean our feet. Guay went about his with comical focus, the tip of his tongue sticking out through his teeth.

The cab-ride downtown furnished us with a lull. Both of us took trembling breaths.

I kept one of my eyes always on the driver, who didn't seem much taken with us.

We were covered in muck. We were young men in shirtsleeves. We were racing the final fatigue of first light.

Child sat between us, uncanny and swaying, Guay's waistcoat encircling his head like a turban. We had closed up his eyes and arranged his mouth open, like the face of a man stupefacted with drink, even going so far as to give him a bottle that the rigours of death anchored there in his hands.

Guay was saying, "Mr. Mumler." His voice had a note of repeating itself.

"What is it?" I said.

"Are we going somewhere?"

"To a man who can help us with our problem."

He lowered his voice. "If you don't mind my asking . . ."

"As a matter of fact, I do," I said.

He glanced at me fixedly, then turned away. And I watched him watch Boston slur past in the windows, its darkened streets gone sleek with rain and we both of us wondered, I think, at that rain, how it had come without our knowing. And then I saw beyond the glass and past the droplets there: my face. At first I'd thought that it was me reflected in the window-pane, and though it was—*was* me, I mean—it wasn't the me that sat there in that cab. An illustration of my face, warping and blurring, caught up with the night, again and again and again down the storefronts, pasted there by Bill and Guay to draw foot traffic toward our doors. The contract drawn up between Fanny and I, I had copied in full at the base of each sign where removed from its context it was an avowal—the Fanny Conant Guarantee.

I even caught a couple of words: ". . . photographic portraitist of eminence and licence."

The hansom swung onto a wide boulevard and soon was ascending from out of downtown.

"What in the hell was you thinking?" said Bill. "Come here with a dead white man."

Guay and I held up Algernon, each to an arm, standing there upon Bill's porch.

Arms crossed, Bill stood, inside the door. I saw, past the after-hours bulk of him, things—a velvet-ish hump of a couch; a cane chair;

a whitewood dinner table with a ring of rattan seats; a woodstove hunkered in the hearth, showing us its glowing grin. We had caught him in the middle of his after-dinner—something. I don't think he was glad to see us. His shift at Fisk's had probably finished no more than an hour before, which meant that three at most remained in which to accomplish our purpose.

Bill Christian gently cocked his ear to somewhere deeper in the house. He was listening to something I couldn't make out; his face in profile, turned from me.

Then he said, "Ain't nothing now. All right, just go on back. Go on."

Bill's undertaker father, I could only assume, shuffled back from the door and away through the house as Bill faced us again.

Foreseeably, there was unease. For all we were on bosom terms, I'd never been inside Bill's home. And now I had perused the place I wondered at its storied purpose. There was no sign in Gothic script announcing the address as Christian & Son; no coffins a-gleam in the foyer beyond, nor bulbs of preservative fluid aswirl. Just telltales of a modest life and the sweetly anonymous voice of Bill's father, anxious for his only son in a world that had never not shown him its worst.

"We figured a dead man should be undertaken."

But Bill refused to take my bait.

"Undertake y'all to the coppers," he said. "Dead white man in my front room." He studied Child from toe to crown, swirling his cordial and clucking his tongue. "And he couldn't be any more deader, could he? Why you a pair of blood-drenched fools . . ."

Here he made to close the door, but I planted my foot against the jamb.

Bill followed through anyway on my toes.

"Move your damn fool foot," he said.

"Bill," I entreated.

"Or I slam it for real."

"So slam it, then," I told Bill calmly. "I can just as well as wait here on one foot as two."

His eyes rested flatly on mine through the crack. He was still exerting pressure on the door and it trembled. But then he let go, made a sound of disgust. The door creaked back upon its hinge.

The door ajar, he turned around and started to hunt about the room. He muttered and cursed and we heard objects clatter.

I urged Guay to join me beneath the porch eaves.

Bill emerged wearing his coat, his stovepipe swinging in his hand and scanned the darkened sitting room before he gently shut the door.

Then he stood on the steps, peering at us, distracted. "How much green you got?" he said.

I inventoried what I had. "Thirty dollars, give or take."

"Have to do, I guess," said Bill.

"Have to do," I said. "So much?"

"Ain't *so* much what you're about. Even black folk have their price. You wait here a spell," he said. "And keep that dead man where he stands. I come back around and you gentlemen moved, forwards, backwards, side to side—"

"—we're statues in an ice storm, Bill. Aren't we, Mr. Guay?" I said.

And then he was off through the dark, down the steps, turning the corner beneath the far lamp, and Guay and I were left there on the undertaker's porch to hold the murdered man upright. In the wake of Bill's footsteps a hush settled in, then a sort of muted dripping. Naturally I figured it for runoff from the storm, dripping from the house's eves, but I soon realized it was Algernon's blood, gathering and falling from the channels of his clothing.

"Shouldn't we move him again, Mr. Mumler?"

After a pause, I replied: "What's the use."

We listened to the blood a while, tolling on the hardwood like the cosmos through its cycles. That, and the shrieking of thousands of rats that even in darkness we saw from Bill's porch, tides of them thronging the rubbish-choked gutters.

"I suppose I should thank you," I told William Guay. "He would've ruined me, you know."

"He would've ruined us," said Guay.

"Yes." I peered into his face. "So he would."

A rather lugubrious pause overtook us.

William Guay said, "You don't owe me a thing."

The coming of the hackney cab caught William Guay and me off-guard.

It was a tattered, lurching thing, and it pressed up the hill underneath the dim lamps like something from a fever dream. Supposing this to be our cue, I took up my end of the corpse and went toward it.

Yet it wasn't Bill who leapt down from the bench and came to meet us at the curb, but rather a tall, light-skinned Negro in black. He did not speak a word to us; in fact, he hardly looked us over but went forthwith about the business of fitting the corpse in the train of the cab. In a matter of moments he had it secured and ushered us into the seat of the cab. Passing in front of the dark, sway-backed mare, long and stringy in the mane, I stared into a ruined eye, yellow and stippled with fly-bites.

The trap started up. Still the man didn't speak.

"Where are we going?" I asked him.

No answer.

"Where is Bill Christian?"

No answer again.

"What do you mean by not answering, man?" I asked the driver, leaning forward.

We'd been travelling faster than I thought for the streetlamps were brighter and shorter between, and now we halted under one that shone full strength into the cab. The hackney's driver whipped around. His face in the lamplight was spotted and swirled, like a botched figure study left out in the rain. His features underneath the blight were softly made, girlish—indeed they were pretty. He did not speak, nor did he frown, but smiled without showing his teeth, almost sweetly, and nodded at me businesslike before turning back to the reins.

William Guay, who appeared terrified—weren't there Negroes in Poughkeepsie?—stole glances at me as the trap went ahead, cresting a hill and then hunkering downward.

Midway down the hill we stopped.

This was in front of a large, handsome building with red brick colonnades out front and one lamp lit above its door. The Negro with the mottled skin came down from his bench to let us out and to deal with the corpse trammelled up in the back. The man was stronger than he looked; he knelt in the street with his back to the train, rose with the body humped over his back, carried it up and then over the curb and paused before an iron door.

"I say, what is this place?" I said.

He gave a great big-bellied knock.

And then I heard a mustering. And then the corpse was floating in. And then the double iron doors appeared to part on Light itself, revealing a vision of glory, Bill Christian, who held a lantern in his hand.

"Witless, Willies. Willies, Witless." He shone the lantern back and forth.

Witless passed the body seamlessly on to Bill who handed the cabman, this Witless, the lamp.

"Witless hears you fine," said Bill. "The thing is he don't talk that much."

Witless turned to Guay and me as if these facts explained it all. That the man was a mute stood to reason somewhat; that he still had his hearing was what had surprised me.

"Mumler," I said and took his hand. His bones were raw and very strong.

Bill Christian walked ahead of us, the slumping corpse astride his back, the lantern falling far in front and too little behind. I stumbled. "Negro," said Bill. "This is no place to wait. Lord, a man could lose his mind."

I stumbled again, this time irretrievably. The dark ground rushed up and I banked my weight left, just missing a grey, perpendicular object. I rose in the dark and looked about and saw, as the lantern played over them, graves.

"Man was dug in like a gopher," said Bill. Witless heard Bill and then ran to catch up. "His people on the hill," said Bill. "His momma mighty sad, I'll tell you."

The ground began to grow uneven, and up ahead the two men stopped. They stood, I perceived, at the edge of a hole. But they weren't looking in it, just left of it rather.

Here two legs in dirt-smeared trousers stretched into the lantern-light.

Witless looked briefly and firmly at Bill and vaulted down into the hole. He beckoned to Bill and Bill vanished from sight and returned seconds later with shovels and picks. He ferried the shovel down into the hole and hung the pick upon a grave.

The two men went about their work. Guay and I mightn't have been there at all. Bill passed Witless Algernon who folded him into the dark at the bottom, an effect of the coffin down there, hid from sight, which Witless began to hammer shut. And every single hammer blow jarred my nerves and made me wince, the cheap wooden coffin absorbing these sounds and pitching them back in my face like light slaps.

The Spirit—the Positive Mind—Reason's Flame, may they protect him all, I thought.

Witless climbed out of the grave with the hammer and Bill and he started to shovel in earth. The shovelfuls seemed to come from nowhere, sailing through the fan of light before raining down on the lid of the coffin. I toured the gravesite as they worked, stepping through the nearby stones and over the legs of the disinterred corpse, whose face I could barely make out in the lamplight, as withered and dark as an overripe plum.

Bill Christian had known this man, which suddenly made our work seem strange.

"Will you take him back to Blackstone square, tuck him in Algernon's bed?" I asked Bill.

"The resurrection game," said Bill. "I don't guess they play it downtown, Mist' Mumler."

"Downtown they call it grave robbing," I said.

Bill Christian shovelled, not pausing for breath. "Lucky for you two gents," he said, "they call it murder everywhere. And I reckon a white man would raise a few eyebrows down at the medical college."

I drew in close to Mr. Friday, angling to see his face, and though the indignities of the grave had made a ruin of his skin, he could not have been more than five-and-twenty, scarcely older than myself.

"Who was he?" I said.

Bill and Witless dug on.

"Bill, who was this man?" I said.

Bill hitched the shovel again. Then he grinned. "A Negro," Bill said. "Y'all know his damn name. You got them thirty greenbacks handy?"

I nodded and dug up the sum from my pockets.

I paid out the cash on the lip of the grave, under the lantern, where Witless could see it. When it was all accounted for, I attempted to hand it directly to Witless but Bill took it from me and folded it up and pressed it on his speechless friend. He pocketed the wad of notes, nodded at Bill, started digging again.

"You two go on home," said Bill. "Witless and me, we can take it from here." But I stood at the lip of the grave, hesitating. "You heard what I said. Go on."

So Guay and I wandered away through the dim, birds waking up all around us.

GUAY PERADVENTURE
November 1858

At night I would gather the Children of God to the Throne of the Son and would there let them lie. I brought Him foxes—badgers—rats—a full wolf cub not yet decayed—and He would hang there mournful-seeming choosing what would be their fates.

Grace Church was a peach to enter.

All you needed to do was to jimmy the bolt up and over the hinge-part that held it in place and the night wallowment of the place was before you, the skin of the Son all the light that there was. I laid what I'd brought on the altar and prayed and awaited the Grace of the creatures to come. I watched the furry strange long bodies pierce the darkness with their eyes.

Some got wind and no one liked it. I was warned to keep away.

Forever have I been a duck and all town wished to see me waddle.

By my father's shame I went and yet I took his poisons with me. I set out from the southern edge of the lake that the Red Men had named Cassadaga and came into a supple land where the winter was starting to loosen its hold. They had called me Trapper's Son—and they had called me Billy Queerly—and they had called me Heretic for seeking intercourse with God but wasn't I a faithful soul and lost to Grace-ways even so.

Each town that I came to I went to the church to sit and hear the Sunday service. I had once walked in Calvin's name though that was all behind me now and in his wake I walked with Mormons—Methodists—Free Baptists—all.

One day I arrived in the town of Esopus, tottering from out the trees.

Congregational Friends of Esopus the banner while Silence the Word that was spoke from the mount.

The Reverend not got up in robes but plain as a farmer at noon in a feed store: his dull cloth shirt—his coat of serge—his wide and mud bespotted brogues.

"You there, Friend," says he to me. "You, child of God, who have come to Esopus. *You*," says he, "are welcome here. You who bear, as we do all, the flame of the Light of the Lord in your breast. Tell us your name, Friend, so that you will hear us when we say to you: come. Be our fellow in Christ."

"I am William Guay," says I. "And I come from Fredonia, sirs, to the north."

At which the Reverend tells me: "*Friends*. Call us friends, Mr. Guay of Fredonia, sir."

Silence was the Word not spoke. "Abide in quiet prayer," says he.

That night in Esopus they set out a meal to welcome me their newest Friend and this in the field out in back of the church where a big wooden table was stationed with benches. Their bread was good—their water cold. I saw the warm entreating faces flickering across a gulf. The Reverend looked down the settings at me and he nodded his head to remember this morning.

A little girl came down the rows presenting something on a plate—and she rounded the head—and she stopped at my place—and she lowered the dish with its napkin upon me. Under the napkin was freshly made cornbread and almost half a pad of butter. She grinned at me a little shy. Then her face flattened out and she ran from the scene.

I ate that bread and ate it well. I ate it gulping bit by bit. Yet no one else but I could see how I sprinkled the poison from one of vials.

It was like almonds to the nose but also bitter on the tongue and then going down something else altogether. But I could see to do that fine.

It was that bending of the head profound—and calm—and fierce at once. How you went to God He did not come to you and closer were you for that fact. I would not take enough to die but I would take enough for cornbread. The girl who'd brought it to my place she watched me just inside the light. I waved at her—and she waved back—and then I forgot all at once where I was but then I remembered with harsh clarity before the world went all to spots.

There were trees in a swirl. There was dark but light too. I parted the fog with the back of my hand. The Quakers were behind me now but I had seen them there of course. They'd been combing the trees at the edge of the light for the man who had followed the taste of the almonds and did I realize. No coat. And did I want it. Suffering, visions. Peter and his flock of beasts.

I continued on over the crest of the hill and when I had reached the far edge I rolled off.

I woke in a sweat in an indistinct room but for the bed in which I lay and all the walls around me white. There was an empty slat-back chair pushed conference-like beside the bed.

"Your spirit moves within you now," I heard a voice from somewhere near. "Your spirit sees such marvels, William. Your spirit traverses the Kingdom of Heaven. And all the while you lie here, peaceful, the temple in you and in all slowly mending, the vastness of your organism gathering upon itself . . ."

Here was Christ or seemed to be or might be yet the Quaker Reverend. A sharp and bespectacled face with a beard that flowed in ridges to his chest.

I meant to ask him where was I but all that I managed to say was: "Esopus?"

He says: "You have come to Poughkeepsie, my son. Or anyway, we brought you here. You lost your way but well," says he. "You have poisoned yourself, Mr. Guay, don't you know."

But then his words took on some weight for I collapsed again right there.

There were slats and un-slats—and white walls furring darkly—and sometimes him and sometimes not the man who wore the chest-length beard—and one time not the man at all but a metal contraption that stood in his place. It stood upon a rounded base that fluted up into a ball surrounded by seven concentric hinged circles. Each circle had writ on its lowermost edge I could see when I looked at the thing very closely a single number I through VI ascending from the outmost in. Until upon the metal ball that marked the centre of the sculpture the letters: S-E-N-S-O-R-I-U-M. The letters were writ small and neat.

"Everything is necessary. The universe reflects," says he. "It shows the beauty on this earth and beauty uncreated yet and so too beauty in its course and *of* its course now passed beyond. So riddle me, William, if beauty is formless and exists of a piece with the words that belie it—nascent beauty, earthly beauty, beauty decayed and transformed beyond earth, which brings us back to nascent beauty—beauty coming into being—if all of this is true," says he, raising his hand from the base of the sculpture, "then what, I ask, is imperfection? *Can* imperfection be said to exist?"

"In death," says I.

"Why death?" says he. "In death," says the man, "we are never alone. Those who have died and those yet to be born are as alive as we are here. The universe reflects," says he, "and in that reflection is all that it holds. *The natural world*," the man pronounced and pushed the outmost ring from him and with a creak it turned in place in an outgoing circuit about the six smaller. "*The Spirit World*," says he and pushed the second inmost of the rings. "*The Celestial Sphere*," says he and pushed. "*The Supernatural Sphere*." Again. And fast upon its heels he pushed the fifthmost of the inner spheres—and named it *Superspiritual*—and stopped to fiddle with his glasses. "Until at last," he says, eyes dry from the whole thing rotating so close to his face, "the veil of the sun, called the *Supercelestial*," and then he pushed the sixthmost ring—and he set the entire contraption in motion.

All of the rings would align for an instant. He followed their arcs with his spectacled eyes—and he ducked in his hand—and he set the ball spinning. "And here, at the centre, our Sun," says he. "These are the bounds and un-bounds of our world."

I said I was a Trapper's Son who might've been a Suicide but he corrected me: "A pilgrim. That is what you are," says he. "I am Andrew Jackson Davis. Or that is what my parents named me. We welcome you only as you are. *We* are Spiritualists," says he.

I soon took a room on the property there. And the Prophet called also the Seer of Poughkeepsie I'd heard from my Brothers and Sisters in Spirit continued to take on healing patients—run his baths—and hold his worships. I lived in a cabin out back of the house among a host of others like it. His Seership, as I'd come to call him, occupied the big main house and that was where he slept and ate along with his partner Miss Mary Fenn Love.

Everyone in the cabins was held to a job. Mine was to slop out the big iron tubs that were crowded about by whole spokes of pale people dousing themselves in His Mesmerized Water.

Sometimes there were daisy chains of telegraphic magnetism where my Brothers and Sisters in Spirit linked hands around a tree His Seership chose at which point he must sensitize it usually amid the dusk. Everyone was awed and gentle. I enjoyed a little talk. I watched His Seership carefully: the muscles working in his jaw—the crease lines etched around his smile—the vast entreaty of his eyes. I watched the words come out of him and form amidst the new still air.

One day I went to watch him work. Somnambulism—mesmerism—animal magnetism too—he invoked in the Room of the Tubs and the Benches. He found out ailments small and deep and these he sought to heal at fee: chronic headaches—indigestion—cankers—impotence—ennui. All of the cures were a matter of blockage not of the intestines but rather the Fluids en route to the head or the sides or the feet and these he would clear with the tips of his fingers.

A man had come to see His Seership ten miles south whence I had come. Or so he said. His name was this: Asahel Lycurgus Nash.

"Your em'nance," says he. "I am come down from Mayville. And I am come to you with grumblings. They are powerful grumblings, right here," says the man, while touching up along his sternum. "And they have made me a mighty phlegmatic Mayvillian. That is a fact you can wear in your button."

Says His Seership: "Pressing pains along the ganglionic nerve?"

"Getting up that way," says he. "It come," says he, "with every meal."

"Center to north of the common sensorium. Recline on your back if you would, Mr. Nash."

The man from Mayville did His bidding. He was a meet and compact man with curly hair and cleanly shaven.

"Mr. Nash, do you mind," says His Seership and pointed to where I stood with several others, "if these pupils of the beast-machine convene around your bed to watch?"

"I don't reckon I mind," says he and looked a little worried then. "The beast machine, you say. Well, I . . ."

His Seership says: "Your body, sir. The instrument that pains you, yes? A curious piece of illogic is man—a luckless breed of beast and angel."

Here the men around me laughed as I was meant to laugh myself but the sound that I made was a hectic and shrill one causing them to look around.

"First and foremost, Gentlemen, we must take a moment to find a rapport. This is best done with the patient reclining as Mr. Nash is doing now. It is optimal, sirs, that your patient be silent. Do you terribly mind, Mr. Nash?"

"You're the doctor."

"Thank you, Mr. Nash," says he.

I gathered in closer around with the others. Mr. Nash had closed his eyes.

"The process itself must begin," says His Seership, "at the *least* unstable of the poles. The fingers or the nose are best. Mr. Nash, do you take snuff?"

Nash's left eye cracked a bit and he sighted the prophet down his nose. "Permission to break the silence, doc?"

His Seership nodded.

"Sure, I take it. What man don't these days?" says Nash.

"Tilt your head back, if you would."

And here His Seership bent in low and looked up Mr. Nash's nostrils. "In the nose passages of a chronic snuff taker the poles have been blunted, more often than not, which is why it is curious," says His Seership, "that Mr. Nash's nose is clear."

"Did I say snuff?" says Mr. Nash. "I mean, betimes, a cigarette. I roll them little spuds myself."

"If you'll lie back again, Mr. Nash," says His Seership. "Gentleman," says he, "observe: rapport is achieved through the lightest of passes. For the sake of our patient, why don't we begin near the body's equator— here at the fingers, then on to the ribs . . ." One by one His Seership took the ends of Mr. Nash's fingers and squeezed them lightly I could see the way that Nash's eyelids twitched. "Now that rapport has been made," says His Seership, "let us examine the patient's sensorium—what's called the hypochondria in non-mesmeric texts," he says. "This," says he and stroked the ribs at which their owner's mouth convulsed, "— this, gentlemen, is the body's equator—the stablest of the vital poles. If I had begun at the head and I might for the eye as a rover prefers north to south, interference from the stars would doubtless complicate my reading. In the same way if I had begun at the feet, the terrestrial fluid that flows south to north would have interfered instead." Says His Seership: "Is there pain?"

"Only from holding in giggles," Nash says.

"I think that you have blockage here. A burning blockage," says His Seership.

"A licking burning," counters Nash.

"By that, I assume you mean flames?" says His Seership, continuing on past the waist to the thighs. "The fluid flows," His Seership says. "The fluid circulates, you see. The fluid that was in your chest may now have travelled to your legs. Just as your sense—your inner man—may wander the spheres under right test conditions and you, sir, may remain behind, lying right here on your back."

"I'm sorry, doc, my inner *what*?"

"Your inner man," His Seership says. "Your self which is a pilgrim, sir. Hither and thither he goes within reason about the land which lies beyond until one day he gets reborn and starts to wander at his will. On that fair day—"

"—*reborn*?" says Nash. "Unless his soul is spoken for."

"Spirits are not spoken for. Spirits, Mr. Nash, are smoke."

"Exile, flames and smoke," says Nash. "I'm starting to see the pattern here."

"I wonder, Mr. Nash," says he, "if you have *come down* from Mayville, after all."

The wire was out before I saw it, the tautened extent of it there in the hands, reaching out for His Seership to trap him and seize him. I bolted forward into them and knocked His Seership to the floor. The assassin buck-wheeled off the bench and crouched down but soon enough we had him pinned. He struggled underneath our weight the garrotte flailing in his hand.

"He waxeth strong in His right hand! He waxeth very strong indeed!"

He kept on yelling this then: "Fool! You have defiled your one true home!"

"You didn't think that through too well," says one of His Seership's interns. "Did you?"

"I am in your gratitude," His Seership tells me wide-eyed—shaking. "In spite of all that I may say I'm not ready to die—not yet." He watched Mr. Nash in his spitting and thrashing and suddenly seemed to become philosophical. "You really must admit," says he, "there is so little time to *do*."

MUMLER ON MARRIAGE

That marriage is a sacred pact among men of all races and creeds is determined. The Anglicans would have it thus and who are American men to say different, unless, in the way of American men, they differ in most everything. For, lo, the American gentleman knows that marriage is a wondrous thing. It is a long and unbecoming cultivation of hardship, and hopes for the future, and faith in each other, and thus can scarcely be confined to what most men would have it be. American husbands apportion to marriage no more than the office itself will return. They are unbounded, in this sense and better fit to stay the course.

HANNAH BETROTHED
November 1860

"Dearly beloved, we are gathered together here in the sight of God and in the face of this company to join together this Man and this Woman in holy Matrimony—an honourable estate, instituted of God in the time of man's innocence, signifying unto us the mystical union that is betwixt Christ and his Church . . ."

Spoke the Reverend before us. Between us. In robes.

Behind us: mother, Negro Bill.

So here is my witness, thought I, *the whoremonger. On this day of all days that I am to be wed.*

". . . and therefore is not by any to be entered into unadvisedly or lightly; but reverently, discreetly, advisedly, soberly, and in the fear of God. Into this holy estate these two persons present come now to be joined . . ."

But there were others in the room. In the giantess shadows my mother and I cast down in the nave of the Neponset Church.

Now sitting upright in the pews. Or leaning on them, loiter-like. Or lying on them facing up as though they were counting the beams in the ceiling. Wandering down and across the slim aisles to always just miss crossing paths with each other. And when they did cross paths, just brushing. Heatless and purposeless. Coat-sleeves and bustles.

". . . if any man can show just cause, why they may not lawfully be joined together, let him now speak, or else for ever hold his peace . . ."

Dead ones did. They said their part. Had been saying their part all throughout the proceedings. Their pointless, unanswered, ongoing laments. All the worse for the fact that they targeted nothing. Declared nothing more than the fact of themselves. How death, at last, could be no mystery. Death was just our waking lives. Death was a stranger, senile and aggrieved, babbling in an empty room.

"—hold my peace, much longer now, when her highness, Madame Antoinette, is so late? Am I to, as they say, eat cake? Or am I to eat what the froggy bitch sells me?"

"—Won't someone tell the hulking fool that I will not be turned away? That Poughkeepsie attack-dog or no, I'll persist—that I will find him out at last!—that I will stand here, in the dark, as deep as I am in my cups until—"

"—woe? Such a pure weight of woe upon me and my cunt? And when I have gone to the chemist's to tell him, has he not been a righteous judge?"

". . . Wilt thou love her, comfort her honour and keep her in sickness and in health; and, forsaking all others, keep thee only unto her, so long as ye both shall live? Wilt thou obey him, and serve him—love, honour, and keep him in sickness and in health—and, forsaking all others, keep thee only unto him, so long as you both shall live?"

"I will," said I.

Or did I say.

But I had said it. Loud and clear.

"Who giveth this woman," said Reverend Not-Hascall, "to be betrothed unto this man?"

My mother, departing the side of Bill Christian. And she gave me her arm. And I felt that it knew me. Partake of this arm, which has trafficked in wonders. And when she had stood there a moment, unsmiling, her hand gave a squeeze and withdrew back to Bill.

Not-Hascall's hand upon my hand. While Willy's hand contained the rings. Bought on the cheap yesterday and left out without the time to box them up.

"With this ring, I wed thee," Not-Hascall continued, "and with all worldly goods endow. In the name of the Father, and of the Son, and of the Holy Ghost. Amen."

And Willy was tasked with repeating his words. The rings were upon us. The rings were our rings. And the Reverend Not-Hascall continued to mutter the familiar, dark prayer of the One and True Lord:

"Our Father who art in heaven, Hallowed be thy Name. Thy kingdom come. Thy will be done—"

First time ever Willy Mumler kissed me, light, upon my lips.

Not-Hascall shut his book of prayer: "And so I say to you—*Amen.*"

THE BOOK OF
THE MORTALS

MESSAGE DEPARTMENT

You fraudulent and forked of tongue, you coveters of fabled ends, what God if any bides in us? What solace is our ill to bear? What second life begins in us, we livers never and again? We tortured dreams and shadow-shapes that mortals yearn to stand too near to demonstrate they walk and breathe, to shore themselves against the end, to show Creation, *We were here!* in opposite to all of them? What makes you think us innocent when we were never so in life, as though death were a remedy for mortal sin, for mortal strife? And whether it be larceny or cruel manoeuvres of the heart or faithlessness or robbery or murder done in money's name, where do they go, these blackened acts, if not with us into the grave, there to perfume the coffin air and gird our pillows as we dream, perhaps of fortunes otherwise than those to which we dead are chained? And yet you set out just the same, though after what we wonder still? What makes you stake your undead souls on what you are foredoomed to lose?

MUMLER IN LOVE
July 1849

Believe me, reader, when I say, though it may seem to you unkind, the day I lost my cousin Cora is one of the fondest that I can remember.

My father and my mother and my mother's brother Asa, and his daughter, my cousin, little Cora Christine, were camped along Nantasket Beach for the handsomer part of a long July day. Dinghies sawed atop the swells. Egrets and gulls skimmed for food in the shallows.

None so favoured as we five, arrayed beneath our little rampart of umbrellas, the elder ones tippled with afternoon sherry while Cora and I, at ten and twelve, roamed the bights and cliffs and grottos.

The Spirit keep my mother in her weakness: she drank laudanum. There were a couple of drops uncoiling at the bottom of her glass. But so do we all have our weaknesses. Yes? And so must we indulge them.

Earlier, in a grotto, beneath a fringe of wet moss, Cora had taken down her costume. I noted that Nature had not found the place between her skinny legs. She posed a moment, unashamed, then she lowered her chest and her groin to the earth, and pressed them there, into the sand, with her eyes resting on me incuriously. When she rose moments later caked in grey from the sand her boldness was imprinted there.

I stared at the ghost of the shape that she'd made and when it subsided again turned away.

Now she looked over, beneath her umbrella. Her costume was purple and flounced at the knees. She dropped her Godey's Lady's Book and her hair whipped away from her mouth in the breeze.

"Willy, come on," she cried. "To sea!"

She raced down the beach, veering into the surf.

I gained some beach on running Cora, my belly shaking out before me, and cut her off on a pass coming in from the shore. Together we stumbled out to sea, our arms around each other's shoulders, kicking the waves as we went.

When our feet no longer touched the bottom, we clung to each other, both paddling in place.

"You're crowding me, Willy," she said.

"I—oh . . ."

"And stop that poking thing you're doing."

"May I kiss you?" I said.

"To be sure, you may not."

"Under what conditions may I kiss you?" I said.

"Conditions," she said to herself, amused. "I will have to think on some."

She launched from my arms, a victorious fish, and rafted away on her back.

"I will swim to . . . there," she said. "And when I come back, you'll have your kiss."

"I will swim with you."

"You will not."

"I won't?" I said.

She looked at me.

"From here to there is far," I said.

This as she began to swim.

Long-legged for all that she was slight, my cousin began to kick and pull, a motion that took her ever further from where I watched her in the calm. How fast she seemed to swim away and yet through the warp of remembrance how slowly, her head, neck and shoulders, all working together, rising, then falling, then failing to rise.

Inconceivable? Yes.

Impossible? No.

In the space of that last breath she took, she was gone.

"Cora," I cried. And cried. And cried. Not tears, but her name, said again and again. "Mother," I begged of the shore. "Mother, quick!" And paddled about to face the beach.

But mother had been there all along. Mother, vague-eyed, had seen all.

MISS CONANT AT A DISTANCE
January 1861

With one of the signs crumpled up in my hands, I did not knock upon the door.

I went, with controlled violence, up the stairs. The Negro was waiting up top, just like always.

"Miss Conant," he said. "Mist' Mumler with clients. Why don't you come inside and wait."

"Detain me then," I told Bill Christian, who took a step back and gazed after me, grinning.

I went at a clip through the sitting room door. Mumler's back was turned to me; he was bent at his tripod as ever, inspecting.

"Mist' Mumler, I tried, but she wouldn't let up, and I told her—"

"—now, Bill, it is perfectly fine. I'm sure that she has got her reasons. Would you like to sit down and wait for me—"

"—in *here*. I would like to wait for you in here," I told Mumler, indicating the very same room he was in.

His sitter, a flushed, older man on a stool, looked unnerved in my presence and then irritated.

"As you were, Mr. Baker," said Mumler. "Just so."

When the sitting was over, they confabulated, the man making grumblings directed at me, but by and by he took the stairs, projecting irate looks behind him. The Negro seemed to know at last that Mumler and I were to be left alone and, hooding his eyes with uncertainty at us, he too left the room to go wait in the stairs.

The room's atmosphere calibrated to hold us, volatile and unconstrained.

Mumler sat on the couch with outrageous bravado, an aura of lewd and majestic dominion, exhaling roughly through his nose, his bicep cast over the arm.

Let him play Henry. Just let him, I thought.

"Won't you take a seat?" he said.

I showed hesitation, the ladylike type. Then I went to the couch and I hovered above it; and I hovered, my bustle sublime in the air, before sitting down on the opposite end. As I arranged my skirts around me, I very lightly touched my throat.

"Where is Hannah?" I asked him.

"Out shopping with mother."

"I'd thought she was your battery."

"She is," he said. He grinned. "She is. Though I don't often need her past two or three shots. And besides," Mumler said with an air of sad wisdom, "it is unrealistic to *always* have ghosts. Three with ghosts and three without—now those are what I call good odds."

I considered his face and then looked to his hands. Today, again, he wore the gloves.

"Congratulations are in order?"

"This thing here," he said. "Of course." And he wiggled a copper or brass wedding ring.

It was sad tragedy for a jeweller to suffer. It was as though the wedding ring were merely an object to anchor the glove.

"Before," I said, "when I came here, irritated with you for promoting your prints, which cost the Banner revenue, not to mention reflected disorderly on us— well I daresay that here, today, you have sullied my trust for the very last time."

Astoundingly, he looked confused—as though in his mildness I really had struck him. And then it seemed to come to him. "The sign postings," he said. "Of course."

"The sign postings, yes, Mr. Mumler, I've seen them. Do you think I am stupid?" I said.

"Not at all."

"Do you think then I didn't know what you were up to? Having me endorse you, sir?"

For a moment the jeweller looked poised to cry "Outrage." Then the impulse left his face. "If you knew I would beggar your interests," he said, "then why did you agree to write?"

"I fear I thought the best of you. I fear I believed in our little alliance."

"Yet clearly you didn't," said Mumler, amused, "if you are as wise as you claim, Madam Speaker."

"You are staring at me, Mr. Mumler," I said. "What is it that you think you see?"

"A woman to be reckoned with," he said to me softly, absurdly.

I scoffed. "And you *have* reckoned—is that it?"

"I've reckoned," he said, sitting back, "but ungamely. How would you have me put it right?"

"Describe me better than you have."

"I see a coquette with a head on her shoulders who wishes to say how this shop's to be run."

"That is better," I said. "That is plausible, even." I touched the buttons on my dress. "Though I am sure that you see more."

He paused for a moment and watched me, gone grinning. He pointed a finger at length, which he dropped. I looked around the studio to see was anyone still there.

I did not care a stitch for Hannah, Hannah's mother, Negro Bill. So I worked at the first of my blocky cloth buttons, not breaking for even a moment his stare as I needed the air rushing in, rushing over, rushing into my neck from cool channels above. I stuck out my knees so they met with his knees and when he tried to move, I held him. It was an alignment of knees, and it pleased me, and I thought to myself, *It is something unspeakable*, and I rapped on his thigh, very sharp, with two fingers, my middle and my index, braced.

"Tonight we will have something straight that you would do better to never forget."

And with those words I took the sign and mashed it, crumpling, in his face. I paid it with a crackling noise across his hot, accepting face and felt his features coming up beneath the rover of my hand.

I felt him through feeling his warmth and his breathing. I felt him though he was not there.

He made, then, to kiss me. I pushed him away. He flopped, awkwardly, on his end of the couch. And there, tumbled over, his hair in his face, not knowing at all what to do with his hands, I think I may have liked him best. I loomed in above him—unswerving, totemic.

"Eyes right here," I said to him and did away another button. And when he moved again toward me, thinking at last I had given him licence, I shook my head at him. He lowered his hands.

"You may extract yourself," I said.

"And I will watch your breast, so doing."

"You will do no such thing," I said. "Your eyes may rest upon my neck."

He did not go about it quickly but lissomely, rather, as if I weren't watching. I could not hear the sounds he made for the deafening sound of my blood in my ears. We sat there in silence but for his exertions, upwards of a couple of minutes.

"Do not finish yet," I said. "So tell me then: what do you see?"

"See?" he said, still working. "See?"

"A woman to be reckoned with? A coquette, as you say, with a head on her shoulders?"

"A whore to be handled," he said.

"Ah—there." The blood in me was everything. "A partner," I whispered, "that's all of these things. A fraudulent queen among whores and coquettes."

"You estimate . . . yourself . . . too high."

"My neck," I said. "*My neck*. Eyes here."

Another button, two, three more and I felt the air rushing, alive, in between me. It was as though the force of him were prying at me to get in.

He groaned and he cramped violently and leaned toward me, and that was when he burbled forth. The milky gouts escaped from him from where he reared up through his shirt.

I leaned back from him not disgusted, not really, but rather confused at my role in the thing. How like a little boy he seemed in the bare aftermath of his gratification. He instantly went about cleaning himself, which consisted of mussing his shirttails together and tucking them into his trousers again. He draped his arm over the couch, breathing roughly "And that was your idea—of what?"

I sat leaning toward him, my dress halfway open. "Of being clear on where we stand."

"But partners. But *equals*." He laughed. "It's absurd."

"You are partners already," I said, "with that Negro."

"Which you'll admit *is* different, Ma'am."

A rage overtook me and then only shame. I clutched my dress lapels together. The room before me went askew behind an imminence of tears.

But then the man's expression changed. His sadness and smugness turned into alarm. This was not, I discovered, because he'd upset me but rather because he had just heard a sound. It was the two women returned from their errand, letting themselves through the front of the shop.

"Please button your dress," said the jeweller.

I stalled.

"Miss Conant, please, you've made your point."

But in my pride I judged him wrong, I had not made my point by half and so I continued to sit there in silence. My hand fell away from the front of my dress.

He smiled at me stiffly, then looked to the door. But when he turned back he was no longer smiling.

"If you would cover up," he said. "If you would," he pantomimed at me, "your dress."

He made the most helpless and asinine motions. I heard a mustering of locks—the Negro's voice—the women, chatting.

"Miss Conant, now is not the time."

"For coquetry," I said, "perhaps. For terms of business perfect, really."

"What business?" he blustered to ask me. "What business?!"

"Yours and mine," I said.

"What *terms*?"

"My terms," I said. "Always, my terms."

As the locks fell away I was buttoning, quick, until I felt the final pinch.

MUMLER AT HAZARD
February 1861

Four months after we buried Child and three after Hannah and I had been married, I got a summons from my mother.

I'd taken off my wedding ring before I even left my rooms.

The house, I saw on my approach, was the most brightly lit one of all the street. It directly abutted the edge of the Charles, save a roadway that circled the city due east, and across from this roadway a narrow worn path to the lowermost banks of the river itself. You could see from on top of that bank, looking down, how the house watched itself in the tarn of the water.

As a boy I'd thrown stones at the not-house down there, wanting to see what it did to the real one. When the house in the water would waver and swirl, I would pivot around to catch sight of my own, certain that the turmoil of the one in the reflection would amount to falling shingles, shattered windows, warping woodwork. My parents, safe but indisposed as the house came down around our heads, I would flee by a boat among cholera cases, disguised by coughing in my sleeve. I had never had a brother or sister—had you guessed? I reckon I am wretched with it.

Now my father stood before me, tyrannically already chewing his dinner. "*Villum—pfah*," he said, "you're late."

"Backlogged tickets, don't you know."

"That *Sveeney* woman's brooch?" he said.

"Mrs. Sweeney. Yes." I sniffed. "Always has the little dog."

Entering the dining room, my mother sat there, facing me, while Paterfamilias encircled the table to sit once again at the head, near the kitchen. My mother looked better since last I had seen her: her face had blood in it; her nails had been clipped. And yet there was something unnatural about her, a brutal, scoured quality playing at health, like a prison inmate who'd been freshly deloused.

A place had not been set for me. I was not hungry anyway. The meal was some old-world concoction of father's: chicken stewed with bits of greens.

"I take it that Hannah is poorly again." She dabbed at her lips with her napkin and smiled. "Your father and I—well we assumed . . ." She looked at my father, my father at her. "At any rate," she forged ahead, "I hope it isn't something grave."

"Hannah's very tired tonight. She was greatly embarrassed," I said, "not to be here. But I said you must save your strength. Your body is your instrument."

"A so-called medium, is she? Some very pretty ones, I hear. My Willy is engaged with one, I tell the ladies down the way and they are impressed, oh enormously, Willy. And do you know what else they say?"

"No, mother," I said. "What else?"

"They say that they are cheats and frauds. Common swindlers, every one! The fairer the cheaper and falser, they say, and yet I am quick to your Hannah's defence. And they say to me, Abby, *is* she pretty? And I to them, *Of course* she is. And they to me, Well pretty how? And I to them, Well I'm not sure! And they to me, Oh sigh. Young love! And I to them, Surpasses words. Now tell me, Willy," mother said. "Which one among us is the fraud?"

I sat for a moment, digesting her words. And then I couldn't help it, I exploded into laughter. Unsure what to do with my hands for some reason, I pointed at my mother, laughing, and pointed at my father, too. As my laughter subsided, I poured out some wine and swirled it around in my glass grandiosely.

"*People*, mother dear, are false. And you will just have to get used to it, won't you?"

"You are a clever boy," she said. "You have always been so clever."

Sternly, she had ceased to eat while father continued to scavenge his plate.

"We have had discussions, Willy. We have had discrepancies. And the girl that you're courting not coming to dinner is frankly the least of . . ."

"What kind of discrepancies, mother?" I said.

"Whatever it is that you're up to," she said, "your father and I will not take part. In fact we feel it best to say . . ."

She seemed to be having trouble speaking. I looked at her setting: her fingers were shaking.

"We feel it best to tell you, Willy, that we will be forced to rescind your allowance. But do not bother to explain. We two will have no part in that."

Do not bother to explain. Now there was a bit of outrageous presumption. Well if I had once had the least inclination, I surely did not have one now. An all-in-or-nothing-ness came over me—a Monte feeling, dangerous. I was also, I realized too late, very angry, the rage of an only and maltreated son, and before I could cotton to what I was doing my wine glass shattered in my hand. A bright, popping sound filled the small dining room and the wine pattered down, with some blood, on the table. When I looked at my palm I was taken aback to see a shard embedded there.

My father stopped chewing, rose up from his seat, leaned over the plates and hit me, hard. He'd hit me in the mouth, back-handed, with plenty of wind-up from his seat and I lurched to the side with the force of the blow, dropping my fork in the process. It clattered.

He watched me a moment and then started eating, miserable bite after miserable bite.

The other time my father hit me, I had been a boy of twelve. That time, I'd discovered a live nest of wasps that hung in a corner of our porch and prodded the thing with a stick that I'd found, releasing the colony into our parlour. He'd hit me just inside the door, his face just beginning to swell from the stings. I hadn't cried but stared at him, not quite comprehending the scope of my crime.

Now I think I understood. I took his wine from him and drank it.

Then I guided the now empty bowl of his glass to underneath my wounded hand. I plucked the glass shard from my palm, dropped it on the tabletop and squeezed my wrist a couple of times so that more of my blood pattered down in the glass. I set the glass before my father, filled up an eighth of the way with bright blood.

He rammed his chair back from his place. He ripped his napkin from his shirt.

"You have robbed us blind," he said. "And now you make *Dummköpfe* of us."

"You seem convinced of that," I said.

"Convinced," he said. His eyes fixed me. "Convinced?" he roared at me. "Convinced!"

He brandished the napkin as if he would throw it. And then my mother started crying, head upon her bony arms.

"Oh your little hand," she cried. "Your tender little wounded hand! It has always been yours, ever since you were small!"

Father looked at her with brief trepidation and lowered the napkin from over his head. He let the fabric slowly down and he folded it into a food-stained rectangle, and when he had it up to snuff he put it at the centre of his plate and walked out.

Mother stopped sobbing and lifted her head. "The man hates both of us, you know."

"He certainly despises me."

"He found I'd been taking the laudanum again. And then he happened on the books. He knew I'd been protecting you before he'd even done the math. And that is why, Willy . . ." She began to break down. "That is why tonight . . ." She sobbed.

"Why you were the one who must say it," I said. "The man had put you up to that."

"Oh but I needed to say it!" she said. "I was—I was not well, you see. Neither of us were," she said. "Both of us were wrong—insane!"

"Yes," I said and reached across to pour another glass of wine, but by that point it made more sense to simply drink it from the bottle.

"And besides," she continued, collecting herself. "Your father only wants what's best. For him. For me. For all of us. Even, if you can believe it, for you."

"Yes," I repeated. "Of course. What is best." I tasted the soil at the base of the bottle. "And yet I suppose that it goes without saying that I shall be out of a job come tomorrow?"

"I'm afraid that the room and the job—nonsense, Willy. You must surrender them to father. But you have other income, don't you? And we will keep in touch, of course. Hannah, whenever you're ready to bring her, is certainly welcome to—"

"—income?" I said. "What other income do you mean?"

"Why Willy," said mother. "Photography, surely."

And that's when The Sadness came over her, too.

"I've never much cared for the hobby," I said and reached for the bottle and canted it up, but I had drunk the last of it and I hammered it down on the table again.

"Oh, Willy." Mother looked exhausted. "What is the use of your saying this, now?"

And then a door slammed, like the crack of a musket, somewhere deeper in the house. Mother jumped and listed left, grappling onto the table.

"Mother," I said, coming over to her. "The man has made you ill again."

I levered my arm under hers and she groaned, this time with a spike of pain and I saw that the arm I had meant to support was the one she'd broken on the ice of the pond.

"We must get you to bed at once."

"No," she managed. "You must go."

"Don't be absurd. I'll go nowhere," I said. "You will not make it on your own."

"Willy, really, you must go. Your father does not want you here. He will be furious if he finds you," she said, "just loitering here after such a bad scene."

"Unequivocally, no," I said to her. "I will not leave you here in pain. If he wishes me gone, he may tell me himself. If he wishes me gone—" we embarked up the stairs "—then father may come out and help you to bed."

"You must not stay," she whispered weakly.

All the fight was gone from her. So too her scoured, alarming freshness. Perspiration at her temples sharpened her face as it climbed in profile.

Her bedclothes were as fiercely made as the napkin my father had folded in anger and all about her tiny room—a room she did not share with father—was further evidence of him, his therapeutic interventions. Bureau clear of smeary glasses; table bare of bloody cloth; vanity rubbed bright as day; bottles of scent in neat rows underneath it. I disarranged his masterpiece and helped her in among the covers.

At once her head dropped to the pillow behind her.

I smoothed the hair back from her brow where it had begun to adhere in the dampness. The hair was lank; it crackled faintly. Her temples pulsed beneath my palm. Before too long her breathing levelled—rasping, really, in and out. Her tiny, reddened eyes had closed and I glimpsed the vein-work just under their lids.

I reached in my coat and took hold of the vial and began to unstopper the cork in the top. She continued to breath in and out, a susurrus.

"I do not think I should," said mother. Her fevered eyes were watching me. "I do not think I *will*," she said, struggling to sit up in bed as I rummaged.

"But mother, you must. You're in pain," I said levelly.

"My pain will pass in time," she said.

"And now," I said, "while it persists?"

"I will sit here very still. I will refrain to move a muscle. Really, you must go," she said. "Your father's bound to hear us talking."

"Bugger what he hears or doesn't. What if he heard you cry in pain?"

"Then he would come to me," she said. "And he would stoop to smell my breath."

"Lie back now," I said. "Lie back."

"I *am* lying back," said mother.

"What I mean . . ." I said. "Relax. Where is your pitcher of water?" I said.

Mother shook her head at me and continued to shake it, fanning wrinkles in her pillow. I held the laudanum up, unstoppered. I imagined the scent of it reaching her, beckoning. She pressed her head back in the bed as if the vision might recede.

"Just a couple of drops," I said, "to temper the worst of your pain," and leaned down.

But she wrenched her head away from me, coughing then retching on air in her throat.

"Mother, dear," I said. "Hold still."

"You get that vial away from me."

"The pain has made you quarrelsome, mother. Another spike will drive you mad."

"I will call for him, Willy—your father!" she said.

"Kindly don't do that," I said.

One hand to her brow and the other her chin, I prized her mouth open as wide as I could. The sweet-sour rot of her was gone, supplanted by another scent, the reek, I recognized, of tea—strong tea, in the gums, without sugar or honey to blunt its bitter aftermath. Mincingly, I tipped the vial. A few drops spattered on her tongue. She moaned but the moan sounded wrong, sounded raw, without the flesh to give it roundness. Deep inside her open mouth I saw its inmost gizzards, flexing. She moaned in despair, snapped her mouth shut and swallowed.

And no sooner done than her head gave up struggling. A torpor settled in her eyes. The yellow witchcraft of the vial had dutifully begun its work.

"There," I said. "Is that not fine?"

"I feel . . ." she said. "I feel . . ."

I stoppered the dosage of laudanum again and made to put it in my coat but then thought twice of doing that and placed it in her bedside drawer. When I looked up again, she was smiling at me. But her smile, like her moan of despair, was all wrong. Her lips were bunched above her teeth and then the lips opened and mother was laughing.

"Willy, I know. I know, you see. I know what you did," she said. "I know what you did," she said, and continued to say in between fits of laughter.

"Mother," I said. "That is all in the past. Shoddy bookkeeping, I'm sure you remember."

"No," she said with glee, almost. "That is not why I am laughing. Wretched boy"—she gulped for air—"I know what you did to *her*."

"Her?" I said.

"Yes, *her*," said mother. "You wanted her, you wretched boy. You dirty, little, wretched beast. You wanted her, Willy, but she wouldn't . . . oblige you. And so you held her pretty head."

Reader, what was I to say? And what am I to say to you?

If saints preside in human form, the Spirit knows I am not one. But take now any bloody crime and lay it writhing at my feet, the death of my cousin that fine summer day—not only her death but her murder, mind you—that crime and that crime alone is one to which I'll not concede. And barring outrage, shock or shame the only thing I felt was Sadness. Not only for Cora, whose doomed stroke and paddle traversed my mind without surcease but Sadness for my raving mother, foundering amidst her bed. For it was then I realized just how completely gone she was.

It was as if the selfsame tide that had taken my cousin two decades before had completed its sweep with the theft of my mother, moment to moment, gone and gone.

"Oh, mother. You know that I'm sorry, don't you?"

"I know what you did," she said. "I know what you did, you beast."

But her voice sounded weaker, less sure by the moment. Smoothing her hair back, I leaned in above her.

"Of course you do," I said. "I too. And now *we* know. The both of us."

HANNAH MUMLER LOUD AND CLEAR
February 1861

Katherine Fox engaged in Boston. Sent her girl around to call.

Sweet Auburn at noon. Cambridge-side of the river. Handsome city of the dead.

Katherine Fox was waiting, unescorted, at the gates. Strollers in the park already. Umbrellas open, should it rain, were passing down the narrow lanes.

We passed the chapel at the gate and wandered down along a road. Avenues had names like Ash and Buttercup and Saffron. Stones in clusters, grouped by clan. Some of them modest, weathered, grey. Others ugly with proclaiming. Stone angels in tears. Gentlemen flying whiskers. Tombs in the Egyptian style. A lot of the graves were streaked with salt. Wore mantles of snowfall on top of their headstones.

She had a daybook and a pencil. Writing down some names she saw.

Romulus Gwyn, Born in 1840, Died in 1859.

Cornelia McDonald, Born in 1834, Died in 1857.

Talked about her sister, Maggie. Lamenting a suitor three years in his grave. Adventurer into the Arctic, said Kate. All he brought back was a case of consumption.

For him to die took two years. Six months in Havana, attempting recovery. The man had sent Maggie avowals of marriage, but he had never made it back.

From New Orleans to Philadelphia, Maggie's suitor's mourning train. Ever since she had taken to drinking all day. As people were wont in the place they were from. But this drinking, said Kate, was new. This drinking, said Kate Fox, was strange.

"It's as if, when she does it, she's breathing," said she. "And the rest of the time she just goes around, stifled. I've talked to him beyond the veil. I've asked him things regarding her. But Maggie, she is unconsoled. She is, by all accounts, too tired. The medium's life is a perilous one in matters of love and affection, of course."

"Were they married before he died?"

"Alas." Katherine sadly shook her head. "Oh Hannah, it's awful, it's *awful*, I know, I mightn't even say the words, but what if he meant to appease her, you know? To cast her finally from his life? And never planned to marry her upon his return from—where was it?"

"Havana."

She looked abashed: "You listen well. You might attempt to sit for circles. For that is all it is, you know. Listening to dreadful things."

And then a rain began to fall. Huge and cold and quick, from nowhere. We ran along Laburnum Path, which coiled down a hill between close-growing bushes. Soon it let us out again at a level much lower than most of the graves. And here a sort of matted lawn, on the outskirts of which sat a few mausoleums. One of them open, its door clanging wide.

HITCHCOCK chiselled in the stone above the dripping archway there.

We huddled in behind the bars. Rain exploded on the grass. Nowhere to sit but a brief bit of ledge that lined the walls that housed the crypt.

"Would you like me to teach you?" said she.

"Teach me what?"

"How to sit for someone sad."

Had picked the conversation up as if we had never been caught in the rain

"First I will do you," said she. "Furnish me with someone dear."

Did not tell her Grace's name. Grace's name would be my secret.

And so I told her of my father. His Sunday Gin. His loose tobacco. Cresting the waves with the seabirds perched on him.

Kate Fox nodded as I spoke. And yet when it became her turn, she did not really seem to see him. See him as he'd been to me. She spoke of him in general terms. Like any father, anywhere. "Ain't you missed me, girl," said he, but in Katherine's voice as she channelled his words. "But ever was I home again upon the wide and rolling sea."

At some point the rain had stopped falling outside. Kate had been speaking for minutes, for hours.

"Now," said she. "Why don't you try. And let us pick someone that matters. My sister Maggie's beau. Do him. Where is he," said she, "right now?"

I combed the small space for a dead one to speak of. Any dead one would have done. A clerk. A red-faced drummer boy. A ruined Narragansett belle.

But none of them *were* here. Not now. Only Kate's imploring face .

I had not seen a single dead one past the cemetery gates.

"Is everything all right?" said Kate. "I haven't upset you, have I, Hannah? Sometimes what comes through . . ." She searched. "Why it can prove *too* true, you know."

"Really, I am fine," said I. "But I am afraid that I can't see a thing."

Not seeing did not last for long. Katherine saw me back downtown.

Along the path that lined the Charles and in the crowded trolley car. Here and there among the throng that pushed in two opposing streams. But always turned the wrong way round. North when they should've gone south. Or vice versa.

Dead ones daft and pale and trackless. Asking me questions I couldn't ignore.

A portly charwoman in only a nightgown. A soot-covered man in a billed cap of tweed. A beautiful boy—the Dauphin of the Hub—wearing just one of his patten-heeled shoes, his blond curls oddly matted down as if he had slept on them wrong in the night.

Had wanted to tell her: *Here they are!*

Had wanted her to take my arm when I saw the young man in the queue at the druggist's. Young man standing, out of place, in a cavalry jacket of dirty blue wool. Turning toward us. Face in profile. Eyes and cheekbones, nose and lips.

The other half was sheered away.

Brightness of bone under wet bands of muscle. Fringe of flesh around the hole. I saw them flex, the chords, the strings, as if he had tightened the jaw when he saw us.

But Katherine Fox had seen him not. She had grown cloistered. Deferential. Allowed the things I could not say with little *hmm's* or little smiles. The new white snow beneath our feet running grey and putrescent with rivers of rain.

Mother in our room as always. Waiting for me at the foot of her bed.

She sat like a man, with her knees pointed out. Her spine girder-straight with her hands on her thighs. Even underneath her dress you saw how poised she was. How strong. Pale winter light from room's single window starkly describing the bones in her face.

"I never had more faith in God than when you were inside me, Hannah. I prayed to God. To Christ, his son. Once in a while, even prayed to the saints. You see, I knew if they were real that they would do all that they could to protect you. And that is why I prayed," said she. "I knew that I couldn't protect you myself."

"I was born in the summer," said I.

"In July."

"It was so hot my eyes were fogged."

"Your barely blinking eyes," said mother. "You were turned the wrong way, shoulders up, in the womb."

"But then you breathed for me," said I. "In my mouth."

I knew the story, how it went. Next she'd say: *We breathed as one.*

"The real trouble only came later," said mother. "I saw you in your crib one day. You were standing or trying to stand when I saw you. You clutched at the bars of your crib and leaned out. And I thought: *Oh,* the little dear. I will come to the crib. I will help her to stand. You were not reaching out to me. And I wanted to tell them: Leave her be! But then I saw your face," said she. And she turned full upon me. Her eyes wide with fear. "I saw you did not need my help. No more than you needed my help to keep breathing."

"You wish that I were not like you. You think that what I am is wrong."

"I wish that you were different, Hannah."

"Different than I am?" said I.

"What you are . . ." Voice dropped. "My child. I'd hoped I was the last, you see. I'd hoped that it would end with you. But it comes in the milk, don't you see? *Is* the milk. In the blood that we bleed, in the urine we pass, in the sneezes we make, in our spit—it is there. But this Mumler," said she. "He is vain and impatient. He does not even trust his friends. And yet there is something unyielding in him. Even something overpowering. One has cause to wonder, child, about the seed of such a man."

"You wish me to bear him a child," said I.

But mother did not answer me.

"I was sixty years old on the day you were born. Before even your father I'd married a man. We bore no child," said she. "He died. Year after they broke her"—she fingered her locket—"I married your father, and then you were born. My mother— Elsa was her name—she married three men in her lifetime alone. The Maier blood is strong," said she—a prayer-song, I felt, that my mother kept singing. "We have always, of course, needed men at our sides."

"You are seventy-five, mother?"

"Seventy-six."

"And grandmother, how old was she?"

"One-hundred-and-thirty-years old when she died. Three husbands— *three*. Outlived them all. And she would've had more had they not broken her. Burned her," said mother, "because she could see."

"Do Maiers *never* die?" said I.

"Not from growing old," said she.

My mother's changeless, handsome face. Like a statue that guarded some old Roman shrine.

"You want me to have Mumler's child not out of love, but advantage," said I.

"You married him out of advantage," said she.

"I married him because you said."

"Better on the whole," said she, "than to spend a lifetime pining after that girl."

"You are terribly, terribly cruel to say that."

Not wanting her to see me cry, I started to go from the room in a hurry.

"My dear sweet daughter, understand," I heard her say, "it's who we are."

MISS CONANT AT HER FURTHEST TETHER
April 1861

At the Rochester Convention for the Vested Rights of Woman, I did not rap three times for yes. And in front of the Womanist's League in Montrose I introduced Constance and brought her on stage to assist in my talk on "the medical folly." And at the Modern Times Experiment in Brentwood, Long Island, I let myself get cold enough I was able to beg off the trance altogether, this being due to the wind off the Sound, battering into my rostrum.

When toward the middle of the crowd, I saw him standing: Shadrach Barnes.

His hair and his beard had broad patches of white. His face was fuller, hung with jowls.

I only realized then, I think, how much like Mumler he appeared.

The people milled impatiently. They wanted me to channel someone.

Barnes looked at me from the thick of the crowd with a cautious yet not at all frightened expression. Somebody yelled to do Luther C. Ladd, the first man shot down in the War of the States; I scanned the crowd to find the voice. When I turned my eyes back to the place I'd seen Barnes, I expected his face to be magically gone, but he was moving down the row, excusing himself through the cluster of bodies.

When I arrived back at the Center again, I wasted no time in beginning to pack.

These last couple of years I had not amassed much. Old galleys of editions of The Banner of Light; ladies' shoes with lead-worked soles; cans of phosphorescent paint; a small lamp with a crimson shade;

bloomers from department stores that I had been given to wear on promotion.

Did I sit on my bed and know where I was going?

I might've gone to Mumler's rooms, not to stay in the long term but, merely, regroup. We could meet in the cellar or down in the shop or one time, even, in the foyer. We had done this less carefully, probably, than ought. In short—and it was often short—any place in the house where "the battery" wasn't. But I could not go to him now. For as soon as I went there and told him my story, then he would know why I had come.

So it was in the act of preparing for somewhere that E.H.B. happened to stop by my rooms. She glanced at me and then my things, arrayed upon the coverlet. I followed the path of my guardian's eyes and saw a stage-set, nearly struck.

"Many clients this morning?" she said.

"Very few. And what about you, Mrs. Britten?" I said.

She smiled and took a shaky breath. "I can scarcely remember a time in my life when so many souls wanted saving at once."

"On account of the war, I suppose," I said weakly.

But then for a moment she seemed to forget that there had been a war at all. "I wonder Fanny dear," she said, "if you have heard the story of my spiritual unfoldment?"

When I nodded at her I had heard many times, she started talking anyway.

"I was under the development of Miss Ada Foy, my one-time tutor at the keys. Piano all the rage those days—" And then I thought, she has digressed and she will say, *But anyway*. "—but anyway, the time had come for us to go our separate ways. I now had clients of my own and the lecturing circuit was just starting up. Have I ever told you of the first one I gave? You can scarcely imagine how nervous I was. Nervous, and yet I spoke fluently, Fanny. A wonder that I spoke at all."

"You were saying," I caught her, "about your unfoldment?"

"After that, Ada Foy and myself parted ways. She remained in her rooms in Canal Street, took sitters, while I embarked on lectures and campaigning like you. Can you guess what she told me the day that I left?"

I smoothed down the hem of a dress in my valise. I started to recite the words: "Forget the dead, Emma, remember the living. The dead will drag you down, down, down. The dead are the dead while the living are—"

"—*here*. Yes, the living are here," said E.H.B. "You and I and everyone, that walks and breathes, that grieves and loves. You always listened closely, Fanny. You always had the keenest ears."

"I cannot stay. Not now," I said.

"I am the only one who knows. You *do* know that, don't you?" she said. "I suppose that is why you have come to resent me."

I thought of the light on the rail platform swaying—hiding her, showing her, over and over. She was a woman who had saved me from a schoolhouse full of monsters. That is all she was to me. And that was all she'd ever be. And yet I discovered: I didn't resent her. For that would mean that she had won. That would mean when I left here, en route to where I could not say, that my spite and resentment would weigh down upon me until I had to throw them off. And then, in spite of spite itself, I would start once again to feel gratitude toward her.

I did my best to look unmoved. "I've decided I do not resent you," I said.

But when she smiled to hear those words I did resent her, terribly.

"Oh how I shall miss you," she said, coming forward, folding her arms around my neck.

GUAY IN DESPAIR
May 1861

His Seership once explained to me that men's impulses good and ill have all of them their complement in the World of the Spirits that borders our world.

And so for every saintly man is a Spirit that cradles that man in its favour. Just so for every wicked one is One that holds him to his ill.

Affinities these ties are named. The wicked ones are called Diakka.

Like angels but with blackened wings, they seemed to flock around my head. They liked to have a lark on me. At night I heard them clambering upon the roof of my hotel, dragging their pale bodies over the slate and scraping the tips of their wings in the gutters.

Mumler was no more at Newspaper Row. Now he was in other rooms just three streets south on Otis Street and these were larger, Mumler said, so as to hold his clientele.

A week passed then of William Guay in search of chairs and rugs and drapes.

The first day we opened for business at large everyone you'd think was there. Hannah's mother in her room—and Hannah in a pretty dress—and Mumler in a costly suit provisioned on His Seership's dime—and then of course there was Bill Christian, lurking, coming in and out.

The day's first sitter came at ten. He knocked his all there was no bell. I drew the door—says to him, "Welcome. Come upstairs and sit," says I.

But then he looked at me cock-eyed for I'd forgot there were no stairs.

When Hannah asked him for his name he said that it was Mr. Hinkley. And then he went on to explain that he did not desire a sitting. Rather it was for his master. This man he declined to name.

Mr. Hinkley bowed to us and then he let me see him out.

No sooner had I shut the door than there was knocking there again and I went down the hall to retrieve Mr. Hinkley. Not only was the knock not him but this new man was tall, well-built, and stood with folded slim white hands. He wore a sweep of waxed moustaches—fussy suit—and bowler hat. The first thing he did upon coming inside was to write down his name in the studio's logbook.

"Mr. Five Hundred?" Mumler says. He checked the shop's logbook again.

"I am the gentleman spoke of," says he. He had a mellow high-ish voice. He was almost a pretty man. His staring eyes were very green and damp as though he had been weeping.

"And what do you do here in Athens," says Mumler, "if we are not to know your name?"

"You came recommended by Katherine Fox on account of your medium, sir, standing there. She has told me that Hannah, if that is her name, would provide me with the evidence I needed for conviction."

"Conviction in regard to what?"

"I hear that your Hannah is gifted," says he. "By some accounts too gifted, yes? While you, sir, were explained to me as a prodigy of science and an artist to bargain. More than belief, that is why I have come. To see a splendid process _happen._"

The way he had said the word happen was strange. It almost seemed to make him giddy.

About my ears the buffeting of claw-tipped black reprieveless wings.

HANNAH EXPECTANT
May 1861

Alone at night. The studio. Alert in a darkness the texture of waiting. Arms parallel to my legs. Hands on knees. The back, the structure, very straight. Peering in an anguished way to see something there in the dim. To hear something.

Some nights he would be out till three. And nights I waited, limbs outflung. Listening for drunken steps.

Meanwhile, the giggling. The bright swatch of purple. Trailing a brightness I saw in the dark. Hid in not-shadow, the loveliness of her. Scampering around my bed.

Grace would help me raise it, surely. Grace would cool its little heels. It would smile with its gums while Grace flitted around it and then, when she got in too close, it would sneeze.

And so I waited. Would it hurt—*yes the man was my husband my husband my husband*—my face averted when he came. My body splayed and darkly open. Watching the window, its limning, its sounds. The rapping, diminishing ones of the traps, and the drunken, diminishing ones of the revelers, and the screams of the horses under winch, and the snuffles and snorts of the ones in the stables. I watched the sounds—*how could it be unless Kate Fox could see them too*—and I watched them along with his footsteps approaching—*how could it be how could it be*—and I watched them and tried to connect them—*to Grace*—until he was there at the side of the bed.

A creak of unbuckling. A sloughing of pants.

A wavering of gritted teeth.

He moved in me and then we lay. But we did not lie there alone.

There was: the policeman. The blue chambermaid. The pair of sailor-suited twins. The man with a collar of blood on his shirt.

"Won't you light a bloody lamp? I daresay, sir, you're used to gloom?"

"Seen a queer sort?" said the copper. "Swarthy and big-boned, his arm in a sling?"

"Where is Clem?" The fair-haired twin. "My one and only brother lost?"

"See here, Hannah," said someone, adjusting what seemed to me very real weight.

Willy, my husband, was speaking to me. Looking at me sideways, mildly.

I lay apart from him, curled up, as I'd been instructed to do by my mother.

"Are you happy here, Hannah?" said Willy again. Had asked me this upwards of several times now, I could hear in the high-ish end note of his voice.

"Happy, oh yes. Very grateful," said I.

"But how can you be happy, *really*?"

"We're safer here," said I. "There's that. And we have our own rooms. And there is steady money in it. And you, sir, are the most—"

"—not that. That is not what I am asking."

Picked up a cheroot from next to the bed. His broad, whiskered face in the flare of the match.

"Did *it* make you happy—the thing that we did?"

"I hadn't yet done it before, Mr. Mumler."

"You needn't call me that, you know. You're Mrs. Mumler now," he said. "You expect me to give you a child, I suppose?"

"I would like it," said I, "but I do not expect it."

"To expect without fear is to truly be happy. I'll do my best to grant you that."

"It's kind of you," said I. I smiled. "I want to be that, in the way that you say."

I rose from the bed altogether and pale and went to stand before the glass. So rarely, if ever, in only my skin. Even by myself at night. This heightening along my flesh. The dwindle of this man in me. I knew his name but who was he.

The jeweller's cheroot jewelled and dimmed, reflected in the pane of glass.

"I am always most happy," said he as he yawned, "when I am looking at the sea. My parents would take me when I was a boy. The North Shore, Hannah. *We* might go. Yes, we might bring your mother there. And then when I say I am happy," said he, "you both will know the thing I mean. In the summer it turns to the colour of sea-glass. But the glass, it melts inward, absorbing your foot. You see, it *seems* solid, but then you approach it and find that it couldn't be softer, more warm. And that is why it makes me glad. To know it can be both, at once."

"Can't you feel it pressing down? Won't you help a girl to breathe? Would you be a dear," said Grace somewhere in the shadows behind Willy Mumler, "and see my Godey's book stays dry?"

"You are fine over there at that window," said he. "But soon you must return to me."

And saw below, on Otis Street, an undead legion on the march. Their progress slow, their heads downcast. As if they walked under incredible burdens. Their matted-down and broken pates passing under the window like strange, trackless worlds. And yet for all that they were young. And yet for all that they were boys. All of them clad in the stripe of some army. Some imminent force that had yet to lock step. Thirty, fifty, hundreds of them. Sun-bleached blues and tatty greys. All a-clatter about them, their muskets and cups, their shot-pouches and soldier's packs. The tassel and the tinsel of them swishing under all the rest. Gouge-headed and missing limbs. Malarial and thin. Scoop-eyed. Grinning though they did not smile. Wordless, tragic. Trudging on.

MUMLER ON CARVING

The carving of meat at American tables may seem, on the face, a pedestrian act. And though this may indeed be true—for carving is carving, is supper well-served—in American lands, in American hands, the act is always more complex. And whether it be chubby mackerel, or leg of mutton, flat-side down, or leg of lamb cut to the chine and helped around the group in chops, the method of carving up dinner is vital. The gentleman carver carves only the prime. What bits remain are merely offal, suitable for cats and dogs.

GUAY IN THE FOYER
June 1861

His Seership proclaimeth: *Each day is a blessing.* And yet I reckon days are days.

Two-hundred-and-eighty days since I had murdered Mr. Child I went to have supper at Mr. Five Hundred's with Mumler—and Hannah—and Bill—and Kate Fox. Though Kate had arrived there some minutes before us.

The servant was that Hinkley man. I went to him to hand my coat which heavens I got stuck inside yet Hinkley was already on me by that point, patiently twisting the coat off my shoulders.

"Mr. Guay," says our host in his sad elegance. "*Bienveue,* my humble home. Mr. Charles Livermore is my name. Call me that."

"Your name isn't Mr. Five Hundred?" says I.

"Disappointed?" says our host. "It is"—he smiled wryly—"my moonlighting name."

"Charles Livermore," the Prophet says. "Of Webster's Bank on Boylston Street?"

"How ever did you guess?" says he.

"Your name is on the door," he says. "I've travelled past it once or twice."

"So you have," says Livermore. "And now, my friend, you have arrived."

With that we adjourned to the grand dining room with Kate Fox and Hannah already in talks while Bill and I came on behind unsure what to do with our faces and hands.

The banker's home was not my home. It branched and tended hall by hall. There were paintings all through it—and bevelled glass panes—and girl-painted screens trimmed with round metal studs. Mr. Five Hundred of Webster's, or Charles depending on what day you asked, he turned to us along the way and reminded us footmen should eat in the kitchen.

But then I saw he meant just Bill.

"*That* man is my associate," Mumler says to Livermore and Livermore held up his hand to gaze at Bill with solemn purpose.

"Force of habit, don't you know. I hope he does not take offence. I suppose I had better start backing in earnest the men that my clients would back to their deaths."

"The Fifty-Fourth Massachusetts Infantry?" says Mumler.

"First nigger outfit in all of the war. But he can stay. Of course he can. Mr. Hinkley, please, a chair."

And I will be a pickled dimwit standing in my unlaced shoes if Bill wasn't smiling at Mr. Five Hundred not with contempt but with shame and exhaustion. It was less of a smile than a dullness with teeth and then Bill says: "I'm grateful, sir."

The firm hot hand of sympathy had closed itself around my heart.

HANNAH AT TABLE

June 1861

A seventh guest at dinner, then. Not beside or across but above the oak mantle.

Portrait hanging, huge and solemn: Mr. Livermore's dead wife.

A handsome lady for the house. Painted eyes so dark they gleamed. A great swirling collar of hair at her shoulders. Estelle had been her name in life. In death just a portrait of oils, staring down. She seemed to wonder: husband's study, husband's desk at Webster Bank. Half-distracted by some dream of where the thing would one day hang.

The conversation was just sounds. Ring of glass and scrape of fork.

But Livermore carved at his lamb as if he could not eat it faster.

Mashed artichokes. Small potatoes. Fresh cream. Bordeaux ferried up from his personal cellars.

Wine was a thing I'd developed a taste for. Katherine Fox took only sherry.

One moment I thought, looking at her sidelong, that Livermore had given her her own private bottle, but then he poured himself a glass and used it to chase down the last of his lamb.

Her plunging face. Her small, coiled ears. The living quickness of her throat.

Livermore was saying something: "Who the devil *are* they then?"

"Devil only knows," said Willy. "Devil of a thing, I'll say. The irony, of course, is this: Hannah can't control what comes."

Wiped my mouth and glanced at them.

"I reckon that is so," said I.

"The dead," said Willy, "are profuse. They are untamed. They go nowhere. Or nowhere willingly, that is. You ask me who are they, these unlucky strangers? Why have they chosen my portrait to lurk in? I say to you: Rejoice!" he cried. "It is only a matter of time until..."

Paused. Then looked above us at the portrait.

"Matter of time till Estelle," said the banker. "That was my wife's name: *Estelle*."

But I no longer listened to what they were saying.

This was because of a man standing near. Just right of the curtain that closed off the kitchen.

He was not a footman. He was not a waiter. He stood with his hands hanging down at his sides.

The serving girl carried a load through my sightline.

"From what I am given to understand, sir, not possessing a medium's gifts myself—and Hannah, dear, you might chime in," I could hear Willy Mumler addressing the banker, "the medium draws with her magnetic sense whatever spirits are to hand and these, well, *accumulate*, sir, thereabout her, in the manner of iron shavings, say, in course of which she sorts them out to find the spirit that is sought."

"Draws the spirits?"

"Ropes them in."

"She importunes their sympathy. So let me understand," said he. He placed his napkin on his lap. "Hannah accumulates spirits around her in the same way that Sumner accumulates zealots, raving on the Senate floor."

"A touch less provocative, maybe," said Willy. "Yet just as momentous, I think you'll agree, provided that we are at war."

"Of course," said Livermore and drank, "our Mr. Sumner has a point. It is by compromise, he claims, that human rights have been abandoned."

A shift of discomfort from Bill, chewing slowly

"Gentlemen," said Katherine Fox, not reproving in the least, but rather as though to assemble the table like five hungry plants round the light of her voice. "While Spiritualism, gentlemen, *has* vouched itself political, we must all of us here at this table remember that spirits themselves have never been. They follow no dogma like our Mr. Sumner. They merely go where they will go."

"Quite right. Quite right," said Livermore. "We all can agree that your spirits are sound ones."

Made up drastically tonight. Or drastically, at least, for her. Bit of pencil at the eyes. Twin blush spots upon her cheeks. Northern light streaks in her hair or was it just the candlelight.

Still: this hangdog, standing man. His two pale hands like ghostly fish.

He was no longer standing just out of my sight but behind William Guay. Standing over him. Watching. Expression myopic and strange on his face. The mantle of blood at his neck, down his shoulders.

"A wonder he can chew and gulp with outright murder on the stomach? A wonder that he doesn't retch his tubers, lamb and all?" said he.

His cranium not right at all. A boneless disuse to the way that it tilted. And a leached shade of blue to the skin on his face, as thought it were partially drained of its humours.

"Hannah," said Willy, "are you quite all right?"

For Livermore was staring, too.

And that is when I rose, with violence. Chair keening back as I pushed it from me.

"Hannah, dear?" said Katherine Fox, rising from her chair in turn.

"I am indisposed," said I.

"I think it is the wine," said I.

"I think that I need air," said I.

But the man wasn't focused on Guay anymore. The man was looking at Estelle.

Stuttering something, the lips. Some avowal. Some question directed at her or her fate.

Here was Algernon Child, bloody-headed, in love.

Inconceivable to me, the séance began. First one in my life that I'd ever attended. But it would happen, here, tonight.

Positives and negatives and negatives and positives.

Willy's large, hot hand on mine. Livermore's cooler by twenty degrees. A practiced hand. A yearning hand. Practiced in keeping its yearning a secret.

His face was pale. Embossed moustaches. Long-lashed eyes held firmly closed.

Across from us there sat Kate Fox.

"Has Rosa come into the form?" began Kate. "Rosa of the cellar floor? Rosa, after days of digging, come to illumine the way?"

(Three raps.)

"Grant us, if you will, a woman, here among patrons, well-wishers and friends. A husband sits here," said Kate Fox. "*Your* husband, distraught, who has loved you so long."

More rapping noises, slow and steady.

"The alphabet is motioned for." And here the rapping sounds increased. Kate Fox smiled, her eyes still closed. "Estelle. It is her name. *Estelle*."

Livermore's hand pulsed in mine.

"How do you wish to communicate, Spirit? Do you wish, in the manner of spirits, to speak?"

(One rap)

"Music?"

(One rap)

"Drawing?"

(One rap)

"Writing."

(One rap)

"None?"

(Five raps)

"The alphabet again."

(The raps ascended rapidly)

"Let the circle note," said Kate, "the letter signalled for is *T*."

"Can ladies be true to themselves?" said a voice. Said the voice of a girl—Grace's voice—in the dark. I tried to cut my eyes and see but the lantern light wasn't quite hitting me right.

"Can ladies be true to themselves?" she repeated. "Can they ever really be? And *if* I am true to myself," she went on, "will he consent to be my friend?"

"The letter *O*. The letter *U*. Your audience implores: more letters! The letter *C*," said Katherine Fox. "*T-O-U-C*—yes, oh spirit? You wish to speak to us through *touch*? You wish to cross the borderlands and lay your fingers on our wrists?"

No raps this time. The sound of steps.

Livermore's hand was convulsing in mine.

Called Grace from somewhere very near: "But aren't they dull and single-minded? Were I to say *no farther please* then do you think that he would stop? If you must make me drown," said she, "then hold my head as if you mean it?"

"Two raps," said Katherine suddenly, "suggests the spirit cannot answer. Are we to assume that the spirit stands firm? Speak or spell to us your need."

A wisp of something. Smoke, perhaps. It rose above the séance table. There was a chill that came up off it. It was coming from under the table. The walls. It blowered hugely through the curtains, sending up a little wind.

"Lower your heads," said Katherine Fox. "Mrs. Livermore's spirit will tell us herself."

And that is when someone, a woman in white emerged through the smoke and came on toward the table. She wasn't Grace. She wasn't dead. She wore a garland in her hair. The dark little hint of her groin. Her slight shoulders. Slowly approached Livermore, next to me, and leaned in close right by his ear.

The chilly smoke was thicker now. I started to cough for its richness. Then others. The woman in the gown, she coughed. In the sheer act of trying to keep his eyes closed, Livermore's face had grown distorted.

The woman in white stepped away from the banker, white robes clinging to her skin. I might've even known her face. Fanny Conant's friend: Miss Moss.

Katherine's coughing fit subsided. Subtly, she cracked one eye and watched the woman walk away.

"The Summerland has been obliging. Is Estelle Livermore's emanation still here?"

"She fades," said the woman in white, walking backwards. Composing herself as she walked, her voice hoarse. "She fades. And fades. And fades. And fades. And fades," said the woman, still backing away. The smoke growing thinner along with her voice.

"Until at last she's gone," said she.

MUMLER IN THE LIBRARY
June 1861

To stay for a drink was not only polite, not to mention savvy business, but for both of us essential, especially after the things we had seen.

The eyes of Livermore were red and his ears were red too with the things they had heard. He sat before a shelf of books with the span of a ladder descending behind him. Just at the level of his head was a narrow shelfless portion of the wall with pictures on it. To these my eyes were slowly drawn.

The top two rows were all Estelle, both during and after her brief luckless life—if luckless, reader, can be reckoned apart from the prosperous net worth of Livermore's holdings.

Estelle and her parents.

Estelle at the beach.

Estelle smiling out from a false bank of clouds.

Estelle amidst her wedding veils, her face composed and somehow sad.

Estelle and Charles on honeymoon.

Estelle on a health cure in some scenic glade.

Estelle holding her only daughter—Lucy Ellen was her name—the girl not more than two weeks old.

Estelle looking piqued in a chair in the garden with Lucy Ellen, aged 7 or 8, at her side. Lucy Ellen seems happy and perfectly poised, ready and able to care for her mother.

And many, many portraits more before we arrive at Estelle in her coffin: a glass-topped coffin ringed around with a party of mourners, all clutching their brows.

Estelle rendered fair by the clever embalmer.

Estelle's gravesite in Forest Hills.

Even more than the punishing need of the thing, I was staggered by its sheer manpower. How very many men had toiled over Estelle Livermore in her statehood.

It was I who spoke first: "Did tonight satisfy?"

"Exceedingly so," he said and smiled, though not without a hint of gloom. "With Hannah on one side and Kate on the other, it seems that I can scarcely fail."

"And yet, sir, you have won," I said. "Was that not the woman herself—your dead wife?"

He paused for a moment, distracted by something. "Her, I reckon, yes," he said. "It *sounded* like her anyway."

"Sounded?" I said.

"When she spoke in my ear."

I waited for him to volunteer and when he didn't, said: "*You* sensed her. Without even looking, you knew she was there."

"I admit . . ." he began, and sipped his drink. "I was somewhat afraid to look. What in the world could I possibly say when she was standing there at last?"

"Hello?" I said.

He hardened: "No. Estelle would scoff if I said that."

"I too," I said, "have loved and lost. You're not ready to see her yet. But a picture," I said. "Well a picture is pleasant. A picture is a middle ground."

He looked at me fixedly, searching, then softened.

"This war will be good to we young men at Webster's, fledgling as it is," he said. "And so, in our turn, we'll be good to the war. A fifty-thousand greenback pledge to Boston's blue boys gone to serve. Less than Suffolk house, of course, but equal to Hovey and Lowell, if I may."

"A pledge?" I said, confused at first.

"A pledge not interest free, of course. A patriotic rate," he said, "for the Minutemen of '61. But we are not the only ones. The Hotel Vedome, the Boston Museum, the YMCA, Batchelder and Snyder, why even the crooked Credit House has offered up a share," he said. "And can you guess what institutions finance such philanthropy?"

"The banks?" I said.

"Here, here." He drank. "To appear to be civically minded," he said, "you must give of yourself to the civic machine. Can you guess what will happen when they return home?"

"The Union?" I said. "If indeed it should win."

"Oh, it will win," said Livermore. "If I ever agreed with our man Mr. Sumner it is in his estimation of what the Rebels do not have. Commerce, railroads, schools, you know. Progress trumps regress, of course. And *when* we win, and win we shall, and Boston's blue boys come back home, can you guess who will give them the money they need to purchase those homesteads in Dorchester, sir? Those homesteads vital and deserved under whose roofs they shall raise up their families?"

"The banks?" said I.

"Three cheers to that. Rah, rah," he said and drank. "The banks."

He set his drink upon the desk. I could barely hear him do it for the feltness of his blotter.

"Which is by way of telling you that money is no object, sir. For I should give it all," he said, "to see her even one more time."

But I no longer looked at him.

For there, behind him, in a picture, in a picture of him and Estelle at their wedding, was a much younger version of Algernon Child. He wore the same moustache, but fainter. His hands were laced upon his stomach. And at his neck a smart cravat that he wore with the evening to come in his eyes.

Charles Livermore said, "I suppose you must wonder why it is that I gave you a fake name at first."

"I figured that you had your reasons."

"I may be honest now," he said, "and say it was, really, I didn't then trust you. And I haven't been able to, well, until now."

I forced myself to look at him, to banish the picture from my eyes. I said to him, "Sir, I am glad that you do. That way we may trust each other."

And then we heard a creaking sound. The banker's eyes were on the door.

"Lucy Ellen," said my host and got up partway from his chair. I saw the briefest swatch of something sucked into the house's gloom. Livermore stood for a moment, considering. And then he slowly sat again.

HANNAH MUMLER AND THE DEAD
June 1861

Afternoons among the graves. Katherine and I shared a few.

Though often I came there a couple of hours early to walk among the morning dews.

The greenness of it, weeping down. The shadows were empty. The hillsides unwandered. It was the only place I walked where dead ones did not walk there too.

Mount Auburn was an antidote.

I thought it would help her. My baby. To be.

Not as my mother would have her, half-blind. The ken in her severed away at the root. But a Maier. My daughter. A seer of dead ones and trained in the art of the dead. Unashamed.

For I would have her just for me. Not for my mother but me: a companion. Mount Auburn in stillness and sunlight. In peace. Would help my ragged womb take up. For though I walked there twice a week, my worries were as regular as Willy Mumler's money.

"Do you think we might *trek* today, Hannah," said Kate. "There doesn't seem a spot of rain."

I held to her. The promenade. She moved from my hand to my arm, at the elbow.

"So tell me," said Kate, "have you found your control?"

"Found my what, Miss Kate?"

"Your guide. Your docent through the great beyond. Every girl who's in spirits should have one," said she. "But you don't need one, maybe, Hannah. Sleeping titan, aren't you, dear?

That little display during dinner," said she. "And then in the séance—those muttering sounds. And Fanny Conant's blowsy girl. It could not have been better brought off in the end had we three of us ventured upon it together. Willy, you and me: a team! For scarcely had I spelled out touch—"

But I no longer wished to hear what she was saying.

"My spirit guide is named Algie," said I.

Which was short, I now realized, for Algernon Child.

"For a man, anyway, he is short," began I. "He is short, with dark hair, and he wears a moustache. Something is wrong with the back of his head."

"Wrong with it?"

Said I: "It bleeds."

She whispered: "Murder! Ghastly stuff. Yet it cannot be so!"

"Why not?"

"Because, my dear, I've seen him, too. Or anyway seen someone like him. My spirit control—*my* Rosa," said she, "had his throat opened up in a hideous business."

Here had come a shift in her. Her old romantic self again. And the business of ice, and the girl, and pretending seemed to leave her all at once.

"You have to admit it is uncanny strange. That both of us have *murdered* men. The man that I spoke of—my Rosa," said she. "He was put in the grave for a large cash amount. About five hundred dollars, I think I recall. He explained it to Maggie my sister and I the first night that we ever saw him. He had worked as a tinker. A seller of something. Lightning rods, I think it was. I suppose that he knocked at the wrong man's front door, years before my family came. He'd been dragged down the steps with his throat leaking blood and was buried ten feet in the cellar, like gold. What is the story of Algie?" said she.

"Algie has no tale as yet."

She looked at me strangely at that. Then she smiled.

"When Maggie and I would rap as girls, Mr. Rosa would rap, and the raps have kept coming. And so when I'm rapping with others—whoever—I'm always in some sense still rapping with him. Constancy is what one wants. From people, of course, but especially men."

Katherine Fox cried out: "Oh men! Terrible, wonderful. Caring and cruel."

I replied: "You mean?"

"The banker. Charlie Livermore, of course!"

Out of nowhere Katherine's words. *Terrible, wonderful. Caring and cruel.* As though she had only just happened to say them. As though she'd been holding them close, in reserve, until she could no longer hold them.

Said I: "Will you marry him?"

"It is for him to ask, of course. He would need to be foolish indeed *not* to know. Which leads me to think he will ask me," said she, "when he is sure that I'm for him. I find it attractive the way he bears up beneath storm after storm with that sad little girl."

Caught up to where she walked ahead and took her arm but she pulled loose. She veered off the path toward a thin stand of shrubs. A scummed-over lake lay beyond it in furrows. Presented me her dark, tense back, which flexed as she manoeuvred something.

From even fifteen feet away I could make out the play of the sun in her hair.

Approaching her she turned around. Wiping her mouth with a blue handkerchief. Came forward and took my hands. Each of mine in each of hers.

"Which is why you must help me—oh Hannah, my friend!" She squeezed my hands.

"But help you how?"

"In order for Charlie to lay her to rest, he must have proof of her, you see. And I can only manifest her . . . just so many times in a barely lit room . . . before . . ." Her grip loosened. ". . . not long from today . . ."

"Before he'll want to see her fully."

"Why yes," said she. "You understand."

"You wish us to make you a photograph of her."

"The very thing," said Katherine Fox. "Men of arithmetic—Charlie," said she. "They're very keen on concrete proof."

The fierce sun continued to shine, off behind us. Framing her face in a terrible splendor. The single time before or since I hated what the graveyard gave.

"Promise that you'll help," said she.

"I promise I will try my best."

"Oh Hannah," said she, and dropped my hands, and took my face in both of hers. "Sweet Hannah, I'm sorry"—she cradled my face—"but that just isn't good enough."

Dead ones out in force today. I clawed my way among them, walking.

Noticed that a single man amid the throng was on my tail.

The man was dressed neat. Tailing me at a distance. Embarrassment of watching me. Coming fast for a time and then slowing, bizarrely. As though to imply he were seeing me home.

When I'd climbed the front steps he gave pause, a block back.

Before I had opened the door to the house he was there, below me, at the base of the steps.

He greeted me as Willy's father.

Shocked. Not only by his clothes. His unassuming modesty. For I had seen him many times for all the times that he'd seen me. And always in those greys he wore, as though he had dawdled too close to a fire. Looking over Willy's shoulder. Patrolling the shop with his hands held in fists.

"And *soh*, you are Hannah, I *tink*," said the man. He was slowly rotating his hat in his hands. "You will do me a favour, young lady?" I nodded. "Please tell him the next that time you see him," said he. "His *muder*, Vilhelmina Marie, she is *det*."

MISS CONANT IN A CERTAIN WAY
June 1861

First couple of months after leaving the Center, I took a room in Parker House.

Of course, it was beyond my means, as Beacon Street was long with lanterns. It struck me as the kind of place that I would've been lucky to sleep in on tour but I angled to stay there as long as I could on what I had put by employed the Center. It was a clean, obeisant space. The sheets were always boiled and crisp. I made sure to sleep and to sleep in them often—to get the kind of sleep I needed. The coffee hour was always prompt with little sugared rounds of cake. The other guests were mostly travellers, to see the leaves turn or the liberty sites. And they passed me in families of four in the halls as a brand new attraction: the unattached woman.

Observe, the fathers might've said, *how high she needs to hold her head.*

And so it was here that the jeweller came calling, two days after planning the Banner together. His bulk was wholly clad in black. His auburn beard was trim and combed. He even appeared to have put off some weight. He happened to mention his mother had died, and that he would attend the funeral.

But then he said the queerest thing.

He asked me if I'd come along.

The service was, in fact, that day. In a matter of hours, according to Mumler, and he had come by on the off-chance, he said, that I would be unoccupied.

But I agreed to go with him. I think it was the human thing.

I saw that my pity was far from ill-founded when he had the hack stop in advance of the park, from whose far edge we went on foot so as to garner less attention.

"I admit that I don't understand it," said Mumler, "how people come here just to *walk*. The Common is perfectly good, after all, and then without the corpses in it."

"On days when there aren't marching bands. Or regiments processing out."

"And yet The Common has no corpses. That is the signal distinction, to me."

We mounted toward a great stone tower. William Mumler took my arm.

You see, he was in love with me. He was, at any rate, enchanted. His hands had touched me, sure enough. But I declined to feel their heat. And so, in this way, they were bunches of nerves that touched on other, separate bunches. The flesh would connect and the chemicals snap. But Mumler never knew the all.

We crested the hill and began to curve downwards. The suddenness of it lurched my stomach. I had to stop there at the crest of the hill with my arms to my sides to resettle my balance. It was as though behind my ribs there bloomed a little patch of moss.

At the base of the hill, in among the first graves, a small funeral party was gathered in prayer. Including the Reverend there were four: two older men and a middle-aged woman.

The coffin hovered, sleek and square, above the long home dug out for it.

"Come along this way," said Mumler, steering us wide of the party of mourners.

We crept along the many paths that made the outskirts of the park and in back of a series of big ornate graves in Roman and Egyptian style, we hovered arm to arm and watched as the prayer finished up and the coffin lurched downward.

Even from here, I could hear the thing creaking. Mumler peeled away his gloves. He put his fingers to his lips and the flesh there turned white from the force of him, pressing.

"You can't hear what it sounds like here. The sound of the dirt coming down on her coffin. My mother is in there," he said. "Do you know what that feels like, Fanny?"

I admitted to him I did not know, that I was sorry even so and that, if he wanted, we might venture closer so that he could bid her a proper farewell.

He seemed to cogitate on this and then he said: "I don't think so. I'm in no kind of mood to converse with my father. No thank you, anyway"— he nodded, as though he understood at last—"I'd so much rather stay right here. Standing here, next to you, I may speak or not speak."

Beyond the mourners and the grave another hill lead to another raised path and, walking along it, I saw Hannah Mumler. She spoke to herself with her hand on her stomach. I do not think she saw us there. He lips were working twistedly and she worried the front of her dress with one hand. Walking along the upper road with the coffin descending directly below her she struck me as a sort of spool that wound the coffin toward the earth.

MUMLER IN A CORRESPONDENCE
July 1861

And here I had always been of the conviction that infamy is never bad. But ruin will call out to ruin and showmanship more of the same, and though I am loath to admit it outright, the bastard had inveigled me.

Mr. Phineas Barnum, dedicated American, defrocked investor, cad and showman had written me letters and I'd written him in a mutual spirit of drapery hanging. Over the course of these letters he'd asked that I send him two of my best spirit pictures to place on display in his Barnum's Museum in the full understanding, of course, that the pictures be viewed and reviewed with respect.

Nobody has not *gained a cent*, Barnum wrote, *in the underestimation of the audience he serves. And what is more, my dear flush friend, the highest aim of art is others.*

Yours In Humbug, he had signed.

Which then, I did not think much of, for he was better known than I for the transparency of his artifice.

So I did what he wanted, I sent him two pictures. Both were crowd-pleasers, displayed years before.

One was just a gorgeous print of "Mutton Chops" Murray, the hair tonic man, Mrs. Murray or someone approximate to her standing off to his left with an armful of flowers. The other was a Senator who'd claimed to recognize his aide, beaten to death at a rally by teamsters. The Senator claimed he'd seen his friend in the face of a man who is clearly his senior, perhaps fifty-five when the aide had been thirty, and yet with resemblance enough to convince him that this had been the man he sought. The foregrounded look to the spirit itself is in large part what renders the picture unique, and the viewer can make out the weave of his tweeds, the cracks that line his aging hands, the charging shadow of his face as he moves through the room, past the sitter, away.

Thinking them impregnable, I shipped off P.T. Barnum these.

But I had not thought wisely, probably.

This narrow outlook on my part might well have been due to my skill as a hoaxer—great, in that I was no hoax!—for there'd always been something of common illusion about my correspondent's work: his woolly horses, Feejee mermaids, giantess ladies and overdressed dwarves. And he seemed, in the manner of most bloviators that seek primacy in their part of the pool, to be more than aware of his many shortcomings, how degraded his craft was compared to my own. While I might've been the inferior showman, showmanship was not my game.

The man attacked me in the press.

He singled out my work uniquely.

Some correspondents will ask me, he wrote, *if I believe that all pretensions to intercourse with spirits are impositions. And I tell those men that if people declare that they can privately communicate with invisible spirits, I cannot prove that they are deceived or that they are attempting to deceive me. Indeed if these men and women can cause invisible agencies to perform in open daylight all of the things they pretend to accomplish by spirits in the dark, I will promptly pay five hundred dollars for the sight of it. In the meantime, I think I can reasonably account for and explain all pretended spiritual gymnastic performances—throwing of hair-brushes—dancing pianos— spirit rapping—table tipping—playing of musical instruments—and flying through the air in the dark and a thousand other wonderful manifestations to be as flat and cold as dishwater. Spirit photography,* he concluded, *is false if not more so than these.*

I'll say it caught me quite off-guard. We were both of us caught off-guard, I think. Put a clever old goat in a room with his junior and you must let them kick it out.

But I declined to stoop to that. I answered him quietly, privately, briefly. I told him he might keep the pictures, hoping they would entertain.

On the night of the day that they published his screed, a brick came through our northside window.

Slipper-shod, I searched the scene for a note maybe tied to the back of the brick, some sinister promise or defaming, but all that there was,

was the hurled thing itself. The incident had roused the women who both ventured down from their garret of night where they stood in the doorway with unblinking eyes.

I drafted a scorching succession of letters, oppressively rhetorical, clad in the facts. Yet I didn't postmark them. I shelved them and waited—ideally, for some hot addendum from Barnum, and when it was clear none was coming, still more.

There was a small drop-off in business. Or maybe not so small, at that. Though I was sure that, given time, this deficit would self-correct.

Yet here was Barnum—spitting, reddened.

I had been the better man.

And yet you will be wondering why Barnum goaded me at all? There'd been that piddling drop-off, yes, in the sitters who came to inquire at my door—fifteen sitters in a week where prior to that there had been nearly thirty. Yet even so the year before had been nothing if not a spectacular year and I had plenty cash already biding in my parlour's chests.

The crux of it was only this: the man had dealt blows to my good reputation.

And that is how it came about that Charles Livermore became all the more crucial.

The man had been in omnipresence all about my rented rooms. He sat there in his tailor-mades, making the modest wallpaper look shabby, or worse would stroll along the walls looking at my spirit pictures and wondering with fierce impatience when his and Estelle's would appear there among them.

The picture of Baker and Child's bloodied corpse I'd immolated weeks ago, though that didn't answer the question one bit of who Child had been to the banker in life. For Child with his head battered in reappeared in several—many—of my prints. He crouched and stood and loomed and lurked and sulked and paced and lounged and peered. It was the highest designation of the fellow's afterlife, I'm greatly saddened to report, to recur in my prints looking not quite his best.

It was a proper haunting, reader!

And so I would double-expose him away, replace him with another ghost and deliver this forgery, priced as before, down into the sad, amazed hands of its owner.

A slippery incline?

Of course it was, reader.

I was well, well aware of the risks that I took.

The banker came two times a week. But today, oh today, it might always be different.

Today he came at ten past eight, and as I led him to his stool once Guay had taken off his coat, he stared at my wife at the edge of the room in the process of warming herself for the sitting. My wife was mustering her shade as a fisherman musters the width of his nets, picking out the kinks and folds so as to throw them best and farthest. Her eyes were fluttering a bit, her gullet working rapidly. It looked as if her cranium were on its way to giving birth.

Katherine Fox was due, and late.

"Mr. Mumler, I wonder," spoke up Livermore, "how Matthew Brady's portraits strike you? Powerful stuff, I am told. And quite gruesome. He means to make us own our war."

I thought of what I knew of Brady: ruined boys and bloody dirt.

"You are all about Boston these days, aren't you, sir?"

Observing me, he sat and smoked. "I'm not withholding confidence that you *will* manifest Estelle. She shall be your Confederate sharpshooter, eh? And all of Boston will rejoice."

When at that moment, happily, Katherine Fox came up the stairs.

For a moment she wavered upon the top step, as though in amazement how she had arrived there. Livermore stood when she entered the room.

"Charlie, I've come," she said. "Hello! Hello to all of you!" She waved. "Say, Charlie: I think we will get her today. I feel she is within our reach."

If Kate Fox was not dead with drink then I was not in need of one. Her feet sounded extremely loud across that many-peopled space.

"You're welcome to take up position," I said, "as soon as you're inclined, my friend."

Livermore sat down in front of the curtain and started to cinch up his tragic cravat.

I asked Livermore, "What *is* Miss Fox's role?"

"The spirit of my wife," he said, "is on good terms with Kate's control."

I remembered the girl from the Spiritualist Center not unbecoming in her robes while Livermore screwed shut his eyes, unwilling or able to see who she wasn't.

"Of course." I smiled at Livermore. "The plates are ready, Mr. Guay?"

Guay poked his head from the closet. "Yes, sir."

"Then I shall calculate the light."

Bill Christian appeared in our midst with the drop cloth and paid it out over the top of the camera.

"Mr. Livermore, you're comfortable?"

And Hannah took that as her signal, rising abruptly from her stool and dragging it right of the shot, just outside it. At this remove she sat again and Livermore responded, "Quite."

And so with the hand that had helped Mother sleep, and the hand that had cramped under scourge of Papa, and the hand that had fashioned my girl-wife her ring, and the hand that had fingered the picture of Cora in the dark of my closet so many nights past, I fitted the plate in the back of the box.

I ducked my head below the shroud.

Beneath the gloom-permitting cloth, I followed the light as it tracked in the fabric and listened to the murmurings of Livermore obtaining poise.

Katherine tittered drunkenly: "Elegance embodied, Charlie."

And then I sensed Hannah was no longer moving, that she had perfected the path of the shot and that she was waiting, her back to the curtain, to see the camera through its work. But not only was Hannah not turned from the curtain but facing its tableau head-on and, to make matters worse, she was violently sneezing, burst upon burst upon burst, *toward* the shot. The motes she blasted from her nose were scrambling up and through the light, and the sneezes came on her with steady control, like shot before a rifle column.

It was all I could do to wait out the exposure, counting off the thirty seconds, while Katherine said: "God bless you, Hannah. Bless you— bless you—bless you—bless—"

"*Mr.* Mumler," said the banker. "Haven't you waited a moment too long?"

I realized, sadly, that I had.

"A grip of sneezes!" said Kate Fox. "But Charlie, we must try again. If you have it in you to keep looking dapper, I'm sure that my Rosa can see to return. Is that not so, my friend?" she said to the still parlour air at the right of her head. And waiting a beat she pronounced: "He agrees."

MUMLER CONFIRMED
August 1861

Reader, I ask of you, what is a month? What is a month in the shadow of ruin? A biddy of a moth, no more, chafing her stick-arms and whirring her wings above the fluid grain of time—so tentative of touching down, of being snagged and snatched away.

So I had bought myself a month. And yet I did not feel I owned it.

In his infinite cruelty and infinite patience, Livermore had sold it to me, not that a month wasn't standard, all told, for producing the six or so prints that I owed. But how unfair it seemed—to me! For I think I began to conceive of the prints that I had made for Livermore as a grouping of cursed and impossible objects whose conjuring I'd had no part in— that had simply appeared there, maleficent, foreign, stern against their cardboard backing, determined to fester my life with unluck.

But allow me to describe them, reader, clad with dread inside their drawers:

More than one ghost would've been bad enough. In Livermore's pictures there are five. They crowded around him on his stool.

Some of them I recognized but most of them, of course, I didn't. You could only see Child on account of the fact that his ghost was, as usual, fixed on the viewer. Around him are shoulders and profiles and hairlines and people's necks above their collars. Why Hannah had ruined the picture with sneezing I could not at that moment say, yet still I must square with a critical fact: the land of the dead was not mine to set foot in. I might schedule the sittings, and work the machine, and jaw pleasantly through the Lahngworthy dinners, but Hannah and her instrument had always had the upper hand.

And so I attempted to muster control; I fumbled about in my arsenal, reader.

Delaying the order, destroying the prints and falling on the banker's mercy, doctoring the prints myself with an image purloined from Charles Livermore's study.

Such were my options. I studied them well. I could not simply give them to him. And still there was the threat of Child—him noticing Child, which he would in short order.

The shades had amassed and the fees had been paid.

At the end of that week, I resolved to do nothing.

Imagine, then, my panic, reader, when I arrived home on the Friday that followed to find Mr. Hinkley, in livery, waiting, upon the topmost of my steps. Hannah was out on parade with Kate Fox again while Claudette, I could only assume, lurked inside—not that she ever went anywhere, reader. It was just Guay and I who came up the front steps.

We were hobbled with bundles and bags from the chemist's. Physically and then besides, the meeting was an awkward one. The footman did not offer aid, just watched Guay and I fight to balance our things.

"To collect Mr. Livermore's pictures," said Hinkley. "He thought they might be done by now. *May* I help you with those bags while we travel inside to collect them?" he asked.

I conferred on his person my three biggest parcels and everyone processed inside.

Into our receiving rooms, I put down my parcels and spoke to the footman. "Feel free to remain, Mr. Hinkley," I said. "*I* will go and fetch the prints."

"I'm sorry, sir. I can't do that. Mr. Livermore was very clear that I vouchsafe his pictures' *freshness*."

"You wish to come into the closet with me?"

"I wish to merely stand outside it."

There was no more sidestepping what now must be done. So I walked to the door in the shadow of Hinkley, and Hinkley himself in the shadow of Guay.

In the end, I went in and came out of the closet.

Everyone was still alive.

He checked the pictures, looked at me, said: "Fifty dollars, is it not?"

"And what do you think of our services rendered?"

But he declined to answer that. When he had counted out the bills he pressed them, springing, in my palm.

"As you can see, *she* isn't there. For that"—I drew nearer the footman—"I'm sorry. But I think you will find, on a closer inspection—"

Yet the footman had moved to the window, surveying, as though I hadn't spoken to him. "If you, sir, are dissatisfied on Livermore's behalf," I said, "then I trust you will out with the source of your grievance before it commences to harden and set?"

Mr. Hinkley continued to stare out the window. And then his eyes grew possum wide. The front door of Otis Street hammered and shook. All of us recoiled at once.

I said: "There's no need, I am coming, do not—"

But whoever was doing the ramming kept on.

The door-jamb retched splinters, the knob jarred the floor, the door itself came quickly after. A column of coppers stood there in the door with a battering ram as the spine of the column. They passed it back, and spread inside, and a bald man in plainclothes came in on their tail.

The man was squat and carven-shouldered. On his head a bowler hat.

"Mr. Mumler, I take it?" he said, very brusquely. "Mr. William H. Mumler of 4 Otis Street?"

"That is the place where you're standing, good man, in case you weren't aware," I said.

"And that is the name of the hand that I'm shaking?"

"But you have yet to take it, sir." I took his hand and said: "Let me."

"But you must wonder who I am. Inspector Marshall Henry Tooker. And I'm come here to tell you," he said not to me, but rather to the group at large and dropped my hand to walk the room, his bowler swinging from his side, "as chief emissary to his honourable mayorship beneath the directive of Article 7 of the Commonwealth of Massachusetts, that you are accused of larceny and fraud against the common man."

"On what grounds are we charged?" I said.

"Your actions, sir, have been confirmed." He gestured at Hinkley, gone stiff in his corner.

"On what grounds are we charged?!" I pressed.

"You're eager for me to pronounce them?" he said.

He seemed almost disinterested. He peered amidst the couch's weave; he ducked into the murky closet; he hunted along the wainscoting as if it supported some structural secret; he cycled by the entry-table, picking up a single card, and skimmed it backward toward its brethren. Then he went by William Guay.

"You are the assistant, I'm told?" And Guay nodded. "Now what can we say is the plural for William?" Trying to think of the right word to call us, his eyes remained fixed on the bumpkin and me. "A skein of geese.

A pride of lions. A murder of crows," the Marshall said. "A confidence, perhaps. Ah, there. A confidence," he crooned, "of Williams. And where is the black one?"

"He's elsewhere," I said.

"And where is the woman? This Hannah—your wife." To this last I did not respond. "I wonder, Mr. Mumler, sir, if *they* would do the same for you?"

And then he softened: "Come," he said, "You are under arrest. Had I got round to that?"

I was a little disappointed when he said that, I admit.

And then we were filing in awkwardness dayward, through the door and down the steps.

I turned to see the shop again and in the window Hannah's mother. She had parted the curtain on the street to show the world her ageless face. I almost had to turn away, so bright with darkness was that look, the way her sighted, sightless eyes peered on toward a future that couldn't mean good, and everything—*everything*—all seemed to char, like a beautiful painting set fire from behind—like the roses in the picture of the girl in her coffin or the blood slipping wildly from Algernon's collar. The ageless face hovered—evoking, accusing. And then the curtain wiped it clean.

HANNAH REMINDED
August 1861

Willy dour these summer months. Sitters coming at a drip.

So it was fitting Kate should call. That Kate should be the place I went.

To the Sunderlands' house. Where she stayed when in Athens. Not so elegant now at the height of the summer. Cornice-clipped and mouldy-looking. Received at the door by the Sunderlands' girl, whose hair was damp with indoor sweat.

Into the foyer and past the front parlour, we stopped before the grand staircase.

"Ma'am," said the maid in a fixed tone of voice. "She's in Sarah's old room. Up the stairs, down the hall."

Rising through the costly air. Everything smelling of wood and glass polish. Room the maid had named, I knocked.

"*Is* that Hannah?" came a voice. "If that is Hannah, do come in."

Beyond the creak lay Katherine Fox. Ensconced in the lacework of Sarah's old bed. A flowered, frosted pink-white bed. Prettified as glassed-in cake.

Shoes and city dress and all, she lay amid a pile of dolls. Porcelain and cloth. Apple-cheeked. Crowded close. Sun pouring in through the back of the canopy.

"Don't be frightened, Hannah, dear. These shrunk ladies are my friends. Isn't that right, little ladies? You, lovelies."

"Kate," said I. "You're still in bed."

"Well I had *meant* to go abroad but here I am all dressed for work. And here you are! You're *always* here. You love me, don't you, Hannah Mumler?"

Inconceivably hot in that room. Windows closed. Some rug at the centre, gone pale at the edges, where light from the garden broke over the boards.

Fanning her arms and her legs in the covers. Knocking a few staring dolls to the floor.

"Maggie and Kate, at ten and eight . . ." she started sing-songing while trying to rise.

Wavering, lay back again

"As soon as I wake in the morning," said she, "I don't remember for a moment. These last several mornings . . ." Katherine looked at the ceiling. "The thing is, I'm happy. And don't quite believe. But then, you see, I *know* again. I know it like my very blood."

"Kate," said I. "What is it, Kate?"

"You should know it relates to your Willy, uniquely. Charlie has—how shall I say it?—entrapped him. Caught him in his wealthy web. Oh Hannah," said she. "It is perfectly awful! What at all am I to do?"

Broke down crying. On her back. Her wrists held stiffly near her face.

"One moment I'm sure that he wants me," said she. "The next moment there's just this—cruelty! And now I know. I really know." She grew violently sober while sniffling her nose. "I suppose, in the end, it is all for the better. Well maybe not for you, poor dear. This way, I may . . . move along. This way, twenty years from now, I won't wake up one day and find . . . And find . . ." Her voice grew thin with tears. ". . . the man has used me as a pawn!"

And here she did break down in wild, ruined laughter.

"Maggie and Kate, at ten and eight, in country darkness lay afraid and so to prove that they were brave, dropped first one apple then its mate."

She paused and leaned down. Groping under the bed. Brought up the last of a bottle of sherry. Gnashed out the cork with her teeth and drank deeply. A little spilling down her chin.

"I have done this, Kate," said I. "I have driven him from you."

"*You* have driven him from me? Would that that were all," said she. "He was never headed *toward* me. I was simply—a bridge! A bridge that he must go across."

Lay on her back. Lightly humming, conducting. The canopy burring along with her arms

"Tied with pretty little strings. We bounced them up and down. Rap, rap. And she and I, at ten and eight, controlled our terrors just that way."

"You and Maggie sang that song."

"Always," said Kate Fox, "as girls. And now you know: I am a fraud. A ridiculous shicker-head rummy, that's all, who loves a man she cannot have."

"The raps," said I.

"We made with fruit. Fruit we tied to strings and dropped! But that was all so long ago. Yes, we have graduated, since."

"You must lie back and sleep," said I.

"But we don't make the rapping with fruit anymore. And we don't make it with our toes. We make it with our knees. The fools! Oh the fools!" cried Kate Fox before turning to stone. Then a grim revelation took over her face. "Oh the beautiful, elegant fool!" she lamented. "He's abandoned me here to my doom—an old maid!"

And fell asleep just as she was. Fully clothed and sweet with sherry. Slept with her head on my breast, where I'd moved—to the head of the bed, I mean, to hold her—*and how could it matter if Katherine was cruel, did Grace not own my heart already*—and Katherine's face purred air. Leaked water. Her hair bent in masses of black on my breast.

And that's when the dead girl unmoored from the wall and walked toward me across the room. The bright hem of her bathing costume rolled between her bony knees.

"Has it occurred to him," said she, "that I am having trouble breathing? A game is always well and good, but hasn't this one run its course?"

"Grace," said I.

The dead girl laughed. A full and larking laugh, cut short.

". . . crossed paths with my pop?" she was asking me now. "How *is* my pop for jowls these days?"

My mother's words: *Go home to God. You are long overdue at his side, darling child.* And the governess, mumbling, had wandered away. And this had been a sort of lesson.

For if you loved them well enough. Or if their madness pricked your heart. Then you might keep them in their grief, if only for a little while.

And so I told her: "Fine. He's fine. Your father is fine—can you doubt it?" said I. "Why just the other day, in fact, I saw buying fresh-cut flowers."

Deeper inside of my shadow, she came. The whey of what had been her face. "Flowers for an entrance hall? Or are they meant for someone's grave?" Continued the dead girl: "Might *I* bring him flowers and hold them above him to bless him, my pop? Might I show him some fair way that I am still his only girl?"

I frowned at her. And shut my eyes. And counted to ten in the dark of myself.

Looked up, and she was Grace again.

Said I: "Just any way you please."

GUAY IN QUESTIONING
September 1861

Things I told to Marshall Tooker:

First things first the Marshall asks: "When was it that you first met Mumler?"

"A year and a half come this August," says I.

Says he: "And that was here—in Boston?"

Says I: "I had come from Fredonia then."

"Expressly to meet Mr. Mumler?" says he.

"That's right," answers I. "For to witness his marvels. On my and His Seership's behalf," answers I.

"By his Seership you mean, Reverend Davis, your ward?"

"Andrew Jackson Davis, yes."

"And what then was your diagnosis?"

"When I first saw his photographs I thought that they were very proper. He has the talent that they say."

"But it isn't *him* with the talent, now is it?"

"Isn't it?" says I to him.

"*She* is the one who produces the trick."

"Hannah makes the trappings, yes, but Mumler always takes the picture."

In silence the Marshall considered these facts and then at length he says: "Indeed. Though I can't but imagine it isn't distracting to have a woman in your shot? Distracting enough to draw the eyes of a good many curious onlookers, surely."

"I don't see what you mean," says I.

"I think you see quite well," says he. "I think your eyes are sharp as diamonds. Tell me, Willy, if I may, by what process these ghosts appear?"

"I told you already," says I. "Hannah's trappings. Willy fits the slide and then . . ."

"Fits the slide?" says Marshall Tooker.

"Puts the plate in back," says I.

"And always with the selfsame hand? Always wearing gloves?" says Tooker.

I was not sure what he was on.

"Mr. Mumler's reported to have certain habits. All within your outfit do. You, sir, have your holiness. And Mumler has his holy hand."

"Her shadow reflects the light," says I.

"The light of the spirits."

"So others have said."

"And that's how the camera is able to catch them?"

"That I have seen it done," says I.

"And what about this man," says he, "who so many people proclaim to be living?"

"There is no man I know of, sir."

He showed me the picture of him I had done for—the one that was taken amid Hannah's sneezes.

"Why that man . . ." I says foundering. "That man . . ."

"Is named Algernon Child," says the copper. "He lives here in Boston— the South End, in fact. Most every person that I've asked attests that he is still alive. And yet here he is in a ghost photograph amid a rather bustling crowd."

"And you have seen him round yourself?"

"I have," says the Marshall. "Conversed with him, even."

"And you are sure that it was he?"

The Marshall was stiff as though swallowing something and then he looked down at his lap.

"But here's a question for you, Willy: what makes you so certain that *you* can trust Mumler?"

"He hadn't cause to lie," says I.

"Why I should say he'd *ample* cause. And now you are complicit, sir. He has lied himself into a corner, I'll say, and he is crowding out your space. Isn't it true that you finance his ventures?"

"Not out of my pockets directly," says I.

"Through Mr. Davis, then?" says he.

"Entrusted by way of his faith in me, sir."

"And so I ask of you again: it that not cause enough to lie?"

"I do not think he would," says I. "Besides that, sir, he is my friend."

Explosively the Marshall laughed and the chair that he sat in appeared to lurch toward me. "Frauds do not have friends," says he. "Frauds do not *need* friends whatever."

"If he is not my friend," says I, "then tell me what he wants with me."

"That, I have already told you," says he. "He wants your money, Mr. Guay. He wants the stamp of Jackson Davis. And while he is at it, I shouldn't much doubt, he wants a pup that he may fetch with. I daresay, sir, that you are that. Maw full of money and useful connections. And here you are in perfect faith, ecstatic to suffer the sins of your master."

"And Livermore?"

"And Livermore! Why, Livermore was just the bait. We've been watching your, sir, for some months at this point. I am happy to say you did not disappoint us."

MUMLER BY MISINFORMATION
September 1861

"When was it, exactly, you met Mr. Child?"

"Two years and two months to the day," I told Tooker.

"You seem to know it very well."

"I thought I heard you say: exactly."

"And *where* was it you knew him first?"

"I met him at a séance in a house in the Back Bay. He was the photographer there and we talked. After that for a while we were friends," I confessed, "as I'm sure Algernon will attest. If you have him."

But Tooker did not hear this last or if he did he gave no sign. "Friends for a while, sir, how long do you mean?"

"The next year and a half I would say, give or take."

"I say that's considerably more than a while."

"It was a while to me," I said.

"And all of a sudden you no longer were?"

"Fairly suddenly," I said. "We ended on bad terms, in fact. Algernon Child was *convinced*"—I clasped hands—"that I was in some way suppressing his talent."

"A case of envy, plain and simple."

"A case of misconception, sir. For ours *was* a friendship of mutual honour. But Algernon could not see that."

"The pictures we have of him," Tooker went on, "all show him rather worse for wear. In fact, he looks a downright mess. In other people's pictures, too. And when they came forward suppose what they claimed?"

"If it please you, no," I said.

The Marshall laughed. "The fools said this: *that* man is not the man you say. That man is my brother, my nephew, my friend for Mr. Mumler told me so. While others said: that man there, Marshall. That man there is still alive."

"If that is true," said I, "produce him."

"Are you implying," said the Marshall, "that for some reason, sir, he cannot be produced?"

"Nothing of the kind," I said. "I myself haven't seen him since we parted ways. And since I have nothing to fear," I pressed on, "when it comes to my work being *proven* a fraud I wonder have you entertained the thought that Algernon is . . ."

"Dead." He looked at me wryly and long, his brow twitching. "How very clever of you, sir."

"But that is purely speculation."

"We cannot produce him," he said. "He is missing. Missing," His Baldness repeated. "Unless . . . But let us circle back to that. You're aware that Child went to the college of art? The man was there three years, we're told. Hazard a guess as to whom he befriended?"

"Why don't you tell me," I said.

"A man named Charlie Livermore. A recent patron of yours, no? Livermore and Algernon, the two of them were friends," he said. "Like you, they had a falling out. All of this started two years after college. Livermore had quit at art. Embraced the banking life full-time. More gainful pursuit than photography, surely. And yet he wished, I do suppose, to keep his finger on the pulse. And so he did what artists do when they resort to making money. He became a board member, if not an aspirant, of the Massachusetts Chapter of the PSAI."

"He denied Algernon's application," I said. "I'd heard as much from Child. But why?"

"In part, I've come to understand, for his entanglement with you."

"I'm not sure that I understand."

"Before he applied to the PSAI, Child had asked Livermore for a loan," said the Marshall. "He wanted to finance some process experiments. He wanted to see how you did what you do. But Livermore denied him that. Spirit pictures, it seems, were implausible to him, believer in spirits though he was. And then when Child dropped off the map at the height of his suspect involvement with you, Livermore, feeling guilty, concerned for his friend, looked into the matter of looking at you. He came to us with his results, and we proposed our little sting. Mr.

Livermore," he said, "was suggestible far in decline of his friend. Care to dwell, Mr. Mumler, on some of his theories?"

He did not give me time to answer.

For by then he'd commenced in a sonorous voice, by way of what the banker told him, to enumerate for me the various ways that I was thought to work the trick. When he was done I smiled at him and eased back snugly in my chair.

". . . Livermore was full of theories. Here's another one for you: Algernon happened on methods," he said. "And *that* is when you murdered him."

"Why this must be some grotesque joke."

"We *know* that Algernon is missing. Along with the fact that when he disappeared, he was firmly in the business of investigating you. Such relative contingencies may not be overlooked," he said.

"And yet your logic has a flaw so far as those prints of him go, Mr. Tooker. For if I am a fraud," I said, "I cannot be a murderer. And if I a murderer, then I can no more be a fraud."

"And so you admit to the first one," he said. "Murder's not your cup of tea?"

"I *freely* admit to none of them."

"And that is why, sir, we've accused you of both. For if we can't have you on murder," he said, "then we will have you on the rest."

"That will never wash," I said. "As you say yourself, Algernon has gone missing. I should think that you might have a difficult time convincing a jury my pictures are hoaxes when you cannot produce the man whose very existence is your only proof!"

"Legally speaking, Mr. Mumler, we won't *have* to produce him, when we're done with you. Our experts and lawmen and rival photographers, not to speak of the people whom you have defrauded, are more than ample cavalry to drag you screaming through the mud."

"And if the charge of fraud should fall," I asked Marshall Tooker, "you'll settle for murder?"

"Murder we are working on."

"Working on," I said, "indeed. Which is to say you have no case."

"In point of fact until just now. It's your accomplice, Mr. Guay. He has just now confessed everything, Mr. Mumler."

MISS CONANT IN CONFIDENCE

October 1861

I kept to my room at the Parker Hotel, to no little degree with the jeweller's assistance.

His and Guay and Hannah's trial for manifesting ghosts at cost was a little bit less than a full month away. The three of them were held at Charles Street, Hannah in the women's wing. So Mumler had put it to Bill—Mumler's man—to see that I was kept in rent. Their coffers were not overflowing. Things were looking ugly for them. But come Friday the Negro, too. He came between clients, the parcel in hand. First he'd close my fingers on it, and then he'd instruct me: "Take care now, Miss Conant."

And yet I wished that he had stared. Untowardness would have been a comfort. It would've made me wonder less on what the folded bills were for.

The jeweller occurred to my mind only sometimes. Most of all I thought of Hannah. I pictured her sleepless and mild during meals. I wondered what dark things were loose in her hair. I tried to envision the face of her jailer—dark serge dress and belt of keys. I remembered the kindness I'd seen in her eyes and wondered was it still alive. And I wondered at kindness—the thing in itself. How it could be killed down in someone.

When it wasn't Bill, or a porter or maid for whom I never had a tip, the women came to sit and weep. And not from the cellar, as one time they had, but in from the heat with their parasols lowered. They were wretched and bitter from nursing their sadness. Oftentimes their mouths smelled stale. It was never a daughter but always some son whose name they came to say, red-eyed.

One woman came in search of this: Private Beecham Tuttle of the 2nd Massachusetts.

She was a lumpen, dark-haired woman. And she had the look, too, of a God-given mother; that was all she'd ever done. She'd been born in some hamlet somewhere in New England, the daughter of some woman like her, and when she'd emerged in a cabin's rank steam she'd known her function even then.

She told me the tale of her son's sorry death. How he'd been under charge of a twenty-inch Smoothbore.

This, according to a friend.

Their last such charge had come at Sharpsburg. They'd been firing the cannon on top of a hill and in a sally it got loose, and Private Tuttle followed it to the edge of the grade and then went over with it. He'd gained some ground upon the thing when it picked up dead speed and came rushing down on him. He was a porridge after that—bones and blood and skin, all mixed.

I began to grow faint, even there, in my chair. The room came in and out of true, the lamp on the table, the woman before it. She came uncoupled from her stamp, and she seemed to retreat down a tunnel of gaslight. A thousand grieving mothers there, two thousand sons and sons' wives. Hers was the haggard face of war, of Lady Liberty herself, of a Longacre penny tramped down in red mud, erupting feathers from her head. And as I sat there, very still, willing the room and the face to stop shifting, I felt my faintness take its course not from somewhere outside me but *in* me, too deep.

It was a sort of siphoning, a slow and heavy drawing off.

And that's when liquid, strange and warm, went coursing down my thighs, my calves. I thought, maybe, I'd spilled my tea or that the woman had spilled hers but realized there was no tea, that I hadn't concocted my usual pot, and that the water came from me.

I had voided my bladder, right there at that table, as sure as the Private had voided his life.

I thought: *it is a part of me but it is not a part at all.*

I tried not to look at the mess I had made—to maintain focus on her face. But she sensed my resistance. And perhaps she smelled something. I was violently embarrassed at the prospect and I blushed.

"Now that's all right, Miss Conant, Ma'am. How far are you along?" she said.

"Only just," I told her, stunned. "I am only just starting just now, Mrs. Tuttle."

"The first six fortnights are the worst. Take it from me, Ma'am, when I was with Beecham. But then, come week thirteen or so, it always gets a little better."

I think my eyes were very hard.

She said: "I *am* sorry. You see, I just meant—it is, of course, a natural thing. You needn't be ashamed, is all. One mother in Christ to another," she said.

Her eyes were half-lidded and kind in the dim.

I gathered myself. "Mrs. Tuttle," I said, "you've lost your son and that's a shame—and then perhaps before his time, but you needn't invent things on my account, Ma'am. A life cannot supplant a death. If you wish to do right by your Beecham," I said, and the woman's kind eyes clouded over with pain, "you must face up to certain facts. You will never hold Beecham, nor touch him, again. Nor hear his voice. Nor smell his scent. Can you concede to that?"

She nodded. Though even I saw she would never concede.

"Good," I told her, better now, the urine dripping from my dress. "The test conditions are in place. And now," I said, "we may begin."

MUMLER IMPRISONED
October 1861

I sit here before you unjustly accused. I sit here at your mercy, reader.

We three sit before you, a congress of rogues, and all our fates are intertwined.

In the days leading up to our spurious trial, with summer skulking into fall, in different branches of the cross that made the Suffolk County Jail, Hannah, Guay and I sat waiting—mute, incoordinate, fearing the worst. Hannah was on the women's wing while Guay and I slumped either side of the men's, though the bumpkin and I might've been different sexes for all we were allowed to talk.

Apart from my counsel, Mr. Townsend, who'd been appointed by the State, I suffered to receive no one and no one paid me mind by mail, though Boston's papers proved adept at meditating on our straits. Every day without fail there'd be Hannah and me, and, boxed in a column adjacent the bumpkin, the scores and notations of Civil War dead beginning to play second horn to us rotting. The only ones of us still free were Bill Christian and Hannah's mother.

Yet I was a lever, while Bill was a cog. Bill Christian got frisked while I reigned in the Globe—but couldn't they be cruel sometimes, calling me Mumbler, and Mummer, and Juggler, prodding at my tender name with keen, commercial impishness. And so while Bill of Beacon Hill of little moment walked the streets, it was I, Willy Mumler of Newspaper Row, photographer of ghastly marvels, who bent his head into a storm of rapists, pickpockets, cardsharps and abusers—in a ten by four space where the sunlight itself, shining raggedly into the arms of the cross, had not the slightest character, the slightest touch of heaven in it. There was always one man, all night long, who keened for just a sip of something and always another, when this man was done, who called to the guard in a seethe of invective. And forever the knocking of implements, scratching, the grunting of a hundred apes, those sad and headstrong bouts of sound that men fallen into the sere will enact.

But I remained completely still.

I wanted to conserve my strength. You see, I wished to feel prepared—stacked up to the task of defending myself—and short of running round my cell or doing smaller calisthenics, which every time I tried to do reduced me to a huffing mound, I determined to sit there, enormously silent, pondering my circumstances.

Yet I did not consider long. Soon the trial was on, full swing.

The state's contention was preposterous. May it please the court, indeed.

Elbridge T. Gerry, the State's prosecutor, with whiskers as full as the Marshall was bald, promenaded back and forth with thespian flair before the court.

"May it please the court," said Gerry, "before stating my case in behalf of the people that we the Commonwealth commend the wide latitude that His Judgeship has shown to the hollow transgressions of William H. Mumler. Your mercy is not strained, My Lord. Nor ere was mercy *ever* so. But plummeteth down through the mists of its maker to soak into the ground below. And so it blesseth he that gives and he that takes in equal reach."

Gerry smiled to hear his words—*The Merchant of Venice*, I believe.

He took a pass around the court. The eminence to which he spoke, a little pressed bug of a man with black hair, nodded his mandibles once and twitched sagely on top of his pulpit surmounting the court.

"A most embroidered quote, My Lord, but also suited to the day. Not only in content, concerning Your Honour, but also in style of delivery, I think. For isn't this Mumler an able embroiderer—and so his apprentices, here in our dock? Have they not taken common portraits—common as the Bard's adage—and outfitted them in the cheap metaphysics that are the bugbear of our age? And have they not taken *advantage* . . ." he spouted.

Sound and fury, on and on.

They brought a so-called expert first: the old wizard himself, Bogardus.

He was just as I'd pictured him, fatter perhaps, with a white mane of hair like a dowager's blanket and a big bushy widower's beard, just as white. It was as though his very life were locked in strife with fickle

Fashion—as though it would've pained the man to dignify a court of law. And in this spirit he went on to hold forth on his breadth of knowing, specifically as to nine methods, in name, by which I might've forged my prints:

One. By inserting a positive plate with a previous image in front of a clean one, so that when the latter came into the completion, the first plate's residual image still showed.

Two. By introducing for a quarter-of-a-minute a fleeting figure clothed in white (for instance, Mrs. Britten's girl) who flees before the plate is done, deploying a shadowy visage behind her.

Three. By the crafting and clever concealment of a microscopic image of the revenant sought in one of the camera's four screw-holes, which is then magnified by a proximate lens and projected to proportion on the surface of the plate.

Four. By concealing by way of the hand a spirit-haunted mica positive and inserting this plate in the shield mid-exposure to achieve the "foggy dumplings" the spirits recalled . . .

Yet to name only four is to name four too many. You heard what Gerry said of mercy.

But on to Bogardus' words about Child—a really, very damning bunch:

"Is it true," Gerry said, "that in this city here in the year of 1856 that Algernon Child was your life drawing student at the Boston Institute of Art?"

"That is so," said Bogardus.

"Were the two of you close?"

"As a student and teacher may be," said Bogardus.

"Forgive me," said Gerry, "my ignorance, sir, but how close might that be? Please, teach us!"

A breeze of laughter swept the court.

"Affinity," Bogardus said. "We have an affinity, each for the other. I felt—and still feel—great affection for him in spite of his unstudied technical hand."

"He was no good at drawing, then?"

"Well he wasn't quite average," said Bogardus. "And yet he was dauntless. Ineptly inspired. His hunger to learn—it was that which endeared me."

"And continues today to endear you?" said Gerry. "I noticed you said, sir—and here see to record—that you felt and *still feel* great affection for Child. Which choice of words would then imply that he is still among the living?"

"Oh, very much so!" said Bogardus, "the wretch. I saw him just the other day."

"Once again"—Gerry smiled—"might you be more specific?"

"This Wednesday past," Bogardus said. "He came to inquire on a technical matter. He was looking rather well in fact—weaning from the bottle likely—and yes, I remember distinctly," he said, his finger raised before the court, "that he came to my rooms around five in the evening."

"Might you tell us then," said Gerry, "the nature of the thing he asked?"

"He wanted to know how to make spirit pictures." A murmur stirred the gallery. "He wanted to know how this Mumler here did it."

"He could not figure it himself?"

"As I said," said Bogardus, "he is not hugely able. Hardly what you'd call a natural. Smart enough in other ways—intellectually smart, you might say—but not technically."

"Do you mean to imply, sir, that you were surprised that Child could *not* achieve such pictures?"

"I was somewhat," Bogardus said. "Most of the methods I named are deductible."

Then tardily, slowly, at blessed long last: "Defence objects," said Counsellor Townsend. "My Lord, what bearing can this have on the fact of Mr. Child's aliveness?"

"Overruled, Mr. Townsend," His Beetle-ship said. "Mr. Bogardus, continue right on."

"I thank you, Your Honour," Bogardus said levelly. "By deductible, sir, I only meant that the process is no unattainable feat."

"And did you inform him of one of these methods?"

"Why I did more than that," he said. "I not only told him the methods, all nine—I stepped him through how they were done face to face."

"You effected *all nine* of the methods yourself?"

"We only had time for some four," said Bogardus. "The double exposure, the miniscule plate, the dumpling effect and the compromised nitrate.

The lady in white, you'll understand, required a bit more preparation. And anyway"—a brooding pause—"Child was disinclined to do it."

"The lady in white, did you say?" inquired Gerry. "The one that needs an actor for it?"

"That is the one," Bogardus said.

"A bit more preparation, how?"

"For one," he said, "a willing body. Two bodies, ideally—a foil and a sitter. The sitter, well, to sit of course while the plate is exposed in the back of the box, the foil to interrupt the scene in such a way his form is captured."

"Captured ghostly," Gerry said, at which Bogardus nodded once. "And why do you think Child himself wasn't willing to be the actor in this case?"

"I'd think that he was very tired."

The counsellor smiled. "Tired, sir. From what?"

"From being Mr. Mumler's ghost."

An excitable muttering burned through the courtroom. Townsend said, "Defence object—"

"—you're overruled," Judge Dowling roared and continued to hunch further toward the proceedings.

It was all, as I'd thought, a preposterous joke. Its logic tangled up in me, a strenuous and stiff unraveling, while the actual murder of Child, as we'd lived it, had been so sudden—been so *simple*!

"From being *Mr. Mumler's* ghost. That is what you said," said Gerry. "By which you mean, I take it, sir, that Child and Mumler are in league. That Child *is* Mumler's ghostly lady—or ghostly gentleman, let's say— who in his wretched poverty, and in his lack of natural skill had been so reduced as to prostrate himself upon the needs of this man here?"

"That is," he said, "what I believe. The compositions show as much."

"The compositions of the prints?"

Bogardus nodded. "See to them. Observe the way the figure stands. Unlike the other ghosts, so-called, in Mr. Mumler's other prints, you'll notice that Child's attitude is contrived. He means, in his gory make-up, to be noticed. He means to unsettle while still being seen. Sir David Brewster's Ghost," he said. "Otherwise known as the lady in white. It has been a trick of our trade, Mr. Gerry, for as long as the camera has been there to make it."

"May it please the court to know that the Commonwealth's witness attests to the following: Mr. Mumler did not manufacture Child's presence. Mr. Mumler employed it, to conscious deception."

"As I said," said Bogardus, "that is what I believe."

"And when he could no longer, sir—when Child had degraded himself good and well—then that is when he came to you to master Mr. Mumler's trick?"

"I suppose he had taken his fill," said Bogardus, "of being Mr. Mumler's boy. Sustenance is sustenance, but all of us must have our pride."

"Did he admit that this was so? That he had tired of Mumler's yoke?"

"Mr. Child did not need to admit it," he said. "His disposition was transparent."

"Let the record reflect that the witness, Bogardus, believes the defendant to be in cahoots with Algernon Child, who is under discussion. But back to those devious methods of Mumler's. Of those you and Child recreated together, which one of the four do you think came out best?"

"The double exposure was bully," he said. "I have it with me here, in fact."

"Exhibit the Second," said Counsellor, striding toward Dowling, a picture in hand, whose contents—thank heavens!—I never made out, inferior as they most certainly were. "May it please the court to know that the picture which Mr. Bogardus has shown not only boasts plainly of Algernon Child, who Mr. Mumler claims is dead, but that the state's witness produced it with ease by following one of the nine stated methods."

"Noted duly," said the judge. "Am I to presume that the Commonwealth rests?"

"Mr. Bogardus, one very last question—and here I'll ask you not to laugh. Have you ever had cause to ascribe to yourself or been ascribed by anyone such abilities or influences as tether themselves to those of ghost-seers and mediums, sir?"

"You mean, am I a Spiritualist?"

"I mean do you possess abilities?"

"Artistic abilities, certainly, sir. Would that I possessed those others. That way, I'd be able to say year to year what will show as the greatest advance in my field. As such I am always discoveries behind."

"Defence objects," said Townsend, meekly. "Clearly, the witness is being facetious. And might I go further in saying, My Lord, that *Spiritualism* itself is not—"

"—sustained," said Dowling, gloomily. "Counsellor should limit his questions to cameras. If Mr. Bogardus is not a believer, it can be no concern of ours."

"Of course, My Lord," said Gerry, smiling.

But the damage, of course, had already been done.

Only later did Livermore—curse him and damn him!—enter the courtroom and climb toward the stand. He did it all with perfect poise, with his spine thrown back straight and his moustache aspirant. He seemed to be scanning the ground that he'd gained for trailing looks of admiration and I would be a liar, too, if I told you that mine was not.

The effect of the words he pronounced on the stand I shall recount for you in full. And not to impress their veracity on you, but rather to show you how needling they were, how venomous in retrospect, and I kept having wavering thoughts of the banker before I had known what a blackguard he was—when he'd stood in my Otis Street rooms, sad and wealthy, searching my face with his striking green eyes.

"Mr. Livermore, welcome," said leading man Gerry.

And Livermore took down the front of his jacket.

Said Counsellor Gerry, "You knew the accused?"

"I do," said Livermore.

"All three?"

"I had entered into business with one of them."

"Which?"

He pointed. "That man, sitting there."

"For the record," said Gerry, "the witness means Mumler. William Mumler is the man with whom he entered into business. Mr. Livermore, tell me"—and Gerry walked wide, round the side of our table then back to his own—"for I have wondered why it was, your business being with *this* man, that you paid Mr. Mumler for services rendered then commended his name to the Boston police?"

"Mumler has a way, let's say, of having that effect on people."

"So that is why you gave him up? His methods seemed to you deceptive?"

"Deceptive, absolutely," said Livermore, frowning. "And sir, I am a Spiritualist!"

"You of Webster's Bank," said Gerry, "*believe* in what this Mumler shows?"

"I believe in the foundations of it—that's so. In Swedenborg. In Jackson Davis. In the midair contortions of Sir Henry Gordon."

At this there were a couple of laughs.

"But I only believe in those things I can see. That is a compact I made with myself upon entering into this Spiritualism. Only stay, I told myself, if you have seen the proof yourself. I must admit, I have," he said. "I have seen many wondrous things. Though it takes more than something just simply existing for me to admit it is widely conceivable."

"And how to demonstrate that difference—between what happens and what is."

This last was addressed half to Charles Livermore, and half to the bustling courtroom at large.

"The life of the mind is perception," said Gerry. "The basis of your compact, sir! What *is* this unique, rarified characteristic you did not see in Mumler's work?"

"Mr. Mumler had his habits. He did things while he took your picture. One of them was this," he said, and drew a camera on the air. "He always slid the plate, just so, by way of his left hand enclosed in a glove."

"Is that all?" said the counsellor.

"No, sir. There's his closet. Never let a soul inside."

"And this," said Gerry, "I presume, is where he perfected the pictures he sold you?"

"I could not tell you at my word for I have never been inside."

"That cannot be all," said Gerry. "That *will not* be enough to damn him. What more besides convinced you, sir, that Mr. Mumler was a fraud?"

"There was also the length of the sessions."

"How long?"

"Never less than one full hour."

"Long enough, would you say, to take *how* many prints?"

"A goodly many, I should think. He would seem to be trying on different exposures like suits of stolen clothes," he said. "And not only that, but the frequency of them."

"The frequency?" said Counselor Gerry.

"He would have me return every week," said the banker, "to make sure that he got it right."

"Got what right? Elaborate."

"A spirit picture of my wife."

"Your wife . . ." Gerry glanced at his notes ". . . named Estelle, who died of consumption. Our sympathies, sir."

"She was," said Charlie Livermore, with a grief-stricken flash of those forest green eyes, "a young woman of thirty-five. Lucy Ellen, our daughter, is not here today—fortunate for her, no doubt."

"And why is that?" said Counsellor Gerry.

"She would be in contempt of court."

"I beg your pardon, sir," said Gerry.

"She would never be able to countenance *him*, who has prospered so well from her dead mother's name."

And here he stabbed his chin at me—his sculpted, resilient, strong-principled chin, and all the courtroom gave a groan: three-quarters bereavement, one-quarter disgust.

"And he never did get her, did he?" said the Counsellor.

"Never quite," the banker said. "Though told me he was drawing closer. And that, of course, would draw me back."

"In the hope that one day he *would* get her?" said Gerry.

He paused. "I had no other choice."

"A steep premium of a prospect, I'd think, to endure on the hope of one day seeing *someone*."

"I see that only now," he said. "I am ashamed to say it, sir."

Those emeralds, faintly damp, turned up. Were there tears in a vial that he squirted *into* them?

I had to turn my eyes away while Gerry processed down the court. He muttered to himself en route. And then he said, "*One*. The consistency, sir, with which he used his leftmost hand. *Two*. The distrust that to all but himself he practised in his secret closet. *Three*. The extended lengths of time that saw him standing at the box. *Four*. The repeated appointments, at cost, that he all but insisted you make to his rooms. Why Mr. Livermore," he said, with incredulous glory in his voice, "this might point to signs of suspicion, I grant you, but could it be the sordid truth?"

"On that," said the banker, "I've no reservation."

And here the degenerate thespian smiled. "Thank you, Mr. Livermore. Now let us speak of Mr. Child . . ."

And so the unhallowed proceedings continued—scurrilous lie after scurrilous lie.

They pissed their blame upon my grave. I hadn't a thing to my name. I had time.

The Sadness blew hot and unclean through my sails.

When Townsend rose, a well-fed man with sprawling, ineffable under-eye bruises, I retained little hope of his tactics reversing the process that Gerry had preached into being. He untucked his glasses from over his ears and polished them at too great length.

He started: "Mr. Livermore, you are a Spiritualist, correct?"

"If you mean am I still one since last I confirmed it, I will venture to say that I am," said the banker.

When the laughter that followed had died on the air, the Counsellor continued: "You might've fooled me."

"And why is that?" said Livermore, behind a haughty half-formed smile.

"Because of what you've suffered, sir, at the hands of this man here before you," he said. "Taking you up to the hub of your trust. And yet it appears that you have little trouble renewing the bonds of your faith in this court."

"The Commonwealth objects," said Gerry. "Objects *resplendently*, Your Honour. What bearing the witness' faith can exert on the blamelessness of the accused is beyond me."

"Sustained," said Dowling. "Please rephrase."

"Your Honour, if I may," said Townsend, and started to polish his glasses again. "All that I mean corroborate, sir, is that through all of this you remain a disciple. Even when, notwithstanding the court's knowledge of it, this is far from the first time you have been deceived."

"You must be more specific, Counsellor."

"I will be, sir," and Townsend smiled, good-naturedly, his glasses polished. "Is the name R.S. Lillie familiar to you?"

"R.S., Counsellor?"

"Rachel Southey?"

"I seem to . . . yes . . . recall," he said, "some person or other who went by that name."

"I take it you are being wry. Could you forget her, really, sir?"

Livermore's eyes went concertedly level. "Miss Lillie was a medium whom a number of years in the past I employed."

"About how many years?"

"Some four or five."

"Just after your wife—God protect her—had died?"

"I was in need of consolation."

"Doubtless, sir, you were," said Townsend. "Nor ever would I question that. But this Miss Lillie, sir, was different. Why was that, Mr. Livermore?"

"She had been surveying my daughter and me. She collected a file of misfortune on us. And then," said the banker, unthinking, provoked, with the lather of something consuming upon him, "she extorted, why, hundreds of dollars from us on the basis that she could see into our hearts."

"But she could not see *in*," said Townsend, "is what you are implying, sir."

"No more than *I* can see," he said, "the object of what you are getting at, Counsellor."

"Indeed," said Judge Dowling. "Be forthcoming, Counsellor."

"She could *not* see in," said Townsend, "and yet you are a Spiritualist. You had been extorted, in other words, sir, by the order to which you now pledge your allegiance. If Our Lord Jesus Christ when he entered the temple had overturned half of the money he saw and pocketed what still remained, might all his disciples have followed him out with the same resolution of purpose, I wonder?"

"I reckon that they might, at that. It was not safe for them to stay."

"A clever, considered rejoinder," said Townsend. "For you are clever aren't you, sir? Too clever, at that, to be taken in twice by so venal a species of liar as Mumler. The witness has a prejudice," Townsend announced to the courtroom at large, "to put it very mildly, sirs. A prejudice, on second glance, that has all the marks of entrapment," he said.

"Objection!" said Gerry.

"Sustained," said Judge Dowling. "I'll remind Counsellor Townsend the witness himself has never one moment been under suspicion."

"True enough," said Counsellor Townsend. "Allow me to rephrase." He paused. "That unfortunate business you suffered with Lillie—how did it impress you, sir?"

"Impress?"

"How did it make you feel?"

"As any man might in the wake of such evil. Violated, sir, profoundly."

"And angry?"

"Well naturally, sir," said the banker.

"In extremis," said Townsend, "and in the long term?"

"No longer," said Charles Livermore, "than was needed. That woman, that Lillie, off-white as she was"—and here a breeze of laughter blew—"did not deserve the energy that it would've cost me to show her contempt. She was a fraud. A parasite. A creature well beneath regard,"—and here the breeze of laughter died as the banker began to show red in the face—"and she no more deserved my impassioned disdain than the right to recite my late wife's blessed name."

"And yet," said Counsellor Townsend, mild, "you do seem very angry now."

"The memory of it rankles me."

"And all of us on your behalf. It *is* an unfortunate narrative, sir.

Though I dare say had suchlike befallen my life—and I am glad it hasn't, sir!— I should not only like to attend where it stings, but rectify it, tit for tat."

"I've imagined it hundreds of times," said the banker.

"Why stop with Lillie?" said the Counselor. "Why not against all Spiritualists who have preyed shamelessly on the stricken and weak?"

"You're asking am I a crusader?" he said.

"A crusader," said Townsend, "seems generous, sir."

"Then what am I?" said Livermore.

"I think you are an inside man who courts an agenda of widespread entrapment. I think you are a shattered man who nurses—"

"I object!" said Gerry. "Counsellor Townsend is badgering, honour!"

"Sustained," said Dowling less severely, as though he were rotating something in mind. The banker was a little whey-faced—not so pretty now, was he?

"I'm curious, Counsellor," said the Judge when by and large the hubbub ceased, "of what might be the benefit behind such—as you have explained it—entrapment?"

"*Mr. Livermore*," said Townsend, affixing the banker again in his sights, "explain to us in layman's terms the concept of Roxbury Unity Lenders."

The banker went more curdled still. "It is . . ."

"Your concept, is it not?"

"My concept, yes," said Livermore. "A sort of, well—a public trust."

"Publically advertised?"

"Publically owned."

"Privately advertised, then."

"Within reason."

"And what would you say," Townsend said, "is its function?"

"To furnish Boston's citizens with a future they might not begin to afford."

"*Begin* to afford?"

"An ungraspable future."

"These are not layman's terms," said Townsend.

"An ungraspable future, at last, that can be. I sell mortgages, sir—I *will* sell them—to soldiers when they arrive home from the war," said the banker.

"Beneath the auspices of Webster's?" said Townsend.

"You might say a sideline of Webster's," he said.

"And so being a sideline and selling, well, something apart from the *notion* of mortgages, surely, how is it you finance your venture?" said Townsend. "This Roxbury Unity Lenders of yours?"

"I offer up securities."

"You have others buy in, do you mean?"

"That is right."

"So that Private Jack Johnson, let's say," said the Counsellor, "who purchases a home in Quincy, obtains said home by leave of you and how many other shareholding investors?"

"Only technically, really, by leave of myself, but if you wish to quibble ..."

"No. I am less interested in how many than whom."

"I could never reveal—"

"Oh you needn't," said Townsend. "For I have got their names right here. Or anyway some telling ones."

Gerry rose spitting, "Objection, Your Honour!"

"Of course you object, Counsellor Gerry," said Townsend. "For your name is among the lot."

A deafening hubbub went up in the court, and Dowling brought his gavel down, and as he whacked it—once, twice, thrice—he said: "You may proceed, I'm sure!"

"I thank Your Honour for his grace." Townsend took down his glasses, wiped at them, replaced them. "I said that I had Gerry's name on this list of investors I hold in my hand. Though that is not quite true, I fear. For the name I have here is not Gerry but Griswold—Cornelius Griswold, to be quite specific—who turn and turn about, I've learned, is none other than Gerry's own brother-in-law. Which development might be coincidence, purely, were it not for a bevy of others just like it. Can you guess what they are, Mr. Livermore, sir?"

"I'd rather you delight me, Counsellor."

"Ferdinand Tallmadge, the cousin-by-marriage of one Marshall Tooker who brought in this case. Benjamin Seybert, the nephew," he said, "of one of your witnesses, Asahel Baker. Samuel Browning, the godson, I think, of no one less than P.T. Barnum, who if I'm not mistaken has been instrumental in bringing this poor man before you to heel. And *would* you like me to go on?"

"I've suffered enough of your humbug," he said.

"It appears that His Judgeship alone," said the Counsellor, "is missing some relative's name from this list. The reason? By proxy and secret design, with nothing forthcoming to link them by name, these men have straw-purchased a paying interest in a confidence scheme of titanic proportions. Participate in Mumler's downfall, profit from a civil war!"

Said Livermore, "Don't be absurd, man—"

"Objection—"

"Order! Order! Order! Ord—"

I volunteered nothing, smiled slightly, perhaps.

When I rose from my bench for the day to be coffled and led through the court to my cell in the jail, I got a glimpse of all the faces milling back beyond the rail. A gallery of rogues, all right—a frieze of faces I had known yet that I seemed to know no longer. Mr. Wilson the tailor, the actor J. Jefferson, Mr. Isaac Babbit of Babbit's Brand Metals, "Mutton Chops" Murray, Reverend Spear, LaRoy and Lucretia Sunderland.

At first I felt only a sort of exposure, rawness to the weather of them, but as I watched them watching me, the milling, rapt ranks of my quote-on-quote victims, I started to feel something else, something finer, the manifest pull of their sundry attentions, and I couldn't help it, dear reader, I beamed.

And I thought to myself: *They have come here for me!*

They have come here, my patrons, to judge for themselves.

GUAY IN DELIBERATIONS
October 1861

The night before I took the stand received me peaceful in my cell.

Then Gerry and the Marshall came. I sat very straight at the end of my cot now allowing my eyes over one then the next one. Counsellor Gerry crossed his legs. He took out paper to record.

Bald head flashing says the Marshall: "Comfortable in court today?"

"As prisoners may find theirselves."

"Comfortable in here?"

"Yes, sir."

"Comfortable then all around, relatively?"

I did not feel that I need speak and so I only nodded shortly.

And besides I had already eaten the meat—and the fruit—and the nuts—and the beer they had sent me—and lain on the pillow of goose-down my head in the stale winding down of the windowless day.

"Any word from your man, Mr. Mumler?" says Tooker.

"A couple of whispers," says I, "in the court."

"And he hasn't attempted to see you inside? Conveyed you messages, perhaps?"

I thought upon the one he'd written: *Do not believe the Marshall's lies.*

Says I: "I have not spoke to him since him and I first met yourself."

"So long as you are sure of that. And ready to testify to it, I trust, when morning finds you on the stand?"

"I shall," says I. And then I paused. "Where," says I, "is Mr. Townsend?"

"You still haven't answered my question," says Tooker. "When you come to the courtroom tomorrow," says he, "on what charge of the State's will you hazard to speak?"

"To that which has been laid on me."

"That charge alone?" says Marshall Tooker.

"Unless there is another one."

"Murder, maybe?" says the Marshall. "Murder dealt and murder done."

Abide in the Light of the Positive Mind. Do not believe the Marshall's lies but here I sat in darkness yet and Marshall Tooker spoke the truth. I made to speak but could not do as courses of doomed icy water ran through me and I says in my terror: "The blow—"

"—yes, the blow?" And Gerry raised his brows at me.

In the face of privation, His Seership had told me, *and in the face of mortal terror.* The man's name had been Algernon and I had stove his head clean in. Diakka brought him back betimes to visit me inside my cell, their black wings revealing his mouldy white skin as they birthed his cadaver back into the world.

"I'll not confess I think," says I and Counsellor Gerry says: "That's fitting. It isn't your crime to confess, after all. We *know* it was Mumler who killed Mr. Child."

"You are no killer, Mr. Guay," says the Marshall once more while the Counsellor kept writing. "You do not have the sand for that. *He* is the murderer—Mumler!" says Tooker.

I screwed my face in panic ways and the Marshall broke down into hard haughty laughter and when he could draw breaths again he fixed me with a sober stare.

"I never in all my life," said Tooker, "have witnessed a man with so sporting a chance so eager to condemn himself. No, no," says he. "We don't want *you.* Solely, your cooperation. Either furnish us with evidence of Mr. Child's murder, which we know Mumler had a part in, or testify he is a fraud in the trust of the good Commonwealth that sustains you."

"Immunity," says Gerry softly putting down his busy pen.

The light surprise of hearing him had caused my head-shaking to cease.

"That's *full* immunity," says he and crossed his tailored legs again and though the Marshall looked on sour did not deny the Counsellor's words. "Tomorrow under oath," says he, "or right here in this room, right now, your words may effect a reversal of fate, so choose them carefully, my friend. All that is left to determine"—he smiled—"is whose fate it shall be and how. And so I ask you, Mr. Guay, of what stuff are your interests made?"

MESSAGE DEPARTMENT

Hannah, traveller, floating haze, who sits confined by walls of stone, what beckons you up from your corner of dark? What bears you aloft over where Mumler dreams behind dark sails of falling hair, the tips of which tickle, just so, Mumler's mouth as he mutters in somnolent, flippant despair? And when you orbit William Guay, lying as stiff as a dressmaker's doll, will you shadow him, Hannah, and dry his wet cheeks? And leaving the cell-block, the jailhouse entire, while to cycle the slumbering earth at your ease and to see Fanny Conant in rooms not her own under mandate that no woman born can appease, until you detach from the ledge of her toes and into the evening beyond where she sleeps, like a shorn figurehead sailing over the earth, the wreck of your ecstasies lost to the deeps? See the governess, loping and blue in the face, and the man in the church with the kelp in his hair, and the grande dame ensconced in her yellowing gown, bent composing a letter that no one will read, and the bludgeoned photographer, pressed under glass, and the drowned girl, the darling, unseeming, at sea? Oh how fair is this wasteland that keeps us no more? Oh how boundless this charnel house, choked with our hopes? Until Hannah's eyes in their fortitude close, and the clouds part before her, and downward she soars?

MISS CONANT IN TRANSITION
November 1861

I could go nowhere else but there. So there must be the place I went.

To afford the hotel, I was down to one meal. My prospects, as such, were uncomfortably barren.

People, I think, had been staring at me as I trudged down the street with my passel of bags. Several had offered to help and I'd thanked them. Concerned, they'd watched me walk away.

E.H.B. was kind but short. "You've come to fetch your curtains, Fanny?"

I stood before her in the door of the CDSK, breathing hard from my travels. "I need somewhere to be," I said. "I hope that you will get my meaning. I know that it's not strictly that kind of house but I hope all the same that . . ."

I couldn't out with it.

She looked at me from toe to crown. A strut gave out behind her eyes.

"People talk," she'd said. "I listen. But I didn't believe it was true until now."

"I will not make excuses for the state of me," I said.

"We harbour our sisters when they are in need."

"Thank you for sparing me begging," I said.

I put down my bags and extended my hand.

She left the hand hanging and drew me against her, lightly and for fairly long. At the edge of my vision, nose pressed in her hair, I saw that her horse-teeth, too large for her mouth, were creasing the flesh of her lip into sections.

"Oh, Fanny," she said. Then repeated: "Oh, Fanny. How singular you are to me."

Miss Moss, without asking, donated her room. I reinstated my possessions—shoes and dresses, lamp, toilette. This room before mine and Miss Moss' had been someone's.

Then I remembered: Lucie Beebe's.

The pale little snot, I had stolen her scissors in what now seemed another life. I'd snuck them from her sewing basket so that Susie and I could construct our sheet-masks and these we had worn, then, to Jefferson's party, out upon that gorgeous lawn, and I had cause to wonder now if I had ever put them back.

The money I'd been putting by from Bill Christian's visits and Parker House clients, I hid beneath the faulty plank that the spirits emerged from in roundtable sessions.

Miss Moss waited on me those first couple of days. She'd grown up lovely, dark and tall. She lit my candles, slopped my pans, brought my meals and poured my milks. She stood, demure, before my door. She even called me Madam Conant. I let it go a day or two.

When at last on a morning she came to my room with one of her pitying pitchers of milk, I sat up as spry as I could in my bed and I held my palm outward to hold her at bay. She did a little startled jump. The milk in the pitcher went sloshing about.

"I've been meaning to ask you what's happened to Constance."

"She is no longer on at the Center, Miss Conant."

"You are, it seems, the leading girl."

But then I saw I had been cruel.

"You prefer her to me. I'm aware of that, Ma'am. You find me—have found me—ambitious, perhaps. Constance has gone to New York, Ma'am, to live. With a man, it is rumoured, and there to tell fortunes."

"Oh," I told Miss Moss. "I see."

Something, an image, began to eat at me. I tried to resist it—to keep with Miss Moss.

"It needn't be me," she was saying, "at all. I will find someone else if it pleases you, Ma'am, and you may even keep my room. I will not be a strain on you in the fragile estate that confines you—"

"—Miss Moss. I am not sick unto my death. The thing I am is mine to bear." Her pretty face dropped further then. "Just the same, I should mention: you've been very decent."

She crossed the room and poured me milk.

I said to her: "How cold it is."

But all I could think of was Susie, nineteen, dragged paraffin-pale from the sludge of the Charles.

From that day on, we mostly talked while I slowly rotated around the apartment. Her family were farm people out in Ohio. Her brother had gone to suit up with the Union. Since the wholesale bloodletting at Sharpsburg, she claimed, they had not read a word from him, but no one had come by or mailed them a notice to tell them he was dead for sure.

I told her her family must be very proud.

I told her I was from New York.

What I didn't tell her was about my own father, a miner whose eyes were as dark and as deep as the mountainous caves that he blasted and scoured. Nor either my mother, a mother by trade. Nor the crisscrossing chutes of the mountains of Roundot.

The Center, I said, had been my home—the place where I had cut my teeth. The Center had been everything until at some point it was only four walls.

Yet scarcely had I told her this, the merest of disclosures, really, than I would trammel up with dread to think on why Miss Moss was there. She hadn't just happened to start waiting on me—to give up her rooms and to start bringing milk. The answer must be E.H.B., who had wanted a tutor for her leading girl. She was nurturing me, culturing me. She lay in wait for me. She was trying to ensnare me in a pretty woman's life.

But then Miss Moss would do something to make my turn of mind reverse and I would feel monstrous all over again for letting the filth of my life overtake me. She would look out the window in sly concentration, fixed on the flowers that waved from the trellis. She would ask me a question, consider my answer, study me long, and then look at her hands.

We mostly walked around the block but always while the air was fine.

And when one day I threatened to burst from my skin with no more than strolling and sleeping and eating, I went to call on E.H.B. in her royal apartments on top of the house.

I call them this because they were: spaciously made, with good carpets and rafters. A tapestry of Joan of Arc in ecstasy arrayed the hearth and yet for years without a thought to the wood-smoke's effect on the weave of the image. Joan, impassioned, seemed to smoke.

E.H.B. watched me approach in the light from the glowing bay windows behind her. Stacked to the height of her chest on the blotter was a rampart of books; she was all head and neck.

"You've been well taken care of," she said, "by Miss Moss?"

"You've made impressive work of her."

"But haven't I, Fanny," she said. "As with you."

"If I am to stay here, I'd like to contribute."

E.H.B. smiled at me quietly; shifted.

"Our purpose—our *mission*—unchartered, I know, but no less noble for that fact—has been the formation of women from girls according to the principles of spiritual benevolence. And not just any kind of woman"—E.H.B. held up her hand—"but one who will speak—who will earn for herself. One who will lift up her sex."

By God, if she wanted a thing, let her say it. Her circling of topics worked in me like lye. Perhaps it was the redcoat in her, careful not to charge too fast.

"If I am to stay here rent-free in *her* room, languishing about." I paused. "I may be slower than I was but that does not exclude me working. There is washing, and sewing, arithmetic, surely—"

"—we will not have you *scrubbing*, dear."

At some point she had risen up and returned with a chair, which she set before hers. "My dear, please take a seat," she said.

As I did, I examined the table between us.

The stacks of text were newspapers, the top two bearing Mumler's face. The headlines shrieked his name, his crimes, his narrowing chance of acquittal, his process.

Juggler's Accomplice in Humbug Speaks Out! Photographer Debunked! Soft Spirits!

"I'm sure that you're aware," she said when I declined to speak at first, "that *avenues* exist, Miss Conant."

"Avenues?" I goaded her. I wanted to hear her pronounce it aloud.

"Alternatives," said E.H.B. "For women of your—latitude. Though I think you will find it is handsomely worth it to visit someone with a name on his shingle."

"And do you think that I would not? Penholders, wire, Pennyroyal, all that?"

"It is merely advice," said E.H.B. "You may take or discard it—whichever you like. But hear these words," she said to me and positioned her hands on the papers before her. "If you're to take such avenues and to take them in the fashion that a woman ought take them, then you will not be needing this." She peeled away the two top layers: William

Mumler's face stared back. "Nor this. Nor this." And peeled still more, a succession of William's and Hannah's and Guay's and Livermore's and all the lawyers. "Nor this. Nor this. Nor any, dear. You wish to contribute?" she said. "This is that. Sacrifice *is* contribution. For sometimes in order to better ourselves we must cut off the thing that enables us most."

I stared at her. She stared at me. And I felt, as we faced off, a welcome exhaustion.

"My feet!" I blurted out at her.

She let go the papers, as if she'd been slapped.

"Your feet?" she said.

"They ache," I said. "They've been terribly swollen and achy of late."

"Ah," she said, brows raised. "Of course."

With her shoulders set toward me, she lowered her head and pushed her chair across the floor. And when she raised her head again and lifted my feet in her lap to massage them, I watched her face soften in peaceful contentment beneath the face of Joan of Arc.

At the end of my walk with Miss Moss the next day, I took my leave of her and wandered. I came by and by to the steps of the court where the circus of shame had been carrying on. I didn't go in but sat down on a bench that faced the Suffolk Courthouse doors and I waited on the exit of the session with intensity.

Finally, at three, it came.

The prisoners left not last but first: Mumler, Guay, then Hannah, trailing. Mumler came on with absurd gravity, as though he were the wounded plaintiff. The man looked prouder even now than he'd looked that first day on his way through my parlour. His beard was in the lead of him, He wore his jailhouse wool like tails. And I tried to imagine a birthing room somewhere—in Mumler's darkroom or in Lucie Beebe's parlour—where I would emit something foul and headstrong the colour of the jeweller's beard. It would march from my womb as he marched from the courtroom. It wouldn't know how it was cursed. Yet before I could really conceive of this fully, the unthinkable-ness yet the imminence of it, I had turned my attentions from Mumler to Hannah. And keeping well beneath the shade I studied her with newfound eyes— how she stumbled among the ranks of men with all her dark and eerie hair.

HANNAH ON THE STAND
November 1861

In court there was a circus of them. Standing at the exits, milling. Arising absurdly behind banks of seats or picking their ways past the feet in the aisles.

"How am I to feed my girls without that swamp soprano's rent? With me laid up in bed like this, how's they going to *live*?" said one.

"Where is my Joe? Did he sleep at my bedside? Am I to suppose that the bleeding has ceased? Am I to suppose that my sweet little bud is slumbering in God's green earth?"

"Can a lady be true to herself?" said another. "Can she ever really be? And *if* I am true to myself," it continued, "will he consent to be my friend?"

"Mrs. Mumler, in essence, enlighten the court on how you *show* these ghosts, exactly? Mrs. Mumler?" asked a voice. "Mrs. Mumler, are you there?"

I gathered a breath. "Thank you, sir. I am fine."

"And so I will ask you again," said the Counsellor, "by what method you show these ghosts."

"The dead ones, you mean. They have always been with me. Ever since I was a girl."

"Of what stuff were the spirits made?"

"Why I should think of flesh," said I.

"*Should think?*" said Gerry.

"Rightly, sir."

"So you are saying, Mrs. Mumler, that after a lifetime of watching these ghosts you never once bothered to touch one?" said he. "I frankly find that hard to swallow."

"You may not be able to see them," said I, "but they are very real to me."

"I don't doubt that at all," said Gerry, a bit of wryness at his lips.

"Defence objects," said Counsellor Townsend. "Counsellor Gerry is coercing."

"Overruled, resoundingly. Mrs. Mumler will answer the question," said Dowling.

Grace or not-Grace. Going here and now there. Could not seem to stay in one place past a minute. Galleried court and the counsellor's bench. Counsellor's bench and the stand where I sat. Stand where I sat and Judge Dowling, beside me, she crouched like a gargoyle, her eyes slanted down. Pushed her palm along her face to rub away the mouldy sheen and a coarse spray of droplets released from the skin. They peppered, though no one there felt them, the court.

"I've never touched one—no," said I. "They do not take so well to touch."

"It angers them?" said Counsellor Gerry.

"It is far less a matter of them than of me."

"The ghosts discourage it, somehow?"

"A flame," said I. "A burning match. You can hold one for only so long in your hand. Can suffer the heat for so long before—pain. That is what it's like," said I, "to try to touch dead ones directly."

"Pardon my ignorance, Ma'am," said the Counsellor. "I am novice in these matters. If roundly they discourage touch, then how else might they manifest?"

"I see them," said I.

"Just as you see me now?"

"As you have a flurry of grey in your hair."

"Age with stealing steps, Madam, hath clawed me in his clutch, it's true." And here the Counsellor gentled back the wings of greyness at his ears. "Not so yourself, I see," said he. "Your vision is minutely keen. Which makes me wonder, after all, if you see spirits here—right now?"

Did not answer right away. The question seemed a sort of trap.

"There are a few," said I.

"How many?"

"Their number fluctuates," said I.

"They come and go and go and come with atmospheres that ward off touch, but how are we the Commonwealth to know when they are in *our* midst? For instance, Madam, might we hear them? What do they sound like, these woebegone dead?"

"They sound like you sound now," said I. "They cannot speak unless they question."

"Ha," said Gerry. Stopping. Smiling. "*Ha*," said he and raised a hand. "Appropriate," continued Gerry, "that their grammar is one of disguise and evasion. May it please the tone-deaf court I should like you to tell us what they're saying now."

"Which one?" said I.

"Whichever best. One that we might understand."

"One of them that's here," said I, "seeks news about her husband Joe."

"This Joe has passed on from the fold?" said the Counsellor.

"*She* has had a business done. A most unpleasant, hidden business. But she never lived to the end of the thing and now she wonders how it was. She wonders at her husband Joe. She wishes to tell him she named the boy Eustace."

"She wishes us to help her, then?"

"Beg your pardon, Counsellor Gerry?"

"She wishes us to counsel her?"

"She is," said I, "beyond all that."

"If so to what end does she speak?"

"No other end," said I, "but that. She wishes only to be heard."

Counsellor considered this. Cupping his chin in the palm of his hand. "I think I start to get your meaning. The dead are anything but shy. Yet still we remain in the dark, Mrs. Mumler, how was it you *revealed* these souls?"

So I told him of the shadow, and the spitting on the glass, and the sometimes unintended sneeze, and the way I would grow very weak in the knees by the end of the long morning cycles of clients.

"To realize the dead, let alone to translate them," said Counsellor Gerry when I had concluded, "are talents that we have not seen to such an extent as your own, Mrs. Mumler. Spiritualism," said the Counsellor, "whatever its basis in verified fact, has grown as widespread in our age as the despotic death that it seeks to combat. But spirit photography, *really*," said Gerry and turned to face the jury box. "Gentlemen, ladies, the camera transcribes. It renders the truth of our world with dispassion, and yet without the fey intrusion native to an artist's hand. Mrs. Mumler proclaims that her very own shadow reflects the light that makes the ghost but need I remind you that light, seeking light, does light of light beguile."

He laughed. Like a madman he laughed and continued to rave.

And yet my attentions were being drawn from him. His voice growing thin and then leaking away.

"Aren't the backs of my hands just an unrivaled horror? Assure me my lips aren't as ghastly?" said she. "Oh who will deign to kiss a girl with lips as ghastly blue as these?"

Crouched there in her bathing costume just below the lofty stand. Pale and small-seeming. A supplicant swimmer.

"Can't you feel it pressing down? Won't you help a girl to breathe? Would you be a dear," said she, "and see my Godey's book stays dry?"

"Mrs. Mumler is not the only one," Counsellor Gerry was saying "to tell us of ghosts. Not a one of the laudable women and men who have come here today in support of this Juggler can be blamed for the sorrow—the grave wishfulness—the hairline cracks in common sense—that have led them each one to surrender twelve dollars, sometimes on repeat occasions. Ben Jonson saw Catholics and Tartars and Turks in a horrible row about his chair. Byron saw phantoms, Cellini the Virgin. Goethe summoned ghostly flowers. Supernatural revelations? Derangement of the nervous system? Enlighten us, Mrs. Mumler," said Counsellor Gerry, focusing again on me, "what symptoms, if any, most often attend these boisterous parlays with the dead?"

He meant the way that I felt now. So I told him my symptoms and then said: "Fatigue. That is what I feel most often."

"And this painful congestion that leads to fatigue whenever the ghosts are nearby," said the Counsellor, "have you always encountered it thus, Mrs. Mumler? Or are such sensations a recent occurrence?"

"Always." I nodded. "As my mother felt them. And her as her mother before her," said I.

Mother's face amidst the court. Twenty years from today when it might show: one wrinkle. Stillness of her watching me. Pale and unanchored to form in the dim.

"And her as her mother before her," said Gerry. "You heard her speak those words yourself. Inherited powers, she calls them, this woman, encountered by way of the feminine gene. Yet it strikes me as no small coincidence, Ma'am—and may it please the court to hear—that what you maintain to be super-cognition is as easily traced to a sort of pathology."

"I don't quite under—"

"—sickness, Madam. An inherited ailment, progressive in nature, that more and more subtly fractures the mind."

"I cannot speak to that," said I.

"Nor ever can the mad," said Gerry. And then he turned back to the courtroom at large. "And so rather than telling you time and again that Mrs. Mumler is insane I will presently seek to show the court and Mrs.

Mumler in her turn how I believe she fits, as such, in William Mumler's enterprise."

Whispers were mounting. The Counsellor's boldness. He was polished again. He fairly gleamed. The dead were shooting up like reeds or crossing braced like darning needles, or making a pass of the court, spitting questions, until they passed from sight again, while Grace in her decrepitude was passing down the eastern wall. How she hummed to herself, absent-minded and sad. One side of her body pressed up to the oak.

"Identify," said Counsellor Gerry, "the photograph I'm holding here."

"If the Counsellor came just a bit closer," said I.

He strode toward the stand. With the picture held high. The first one we'd taken together. With Grace. Her palm held out. Her hair in rags. While I am tipping from the frame.

"My first ever picture with Willy," said I. "Taken two years ago now, Counsellor Gerry."

"And who are the persons," said he, "it depicts?"

"Her name," said I. "Her name is . . ."

"Yes?"

But could I say it. Really: Grace. With Grace so near. So dead and sad. So little and wet with the mould on her cheeks.

"Her name is Grace Fanshawe," said I.

"*Really?*" said Gerry. He stalled for a moment. As though I'd caught him quite off guard. Then, nodding his head, he returned to his bench, where he rifled a while among his papers. He made some selections. Approached me again. "That name is familiar to me, Mrs. Mumler, as it is familiar to you, I am sure. Would you like to know what we uncovered about it?"

Vigorously, he consulted his notes.

"Daughter of Lilla and Joseph Fanshawe. Born in Providence, June, 1841. Lived there for seventeen years with her parents a rung above the merchant class until, in 1858, they moved to Block Island where you, Ma'am, are from. There they planned to start an inn for travellers along the coast from what they had put by in previous ventures. Retire there, I reckon. An untroubled life, as all of us may hope to have, and that is when Grace met *you* there," said the Counsellor. "The two of you became fast friends.

"After you and your mother were run out of town for a murky, unspecified reason," said Gerry, "Grace Fanshawe was shipped to a girl's school, Mrs. Prury's, to finish out her comprehensives. There she wrote letters—addressed to you, Ma'am. The majority of them I have with me here. Very few of these letters, however," said he, "ever reached Mrs. Mumler or anyone like her. And yet you claim"—he turned to me—"that *this* is Grace Fanshawe, right here?"

Brandished the picture and waved it above him.

Meant to say, "Yes," but the words slipped away.

"See this letterhead," said Gerry. Unfolding a sheet as he came toward the stand. "Tuesday November the 3rd 1860. Mrs. Mumler professes to manifest ghosts that speak their bloody woes aloud and yet it seems that Grace Fanshawe is a most literary phantasm indeed. For if Grace wrote these letters I hold in my hand then Grace Fanshawe is still alive!"

"I never saw those letters there. The one was all I ever got. Why I even remember the date of it, Counsellor: April the 16th, 1859."

But Counsellor Gerry raised his hand. "It cannot matter *now*," said he. "For the girl in the picture you took isn't her."

Waves of whispers swept the court.

"If it isn't her then who is it?" said I.

"Well who did Mumler say it was?"

"His cousin," said I. "Name of Cora Christine. Willy Mumler is honest but he is mistaken. I never had the heart, you see, to tell him that it *wasn't* her."

"This person here?" said Counsellor Gerry, extracting a new photograph from his pocket. Held it up next to the first, side by side.

A cameo portrait contained by a frame not unlike the one of my ageless grandmother. But this was a girl, maybe ten or eleven. A family photo, her mother beside her, a Christmas scene behind them both. The mother's colouring like Willy's: auburn, soft and very fair. The girl's hand pushes at the viewer. Not wearing a bathing costume but a dress. She is pushing her palm at the viewer while smirking. She is not yet a woman but hardly a girl.

"Are you saying," said I, "that the picture's not real?"

"Both pictures are real in a sense," said the Counsellor. "The first one of you and the second of Cora. But graft them together as Mumler has done—as Barnum has done with a fish and a chimp!—and what you get is real as pinchbeck. Photographic sophistry. Like all of Mumler's clientele, you saw what you wanted to see, Mrs. Mumler!

"But true duplicity," said Gerry, "is always more than just itself. It must have strategy to work. Which explains why this man needed someone—a woman—for women *are* best in this Spiritist business—to accomplish not only the external work of convincing his clients their portraits were real but also that other, insidious kind of being convinced of her powers herself! And being *so* convinced of them"—and here the Counsellor paused to mark me—"that she would be willing to testify to them even in a court of law. But she is not the villain here! For Mrs. Mumler never faked. This Mumler—this Juggler—this duke of deceit—and yet nothing more than a confidence artist—has basely, egregiously taken for ransom a woman unable to care for herself. And not only her but her suffering mother, both of them decent and both of them ill. Isn't that right, Mrs. Mumler? So, say it."

"No," I told him. "You are wrong."

"Why keep up this ruse any longer?" said Gerry. "My dear, you are in need of help. Let the next words you say in the lap of this court be the first in a series toward your liberation!"

But only then. In Grace's face. Here was a doubt like a vise, tightening on my throat.

GUAY UNMADE
AND MADE
November 1861

The Positive Mind protect her soul she had not had an easy time and I began to see at last that I wasn't as crucial as I had imagined. On the first Hand of Fate there was serving His Seership and then on the second to serve William Mumler and yet on the third serve the Marshall and Gerry in a way that embattled the first pair of hands.

But these eight hands were preferable when in former times I had served just Diakka

About my head the buffeting and always blackly of their wings.

In these conditions I abided, thinking waiting in my cell. I'd told the lawmen on my faith that Mumler was the murderer and told them too in what queer place and how deep down Child's corpse was laid. But my time on the stand could no more put off.

When Counsellor Gerry questioned me it had been as he said a "formality only."

—*Deception not that I had seen.*

—*The Spirits were as real as any.*

—*The man himself oh most integral kind and even brotherly.*

Piety was sacrifice and sometimes yes of lesser lives. The Mumlers *were* my sacrifice as Child had been one in his turn to the Mumlers.

For everything was necessary. Everything was perfect too. The universe reflects I knew and in that reflection was all that it held.

During that day's adjournment they paid me a visit, setting stools before the bars. The Marshall had not been in court though here he turned up red and chafed as though he had been in a strenuous hurry. Gerry wore spectacles over his whiskers so bright I could not see his eyes.

"He's a fiendishly clever one, no?" says the Marshall. "More clever, surely, than he looks."

Says I: "Is there something wrong?"

"Oh plenty!" says Tooker "And yet you seem to have no clue."

"Did you go where I told you?"

"Indeed sir," says he.

"To the Negro churchyard at the base of the hill?"

"It goes by some exacter name?"

I could not see to answer that. I says to the Marshall: "Well what did you find there?"

"A mute set there to guard the gates."

I swallowed stones I could not breath. "But what did you find in the grave, Marshall Tooker?"

Marshall Tooker took the time to build and light a cigarette and when he had it smouldering he glanced at the Counsellor and says: "Not a thing."

"The plot was empty," says the Counsellor tipping down his spectacles.

"But that cannot be true," says I. "I saw him buried there myself."

"You saw him buried," says the Marshall. "Someone saw him out again."

"You have perjured yourself, Mr. Guay," says the Counsellor.

"For all I knew he was right there. For all I knew, my lords, believe me. If he were moved, I don't—"

"—please, sir. Preserve what honour you have left. Mr. Gerry and I have conversed," says the Marshall, "and here is what we've come to think. You are a saboteur, of course—possessed of a certain rudimentary cunning that we were too proud to detect at first glance but now we have you in our sights we'll not soon forget it, of that, I assure you. Which brings us to your strategy."

"Your aim in all of this," says Gerry.

"To destroy, on the one hand, the state's case for murder by having the body removed from the plot, while planning, on the other hand, a straw indictment of your friend. You would see William Mumler fall, but you would play no part in it. You would let Hannah, mad, do that. As Hannah, mad, has surely done. You'll notice Counsellor's time with you was not exactly probing, was it? Nor were your answers quite up to the promise you made in exchange for immunity, sir."

"We might've delayed your testimony until after we'd dug up the plot," says the Counsellor. "Yet alack and alas, we could no longer do. And so we have ourselves to blame."

"But you are far too clement, Counsellor. *We* are agents of the law. Mr. Guay of Poughkeepsie," the Marshall begins in the voice of a stuttering ignoramus, "is all but the commonest c-c-criminal, Counsellor, lest we fail to recognize. Add to that: a common coward. But wouldn't you guess it, Mr. Guay, we too have our insurance policies."

"Plenty of them, Mr. Guay." And here the gaslight down the block twinned hell in Counsellor Gerry's lenses.

"See if this one fits," says Tooker. "The trial will go on unabated. If murder cannot be the charge, let fraud and larceny stick deep."

"Let fear of *us* stick deep," says Gerry.

"But not of us alone," says Tooker. "Let the fear of this Juggler stick deepest of all."

"Mumler?" says I.

"Juggler, sir. For that is what this Mumler does. He has juggled alliances, enemies, all, in arcs too high and wide to gather and they have fallen round his feet in patterns most desperate indeed," says the Marshall.

"But I have not betrayed him, sirs!" says I to these men of the law rising up and Tooker and Gerry they backed from the bars as though they were afeared of me.

And Marshall Tooker says to me: "Remember where it is you are."

"But I have not betrayed him, sirs!"

And Tooker says: "Successfully. Which does not mean you haven't tried. But how should Mr. Juggler know, attempting to stand beneath so many baubles?"

"We *will* make sure he knows, is how. You can depend on that," says Gerry.

"Once a jeweller, always one."

"Once a killer," says the Counsellor.

"You can always depend on a jeweller," says Tooker, "to make right his assets before closing shop."

Tooker stood there at the bars his baldness and his knuckles bright. His eyes were on me hard as slate his skull vibrating in its casement but then when he saw me. I mean really saw me: sprawling tearful on the floor his eyes lost their sheen for the wretchedness of me.

And then he slowly backed away.

That night I did not sleep a murmur lying wide-eyed in my cell as the branching and winding of all I had heard brought me skinning my bones on the selfsame terrain.

And yet after a certain point I did not think of anything but the small Quaker girl with the Light in her eyes who had brought me the bread when I came to Esopus. She had bounded right up to the place where I sat. She had not been afeared of me. She'd given me the cornbread hot in its straw-woven basket and under its cloth and she had raced away from me and waved to me along her way and I had ate it pinch by pinch while sprinkling the powder from one of my vials.

I was not nor had been anything in my life. That little Quaker girl was all.

When finally they came for me to bring me to the court of law my eyes were so starved of the morning's last dark that they refused to open fully. But my vision cleared some at the door to the jail where there were figures standing, waiting.

It was the Mumlers, flanked by guards.

The figure of Mumler was bristly and big while the figure of Hannah was tattered and thin and pressing in around their bones a pulsing robe each one of Light. While out beyond the metal doors that led to the courtyard that led to the court there stretched a sort of Maw of Light that swallowed everything save them.

Mumler's figure nodded once. And then I could see him distinct at my side.

"Good Morning, Mr. Guay," says he. "A little sleepy are we, then?"

He smiled and then he clapped my shoulder. "Today, perhaps, shall be *our* day."

I looked at him and looked at him for any trace of what he knew and when I saw that he did not I nodded at him lovingly. And then I tells him: "After you." And William Mumler smiled again as if to say: *I am obliged.* As if to say all is forgiven good sir whatever it is that you think you have done for it could not be helped one bit. And Mumler and Hannah they both took a step and then the Maw of Light unhinged and just as my arm raised to block out the glare it took them ranks of guards and all.

"You're waiting on me to remind you how to? One foot goes in front of the next," says the guard.

So I squinted my eyes and I followed them forth until the brilliance claimed me too.

MISS CONANT IN TALKS
November 1861

Dimmer, darker, by the key, the gates of Suffolk fell away. Pawing hand by matron's hand, my belongings were rifled through, charged and accounted. Mainly, I carried the creature inside me which I hadn't done much to conceal by design. That and a galley of the Banner, which I held folded in my hand.

They patted my ankles for chisels and pins. They ruffled the place where my thighs met my groin. They left the comb that held my hair; it was whalebone and bright, a luck-charm from Miss Moss.

I liked the way it hugged my scalp and made my shoulders prone to lift.

Inescapably, one of them stopped at my stomach. "Oh," she said lightly. Her key ring went swinging. She started again beneath my arms then gave her inspection a cursory finish.

"Couldn't keep them legs closed, could she? Slattern walking!" called a voice.

Then: "Miss! Oh, Miss! A handsome comb! A lady needs a patron, Miss!"

My wooden heels went marching off. The deeper darkness smelled of piss. A lantern of misery swayed in dim arcs across the slick, ill-sequenced stone.

Hannah Mumler's prison cell was the very last one in the block, on the left.

She sat there with her knees drawn up, her pallet pushed against the wall. Her pale arms encircled her knees for protection, the right hand encircling the wrist of the left. Her hair was curtains fallen to; it revealed just the tip of her straight, skinny nose. Were it not for the faintest gestation of breath along the ridgeline of her shoulders, she might've been a carven woman—pale like paraffin or soap.

I'd long since glimpsed the morning's headline: *Perfect Battery Imperfect.*

A chair knocked behind me, as though out of nowhere. I sat in it, lifting and smoothing my skirts. Some stealth juggernaut of a matron had brought it. I watched her backside roll away.

"Miss Conant?" she said.

She'd been looking right at me.

"I was sorry. . ." I swallowed my words, ill at ease. "I was sorry to hear of your troubles," I told her. "Yesterday can't have been easy for you."

She paused before speaking. "Some say I deserved it."

"Did William Mumler say that, then?"

"Willy would never say that," she told me. "Willy puts great trust in me."

"And you in him?"

Her posture loosened. "Willy dotes on me," she said. "I believe he would be here right now if he could be. But the gentleman's wing, it is so far away. I am here alone, Miss Conant."

"Not all alone?" I said.

"Yes, Ma'am."

"There are no spirits here with you?"

"I'd rather not to speak of that."

"Would rather not or cannot, Hannah?"

"Would rather not," she said, "Miss Conant. I shouldn't talk of spirits, now."

"Why not?" I said.

"They said I shouldn't."

"The spirits said?"

"The Counsellors, Ma'am. The Counsellors have said I am past them, such things. They say that I have dreamed them up."

"But you did not do that, did you? The spirits exist, don't they, Hannah?" I said.

She looked at me a touch too long. Her eyes were dim sparks in the cave of her hair. But a glimmer had showed in them—*was* them, a moment, when I had told her I believed.

"You'd pretend to be somebody else for their sake?"

"Not for them," said the girl. And her head tilted up, and her hair fell away to the side of her face, and the look there beneath it was calm, beatific. It was, I thought, a look of faith. "It's for him," she continued. "For Willy's sake, Ma'am. They say that I will ruin him."

"And what of you?" I said too loud and Hannah went flinching back into the shadows. "One should always be careful to speak for one's self," I said to Hannah Mumler, softer. "Otherwise one might end up with a far different life than one ever imagined."

"Why have you come here to see me, Miss Conant?"

"I have come here to give a proposal," I said. "But first I feel it best to say . . . Which pertains after all to the reason I've come . . . I feel it best to tell you, now, that I come bearing William's child."

So there I had said it and now it was said.

And I thought: *it is something that is—in this world.*

She studied me slowly, serenely. Those eyes.

"Oh," she said. "I didn't know."

I watched her watching me: "Well, then."

"*I* tried," she said, "but we could not."

She spoke those words without a hitch—there could be nothing strange about them—and I thought to myself: *Am I still human, then? When a person turns into a monster, what happens?*

Yet I said: "I am sorry to hear that, of course. And furthermore, Hannah, I *will* understand if you hate me and wish me . . ." I quavered my voice. ". . . if you hate me and wish me to go, right away. For William Mumler is your husband. *That* is cause enough," I said.

She didn't nod or shake her head. "Does Willy know?" said Hannah Mumler.

"Locked up in here these many weeks I don't believe he could," I said. "But of course if you wish me to tell him, I will. . . ."

A burden seemed to weigh on her. "Right now," she said, "it seems unfair. I think we'd better not to tell him. He's had trouble enough simply clearing his name."

"He isn't a bad man is he, Hannah?" The girl shook her face—a convulsion of hair. "He is merely a man in bad circumstance."

"They have trapped him," she said. "They have made him to kneel."

"And *you* are caught between them, aren't you? You are in a quandary. *You.*"

"They're keen to correct me for helping him, Ma'am. They're keen," she said, "to teach us both."

"You want to be helpful?" I said.

"Yes, Miss Conant."

"Then what if I told you there must be a choice."

"Between Willy and me?"

"Between him and this child."

"Your and Willy's child."

"*This* child."

"I'm not sure that I understand."

I took a breath of competence which seemed to garner her attention I said: "His chances are not strong. Neither of yours are—together. One needn't look farther than headlines to see it: the Commonwealth will bury you. Most certainly William Mumler, they say. And Guay will be collateral. It's you alone who stands a chance. You alone *alone*," I said.

Huddled there, she squirmed a bit. "You really think I have a chance?"

"Right now is your chance if you have one," I said. "They think you are insane, don't they? They think you've made the spirits up? But you are not insane. You're not. Those barristers have skewed your mind. They mean to make you doubt yourself. So simply let them think you *are*. Play into their hands," I said. "And win your freedom just that way."

"But why would I do *that*?" she said, as if it were the strangest thing.

"So you can tell this child," I said, "that baseness is not in its blood."

At once, Hannah let go her legs and stood up. She made a circuit of her cell. She absently, forcefully rubbed at her stomach. She seemed to say a couple of things to parties whom I could not see while tracking matter with her eyes that seemed to move from place to place.

"But first we must make sure," I said.

"Make sure?" she said and paced again.

"Make sure that William and not you is martyred by the Commonwealth."

I felt the monster in me stir, the woman part of me was gone and I thought to myself: *it is no more than this. It is no more than what I will presently say.*

I looked directly in her eyes. I told the medium my plan.

Miss Moss would be the centrepiece. Had Hannah ever seen her hair, how fine and dark it hung from her? And then I folded out the galley, the first one that Mumler had taken of Cora. Did Cora not bear a strong resemblance to dark-haired, pale-skinned, lean Miss Moss?

It would transpire like this, I said.

We'd coach Miss Moss to be that girl (the "cousin" that Mumler was sure he had captured): David Brewster's Ghost revealed. We'd place her on the witness stand, and see him put away for fraud. Meanwhile

Hannah would persist in playing the crazed innocent from Rhode Island by professing to have not the slightest idea that Mumler augmented her gifts on the side.

She must stand by these gifts, of course. For were they not *her* granted gifts?

And so in the course of the scheme I proposed she would never, herself, be compelled into lying.

It was risky, I told her, but more so contentment—riskier to just sit here. And as she kept pacing she seemed to go firmer—seriouser, anyway. She had even stopped rubbing her stomach. She stood there.

"If I may speak immodestly . . ." said Hannah Mumler, eyeing me. "What are your plans, Ma'am, to do with the child?"

I thought to lie to her again as I'd been doing this whole time, but then I said: "I cannot think that I would be much of a mother at all."

"Will I play a role in its life?" she asked plainly.

The monster in me said: "Of course."

"Thank you! Oh thank you, Miss Conant!" she cried. "Oh praise the spirits, oh! Praise God."

Yet the plan we'd agreed on was never to be when the case was thrown out at defence's first witness. Despite his seeming prejudice, Judge Dowling was the one who'd done it. Counsellor Gerry's case for fraud was nothing if not well-constructed, but it fell in the path of the ultimate fact that Child was nowhere to be found. It was the case's fatal flaw and one that Judge Dowling had long overlooked. Now, he announced, he must tighten his belt.

And then he went about the task of acquitting the lot of them, one by one.

MUMLER ON THE PROMENADE

How joyous is the promenade, in every nation on this earth, a venue for strolling and taking the air whose plenitude all men do breathe. The Brit and the Dutchman, the Norse and the Frenchman, the Guinea-Coaster and the Swede goes each at his appointed hour along bright esplanades that give way to the sea, across moors in the mist and on greenways through parks. The American gentleman is no different. He too treads with vigour the promenade's windings with colleagues and relatives, lovers and friends and he goes with his hat on, his cane striking earth, his footsteps as evenly paced as a waltz. He meets the stares that rub him raw. He greets the rumours said about him, sober, with an even mouth. He skirts the wallow of despair. And in many a mind he walks taller, this man, American in every sense.

MUMLER AT LARGE
November 1861

That His Beetleship's gavel drove thundering spikes through Gerry's sour nut of a brain, I am certain. Some among the court dropped eyes or stood up halfway in their seats. Others of them raised their arms and whispered to the person near them. And all at once my chains were dropped like the chains of the slaves being freed round the country, and as my shattered coffles rang upon the marble floors of justice, I went on toward the busy street—Suffolk Street, as was the case—while Hannah and Claudette regrouped and Guay perused the crowd for no one.

I burst through a column of newspapermen, my arms like axe heads at my sides, and I made for the regions beyond the grand steps, determined to savour my triumph in private.

As for the men who had sought to destroy me by confidence schemes of their own, what about them? They were slaves to the dollar, bloodhounds for the dream, whereas I was no less than an artist who earned! It had been a heady thing to watch them drubbed in open court.

I should've felt happy or merely at ease and yet I was conscious of something not there.

Hacks were still moving outside in the street, and people passing by with purpose, and superintendents of the law were conveying now here and now there with their charges, and a horse, yoked to cartloads of what I assumed were beams for a construction project, beshitting the pavement with prodigious ardour, letting off a little steam.

At the discharge and crumbling apart of that shit, my heart surrendered altitude and the fact that the world *hadn't* changed in my absence felt more deflating by the instant. And as I stepped over the shit, headed home, past faces that fleetingly recognized mine and faces to whom I was no one, I started to view the ordeal of my trial and my public besmirching with sharp irritation. It was, for a moment, the one thing I felt. And this irritated me, too.

I grew tetchy. The day was starting to go cold.

I did not slow my pace for Hannah. Hannah Mumler would catch up. She shadowed the progress I made even now with her mother-retainer, her hair in her face.

I hurried on toward Otis Street for where else, reader, would I be?

I was in the main anxious to recommence business. The box had been too long without me. And imagine the backlog of long-standing orders that had gathered these last couple of months in my absence; I almost expected, I freely admit, to be met with a wild, distraught queue of petitioners—a funeral train's worth of calcified souls that I would endure with a wave of my hand.

But what I saw instead was Bill. He stood in the studio's window a moment, his face like the face of some Guinea-Coast-God.

A regular butler in teakwood was Bill. He must be on a homecoming! He had swept the crawlspaces, and batted the curtains, and refilled the oil-lamps, and scoured out the sinks, and plumped the couch cushions, and waxed down the mantle, and polished the windows to better the light in these vacated rooms where I'd taken my pictures. And where I would take pictures still.

He said at the door: "Mist' Mumler, you're back."

I thought: here is a different Bill than the one I'd entrusted to safeguard my office and, different chiefly, because of the fact that Bill and I now shared a history between us. We had both of us been bound by chains and both of us in good faith freed. It made us equals, at the last.

It made us, truly, timely, friends.

"I am returned," I said to Bill. "And in no little part thanks to you, I should say."

I reached out for Bill Christian's hand, but Bill shook his head—without malice or spite.

"There you stand sure enough, Mist' Mumler," he said. "But you no longer welcome here."

"Not welcome," I said on the verge of a laugh.

But what I saw beyond the door behind Bill Christian stayed my tongue.

The scuffed velvet couch, and the old easy chair, and the whitewood dinner table with the ring of rattan seats that had formerly been in Bill's rooms, now in mine. All of this and plenty more formed a sort of blockade before all that I owned, each piece leaning into or bracing the next. The grandfather clock given me by LaRoy to honour our third fruitful sitting together now leaned in a corner wedged in by a table. Resting in the crevice that the edge of it made with the hip of the grandfather clock, shades from lamps—dunce-cap of them teetering above the whole confused morass.

"Not welcome. So I see," I said. "Well aren't you going to tell me why?"

"Nothing personal now, Mist' Mumler," said Bill. "It's just that these rooms here are mine and not yours. They're paid in full, a week today."

"You cannot own this house," I said, "for I have never sold it, Bill."

"You never owned it, Mist' Mumler. It gone into 'rears the first month you in jail."

"In arrears, you mean, Bill?"

"If it please you," said Bill.

"You paid for the house with *what* money?!" I said.

"You ain't the only man," said Bill, "can turn a nickel in its traces."

"You did it with pictures," I said. I was laughing. But Bill's features were deathly still. "With ghost pictures! You thieving wretch. You stubborn, black son of the devil's own nig—"

"—all right," said Bill Christian. "Okay, Mist' Mumler."

"You stole my life."

"I had my eye. Claudette has helped me some, of course. You needn't to take it that hard, Mist Willy."

And here he was—old Bill, my Bill! But then in a flash he was gone.

"Damn you, Bill."

A shape drifted into the door behind Bill: the ancient undertaker father. He was a feeb in loose tan slacks with an overgrown iceberg of black and grey hair, and he dithered obscurely just right of his son, peering at me from the shade of his hair.

But I would not barge in past the man. No, I would not provoke a scene!

I was a gentleman, and white, and one to wit of some repute, and I would not be taken in by any substandard—and then I pushed past him.

He did not really block my way.

Maybe only to take back a few of my things—say, a couple of lampshades, the scuffed logbook stand. It was all of it mine, after all, was it not? From the stains on the flock, to the cobwebs in corners, to that old Negro woman right there in that chair whom I hadn't been able to see from the door and who tilted her face up at me as I passed with a mild-mannered look of inquiry. Then smiled.

She tented the book she was reading to mark me.

We remained there observing each other a while, like acquaintances summoning probable names. "Why, you must be the photographer man. I heard a goodly bit on you. You the luckiest man that I reckon's alive, the mess you got out of today," said the woman.

She was, of course, Bill Christian's mother.

But that was all I heard her say. For Bill had sauntered up behind and quietly restrained my arms. I let myself be led back out.

It had all of it, terrible, happened so fast!

Bill's mother accosted by slave-monger jackals and tossed into a grave indeed. For now, I slowly realized, I did not know a thing about him.

The Sadness, profound and accumulate, took me.

Bill's mother and father appeared behind Bill. And yet they were not watching me.

They were watching my wife and her mother, behind me, having followed at length from the courthouse to here. Hannah still sported the rank, off-white apron they'd given her to wear in jail and she stood there submissive, her hair in her face. Claudette and Bill exchanged a nod.

"You need me to hail you a cab, Mist' Mumler?"

"No," I said. "I don't think so."

Bill stood for a moment then seemed to recede into memories fonder by far than the present. "You were me, Mist' Mumler . . ." he started in saying. "Well, anyway. I think you'll do."

MISS CONANT DECIDED
November 1861

She was, I'd heard, a youngish woman.

A spirit medium, like me. She'd been unmarried all her life, not that she discouraged asking. She was pretty, they say, even beautiful, sometimes, when the lamps of the séance were burning quite right. Her showings were reputed to be "physical" in nature. Which meant that, according to hearsay, she *showed* as the strife of the spirits afflicted her flesh. She would, for instance, start to cough and a spirit miasma would slip from her mouth. Another time she'd offered up, in between pointer finger and thumb, shards of light.

When one day she showed in a whole other way: a flexible mound at the centre of her. She manifested all the symptoms. Her stomach was ripe in the morning—most mornings. Her breasts were painful to the touch. She hadn't yet been with a man to her knowledge, which was of course what they asked first and when they had reckoned with all that she told them she continued to service her roll call of clients. When finally her time arrived they took her to the birthing room and she gave vent to something not dead or alive: a slithering of ectoplasm. When she returned to her previous form, she claimed to have mothered the spirits themselves.

She titled her ability what would come to be known as the New Motive Power.

And so if someone saw me now as I carried myself to the city's north side, this story—E.H.B. and myself had agreed—would be the story that I told.

Perforant objects resulted in bleeding. Steam from a bucket would cook you inside. The pills that they gave you would tangle your guts when just as well you'd had the poke. The best you could do was curl up on a bed and, if you were lucky, decide not to die.

The woman's name was Mrs. Luft. She had a worthwhile reputation in such matters, as they went. Her name and her address—in Boston's North End—were given to me by Miss Moss.

Mrs. Luft worked as a seamstress by day.

The North End was warrens, ill-favoured of lamplight. Chimney smoke boiled from the tops of gaunt houses, windows weak with bedtime prayer. A man-shape approached me, his silhouette awkward until I could peg him for missing an arm. While in among the crevices that marked the beginnings of new, twisted alleys, there were parchment-and-tin dioramas of saints.

They glittered in darkness like broke-open ore.

St. Stephen's Church, with its new clock and cross, announced a final branching on the map I carried with me. I stopped there a moment. I knew not for what but that lamplight illumined the church's pilasters. And in fact, as I stood there, some six trembling Catholics either mounted the steps or came out through the doors.

My words, as I said them, were matter-of-fact. It was something, I think, about not dying yet. It was not a prayer but a conscious desire.

Someone bucked out of the doors and came toward me, something hunched beneath his arm. I might've mistaken him, say, for a beggar—many in these varied parts—or an overgrown child with a long, jagged head, but I looked closer still.

It was William Guay.

He had a clutch of bags about him. He loomed and went loping away through the lamplight.

The clock had yet to chime my time. I had gotten there early, of course, due to nerves.

And wondering what spurred him on, especially now, with the favourable verdict, I tucked the map into my dress and rounded the corner some distance behind him.

He kept straight for a time down the more major streets. He did not seem to know these regions. He had a natural furtiveness, as anxious and black as the rats underfoot.

By and by, he reached the place. I bided down the block behind him. It was a typical block in that part of the city, dark and swaybacked in its paving. The place that he had come to was a boarding house or warehouse, its higher stories all alight. He hoisted the bags that he carried and knocked.

A beat, and he was let inside.

I abandoned my post at the corner and crept. A window showed along the side. I stood at the top of the long, deranged square that the lights from inside had arrayed on the sidewalk.

The room was incredibly bright, too bright: it had the sick sheen of magnesium burning. Guay entered the room and went through it, back to me. He set his bags upon a table—a dining room table worn to shreds, as though they had salvaged it, brought it here, cleaned it. Behind the table, facing me, I saw the jeweller clad in sleeves. He looked at Guay—a vexed, red look—and commanded him something and Guay reeled away.

Now I heard the clock at ten.

The verdict had been innocent, which at first I determined had given me options, but here was I and there was he and I was not prepared for that. I had been on the verge all this time of returning, of turning around toward the CDSK but when I saw him there, enthroned:

There was something about, well, the attitude of him. The way he looked upon the scene. It was a sort of blamelessness, the innocence that children have, but also a madness somewhere near the surface, as though he could not help himself.

I rounded the edge of the light from the window.

In the corner that now came to light was Claudette. She sat there intent on the dark of her lap; I had never felt right or secure in her presence. She had a sort of faceless force, a thing that moved ahead of her, so even when you saw her near she had always been there in some sense, next to you. Her hands, above a wide-lipped bowl, were spitting out a small, white rain. Her expression was trained on the floor of the room.

Then, upon the nearest wall, a shadow flickered, rolled, was gone.

I adjusted my vantage again.

The clock ceased. *This one*, I said to myself, *or the next one.*

And there in the wake of the shadow went Hannah. She hunched, her arms held straight along. Her hair swung and parted, and parted and swung before her lightly charging face. I remembered when I'd seen her in Mount Auburn cemetery, rubbing her stomach among the grey stones and she had seemed a sort of spool that wound the coffin toward the earth. Her footsteps were short but remarkably fast, as though she went at some instruction. She looked at nobody, not even her mother, on her way to the wall I was facing onto.

Which wasn't, quite, a wall at all; it was a sort of screen or curtain. And Hannah was testing her shadow upon it.

Guay came into view again, conveying a big, rippling cloth, which he lowered.

A cataract seemed to descend on the room, as though it were shrouded along with the camera. But it was only Hannah's shadow, spreading like a pair of wings.

And then I saw, as in a flash, that she had never lied at all.

She had no reason to, not now. There was nobody watching her—no one but me and I did not care either way to verify the thing she was.

But Hannah was herself enthroned. The wings of her shadow extended out from her and the dark majesty of the things she would see was already with her, already among us.

Guay paid out the cloth, stepped back.

No one sat before the screen. It was to be only a picture of absence, roosting under Hannah's shade, but there were figures in it yet like fishermen in waist-high fog.

And Hannah, as though hearing something—as though hearing me as I took in a breath—turned toward the window, emerging through hair, to show the street her sad contentment.

I will do it. Go now.

But I didn't. I stood there.

And finally my second came.

MESSAGE DEPARTMENT

What moves our tongues to speak your names, you mortals who tend on the ways of the spirits? Why do we cross over if not to abide and why cry out if not to mean? Why to watch over if not to protect and why to wake if not to love? And what makes you think you could even perceive us, you mortals, you darlings, who conjure us forth, when walking, say, amid a crowd you grasp an arm you recognize and you behold a stranger's face, corrupt behind a wall of flies? But would it cheer you in your beds, in which you wake and wake with age, that every last spirit among us is reaching to make a mark upon your cheek, the imprint of a pressing palm that throbs with heat when we are near and keeps you for us, sad and bright, until the day you walk along? So what do we say to you? What do we say, you wilters and strivers, you cursers, becursed? Why must we bother to explain what you one day too soon will be?

MUMLER ASCENDING
November 1872

With the Irish arriving in still greater seethes, and the swamps being stylishly choked with fresh gravel, and the Rail Splitter dreaming in midwestern loam, and the great war of Southern Aggression concluded for us regrettably too soon, and Spiritualism gone to ruin when Kate Fox admitted to juggling fruit and promptly drank herself to death—with all of this come down at last like a dynamited avalanche of unrefined granite, Hannah, her mother and I persevered, buying out rooms in the cheap of downtown, and there continued in our trade just a couple of blocks south of the place it began.

Ours was a business arrangement, no more, in these rooms where we captured the soul's transmigration and now reproduced at eight dollars a print—a reduced bill of sale but still true to our mission, may it succor the Spirit in these trying times.

Hannah continued to give of her shadow, grown duller perhaps as the years scraped along but reflecting enough of the Summerland's light to betoken a budding in long barren hearts. Yet the spirits themselves came more randomly now, more contorted and shambling, their faces averted. On more than a couple of occasions those days, hard up for a way to explain who appeared, I'd been driven again to the fraudulent tricks I'd had to adopt in my struggles with Child—double-exposing the strangers away, replacing them with someone loved. And while the murdered man himself no longer lurked inside my prints—a reversal on which I'll elaborate later—it always gave me fleeting shame to have to fall back on such methods with others. This was never of course on behalf of the sitters, who had laid their breasts bare to my intrigues in coming, but rather on my own account, as though I had deceived myself.

Hannah never knew the difference. Hannah did what Hannah did.

But all the same, I bullied her.

I could not seem to help it, reader!

She was just so inviting of cruelty, finally, for all she barely slept and ate, her faculty weakened by punishing "spells" she endured in the room that lay under her mother's. Sometimes I even told her this: she did not see the ghosts at all. It was only a fiction that I had enabled by way of the humours I poured on the glass. She would go very sheepish then, if only for a couple of hours. And I would have to build her up from the unhappy rubble to which I'd reduced her.

Predictably, the house seemed small. But perhaps I am getting ahead of myself?

It seems I've forgotten to mention the boy, though how could I forget him, reader. That boy and his feet even now at their scrambling's, and skidding's, and charging's, and hammering's down; and his baubles of soap on the stairs and his wailing's all throughout the first two years until the child's tantrums found focus at last in a general inanity and vehemence of temper, for he'd become that dreaded thing: a healthy boy of nine, cooped up.

In March of 1862, the boy had been left in a dressmaker's box at the door of the warehouse where we were then living. The dress-box itself, on that early spring night, had been padded inside with torn pillowcases and nary a note or Christian name to mark his being in this world. He was all but an infant, still choke-faced from birth, with hair that grew blonde for a time and then black.

It had been Hannah and not me to insist, passively, that we take him inside.

Surely I must owe her that or something else, reader, to placate her need, especially now that she no longer came like some countrified Lilith to sup of my essence.

She had named the boy Heinrich, a squat, old-world name, and she loved him against her ruin. For hers was a terrible, soul-leaching love, as she practised in everything.

And as he grew older, the boy felt it, too. Though mostly he was strange to me.

That Guay had seen to end his life by drinking a glass of developing fluid—not long after which Child's ghost disappeared—or that I'd seen Bill Christian once in the long line of mourners outside of South Church to lament, at a distance, the murder of Lincoln, made it all the more lonely for me in those days with the two generations of weird, resigned women and that child, their rambunctious familiar, for company. Fanny I'd not seen in years, since even before our acquittal for fraud. In her words she had been my own whore to be handled. She was also the most refined woman I'd known. The original stamp of the signpost endorsement that a decade ago I'd insisted she write, I kept folded up in a drawer in my closet—as yellowed to date as the picture of Cora. I would straighten it broadside and tamp down its corners and pore for a while on the shape of her words and sometimes even told myself that the ink had dried there but a few hours before.

What was it about her?

Austerity, maybe.

I often missed her terribly.

So you will forgive me for misrepresenting when I said that I persevered.

I mostly had cause to bewail a spent life, as orphaned of friends as it was of good fortune. I allowed it to burn from the prominence of me, quickly turned to other things.

Not least among them Madam Fisk's, my cathedral of flesh at the top of Copp's Hill.

Brianna was no longer there. Brianna was no longer there, and yet there were traces of her everywhere—in the rooms that I heaved in, the water I laved. It wasn't that I missed her, quite, but missed the thing she'd made in me and liked to go in search of it in the arms of the hags she had left me for congress. They were canny, used women, long stripped of their mystery, save what disease they might pass on. I combusted inside them with worrisome violence.

Once I'd found myself unstirred.

"It's fine ain't it, though," said the woman beneath me.

She had risen from bed and began to heat water.

So it portended handsomely—returning at last to the lackluster present—when one fall evening, near to six, in the Year of Our Spirit 1872, that another sort of woman came to see me at the shop, her face obscured by widow's weeds.

It was well past the time that I entertained sitters, especially ones strange to me. Though still there was something about her, this widow, untold behind her blackened shroud. And I at last a gentleman.

Accordingly, I asked her in.

She was, I saw, a Lahngworthy, from the way that she bore herself, studied, polite—and yet with a sort of hard-bargained steadfastness; as though without purpose to power her forward she would probably slow with a moan, hunker down. She reminded me, reader, of red-letter days when I had been a personage of "eminence and licence," and when it had always been women like this who came to sign their names and sit. Our recent clientele, you see, had been less and less choice by the signature, reader, the writers and statesmen in steady decline in favour of bondsmen, bricklayers, beer-brewers.

I bade her sit and sign the book.

She signed her name as *Mrs. Lindall*.

I went to fetch Hannah who answered her door in a fierce flush of horseplay with Heinrich behind it, and as I briefed her on our guest I could hear him off thrashing his toys or some rot. She fussed for a while, making sure he was happy—god forbid she should leave him for only ten minutes!—before trailing me, tugging her skirts, to the parlour where we went about the science of arranging Mrs. Lindall at a coordinate of curtain that was favourable to Hannah.

When everything was in its place I turned to the woman, who sat there still shrouded. I asked her might she move her veil.

The woman told me only this: "When you are ready, then I shall remove it."

"But I *am* ready, Madam," I told her. "Quite ready."

She stalled a beat, then pushed it from her.

I am willing to admit at first that I didn't fully understand the tentative solemnity with which she'd invested herself at this juncture. For this woman, de-weeded—this stubbed Mrs. Lindall—was nothing if not commonplace, with her mound of a figure, her veil-to-toe black.

But that was when I recognized her.

Monsieur D'Tocqueville, when he came to this country, chirping of democracy, would've praised us to the very stars had it not been for what he termed "the bootless chase" of heedless fortune. What he meant was our pursuance of elusive main chances, of the one combination that made it all work. Well, whatever the intention or inflection of that statesman, *this* woman was my own main chance, sitting there on her stool with her pushed-aside veil after so many years of deplorable sameness.

She was Mary Todd Lincoln, last bloodkin of Abe. Exposing her, I might've trembled.

And that's when that sniveling nuisance in sockfeet came hoof-pounding into the room at that instant. He planted himself at its edge for a peek.

Instantly, Hannah moved off to contain him.

"Heinrich," she scolded, too gently, I think. "Heinrich, my child, you are not to be down here."

But he stayed in the doorway, confused, maybe daft. Hannah took a few steps closer.

I said: "Our little foundling, Henrich."

Mrs. Lincoln fixed me with a muted distaste—what in the world had I said to offend her? She turned to Hannah, then the boy, and then she said: "Your son, I take it?"

Hannah Mumler told her: "Yes."

"I am partial to children. All kinds," said the widow—the widow of Lincoln, need I be reminded!—who sat here now before my screen in a weathered pursuit of this Spiritualism beyond even what promised to be its disgrace. Katherine and Maggie, just eight months ago, in mutual decline toward drink, had admitted that when they heard rapping as girls it was only the dropping of fruit tied to strings.

Granted, so to speak—ah, reader, I love a presidential pun!—I'd heard that Mary Lincoln was a Spiritualist herself, that she had sat for mediums and put on séances while still in the White House, though her coming here now, in so desperate an age, impressed me as not a jot less than fantastic. For an instant I feared I'd embrace her right there.

Her husk, which had buried her husband and son all in the space of a few thieving years.

But I didn't embrace her. I said: "Heinrich, come."

The diminutive wretch looked afraid for a moment as he so often did with me. He approached Mrs. Lincoln a-twitch and a-twitter, his hands unappealingly rumpling his pockets.

"Have you come down to watch us then?" said Mrs. Lincoln, smiling warmly. Simple Heinrich did not speak but continued to lurk there like some sort of changeling. "Well, have you?" she pressed him.

"Yes, Ma'am," the boy answered.

"How silly you must think us, dear."

He said: "I like the pictures, Ma'am. I like how they look when they're fresh from the bath!"

And cramping with shyness, he heeled from the room.

"Isn't he a cherry, Miss," the woman pronounced, with a flattish inflection.

Hannah thanked her, muttering. She nodded and then turned to stone for the picture. Mrs. Lincoln paid her monies, complimented our tact and then hurried away.

But not before writing, in next to her name, a day that would suit her to come for her prints and, making note of it too well, I shut the book on hours well spent.

I subjected Mary's sitting to the firstlings of development and having done so went to bed.

But I didn't sleep long before I was awoken.

Something rankled on the air. I sat up in bed in an unnatural sweat. The room, I slowly found, was baking, and I tried through my grog to align the strange smell with the reason I should be so hot. My curtains, which faced on the north side of Milk Street—velvety, black ones that meted the sun—were alive top and bottom and down through the centre with a queer agitation of ambient light. I thought that it looked like a portrait of hell—a negative of hell, perhaps. As I walked from my bed to the street-facing window, wiping that freak of night-sweat from my brow, I *heard* the sounds of hell unreckoned, a popping and grating and crashing. Then screams.

I parted the curtain to look on what bedlam.

The building next to mine was burning. It had recently trafficked some manner of textile and now as I watched it be eaten by flames in the foreground of other such buildings, half eaten, I fancied I could hear the sound of the bed-sheets or rugs or whatever inside it flaring and whooshing and crinkling to crisps.

Was the whole blessed city on fire?

So it was.

Crazed, I wrenched the curtains closed. I even cried out—an absurd, sincere cry: "Why has no one come to warn me?!" And then as though without a thought—with less than a thought, the abeyance of thinking!—I raced in my bed-shirt downstairs to the street. And when I arrived there amid the melee, my bed-shirt clinging to my bulk while the shop next to mine, now a banquet for flames, began to nibble at our mansards, I was startled at last at my own cowardice.

I had never paused once to alert the two women.

I'll admit that for more selfish reasons than right ones, I did not wish them both to die—though if I had my druthers, reader, I would've elected Claudette for that outcome. And yet I discovered that I'd been unable to think of anyone but me. I had woken, felt heat, sniffed at smoke, reckoned danger, transported myself at a clip from its clutches. I had not even brought the prints that I had made of Mrs. Lincoln and though I thought to rush back in and cradle them, sweating, away from the flames, I could not will myself to do it.

A black-winged inertia held me to the spot. Yet still I felt resilient, reader; many times in my life, even, favoured by chance.

A notion perhaps superseding belief as flames began to take the shop but one I was willing to—*must!*—believe in as I commenced to walk away. And so did the H.M.S. Mumler set sail for what new shores I cannot say, only that when I got there—yes, missing the prints and without the weird women required to make more—there always would be Mrs. Lincoln's, Hannah Mumler's, hopes to hope.

I ran down Milk Street bound for Summer with the logic that I would be safer near water—the sort of idiotic thing that occurs to one, reader, in such situations. But I found as I ran that the fire was well-fed by mansard rooftops cheek by jowl, not to mention the porous beige bulk of old granite, which now, all around me, began to combust in a walled-kingdom wreckage of battlements breached, huge hunks of it cracking and taking to air to crater the ash-sifted street with its ruin. The cauldron shapes of firefight troupes were grinding up and down the main, doing their best to spout impotent ropes across the spreading of the flames. The firemen shoved, and punched, and swore as to which troupe among them would herald a savior while the horses attached to their engines stood still. They were baleful and black and they bowed their rank heads, as if at my prospects of getting away; and that was when the ghost of something—something large, grotesque and bubbling—rose out of an alleyway off to my left in a great gathering of opaque, gaseous matter and when it reached the highest point, the size of a book-spine between the two rooftops, concussed in a torrent of gas set aflame, coating the frail world below with hot rubble.

A goodly portion found me out, pinging off rooftops and walls, breaking windows, but always, *always,* missing me, and I fled ever farther, the whole world aflame, like a sinister throat that was coughing me out.

And then the bedlam seemed to stop.

The horses perked their scabby heads. The firefighters no longer fought. All were looking at the sky.

And William Mumler, too, looked up to see what drew the others so and saw far out beyond the roofs, unfurling each a tail of flame, a burning migration of geese toward the ocean. Any second, they'd crash down. Their wings would dip in singed surrender. And their feathers would flee from them, blackly, in torment, as they went into mostly dead spirals and sunk.

When I lowered my eyes to the street once again, the scene around me had resumed. The inferno was popping, the water was lashing, the people were running, the children were crying, the horses were snorting, the firemen were brawling, and yet I could not feel a thing.

It was as though an atmosphere impassable to earthly force had gathered around me the place where I stood.

And suddenly I realized I'd no idea where I was.

Not only geographically in terms of where I had come from, but also the street that I stood in, the city; I might've been in any one.

So I ran to the end of the street I was on to commit to my memory the name on the sign with the logic that if I forgot it again then I might remember it, sooner than later. But there was no sign there at all, just a shattered gas-lamp at the top of a pole that was bowed at the middle and faintly on fire, and turning I ran down the street whence I'd come, or had it been another street, and kept on running through the dark where the fire showed in grotesque displays on the brick.

At the end of that street, I turned left and then right; then right again, then left once more, at every branching looking up to see if I could read the sign. But most of the time there was no sign or the words were so worn I could not make them out. Or maybe there had been a sign but no sooner seen than forgotten again, as though my mind could not retain the letters as they were arranged.

"Can somebody tell me the name of this street?" I shouted at some passersby. "Is there one cursed street in this Sodom," I said, "that wears a sign upon its post? How is a gentleman meant to discern the place he is headed, one block to the next?"

But the people I'd shouted at didn't respond. They did not even turn around.

When turn and turn about I came to a street in the darkness that, somehow, I knew. I am not sure why I felt this. And yet I had the *certainty* that I had been there once before and when I had, a few years past or maybe only fifteen minutes, that all the jewels of happiness had lain assembled in my palm.

Where was I? I wondered. *What had I been doing?*

And then I remembered: *a city on fire.*

Three people emerged from a two-story house across the street from where I stood. They were fleeing the drawn-out and deadly collapse of the structure entire as its upper floors caught—two adults, I could see, with a boy in between them. The boy was coughing violently, that quick, raw cough small children make. The adults were both women: one older, one younger. The older one was in the lead. And while her eyes were vague and strange, her jaw was set ahead of her—not to such a degree as to make her forbidding, but only concerned for her grandson and daughter, intent on conveying them out of harm's reach to somewhere better, somewhere safe.

At first they were familiar but then I thought I was not sure. There was something about them, the way they appeared, familiar yet also indelibly strange, as though I had known them in some other life.

They seemed a loving family, yet suddenly I felt ashamed. Not only because I was filthy with ash or in a state of half-undress but rather that I could not say the way that I appeared at all. I was utterly, darkly unknown to myself, a mirror at a canted angle. And I couldn't be sure from one beat to the next either what I would say or attempt in their presence. It was almost as though I were propped in a coffin, the sort in which killers are propped for displaying behind the glass of druggist's shops, and though I lay there dead to all I could hear every word, I could track every movement. The beautiful family had but to go by me, to tilt their eyes toward where I leaned and they would see my helplessness, my fallen and decaying face.

I wanted to ask them: "What street are we on?"

I wanted to ask them: "Have we met before?"

I wanted to ask them: "Assuming we have, did I cradle your hands to my mouth for a kiss? "

But I said none of this. It was too, too absurd. Embarrassed, I found out the shadows again. They stood a moment, conferencing, and then with the boy in between them they vanished.

"Where am I, exactly?" I said. "In what city?"

And when nobody answered: "To whom am I speaking?"

The answer is speaking to you, faithful reader.

I have now and forever been speaking to you.

HANNAH MUMLER TRUE AND FALSE
November 1872

Willy kept out late tonight.

Had taken one brandy too many, perhaps. As he was given to most nights. Gone to sleep at the tavern, one time in the street. But we could see to warn ourselves.

The heat and the smoke and the warping of wood and the shouts of the injured and dead were enough. I stood at the door to the room that we shared, Heinrich on the bed behind me.

"*Stay*. You stay right here," said I.

"I don't want you to go," said he.

"It's all right. It's *all right*. You must sit and be brave. Bravery smothers the fire—did you know? I will be back in . . ." I smiled to myself. ". . . in how many blinks of an eye, do you think?"

"In thirty blinks?"

"In twenty-five."

"I will start them now," said he.

I paused when I had reached the door. "I do not know what I should do were I to come back here and find you *not* blinking. I do not know what I should do. Do you hear what I'm telling you, Heinrich?"

"Yes, Mommy."

Closed the door and tested it, and climbed the attic staircase slowly. Here the smoke from the fire of the building next door fingered out from the walls like a dangerous scent.

The door to mother's room was hot. Had to bunch my skirts to turn it.

Already awake at the end of her bed. Sitting with her back to me. Dress the colour of ash that fell down past the windows. Bearing witness to the world, her dolls beside her on the floor. Lining the bucket in which they'd been made in a tilted and gathering spiral of figures, wrapped each one in dunish crepe. There were these and a few random dresses. Her knives. My mother, my maker, was already packed.

Helped her to go down the stairs to the landing, pushed the bedroom door inward. "Come, Heinrich. We're going."

"I waited!" said he.

"A whole thirty blink's worth?"

"I counted to forty."

Said I: "Needn't worry. Grandmother is with us."

When he looked at my mother his eyes were black pools.

Came down the staircase with Heinrich between us. The side of our building already on fire.

"Are we going to die now?" said he, looking back. His frightened, disbelieving face.

"One foot and then the next," said I.

"Are we, Mommy?"

Smiled. "No, dear."

"All right." He gripped my hand. "All right."

Finally we reached the bottom where Willy's rooms were, the developing closet. Here I determined to usher them out. But then at the very last second I stopped.

Cut my eyes toward Willy's door. A jittery glow in the crack of the frame.

I tipped the door wide with my foot and edged in. The bed was completely on fire. And the curtains. They withered like bacon and dropped to the floor where they made other fires that began to grow taller. I strode through the flames to the door of the darkroom, and when I had reached it I gathered my skirts and pushed the door, unlocked, from me.

The negative had been completed. On the counter it sat, freshly dried from the bath.

The woman occupies the foreground. Her hands clasped before her, her mouth a grim line. While Willy, my husband, is standing behind her. Willy, who'd taken the picture himself but also there inside the shot. Already concealed and revealed by my shadow. His body cocked slightly. His head gazing up. The expression that colours his wide, fleshy face no more than one of vague surprise. As though he is seeing, perhaps, a rare bird arranging itself on the window outside.

The negative I wrapped in cloth and holding it to me I rushed from the closet.

The chaos was general. Boston in ruins.

A spout of flame and blasted stone from the upper west side of the block. People crumpling. Crumpled horses crumpling too, beneath the soaring sheet of flame. And Heinrich, beside me, cough-squinting, dry-sobbing while trying to hide in the folds of my skirts.

Mother, calm, surveyed it all. "We should make for the water," said she, facing forward.

"There may be fire there too," said I.

"No matter," said mother. "At least there'll be water. And there is nothing for us here."

"Mommy," said Heinrich. "Burning birds!"

He was tugging my skirts. He was pointing. Exclaiming. My mother beginning down Summer Street now. The path that she carved through the wreckage a good one. The ashed lakes of water, congealing to mud. And sometimes, too, the charred, dark forms. Their faces burned away wholesale or turned to ground from deadly falls.

"There!" said Heinrich. "Watch it, there!"

The water arcing overhead. He bounded ahead of me. Laughing, unthinking. I wanted him to laugh, of course.

But all I could think was: this step or the next one. This fire, which is the whole wide world.

As we went, the fire dimmed down. The muscle of it mostly north. Chalk it up to puddingstone, which did not burn like granite burned.

A little girl stood at the edge of a lawn. Refugee among the many. Looking up at her house, which had been mostly spared. All except the upper floors, which were singed at the edges from skirmish inside them and a window that bristled with torn wood and glass where someone or something had gone pitching out.

Below it a white shape. Onlookers around it.

A person draped under a sheet stained with blood.

The girl on the lawn in a terrible state. Her face was smeared with dirty tears. And her hair was soaked dark from the engines' exertions.

The name of her mother, who lay in the grass, she partly screamed and partly sobbed.

Above the body on the lawn stood a man in a vest greened with age. Golden fob. The singed stateliness of his house all above him. A couple of neighbours stood by in concern.

I saw my mother mark the man. The girl upon the sodden lawn.

And then moving forward, head turning away. Still bent on existing, on being somewhere, for as long as the grail of her blood would allow her.

"Why is she crying?" said Heinrich.

"Who, dear?"

"That little girl." He pointed. "There."

"That little girl"—I studied her—"has lost somebody that she loves."

"Can I go to her, Mommy?"

"No, Heinrich. Not now."

"But Mommy she needs me. I can't—I can't leave her." My mother paused at Heinrich's words. "Can I go to her, grandmother, please?" said the boy.

I started to scold him for asking her, too.

Mother showed me her palm. Not a threatening motion. Yet one that impressed me as purposeful, solemn, as though here in the burning and burned Boston street, she would finally do it. Be family to him.

She took up his face in her thin, able hands.

And she turned it, not speaking, this way and then that as the ghost of the firelight played over his cheeks,

"On one condition you may go." He started to run but she caught him: "Stop squirming." She straightened his posture. Brushed ash from his face. "You cannot say just anything."

"I will tell her I'm sorry she's sad," said the boy.

"That girl needs more than friendly words. She has just lost her mother—you see that, don't you?"

He fidgeted. And looked away.

My mother caught him: "Look at me. You must tell her the truth: that her mother is with her."

"But I don't even know what she looks like," said he.

"Then you must imagine her, dear, mustn't you? And then it will become a game."

"But she wouldn't believe me, grandmother, would she?"

"Some part of her may not at first. But that," said she, "is why we're here. You have only to point to the two of us, child. Here, now." She took hold of his arm. "Let us try it."

She guided Heinrich's arm away. His finger extending. As though at her urging—as though she plucked the very nerves. Until at last it came to rest on the girl in the gown at the edge of the lawn.

"What do I say to her now?" said the boy.

"'See them over there?' you'll say. 'Those women there beneath the trees. Those women, so dark and alike, do you see them?'"

"I see them," said Heinrich. "I'm pointing. Look, Mommy!"

"Go greet them then," my mother said. "Commend them to your father's favour. They have so much to show you—so much to reveal. Feed them. Warm them. Ask them in."

ABOUT THE AUTHOR

Adrian Van Young is the author of *The Man Who Noticed Everything*, a collection of stories, which won Black Lawrence Press's St. Lawrence Book Award in 2011. His fiction and non-fiction have been published or are forthcoming in *Black Warrior Review*, *Electric Literature's Recommended Reading*, *VICE*, *Slate*, *The Believer*, and *The New Yorker*, among others. His work has also appeared in the anthologies *States of Terror II* and *Gigantic Worlds*. He has twice been nominated for the Pushcart Prize and is a regular contributor to *Electricliterature.com*. He lives in New Orleans with his wife, Darcy, and son, Sebastian, where he teaches creative writing at Tulane University.

SOURCES & ACKNOWLEDGEMENTS

Although *Shadows in Summerland* is a work of historical fiction, William H. Mumler really did claim to photograph spirits in Boston and New York in the 1860s with the help of his wife, Hannah Mumler, the medium J. H. Conant and the Spiritualist "investigator" William Guay. And while I have taken significant liberties with the chronologies and personal details of the lives of Mumler and his cohort, as well as all those actual historical persons whom Mumler would've encountered in Boston Spiritualist circles, the following works were indispensable to me in my research, my world-building and my consideration (and sometimes subsequent discarding) of historical fact:

The Strange Case of William Mumler, Spirit Photographer by Louis Kaplan (University of Minnesota Press, 2008);

Confidence Men and Painted Women: A Study of Middle Class Culture in America, 1830-1870 by Karen Halttunen (Yale University Press, 1982);

Radical Spirits: Spiritualism and Women's Rights in Nineteenth Century America by Anne Braude (Indiana University Press, 1989);

Modern Spiritualism: Its Facts and Fanaticisms, Its Consistencies and Contradictions by E.W. Capron (B. Marsh, 1855);

Talking to the Dead: Kate and Maggie Fox and the Rise of Spiritualism by Barbara Weisberg (HarperCollins, 2004);

A Practical Guide to the Collodion Process in Photography: Describing the Method of Obtaining Collodion Negatives, and Of Printing Them by George Washington Wilson (Longman & Co, 1855);

This Republic of Suffering: Death and the American Civil War by Drew Gilpin Faust (Vintage, 2008);

The Harmonial Philosophy: A Compendium and Digest of the Works of Andrew Jackson Davis, The Seer of Poughkeepsie by Andrew Jackson Davis (William Rider & Son, 1923);

A City So Grand: The Rise of an American Metropolis, Boston 1850-1900 by Stephen Puleo (Beacon Press, 2010); and

Civil War Era Etiquette by R.L. Shep (R.L. Shep, 1988).

I am also indebted to Professor Stefan Andriopoulos of Columbia University, who provided me with many valuable leads as I began my research into Mumler and spirit photography. Ditto the town of Lily Dale, a.k.a. "The City of Light," a.k.a. "The Town That Talks to the Dead," for hosting me so openly and warmly when I visited there on a research trip in fall of 2009. And most of all, perhaps, The Metropolitan Museum of Art for curating the exhibit "The Perfect Medium: Photography and the Occult" in fall of 2005, where I first conceived of writing a historical novel about William Mumler. Eleven years later, here is one.

Nor would this book have been possible without the sage guidance and support of writers, editors, friends—and you, reader. So thank you to those who read and helped make over early (and much longer) beta-drafts of this novel: Darcy Roake, Lincoln Michel, Anya Groner & Nicole LaBombard. Thank you to those who both published excerpts from the novel, and other bits of Spiritualism-related output that I completed in the course of writing it: Ryan Bradford in *Black Candies*; Tobias Carroll in *Volume 1 Brooklyn*; and Heidi Julavits and Andi Mudd in *The Believer*. Thank you, too, to the literary mentors and models without which *Shadows in Summerland* would have withered on the vine: John Wray's *Canaan's Tongue*, Hilary Mantel's *Beyond Black*, Sarah Waters' *Affinity* and Henry James' *The Bostonians*. Thank you to Laird Barron, Julia Fierro, Bennett Simms and Michael Rowe for the blurbage, given with grace. A table-tipping, violin-weeping thank you to everyone at ChiZine Publications and their affiliates: Sandra Kasturi, Brett Savory, Erik Mohr, Samantha Beiko, Bracken MacLeod, and Michael Rowe, yet again. And last but not least to Ashley Brett Chipman for the frightfully elegant book trailer. Finally, thank you to the greater New Orleans literary community, each of whom, in some small way, helped see this novel into being: the No-Name Writing Group, Matt Carney & Gladin Scott at Maple Street Books and Nathan Martin and Sara Slaughter of the Room 220 Series, among many others.

And then there are those without whom, not a thing:

My extended family, blood-related and non, but especially Anne Guite and Matt Nimetz, who granted me invaluable access to their property in upstate New York where large chunks of this novel were written.

My sister, Marin Van Young.

My parents, Marjorie Milstein & Eric Van Young.

My Little-Face, Sebastian Roake Van Young.

Darcy, Darcy, Darcy, *you*. Somewhat mystifyingly, Andrew Jackson Davis, the grandfather of Spiritualism, wrote: "The association of particles or spirits, thus drawn together, is an outward expression of inward marriage . . . Heart calls to heart." So too our hearts, Darcy dear, in this life and the life to come.

EMB
RACE
THE
ODD

ALMOST DARK
LETITIA TRENT

Claire, a private and outwardly content librarian, carries a secret: she is wracked with guilt over her twin brother Sam's accidental death fifteen years earlier. Claire's quiet life is threatened when Justin, an aggressive business developer, announces the renovation of Farmington's oldest textile factory, which is the scene of Sam's death along with many other mysterious accidents throughout its long history. Claire not only feels a personal connection to the factory, but she also begins to receive "visitations" from her brother, which cause her to question her sanity. As Justin moves forward with his plans to renew the factory, Claire, and the town as a whole, discover that in Farmington, there is no clear line between the past and the present.

AVAILABLE APRIL 2016
ISBN 978-1-77148-336-0
eISBN 978-1-77148-337-7

CHIZINEPUB.COM

THE RIB FROM WHICH I REMAKE THE WORLD
ED KURTZ

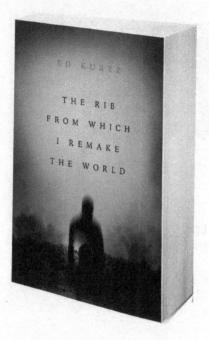

In a small, rural Arkansas town in the midst of World War II, hotel house detective George "Jojo" Walker wearily maintains the status quo in the wake of personal devastation. That status quo is disrupted when a "hygiene picture" roadshow rolls into town with a controversial program on display and curious motives in mind. What begins with a gruesome and impossible murder soon spirals into hallucinatory waking nightmares for Jojo—nightmares that converge with his reality and dredge up his painful, secret past. Black magic and a terrifying Luciferian carnival boil up to a surreal finale for the town of Litchfield, when truth itself unfurls and Jojo Walker is forced to face his own identity in ways he could never have expected.

AVAILABLE JULY 2016
ISBN 978-1-77148-390-2
eISBN 978-1-77148-391-2